A QUEEN

COMES TO

POWER

SHE WILL DEFY

A QUEEN
COMES TO
POWER

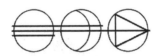

CHLOE C.
PEÑARANDA

LUMARIAS
PRESS

Published by Lumarias Press
www.lumariaspress.com

First Edition published August 2021

Map design © 2021 by Chloe C. Peñaranda
Cover illustration © 2021 by Alice Maria Power
www.alicemariapower.com
Cover design © 2021 by Lumarias Press
Edited by Bryony Leah
www.bryonyleah.com

Identifiers
ISBN: 978-1-8382480-5-5 (eBook)
ISBN: 978-1-8382480-4-8 (Paperback)
ISBN: 978-1-8382480-3-1 (Hardback)

www.ccpenaranda.com

Content Warning
Some scenes contain brief sexual implication. Death of a child. Fantasy blood
and violence detail.

DEDICATION

To every dreamer

I see you…and I hear you.

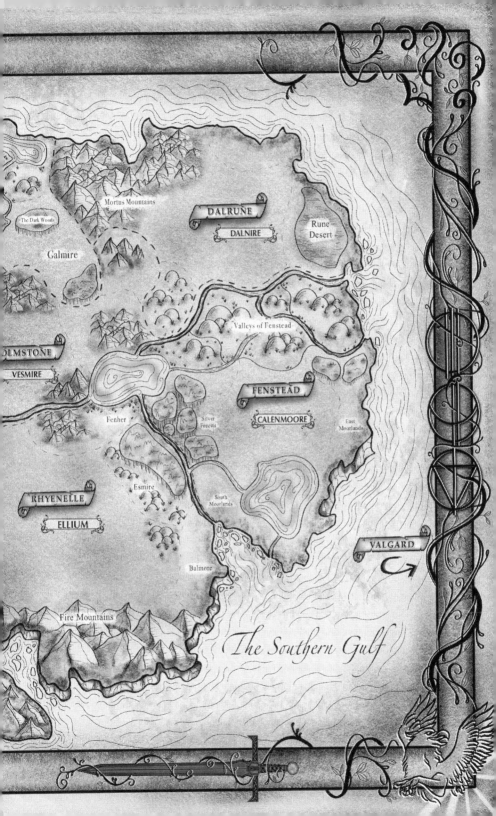

PROLOGUE

Reuben

D ARKNESS. THAT WAS all he knew.

The darkness of a cold, barren cell. Of his desolate thoughts. Of a lingering death.

What he dreaded most was the darkness that took his sight as he was led from the prison, his sanctuary. He did not fear the bars that kept him in as long as they kept the monsters out.

Every time they came for him, he was blindfolded but not restrained, as though they knew terror gripped his ability to move beyond the vacant steps he took, guided by a hand that held him loosely. To run or fight—he didn't have that courage, not even when a childhood friend's voice urged a response in him.

Nothing was worse than the feeble submission he'd been reduced to.

To grapple onto his fading sanity, Reuben thought of Faythe, of his mother, of Jakon and everyone else he left in High Farrow. He didn't know how much time had passed since he was met with this terrible fate.

A door opened with a faint creak. More shuffling. He wasn't

embarrassed by his fumbling footsteps; part of him hoped to trip himself, if only to delay the confrontation for a few seconds longer. Then they halted. Reuben couldn't hide his trembling.

His blindfold was snatched away. He kept his eyes closed for a moment longer, wishing for darkness in place of the piercing light that tried to penetrate his lids. When he found the courage to flutter them open, he blinked rapidly to adjust, and upon spying the waves of flaming red hair across the room, his heart began to pound.

She kept her back to him for a moment, looking out over the clearest waters and purest crystalline snow from the wall made completely of glass. Reuben stood still. Despite the warmth of the room, he felt as cold as the icy sheets that sparkled beyond.

The beautiful fae twisted to him like an elegant wisp of wind, but the fire in her blazing amber eyes was ice-cold as she fixed them on him.

"I have offered you everything," she said, her voice sending a shiver to make every hair on his body stand. "Everything you could dream of in your miserable human life, for your allegiance to me. Yet still, you resist." The enchantress floated to him, slow steps that lapped the waves of her gown like a ruby sea. "Why?"

Reuben couldn't speak. His answer was there, but it was wholly traitorous to her plan. He could not betray the names he chanted nightly in his lonely cell. He could not betray the one she sought the most.

The red-haired fae stopped close enough to touch, and his whole body stiffened. How could such evil lie within such devastating beauty? A combination of the most lethal kind.

She raised a delicate, slender hand, and Reuben flinched. Her fingers curled around his jaw, turning his face to hold her stare when he tried to avoid it, for the color struck him with conflicting emotions.

"You let your fear consume you. It is not your fault." Her hand caressed his cheek—a loving gesture that held no true endearment.

"I really hoped it would not come to this, Reu." When he tried to look away again, her fingers gripped his jaw with more force. Her sharp nails dug into his skin, and he winced. "I am going to break you," she hissed so beautifully, but laced with poison. "Only then can I mold you into my own perfect weapon. Only then will you see that I stand to better this world."

She stepped forward, and he had no choice but to retreat backward while she held him firm. He stumbled all the way until he hit solid wood and became trapped.

Before he could even consider the thought of a possible escape, he felt another presence there. In his mind. A gasp, and coils of shadows were circling his thoughts, searching, listening. They formed into claws, scraping along every corner, violating every private memory. Everything he was surfaced at their command.

Then, without warning, fire erupted in his head.

Reuben screamed, but the echo around the room was swiftly cut off. His cries still rang in his mind, and her hold on his chin loosened to begin a soothing caress of his face once again.

"It will be over in a moment," she cooed.

Every time one of those shadow talons sank themselves deep, they scorched a new line of searing pain until they nestled in his mind. Again and again and again. They would kill him, each wicked claw taking hold to shatter him completely from within.

He felt the darkness calling. This one he welcomed. A darkness so free and final.

Just before he could fall into that blissful oblivion…everything stilled. He closed and opened his eyes.

Quiet, peaceful nothing.

The stars that scattered his vision began to fade. He didn't fear. He didn't feel anything. He looked down at the presence in front of him, and she was the most breathtaking thing he had ever laid eyes upon. Fire with the heat of a thousand suns. He wanted to fall to his knees before such a magnificent creature.

As her touch on his face registered, he felt the need to return it.

Slowly, his hand raised to cup her cheek, and she smiled. It wasn't sweet or kind or tender. It was pure, blazing triumph. Both her hands laced through his hair and tangled there as she brought her face to his. He didn't object, didn't want to retreat as he kissed her back. He felt nothing from it. But the way she moved was all he cared about. His kiss seemed to please her.

When she pulled back abruptly, the curl of her rouge-painted lips was nothing short of devastating. Reuben shivered.

"You are mine," she purred.

"I am yours."

He would kill for her. He would bleed for her. He would do… anything for her.

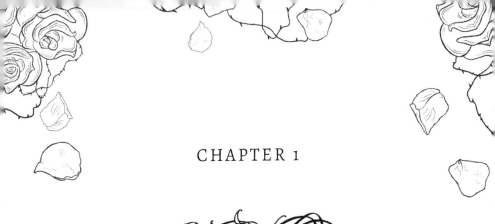

CHAPTER 1

Faythe

AS THE KING'S spymaster hurtled through the bright, wide hallways, the tapestries and sculptures blurred into waves of deep blue and white. The fast clap of her feet against the marble overtook the tempo of her racing heart. Her lungs burned, breathing uneven and short from the exertion of her sprint. In her urgency, she skidded and twisted around the few servants who littered the hallways. They shrieked, attempting to dart out of her way before she could knock them off their feet, and she called her apologies to them over her shoulder, not slowing her pace at all. The tail of her jacket billowed behind her, along with wisps of her half-unbound hair. With her neck on the line, she didn't have time to consider how frantic she would appear to those she passed.

The few guards she came across were halfway to drawing their swords, their fae ears alerted to Faythe's fast, thundering footsteps long before she came into view. Upon seeing who was to blame for the commotion, they relaxed, and she winced at their disapproving glares and disgruntled head shakes.

She was already running dangerously late and had decided to

take the long route to the council chamber to surreptitiously enter through the back door instead of the front, hoping no one would notice her tardiness. Especially not the King of High Farrow. Sweat beaded on her forehead, and her breaths cut like broken glass in her throat as she stumbled clumsily around the last corner into the dark, narrow passage that led to where the lords' meeting was due to take place.

Damn rutting Spirits, let it be delayed…

It was all she could do to keep her jittering nerves at bay.

Two royal guards stood posted outside, and Faythe slowed to a walk as she approached, straightening the jacket of her uniform while regaining her composure. At first, she had felt ridiculous when she was presented with the royal blue and silver-accented attire that closely resembled that of the guards. It was far too elegant and formal for her to ever feel accustomed to. The only distinguishing feature the guards had was their shorter jacket and the matching blue shoulder cloak Faythe was spared from trailing behind her all day.

"You're lucky. A few of the lords are still to arrive," the guard, Caius, said. He was one of the friendlier fae Faythe had become acquainted with during her three months in the castle. Younger than most, he was the first in the guard to ease her tensions, and she'd even come to consider him a friend.

In fact, she was pleasantly surprised by just how many of the guards had warmly welcomed her into their ranks, albeit she still felt at odds being shuffled among brute warriors. Nothing they could dress her in or title her with would ever be enough to make her blend in, and it had taken a long while to get used to. There was also a large number in the guard who remained uneasy about her presence in the citadel, specifically for her ability, and she couldn't blame them when they avoided her eye. She was only here for her talents after all, as the king's reluctant *spymaster.* It was only natural to be untrusting of anyone with such a title, and they knew that if the king commanded it, she would be at his mercy to invade any one of their thoughts.

"That's me, just a fountain of luck," she grumbled flatly. *Damn, a loose button.* She fumbled to knot it closed, muttering curses under her breath.

Caius chuckled at her flustering as she checked over the rest of the attire she'd all but flung onto her body before flying out of her rooms. The other guard didn't even try to hide his scowl, and she pinched her face right back at him in irritation.

She was running late thanks to this morning's training session with Tauria. What was intended to be a quickly crammed-in solo hour in the weapons room ahead of the grueling meeting had turned into an intense combat lesson with the king's ward who had tracked her down there. They lost the concept of time. Faythe became fully engrossed in learning maneuvers with a long staff instead of steel. It was Tauria's weapon of choice and apparently a custom in her home kingdom of Fenstead.

One of the most dumbfounding revelations Faythe had learned about the golden-skinned beauty was that above being the King of High Farrow's ward, she was the sole heir to the Fenstead throne. *Princess* Tauria Stagknight.

Lost in the action with iron-tipped wood, it was only when Faythe's wonderful handmaidens Elise and Ingrid came looking for her that she was enlightened to the time. She sprinted to her rooms to frantically dress before hurling herself halfway across the castle to make the congregation on time.

The king never let her forget that her life hung in the balance of his mercy, and it made her constantly on edge that he always seemed to be *looking* for a reason to go back on the bargain to spare her life. One slipup could result in the end of her days. And not just in the castle.

Caius's quiet rumble of laughter sounded at her back as she stepped up to the door, creaked it open, and slid in through the smallest gap she could manage. The low chatter of voices disguised any noise from the shallow creak of its hinges and her deliberately light footsteps. Upon discovering the meeting had yet to begin, Faythe sighed a breath of relief that dropped a weight of mercy in her stomach. She noted the few empty chairs yet to be filled.

The king's council chamber was far smaller than the throne room but still big enough to warrant four guards. They were posted two to each wall, standing formally parallel to each other. A massive deep oak table occupied the center, at the head of which the king was already seated in his grand throne with his back to her. Prince Nikalias was to his left and spied Faythe as soon as she entered, shooting an amused smirk in her direction. She glowered, not paying him any attention as she glided in and took up position against one of the walls, an even space away from the other guards. She stood straight and poised, clasping her hands behind her back, and didn't dare a glance in the king's direction to see if he'd noticed her late arrival.

More Lords of High Farrow filed through the door until every seat was filled. Then the ornate main doors were closed so the meeting could begin.

This wasn't Faythe's first time being used for her ability. Not even close. The king had several different gatherings with lords, councilmen, war generals, and other members of the royal court on at least a weekly basis. In the beginning, she struggled with morality for what she was doing and had to swallow her revulsion at herself for what she was, peering into the minds of the unwitting subjects. She had learned to live with it by not diving too deep unless there was threat or suspicion. She *had* to live with it, and she knew she could shoulder the burden of a tarnished soul as long as it kept her friends safe.

Most of the time, Faythe was only forced to listen to her own bored thoughts and the occasional rude remark about the king's actions and strategies. But Orlon would quickly find her of little use if she never reported anything he didn't already know. So, while it pained her to do so, she had exposed a couple of councilmembers who were conspiring against him—an entirely foolhardy plan—as well as a lord who sought to gain more power and wealth through illegal trade. She never learned the outcome of their fates, nor did she particularly want to, preferring to remain blissfully ignorant to her third-party involvement in their probable deaths.

Faythe had become fully acquainted with her ability, and it no longer doused her with dread to use it. Instead, she harnessed it; became the power that hummed in her veins, far more prominent since those first months of teaching with Nik that seemed so distant now. Her time as spymaster had at least earned her practice and taught her self-control. Collecting thoughts had become like breathing air. And the deeper skeletons those in high places often harbored—they were a game to find, something to offer the tedious meetings a little entertainment. While an ignorant eye would glance over the room and see a gathering of highly respected courtly individuals who carried themselves with an air of importance, Faythe saw what they truly were inside: a congregation of greed, adultery, and spite.

There were other stems of her ability she was less acquainted with. Faythe had only been made to use compulsion once, during a vote for the king's proposal to remove the fae soldiers stationed in the town of Galmire. This would leave the town on High Farrow's edge, which shared a border with the conquered kingdom of Dalrune, completely defenseless. The king was many hands short, but with a subtle glance at Faythe, the scales miraculously tipped in his favor. Faythe knew Galmire was a fully human-occupied settlement, which made her part in securing the vote hurt like a painful twist of the dagger constantly piercing her chest. It was not something she was proud of, but it was certainly not her place to have a voice on any of the matters brought into the council chamber.

The meeting was fully underway now, and Faythe had already met the eye of all the lords facing her and captured a glimpse into their minds. It was easy enough to project a thought for them to look at her, and once she caught their eye, she no longer needed to hold their stare. Even when they quickly averted their gazes from the strange human standing in the shadows, she would still be riffling around their heads.

They all noted her presence with a curiosity and distaste that was strongly reflected in their thoughts, loud and clear for her to hear. Their obliviousness was too amusing for Faythe to be insulted by their internal slander. The only humans any of them were used to were the ones who kept their goblets topped up. Faythe no longer felt bad for the invasion of their minds, finding most of the lords to be as imperious and arrogant as the king himself.

Faythe inconspicuously floated herself around to the other side of the room to stand mirroring her previous position, as she always did, and began probing into the minds of the lords who had been seated with their backs to her. It was deliriously dull, and she was exhausted from her exertion that morning, both in the training room and her wild sprint. Her eyelids drooped a couple of times, and she was jerked awake every time a new voice fought to be the loudest in the room. She didn't pay any attention to the tiresome affairs they conversed—or rather, argued—about, instead counting the minutes internally with no way of knowing how much time had passed.

After what she gauged to be close to an hour, the king bellowed over the petty squabbling of high fae, silencing the room immediately. Faythe refrained from slouching in relief as he relayed his conclusion to the rather pointless formal gathering. The only time she ever longed to hear the wicked ruler's voice was to signal that yet another exasperating meeting was adjourned.

The Lords of High Farrow stood, chatting idly to each other as they slowly filed out of the room. She watched each of their backs as they exited, far too slow in her impatience. The king and prince remained in their seats, and Faythe didn't flinch from her position until every other noble set of pointed ears had left and the grand doors were closed once again.

Faythe visibly relaxed the moment she heard them groan shut, rolling her stiff shoulders before sauntering over the king. She stopped and braced her hands on the back of an empty chair.

"Anything to report?" the king asked, sounding as bored as she felt.

She rubbed her right temple. "Lord Devon thinks he's being very undermined and that his lands are not big enough, if that interests you."

The king only scoffed.

She went on anyway. "Lord Vactus feels your plans for the fortification's defenses are weak, but he's too afraid to speak out. Lord Folly detests the sound of your voice. The repetition of the word *fool* was hard to ignore. But you can't please them all, right?"

The king's jaw flexed at the insult while the prince's mouth twitched at one corner, fighting back amusement.

"No one's planning or conspiring against you as of late. It's all getting a bit dull, really."

Orlon leaned back in his mighty chair, propping an elbow on the velvet-clad arm to hold his powerful jaw in quiet contemplation. He didn't need the grandeur of a throne to assert his dominance as it radiated across the hall, yet she couldn't imagine him seated in anything less.

Faythe stayed silent, waiting for her dismissal, which was usually quick. When he didn't immediately relieve her of duty for the afternoon, her stomach started to knot with dread.

Orlon took a long breath before he spoke again. "High Farrow is to host King Varlas of Olmstone and King Agalhor of Rhyenelle next week. They will be staying with us for one week for the kings' meetings."

Faythe's fingers curled around the wood of the chair tighter out of nervousness. She silently damned the Spirits to burn, already anticipating the dangerous proposition that was about to fall on her shoulders.

"I shall require your presence to confirm their loyalty in the alliance is true, and I should like to find out their defense plans for their kingdoms above what they might disclose."

Hearing it out loud still made her blanch in horror at the thought of prying into the minds of the ancient and powerful rulers of Ungardia. She dropped her limp arms to her sides.

"With all due respect, Your Majesty—"

"Let me be clear: It is not a request," he said firmly, swiftly cutting off her protest. "I hope you have mastered your little mind tricks, *spymaster*. If one of them discovers you poking around, make no mistake, I will gladly hand you over to them and deny any knowledge."

Faythe swallowed hard, though it did nothing to relieve the dry pain in her throat.

King Orlon waited expectantly, and she reluctantly offered a small nod of obedience. A sly, satisfied smile spread wide across his cruel face. The look twisted her gut. Then he waved a lazy hand in dismissal, and she stumbled back a step, bowing her head before twisting sharply to storm for the exit, desperate to leave before the air in the council chamber became too thick to inhale.

Making haste through the doors, she remained rigid, marching through the halls while her mind reeled over the insanely daunting task bestowed upon her. She had only just grown accustomed to filtering through the minds of the Lords of High Farrow, and she had the protection of the king if she happened to be discovered. He would be able to silence any of them to keep his secret weapon from public knowledge. To spy into the mind of another *king*, however… There would be no salvation if she were caught, and the consequences didn't bear thinking about.

Her hands trembled, and she clamped her fists tight, fingernails biting into her palms out of fear and anger. She felt hot and restricted, unbuttoning her jacket in the hall before her rooms, thinking she might suffocate if she waited any longer. She wanted to burn the uniform to ash—the thing that made her shackles as the king's slave visible for all to see.

Barging through her chamber doors, she tore the royal blue coat from her shoulders, tossing it onto the bed and untying the top of her shirt to allow the air to breeze across her chest. Hauling open the balcony doors next, she took a long, deep breath of the bitter winter air that had chased away the autumn all at once last month. Winter was always the longest season, but Faythe welcomed the extended nights and chilly wind. The sun didn't shy in the presence of the coldest season and still beamed its powerful rays down on the marvelous, impeccable city. The reflections off the tall glass and white stone made it a sea of glittering crystal to look upon.

Today's sun offered no warmth, but as a tendril of its light fell on her face when she stepped out farther, Faythe closed her eyes at the comforting feeling. When she opened them again, she thought she could feel the ethereal presence that embraced her through those rays, bringing the Goddess of the Sun to mind. She had not visited Aurialis since her last rocky encounter with the Spirit of Life. Over three months later, that felt like a lifetime ago.

Everything had changed. Within herself and in her turn of circumstances. While her soul remained bound to the Eternal Woods until she returned the temple ruin—a reckless bargain made in the heat of a desperate moment—her mortal existence had now befallen a different kind of life sentence. A permanent tether to the King of High Farrow.

She had nothing left to barter with and had recently felt the crushing confinement and terrifying notion of not belonging to herself anymore. What hurt the most, and what had kept Faythe in low spirits since the day she signed her life away to the demon in the castle, was the heavy weight of sadness at her human friends being ripped away from her. They were safe, which was all she could be grateful for in the darkness. But it didn't ease the ache in her heart from their absence.

To assert his control, or perhaps to torture her further, the king had ordered that she was not permitted to leave the castle grounds even with guards. The stone walls had slowly been closing in on her, close to shattering her spirit completely if she was stuck between them any longer.

Faythe owed a lot of her remaining sanity to Tauria. It was amusing to think how they'd met, with Faythe holding a dagger to her throat to get the king's attention. They'd laughed over it later, after Faythe profusely apologized, guilty at knowing how kind and welcoming the ward really was. The shape of their ears was no more prominent than their different skin tones. None of it mattered to her, and she cherished the comfort and distraction from a certain blonde whose company she pined after.

Just as her heart began to calm and the air filled her lungs anew, a knock sounded at Faythe's bedroom door. She groaned out loud, in no mood to see anyone. Without giving her a chance to call out and dismiss the intruder, they opened the door with a creak, and she knew exactly who to expect from the lack of formality.

A familiar wave of sleek black hair came into view. Nik's emerald eyes glittered hues of a brighter green as he stepped outside to join her. He slid his hands casually into his pockets, eyes closing on a deep inhale while he basked in the sunlight. Tendrils of light kissed his fair skin while dark lashes cast soft shadows over his cheeks. Faythe looked away from him to lean over the stone railing, unable to silence her tormenting thoughts of how effortlessly beautiful he appeared.

"I thought my father was about to combust at hearing you call him a fool," he said by way of greeting.

Faythe laughed through her nose. "*I* didn't call him anything. He wishes to know what his company thinks. If His Majesty is so sensitive to getting his feelings hurt, he should be more specific about what he wants me to filter out."

"While that may be true, you should be careful. He might find your usefulness doesn't outweigh your brazenness."

She waved a hand, nonchalant. "He delights in knowing exactly what the people around him think, good or bad," she said confidently. "Besides, what's trading one life sentence for another if he does find me redundant?"

The prince frowned deeply. "Don't think like that."

"How am I supposed to think, Nik? I live by his command, and I'll die by it too."

"You're not a prisoner."

"Because I don't wear chains of iron? The bonds are still there —don't tell me you've convinced yourself otherwise."

His face fell, and she turned back to the city. Her nerves for the week ahead, the looming confrontation with the Courts of Ungardia, rattled in her mind, and she feared she would take it out on Nik if he stayed.

"You should go," she said quietly.

"Actually, I came to tell you to dress nicely tonight. I'll be back to get you at nine," Nik said, turning on his heel to return to the bedroom.

Faythe followed. "Why? What am I needed for now?" she grumbled, crossing her arms.

He paused at the door and turned to her with a bright smile. "You didn't think I'd forget, did you?" At her pointed look of question, his grin widened. "Happy Birthday, Faythe."

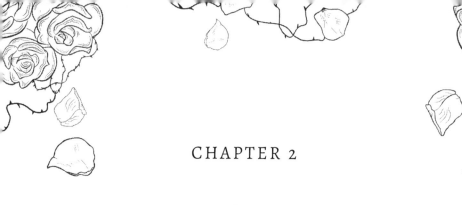

CHAPTER 2

Faythe

FAYTHE NERVOUSLY RAN her hands down her white-and-gold gown, feeling a little overdressed. She wasn't permitted outside the castle gates, so whatever Nik had planned for them must be within the confines of her stone cage.

While she was used to being dressed in pretty ornate gowns to blend in with the ladies of the court, she felt particularly pretentious in the dress that looked fit for a princess. It flowed with her movements, its colors giving her the familiar comfort and illusion of her subconscious mind.

Faythe found herself sitting in the white-and-gold mists of her mind often, reliving better times of freedom in the outer town with the two people dearest to her. It relieved her pain as much as it caused it. Reflecting on joyous memories was also a solemn reminder that she was banned from making any new ones with Jakon and Marlowe indefinitely. The torture of seeing them without physical touch was only made bearable by the knowledge it was a way of keeping them close while they were far. She realized this was the longest time in over a decade she and Jakon had been apart. Faythe felt as if she were missing a piece of herself in his absence.

Elise and Ingrid fussed over her hair, styling half of it back in a variety of braids as usual. Pretty as it was, Faythe always looked forward to relieving her head of the tight pressure and letting her fair brown waves loose by day's end. It wasn't customary for ladies of the court to have unbound hair, and she was already a far cry from their elegance and poise without defying that rule.

Faythe stared into the vanity mirror, and it unnerved her that she wasn't sure who was staring back. It was her face, but she didn't think it belonged with the diminished spirit inside anymore. The longer she remained a puppet to the king, the more she began to slip from herself. Her thoughts and opinions were silenced in her position of bound obedience. Every time she wanted to scream, cry out, or disagree, it was as if her head were underwater. Not even Nik was able to save her from drowning this time.

"Maybe it's a romantic tour of the gardens," Elise pondered with a giggle while securing a braid.

"No way. It's far too cold at this hour! And not to mention dark," Ingrid countered, fiddling with the stubborn strands hanging loose around her face.

Faythe rolled her eyes, though it was amusing to watch them excite over what Nik had planned. Their infectious enthusiasm lifted her somber mood.

"I hate to disappoint, but I can assure you, romance will not be playing a part tonight," Faythe cut in.

She caught the playful discontent in their expressions in the mirror's reflection. They knew of her history with Nik, had pressed and listened to every detail, and it felt wonderfully freeing to speak of it so openly without fear of the information ever leaving these walls. Faythe trusted them. Though, despite her persistence that whatever romantic feelings she and Nik had shared had been felt and left in the Eternal Woods, when the spymaster and the prince were simply Faythe and the fae guard, it didn't stop their fairy-tale minds from indulging on the fantasy.

When the door knocked at precisely nine o'clock, they knew exactly who was on the other side. Elise cast her a teasing look, and Ingrid released a subtle squeal and moved to answer it. Faythe couldn't prevent the heat that flushed her cheeks at their reaction.

Nik slipped into her rooms, and the two handmaidens bowed low to him before shuffling to leave. At seeing their fleeting giddy looks aimed at Nik's back, Faythe had to refrain from scowling as they left.

When the door clicked shut, she went to stand, but Nik had already taken the few strides over, putting a hand on her shoulder for her to remain seated. A delightful shiver trailed over where his fingers grazed the bare skin near her neck, lingering a little longer than necessary.

"I see you got my gift," he said, inspecting her gown in appreciation.

She raised her eyebrows as she looked down to observe the shimmering fabric. The colors seemed more fitting now as he was the only one who knew what they symbolized.

"Though, it's missing one small detail." His hands came around both of her shoulders with deliberate slowness, and she inhaled a breath. When something cool fell against her bare chest, she released that breath, glancing at the delicate eight-point gold star pendant now hanging there.

"It's beautiful," she breathed, stunned by Nik's thoughtfulness. She met his eye in the mirror. "Thank you."

Faythe stood and turned to him. Nik's eyes searched hers for a tender moment, and she thought she caught the flinch of his arm, which he forced down as if refraining from touching her. While it triggered a faint pinch in her chest, she knew it was better, safer, for both of them this way.

"You make it impossible not to love you," he said quietly.

Though it wasn't a comment made about a romantic feeling, it warmed her all the same. "I'm not sure everyone shares your view."

"Those who matter do."

His attempt to lift her fading spirit worked, and she couldn't hold back the desire to embrace him for it. It was exactly what she needed to hear after her long months of self-doubt, and he didn't even know it.

Nik held her tightly with his strong arms around the shoulders, savoring the comfort as he pressed his cheek to the top of her head. When she pulled back, their faces came so dangerously close past feelings flooded to the surface, making her breath hitch. But Nik quickly cleared his throat and stepped out of the embrace completely before either of them could give in to reckless impulses. He smiled brightly, and it dissolved any sad feelings at the lost opportunity for a kiss.

"We should go. The other half of your gift awaits."

Faythe furrowed her brow. "This is more than enough. What else have you done?"

He ignored her, grabbing her hand to lead her out of the room with a childish excitement she had never seen before. It almost seemed ridiculous to have the Prince of High Farrow escorting and fussing over *her*.

Everything was so easy with Nik that she often forgot his high power and status. Forgot he was fae, centuries-old, and heir to a mighty kingdom. None of it seemed relevant with the strength of their friendship. Even though he had lied about his true identity in the beginning, meeting with her outside the city walls under the false pretense of being a mere *guard*, in hindsight, Faythe was glad he did. It gave her the privilege of knowing him without the stigma of the title and crown he bore.

Nik dropped her hand when they emerged into the bright open hallway, falling into a casual stroll beside her and maintaining a respectful distance. In the public eye, they remained little more than strangers. His visits to her rooms were few and far between, but sometimes, he would risk visiting in place of sending Tauria to check on her well-being. It was not without careful approach, knowing the guard rotations, and with the help of Elise and Ingrid, so he wouldn't be seen entering or leaving. For both their safety, it was best they didn't draw suspicion to how well they knew each other and how close they really were.

Aside from her handmaidens, the only person they had mutually confided in was Tauria. She found the prince's artful ventures to the outer town all those months ago deeply amusing and admirable.

Nik led the way down two spiral staircases onto the ground level, and Faythe had no clue where he intended to lead her. The passageway she had come to memorize only led to the servants' quarters. He didn't give anything away as he ignored her pestering observations and guesses. Patience was never one of Faythe's strongest traits.

"If we're going to be cooking, I think we're both a little over-dressed," she commented as they approached the kitchens.

"Can you ever just be quiet and trust me?"

She was about to retort when he gave a mischievous smile and took a sharp right, passing the culinary quarters and heading straight down another dimly lit hallway. He stopped abruptly.

"Here we are," he announced, halting outside a small wooden door. It was closed, and while she stared at it warily, his grin stretched wider. Then he gripped the handle and strolled inside.

Faythe hesitated at his unusual eagerness then took a few tentative steps forward.

The room was small and had no windows. It was warmly lit by a fireplace, and some tall candles created the centerpiece of a humble dining table. Faythe walked farther into the room, noting the three table settings laid out, and figured Tauria must be joining them.

"You brought me all the way down here to have dinner?"

Not that she was unappreciative of his efforts—the food looked positively divine and already had her mouth watering. In fact, she was glad for the modest setting in place of the grand spectacle of a hall. Perhaps Nik saw the benefit of a little privacy to be themselves without worry of interruption or listening ears.

"Yes, but not with me," he said, casting his eyes to land on something behind her.

Faythe's eyebrows knitted together, and she turned back to see what caught his attention. At the sight of who stood there, a shallow cry came from her lips. It took a few seconds for her overwhelming shock and joy to subside, but then she ran the few strides before hurling herself at Jakon.

He caught her around the waist, and she burst into an ugly sob as the weight of missing him for over three months crushed her all at once. She couldn't let him go, and he made no move to release her as she cried, not quite believing he was physically here and in her arms.

"I've missed you like crazy," Jakon mumbled quietly into her hair.

She finally pulled back to look at him, touching his face. "You're really here," she breathed with immense elation.

He nodded with a small smile and released her. Faythe wanted to protest, but then her eyes landed on another wonderfully familiar ocean-blue set to his right, and another whimper left her.

"Nothing's been the same without you," Marlowe muttered sadly, embracing her tight.

"I want to know everything," Faythe croaked, wiping her wet cheeks with the sleeve of her gown.

"You should be safe down here for a couple of hours. I'll come back at midnight to get you both back to the town," Nik said.

Faythe spun around and found the prince standing directly behind her. "Thank you," she said, though words couldn't even come close to expressing how grateful she was. He'd risked everything to give her this night with her friends.

He only smiled and gave a small nod in response. Jakon and

Marlowe also uttered their gratitude, and the prince left without another word, closing the door behind him.

The trio took their seats around the table, but no one moved for the food. Faythe sat at the head so she could be beside both of her friends and spent a long moment simply looking between them as if they might vanish before her eyes. It was Jakon who broke the silence.

"Looks as if they've been treating you well at least," he observed.

Though he tried to hide it, Faythe knew him well enough to detect the hint of bitterness at her new status and way of life and how it was bestowed upon her. She didn't let the hurt show. Jakon didn't blame her for anything—she knew this—and she didn't blame *him* for his hatred toward the fae king who controlled her life.

"I would trade it all for a night back at the hut," she admitted.

Marlowe's soft voice chimed in. "I've been staying there with Jakon since you left. I hope you don't mind."

Faythe looked to the blacksmith, and the sorrow in her eyes told of something unspoken. Her stomach dropped at the sight.

"Of course not. Though you might want to look into getting a proper bed." She laughed weakly. Neither of them matched her humor, which only added to her sinking feeling. She dreaded to ask, "Did something happen?"

Jakon shifted his eyes to meet Marlowe's, leaving it open for her to choose whether she wanted to explain herself or hand the task to him. The blacksmith's brow creased tightly as if holding back the pain.

"My father...he passed away just a few weeks after everything happened." A single teardrop ran down her cheek, and she quickly brushed it away. "I think it was the stress. He was complaining of chest pain for months."

"Oh, Marlowe." Faythe took her hand. Her own eyes burned for her friend's grief and also in anger that she had been confined to the castle walls, completely cut off and unaware of Dalton's tragic passing.

Marlowe mustered a small smile. "We were both going to stay at the cottage for more space, but I couldn't bear going back there yet knowing my father never would."

Faythe's already fractured heart shattered completely then. She squeezed her friend's hand.

"I can't tell you how sorry I am. I should have been there."

Marlowe shook her head weakly. "It's not your—"

"It *is* my fault," Faythe cut in before her friend could try to give reason for her absence when Marlowe needed their support the most.

"It is my fault you were ever taken. It is my fault Dalton went through the terror of your capture. It is my fault both of you went through the horrific ordeal that landed me here, and you out there."

Neither of her friends protested or spoke out against her statements. Faythe took the silence that settled as their agreement. Jakon and Marlowe exchanged a look, something silent passing between them. Faythe had to drop her eyes to her plate, hating the sharp sting that almost made her wince from witnessing their unspoken language.

Her mind raced, taunting her to conclude what it meant. It was as though they were reflecting on some past conversation—about *her*. Perhaps they had been waiting for her to own the blame they had already cast.

Faythe's body flushed with guilt and humiliation, but she steeled her face. She fought the urge to shorten their time together and allow them to return to their safe and carefree lives. To spare them from the mess and danger that hovered over her like an angry storm cloud and broke whenever those dearest to her got close.

Marlowe's distant voice cut through her dark, spiraling thoughts. "If this is the only night we get to be with you for a while, we should try to enjoy it."

Though even as she said it, Marlowe didn't meet her eye.

It felt like a carving in Faythe's chest, as though her apology had been heard but not accepted. Not fully. But Faythe couldn't blame Marlowe—not after everything. After all, any protest might make her friends' opinion of her even lower. And with the grief of losing her father still fresh, it didn't feel right to beg for Marlowe's forgiveness in that moment. Perhaps it was better to set her insecurities aside and enjoy the moment. There would be plenty of time for self-pitying thoughts when she was alone in her rooms later.

"*Try* to enjoy it?" Faythe fixed a smile and met her friends' eyes. "I'm with my favorite people in the world, Marlowe. Enjoying your company is as natural as breathing air."

She was relieved when their features softened and the tension visibly cleared.

Faythe didn't particularly care that it was her birthday, but Nik had given her the most precious gift she could have asked for, even if she was only seeing her friends for a night. She made a promise to herself that she would figure out a plan to get the king to agree to relax the leash he held and give her some freedom within Farrowhold at least. She would do whatever it took and whatever he asked of her for the chance to be with her friends. Faythe owed them whatever fight she had left in herself. For everything they had done.

Jakon leaned forward in his chair, rising to grab the jug and refill his cup. He clenched his teeth and tried to hide the hiss of pain, his hand rising to his abdomen as he moved. Faythe's eyes fell to his stomach, and she frowned.

"I thought you were fully healed." She winced at the memory of Jakon's stabbing at the hands of crooks she'd foolishly fought in the Cave. She had to swallow the hard lump of guilt.

"I am. But a fatal wound healed by magick is likely to have flare-ups now and then." He added a chuckle to wave off the pain.

Faythe's stomach sank further. "How long has it been hurting?" she pressed, not convinced it was some side effect when he had assured them it had fully healed months ago without any lingering tenderness.

"Not long—"

"It comes and goes," Marlowe cut in, shooting Jakon a look of apology. "But it's been getting worse lately."

Faythe could see the silent scolding in Jakon's eyes as Marlowe confessed for him. Knowing her stupidly selfless and overprotective friend, Jakon would never have mentioned it at all if he hadn't slipped up enough for Faythe to notice.

"It's honestly nothing of concern," he dismissed.

Faythe gave a pointed look to where he still held his hand over the scar beneath his clothes. She had to focus her mind not to flash back to the image of the dagger protruding there and his blood staining his pale skin.

"It doesn't seem like nothing," she accused.

He removed his hand from his stomach and waved it lazily at her, reaching for the jug once again and topping up his wine. "I'll live," he mused with a crooked smile.

Faythe wasn't so convinced. He was healed by the yucolites— by Aurialis's light magick. Faythe's side of the bargain remained unfulfilled, and perhaps this was the Spirit's way of getting a message to her. A coil of dark, cold dread knotted in her stomach as a daunting thought crossed her mind: Was it possible for Aurialis to undo the magick of her yucolites? Faythe had been content to ignore her unfulfilled end of the bargain for as long as possible, but if there was a chance the Spirit held the ability to take back her magick…

She swallowed hard and mustered a smile in response to Marlowe as she tried to divert the conversation to something more lighthearted, noting Jakon's discomfort at the topic of his pain. But the air remained tainted, and she wondered if they felt it too. The faint essence that left a friction, a *divide*, between her and her two friends, which she couldn't shake.

For the next few hours, they caught up on both the pretentious and painstakingly dull affairs of court life and the same dreary routine of the outer town. Apart from the devastation of Marlowe losing her father, everything was reported to be as bland and somber as she remembered. The young blacksmith had taken over the business full-time and was making it thrive, while Jakon kept his job on the farm, both of them welcoming the distraction from the hollow void that was left behind by Faythe and Dalton's absence. The only time Faythe could muster any positivity in her voice was in speaking of Nik and Tauria. She told her human friends all about her fae companions on the prestigious side of the wall. Part of her wished they were here so she could see all her friends together and damn the social divide. It didn't matter to Faythe, and she was confident they too would forget the physical differences and status that set them apart to find friendship if given the opportunity.

She wanted to stay in that small room and talk the whole night away. Then, all too soon, the dainty wooden door creaked open and Nik entered with a sad look on his face, regretful he was the signal for them to be taken away from her once again. Her heart dropped, and she embraced both her friends tightly, promising she would see them soon.

Perhaps it was selfish of her to need them, their friendship and comfort, after all she had done, but until they gave the word they were wisely seeking distance from her...Faythe would harbor that kernel of hope. Hope that one day, she could offer them something in return other than danger and misery.

Seeing Jakon and Marlowe sparked the slowly dying embers within Faythe, and she felt the fire rise, pulsing through her veins once more. In that moment, she struck a private oath: that she would not lose herself or allow herself to be tamed, silenced, or controlled within the evil grasp of the king's desires. For her friends, she had to keep fighting.

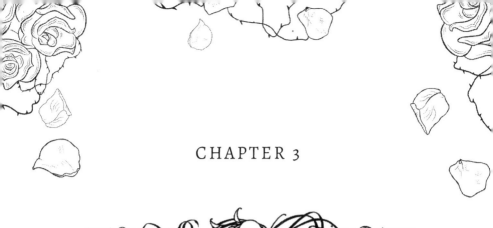

CHAPTER 3

Nikalias

U NDER THE COVER of darkness, Nik cautiously took a route he was all too skilled at maneuvering through undetected. He didn't forget about the two humans he had the job of leading to safety, and luckily, their dull senses and comparative lack of stealth didn't prove to be a problem in getting to the hidden drain tunnel.

Down the dark alley, he spied a figure leaning casually against the wall. Jakon and Marlowe seemed to slow at his back, but Nik detected the stranger as a friend, not foe.

Caius peeled himself from the stone with a beaming smile when they approached. Nik had asked the young guard for his assistance specifically, observing how welcoming he'd been with Faythe. That, and Caius was one of the very few in the know about his inconspicuous endeavors into the town through the dark labyrinth below. His loyalty was unquestionable.

"Your Highness." He bowed slightly.

Nik cringed at the formality, strangely more so in the presence of Faythe's friends. He didn't think they fully forgave him for his months of deceit to her, hiding his true identity while he helped to train her mind abilities.

"Thank you for this, Caius. It won't be forgotten," he said gratefully with a hand on his shoulder.

The young guard gave a humble nod in response, bending down to haul open the wrought iron seal on the drain hole.

Nik turned to the humans, feeling a little awkward that he didn't know how to bid them farewell. It was ridiculous—he was a crown prince, heir to a great throne, yet he was shy in the presence of two ordinary mortals. He cleared his throat and straightened.

"Caius will lead you out through the underground tunnels. You'll be safe with him."

The blacksmith stepped forward to go first but stopped in front of Nik before she descended the ladder. "Thank you," she said, soft and heavy with bittersweet gratitude.

Nik wished he could have given them more time.

He didn't respond. He couldn't make empty promises that they might get to see Faythe more often, as it wasn't entirely in his power to grant her such movement. He gave a small, tight smile, but his fists curled at his sides at feeling so useless against his father who had deprived Faythe of her most basic right: freedom.

Marlowe crouched then disappeared down the dark hole. Looking to Jakon, Nik almost recoiled to find him already staring with a contemplative frown.

"I didn't want to like you, and I'm still not sure I trust you," Jakon said, using his whole body subconsciously to try to level with him in dominance. Nik had to admire the human for his bravery, if anything, even though his fae instincts flared at the hint of challenge. "But Faythe trusts you, and that's good enough for me. She's strong, but not unbreakable. Keep looking out for her in there, will you?" His tone was almost pleading, a small wavering of his bravado Nik understood.

Jakon didn't have to ask. Nik was certain there wasn't anything he wouldn't risk to ensure Faythe's safety against his father's cruelty.

He appreciated that although the human expressed his reserves about the prince, he *did* trust him to protect the single thing dearest to him alongside Marlowe. Not only Faythe's life, but her internal well-being while she remained distanced from their comfort and friendship.

"Always," Nik promised.

The next morning, Nik's father summoned him early, much to his irritation after having little rest.

Once he'd delivered Faythe's friends into the capable hands of Caius, Nik had ended up outside Faythe's door, not entirely of his own conscious decision. As much as he tried to stay away from her, maintaining distance for both their safety, he couldn't stop himself from checking she wasn't breaking down at having to be separated from her friends again.

He was surprised to find she was in the complete opposite mood when she invited him in, and they talked into the small hours of the night about her plans to be granted access to the outer town. While her confidence and bravery was something Nik had greatly appreciated about Faythe from the beginning, he was wary it would be the thing to land her life in peril if she tested it too far against his father. But there was no dissuading her from her course of action, and Nik could only pray the king would see reason.

Nik acknowledged the guards with a nod of respect as he slipped into the council chamber.

During Faythe's first week in the castle, Nik had gone discreetly to each of the guards in an attempt to put their minds at ease about the unknown human telepath in their court. He hoped to convince them she wasn't a threat and help make her feel at least slightly welcome in a castle full of strangers who weren't even her own species. It seemed to have worked for some of them; he saw them engaged in occasional friendly conversation with the king's spymaster.

The room was empty aside from his father, who stood over a map with counters and wooden figures spread across it, and a couple of guards as usual.

"You wished to see me, Father?" Nik stopped halfway down the long table and stood straight to address the king.

"Ah, yes. I would like to discuss arrangements for the kings' meetings next week." He tore his eyes from the map to look at him. "I've been thinking about propositions for my spymaster."

At the mention of Faythe, Nik shifted nervously but waited in silence for him to continue.

The king walked a few paces to stand at the head of the table, resting a hand on the back of his throne with a creased brow while he pondered his own thoughts. "Having her in uniform posted next to the guards won't give her the opportunity to engage and gain trust among the other courts. There is only so much she can find out in a few meetings," he said, fiddling aimlessly with the sigil ring on his finger.

"What do you propose for her?" Nik asked, antsy with anticipation.

The king's eyes met his once again, stark black that had chased away all hues of brown over a century ago. Nik thought nothing of it at first; perhaps it was only a trick of the light. But along with his eyes, he didn't fail to notice the inner change in his father also. He hadn't always been so harsh in his discipline and ruthless in his plans. For a long time, there had been an added layer of cruelty Nik could only pin down to the aftereffects of the Great Battles, then losing the queen, Nik's mother.

"I wanted your thoughts on presenting her as a lady of the court instead."

Nik's instinct was to splutter or laugh or ridicule the idea, though that would be highly inappropriate given his company, so he kept his face placid despite his internal conflict.

"She will dine with us on the first night, charm the other courts, and it will give her a means to engage with them outside of meetings to dive in for further information."

It was a smart plan with one glaring problem: Faythe was as straight as a die with her thoughts and emotions. "Charming" was a far cry from what he anticipated from her in the presence of fae nobles. It was one thing for her to stand in silence and get the information the king wanted, and a whole other to ask her to lie through her teeth and be pleasant while she racked the minds of unwitting foreign court members.

"It would be a fine idea, but I fear she is not well-educated in court life. And she's human. It might be too difficult a lie to spin," Nik said cautiously.

"You will teach her," the king answered a little more cheerfully than Nik expected, clearly reveling in his own brilliant plan. "It is the perfect cover. And I do not need to remind you or her that her position could change any day I see fit."

Nik didn't miss the hint of a threat in those words and didn't feel it was solely directed at the spymaster either. It shook him with mild alarm. Did the king know more about his relations with Faythe than he let on?

"Of course. I will see to it that she is prepared, and if she tries anything smart, I will personally bring her to you in chains," he said as confidently as he could.

It must have been convincing enough as a cruel smile split the king's face. "Excellent. I know you will not disappoint."

Just then, the doors groaned open, and the prince's heart skipped a beat when the spymaster in question glided through the door. Wisps of lilac and white from her delicate gown trailed after her, and she strolled in with an air of confidence to address the king. Nik would have admired her beauty in the court's fine silks as he always found himself struck by it, except he was too overcome with dread at knowing the purpose of her visit.

"I need to speak with you, Your Majesty," she asserted, and Nik's nerves rattled. Faythe stood firm, not even offering a bow.

It didn't go unnoticed. The king's eyes flashed at the lack of respect.

"Then speak," he said in a low tone that would have most fae quivering in their boots.

Nik watched Faythe's chest expand as she took a long inhale and braced himself for the worst.

"I want free movement to go outside the city walls."

Not a question. Not a request. Spirits have mercy on them all at the spymaster's boldness. Nik dared a glance at his father and caught the flinch of his narrowed eyes.

"Your wants are not my concern," he said simply. "I will not risk you using mind tricks to elude the guards and escape."

"I have been here for months and done everything you have asked. If I wanted to escape, I would have managed that long ago," Faythe said, and he knew her well enough to note the rise of her temper in her tone.

Gods help them.

The king's jaw flexed at her insolence. "Perhaps I should have you chained when you are not needed then, *girl.*" His dominance in the room rose as the king and the spymaster faced off in a lethal battle of wills.

Nik wasn't sure if he should admire the human who was brave enough to stand up against a fae king or chastise her for her stupidity and complete disregard for her own life.

"You could have kept me in chains from the beginning, but my cooperation makes things easier for you."

Nik could have collapsed at her defiant stance. Even the few guards shifted a little. He wasn't sure who unsettled them the most.

The king stepped away from the chair he was leaning on and slowly walked closer to Faythe. To her credit, she didn't balk at the dark force that crept up to her. Instead, she stood straighter and raised her chin.

Nik didn't move, didn't even dare to breathe too loud, afraid any interference would be the catalyst for the pair to explode.

"You forget that you are only *alive* out of my mercy, girl. You are not irreplaceable." The king's voice rumbled low and deadly.

Faythe took a step toward Nik's father, and he jerked a fraction in response to the lamb recklessly approaching the predator who could end her with a single strike. "Am I not?" she challenged audaciously, and Nik knew that if she made it even halfway through her mortal lifespan with those wits—or lack thereof—it would be a miracle.

He noted the twitch of movement in his father's arm as he refrained from reaching for his mighty blade, the legendary Farrow Sword with a Griffin-carved pommel, to bring it down on the human right there. "I have many skilled Nightwalkers who are not so different from you. The information may come at a slower pace, but do not make the mistake of thinking I won't hesitate to end your pitiful existence."

Faythe took another step toward the king, and Spirits be *damned*, Nik had to brace a hand on the table in front of him to stop from lunging over it and placing himself between them. "Yes, you do. Your own son is a fine testament to that," she said, but she did not remove her eyes from the king. "But can your Nightwalkers bring your enemies to their knees before you without touching them? Can they bend their will right before your eyes? Can they reveal secrets and lies straight from the mouth of the deceiver?" She tilted her head as if offering the king a chance to counter her statements. *Gods*, the woman had a daring nerve like no one he'd ever known before.

When the king didn't respond, she continued. "Perhaps you want a demonstration. Is the captain available for another show?" Faythe glanced around the room, and every guard shifted on their feet, averting their gaze.

"I will kill you for your impudence alone, girl. Don't overestimate your use to me."

33

Nik didn't doubt his father would hold true to that threat. He wanted to whack sense into her. Picking a fight with the King of High Farrow was a whole new level of foolishness for Faythe.

"I'm bound to die at your hand anyway. By life imprisonment as your puppet, or by your sword—it makes no difference to me."

The pair faced off for a long moment, and the weight of the thick, rising tension in the room was crushing.

To Nik's absolute shock, the king conceded first, though the rage still simmered in the crevices of his face as he turned away from the spymaster and strolled back to the head of the table. He was silent for a moment, and Nik knew the look that glazed his father's eyes as if he could see the cogs turning in his head.

"Very well," he said in a calm tone that made Nik tremble. "You will be allowed access to the outer town."

Faythe relaxed a little in surprise.

"But…you will go in uniform and as part of the guard patrol."

Nik snapped his head to his father at the proposition. The king nodded at his own cunning plan.

"Yes, this could work to our advantage. You will have your freedom, and in return, the humans will be grateful to see one of their kind has been given such a generous placement within the castle. They will thank their king and know they are not left without a voice in the outer towns. You will be it for them. In appearance," he finished with a wicked smile.

Anger was written on Faythe's face at the additional terms to her small dose of freedom. She was to be paraded to her people as a lie. The king had no intention of listening to the woes and sufferings of his human subjects, but her presence out there, in a royal uniform, would earn him all the favor he needed to keep them quiet and even more obedient.

Faythe looked as if she was straining against protesting further, but mercifully, she saw it was the best she was going to get from the king and nodded once.

His father grinned triumphantly, but the grin subsided as he said, "Good. Now, get out of my sight before I decide your skills aren't worth that arrogant mouth of yours."

The spymaster didn't hesitate nor even glance at Nik as she spun on her heel and the guards opened the doors for her to leave. He didn't take the lack of acknowledgment to heart. As soon as she was out of sight, he physically relaxed, realizing he had been painfully rigid in fear and anticipation since Faythe first set foot in the hall.

"I shall leave you to inform her of her new role for the forthcoming week."

Nik met the black eyes of the king at the sound of his voice.

"She will not speak unless spoken to. She will hold that tongue of hers, and she will not get the chance to undermine me in my own court again," he said in a deadly warning Nik knew was as much for him as it was for Faythe. She would be his problem to handle and his punishment to face if she stepped out of line.

The crown prince swallowed hard but gave his father a firm nod of understanding. Even though he knew the Spirits themselves could not tame the fire that burned eternally within Faythe.

CHAPTER 4

Faythe

T HE DAY FOLLOWING her confrontation with the King of High
Farrow, Faythe enjoyed a walk through the castle gardens
with Tauria, feeling as if a weight had been lifted at her small
victory. The king's conditions still pierced her heart with another
dagger of control. He gave nothing without working it to his ulti-
mate advantage. The price of seeing her friends beyond the wall
was to submit to patrolling the outer town as a walking lie, a false
frontage, to make them believe the king was generous and caring of
their lives when he would sooner let them all perish outside the
walls than offer sanctuary in the face of an attack.

It was a dangerous gamble to confront the king—one she really
wasn't confident she would walk away from. But in an act of pure,
reckless insanity, she finally snapped, damning the consequences to
finally take back some of her lost voice.

The bitter air nipped at her cheeks as she strolled slowly over
the pristine stone paths alongside the ward. Though beautiful and
well-kept, the gardens didn't compare to the Eternal Woods. Every
piece of nature she encountered now, Faythe couldn't help but

notice the grass was a shade duller, the flowers not as bloomed, and the water murkier.

She found herself missing the spot she frequented with Nik. It was the one carefree, safe space she missed the most, free from any wandering eyes and where she was liberated to be completely and wholly herself. Her heart ached in longing to have those moments again. She mindlessly reached a hand under her cloak to grasp the gold star pendant that lay there.

"From the prince, I assume?" Tauria's voice of song lifted her from her reflections.

It took Faythe a moment to realize she meant her necklace, and her cheeks flushed. Dropping it, she nodded. "A gift for my birthday."

The ward smiled warmly. "You have his heart, you know?" she said casually.

Faythe detected a hint of sadness on Tauria's smooth tan face, though she insisted there was never any romantic history between her and Nik during times when Faythe had needed to curb her curiosity and guiltily soothe her jealousy at the thought.

"There's a bond there for sure," Faythe said.

Tauria's courtly life made her a master of masks to hide her true feelings in the presence of high-born nobles, but Faythe picked up on the slight twitches that gave her away. Averting her gaze for a second when she heard something she didn't like was one of them.

She added, "But it's the same bond I have with my friends, Jakon and Marlowe."

Tauria's lips curled up a little, but not in happiness. "You're lucky to have friends you can trust. Court life can be lonely. I can never be sure which of the lords and ladies want to know me for me or my status as the king's ward." The perfect golden skin on her forehead creased in suppressed sadness.

It filled Faythe with guilt. She had spent all her time in the castle complaining about her own misfortune and never considered how tough life could be for someone like Tauria who suffered under the king's rule daily. A ward, a *princess*, who appeared to have everything on the outside: beauty, luxuries, the king's favor. Faythe figured no one realized it all meant nothing without the fruits of life's labor—the real connections made along the way.

"You know you have a friend in me, always," Faythe said, and she meant every word.

Tauria smiled in appreciation. "There's something about you, Faythe. I don't know exactly what it is, but it gives me hope for us all."

Faythe was about to laugh at the ridiculous compliment, but one look at the ferocity in Tauria's face made her nervous smile drop. Her searching brown orbs almost set her in a trance, and she realized they had stopped walking.

"I'm just a tyrant king's spymaster," Faythe said, averting her gaze out of shame.

"No. You are so much more, and you cannot let him break you."

From the moment Faythe first spoke to the ward, that night on the balcony when her fate became sealed to the king, she knew Tauria was not the simple, polite court lady she had deceived everyone into thinking she was. No—behind the innocence of beauty, there was a fierce warrior who would bow to no one and stop at nothing to see her kingdom returned to her and her parents avenged. She had yet to open up to Faythe about the dark days over a century ago that saw her home kingdom conquered and her family slaughtered, or how she managed to make it to High Farrow to find sanctuary. But Faythe wouldn't push for the story that clearly haunted the ward all these years later.

She cleared her throat and linked her arm with Tauria's so they could resume their leisurely stroll. "Tell me more about Fenstead," she said to divert the conversation away from herself.

Tauria beamed at the mention of her home and started an immersive description of the beauty of the lands and the wonders of the people. It was a rural kingdom with far more open hilltops and forests, which made their sigil of a stag seem all the more fitting. The ward's face lit up with brightness and enthusiasm when she spoke of her people and homeland.

"I hope you get the chance to see it someday," she gushed.

Faythe gave her a weak smile, but even in Tauria's eye, a glint of dejection gave away her wishful thinking. With a mortal lifespan, it was unlikely Faythe would ever see the day the princess took back her kingdom and throne.

Never before had she longed for any more years than her human body would sustain her for. Yet now, having two friends who would hold their youth while she turned gray and frail, her stomach sank horribly at the thought of ever parting with them. There would be so many things she would miss out on in Nik and Tauria's lives thanks to the wicked curse of time.

Noting her sorrow, the ward nudged her shoulder. "Watch this."

Faythe's eyes followed as Tauria glided over to the dull bushes, bare from the effects of winter, and raised a delicate hand to them. Right under her fingertips, a fluorescent green stalk spiraled from the crooked brown branches, and a rose of the purest white bloomed out of its bud. Tauria picked it from the gloom of the shrub and held it out to Faythe, who took the thornless rose in awe.

Tauria was wonderfully gifted in elemental magick, a Windbreaker with the ability to command the air around her, but she had also inherited some of her mother's talent as a Florakinetic and could easily manipulate nature.

"I'd trade my ability for yours any day," Faythe said, admiring the perfectly blossomed flower.

"For mind control? It's a deal."

Faythe chuckled, and they linked arms for the rest of the walk around the gardens.

They strolled lazily, chatting aimlessly, until the sun started to fall behind the impeccable white buildings with a last wave from its fleeting rays before dusk welcomed the night. The air dropped to a temperature that had them shivering, and Faythe was surprised by how much time had passed. She welcomed the mundane distraction. It was a feeling she had been missing from her blonde friend over the wall.

When they were back inside and warm again, Faythe announced, "I have to go—I'm heading out with the outer-town patrol tonight."

She wasted no time in finding out exactly when the day and night patrols were scheduled to leave each day and jumped on the first opportunity to see her home again. She made note of exactly who would be given each assignment. A few of the guards were friendlier to her than others, and she had plans to divert herself from the group to see her friends.

"Can I come?" Tauria asked with a beam of excitement.

Faythe raised her eyebrows at the ward's eagerness, not expecting her to be the least bit interested in the dreary town.

"Please? I hardly ever get to go outside the city walls."

It was an absurd notion that Tauria would ask Faythe's permission for anything. She even felt silly for not knowing how to respond as it wasn't exactly within her authority to tell a princess what to do.

Faythe hated herself for even thinking it, and she winced as she said, "Are you sure the king won't mind?"

The ward waved a dismissive hand. "He's not my keeper. Besides, he hardly keeps track of where I am anyway."

Faythe didn't know the exact relationship between the ward and the king, or why such a cold-hearted male as Orlon would not only offer sanctuary to the foreign princess, but station her as his *ward* to be by his side at all times. Perhaps there were more layers to the King of High Farrow that Faythe should reserve judgment for.

"Well, I have to change into uniform," she grumbled reluctantly. "Meet me at my rooms in an hour?"

Tauria squealed in joy, giving a quick nod before turning on her heel and near skipping down the hallway to her quarters.

Faythe stood in the silent hall until she was out of sight. She was a little apprehensive of allowing her to join in case it put her agreement of freedom in jeopardy. But who was she—or the king for that matter—to tell a grown fae, a *royal* fae, where she could and couldn't go?

Fastening the final button of her uniform jacket, Faythe was giddy with anxious excitement at getting to see her quaint little hut in the outer town again. Her living quarters in the castle were lavish, and she had no complaints with the generous space and soft furnishings. Despite this, it had taken a while to get used to the large, plush bed. She strangely missed the cramped, awkward arrangement of the wooden dwelling she shared with Jakon. Most of all, she missed the soothing nighttime comfort of his breathing and soft snores before she slept. She had spent many painfully restless nights during her first weeks in the castle trying to adjust to the new stillness and silence of her lonely rooms.

Looking at herself in the full mirror, dressed in the king's colors, Faythe couldn't help but feel stupidly nervous to see her friends. What would they think of her parading around as if she were proud to serve the demon with a crown?

Before she could work herself up and lose her nerve to go, there was a knock at her door. Faythe called for the person to enter, doing a double-take when instead of one body, she spied two entering her bedroom in the mirror's reflection. She whirled around, raising her eyebrows at Nik who was dressed in a similar attire to her own, like a royal guard. She was about to ask why he was here when Tauria saved her the bother.

"He passed me in the hall, and I told him about tonight. He insisted he was coming too," she explained sheepishly.

Faythe folded her arms. "I thought you weren't allowed to be seen outside the walls?" She cocked an eyebrow, remembering his excuse for why he was always so secretive during their encounters in the outer town. If only she knew then what his real reason was for going incognito.

"I'm not going as myself. For all my father knows, Vixon is still out on patrol, and *I* am simply indisposed." He grinned mischievously. "You're not the only one missing the rustic views of the outer town. The inner city can get a bit claustrophobic."

Though he teased, Faythe knew he was only insisting on coming along to keep an eye on her and Tauria. She noticed his overprotectiveness extended endearingly to the princess too. Sometimes, the way Nik looked at Tauria, whether the princess saw it or not, held a depth that dropped a sadness in Faythe's stomach. She never gave the ugly sinking feeling a chance to settle.

"So, you paid off Vixon to cover for you," she concluded. His answering grin was all the confirmation she needed. Faythe huffed. "You've definitely used that trick before. At least now I know how you ended up at the summer solstice bonfires." She shot him a playful, accusing look while Tauria's lips parted in surprise. Clearly, the prince was far more cunning and secretive than even his closest companion knew.

Nik had risked a lot to venture into the human town and remain undiscovered. Faythe understood why he wouldn't confide in the ward about those particular antics, at the risk of implicating her too if he were caught.

The deviance on his face made Faythe's mouth twitch up in amusement.

"That was particularly difficult. I had to come up with a perfect excuse to get out of the solstice ball here at the castle and not have someone come looking for me." He cast a lighthearted smirk at the ward whose tan cheeks flushed a shade of rose as she quickly averted her eyes.

"There's really nothing that eventful out there. I don't know why either of you are bothered." Faythe grabbed her deep blue cloak with the king's sigil of a winged Griffin as the clasp across one shoulder—an extension of her prison-wear.

"Adventure is what you make it, Faythe," Nik quipped.

With a roll of her eyes, she answered with sarcastic enthusiasm, moving past them and out the door. "Then the great quest of the outer town awaits."

They met the other two night guard patrol, Caius and Tres, by the servants' exit. At the sight of the prince and the ward, both of them blanched.

"Keep quiet. Let's go," Nik instructed, leaving no room for argument.

They both hesitated, clearly debating the punishment if the king found out about their added party members. But with a glance at the prince's stern face, they nodded.

Nik already had a plan for how he and Tauria would get out of the city unnoticed by the other guards: through the underground labyrinth. Faythe shuddered at her recollection of the dark, grim passageways she had only ventured through once before—with Jakon, in their reckless failed attempt to infiltrate the castle and save Marlowe's life. She wanted to slap herself for the brash plan that had landed her in the Netherlord's service.

Nik and Tauria kept the hoods of their cloaks up and their heads bowed low, trailing slightly behind the patrol. Once they were through the side gate, the two of them broke off to take the inconspicuous route. They would merge again once in the safety of the outer town.

Faythe followed close to Caius, diverting to take the main street out of the city. Only now did she feel riddled with anxiety. She subconsciously adjusted the clasp of her cloak, all too aware of the flood of royal blue. Paired with the rounded contours of her ears, she felt as if even the mortar of the pristine white buildings weighed judgment on her.

All of them stayed silent as they marched through the inner-city streets, and Faythe was grateful for it. Her throat became hoarsely dry as she craned her neck to gauge the full height of the daunt-ingly tall dwellings. She had only ever admired the gleaming city from afar, and never in her lifetime did she think she would stroll so casually across the smooth paths. Her nerves were momentarily subdued by her awe. In stark contrast to the uneven, harsh cobbled streets of her human town, the ground here was level and clean. She almost felt as if she were gliding.

Every now and then, she had to hurry her steps to catch up with the guards after she slowed to take in the marvelous beauty. She tried not to pay attention to the few fae they passed, but her curiosity got the better of her, and she felt her confident poise falter every time she caught their wrinkled glances of distaste and confu-sion. It made Faythe feel horribly out of place. She wanted to shrink out of the blue attire and dissipate into the wind.

She noticed the flickering lapis flames that danced in ornate, floating white baskets along the sides of the buildings—something she had found oddly alluring the first time she saw the obscure color of the fire months ago. She turned her head to Caius.

"How does the fire burn blue?"

He glanced at the baskets. "Firewielders," he said as if it were the most obvious thing. "They create flames that give off heat but don't require wood or coal to keep burning. They won't go out without their command."

Faythe raised an eyebrow in curiosity at the eternal flames forged by those with the elemental gift of fire. She wondered just how many different abilities there were, impressed by each new talent she discovered. She was lost in this city of magick and perfect sculpture. Not a lick of paint was tarnished, and there were no discarded crates or really anything out of place on the immaculate walkways. It was beautiful...yet artificial.

When they reached the wall and stepped under the archway, it was as if someone had snuffed out all the lights, leaving only the dullness of the grim, tattered brown town. However, it allowed the glittering stars to shine confidently against the dark night sky without competition. Below them, Faythe had to blink hard a few times to adjust to the change in luminance. She never realized just how cold and run-down her dreary town was. The sad, worn buildings and orange glow of the torches made it look all the more impoverished in comparison. It wasn't high and lavish like the inner city, but it held a humble warmth and comfort that welcomed her *home*.

Faythe and the two guards fell quiet again as they ventured down the nostalgic streets she grew up in, the ones she was confident she could find her way through if anyone took away her sight. She didn't know how far behind Nik and Tauria were for taking the underground route, but she kept calm as she waited for them to make their appearance.

"What do you usually do out here?" she asked Caius out of curiosity as they weaved through the uneven paths.

"We have to do the rounds. Mostly just check up on the main parts of town, make sure everything's in order. It usually is and can be pretty boring," he answered simply.

Caius had a wonderful way of humoring her questions without any judgment or irritation. She felt relaxed around him, knowing his friendliness toward her wasn't fake because he feared her for what she could do or because of her status to the king. It was genuine, and he was invaluable as a friend among the guard ranks, knowing how to ease her nerves.

A sharp whistle stopped Faythe dead in her tracks. She jolted back to look down the alley to her left. Nik's eyes were bright, his smile amused at her obvious fright. She refrained from whacking his arm in annoyance when he and Tauria emerged from the shadows to join them.

The prince turned to the guards. "You two carry out your duties. We won't be far, and we'll find you when it's time to go back."

Caius's eyes darted between Nik and Faythe, and she could see he wanted to protest. He was likely under strict orders to keep an eye on her at all times. Faythe thanked the Spirits for Nik's presence then. He knew her intention was to divert from the patrol to seek out her friends, and his influence took the task of persuasion off her shoulders. Thankfully, Caius said nothing, giving a short nod of understanding.

Faythe didn't waste any of the precious time she had been granted. She turned on her heel to take the street to her right with the prince and ward in tow while Caius and Tres continued straight on. Reaching her destination in a few quick minutes, she paused outside the familiar crooked brown door of the hut, heart wild with nerves, wringing her hands.

"What's wrong?" Nik asked softly.

She wasn't sure how to answer, caught up in a mixture of joy and sadness at seeing her home that felt strangely foreign all of a sudden. Then, thinking of her two friends inside happily living their lives, which she was about to barge into wearing a guard's uniform as a completely different person to the one who last stepped inside the feeble structure, she realized she felt guilty for bringing her mess of a life to their door. They could live a perfectly mundane and fulfilled existence without her. It was Faythe's own selfishness that brought her here.

"This was a mistake," she muttered quietly. She turned to leave, but Nik caught her by the shoulders.

"I don't need your ability to know what you're thinking, Faythe. Don't take that choice from them."

Tears nipped her eyes as she met the prince's green gaze and saw the determination behind it. He wouldn't let her self-destruct.

"They deserve better."

Nik shook his head. "They deserve a friend who will stick by and fight for them. And that's what you're doing by coming here tonight." His hands fell away, and with that, he left her to make her own choice.

Faythe slid a look to Tauria who offered a warm smile of encouragement. "I feel as if I already know them from how much you talk of them. It would be a shame not to meet in person now we're here," she mused lightly, but in a way that still left the decision in Faythe's hands, without any judgment.

She wouldn't cower, and in that same decisive moment, Faythe banished all thoughts of knowing what was best for Marlowe and Jakon. If they decided they would be better off without her mess and drama, she would respect their choices to lead their lives without her. Until they gave the word…

She took a deep breath and spun around to the door, rapping her knuckles twice against the wood before she lost her composure. It felt odd to knock, but at the same time, it was no longer her home to welcome herself into. She trembled with anticipation, the coward in her hoping they weren't even home to save her the emotional stress. Then the unchanging sound of the front door's creaking hinges being pulled open revealed the disheveled brown hair of her dearest friend.

Jakon stood silent, stunned, and neither of them spoke for a few painfully long seconds. Faythe waited outside the threshold, giving him the chance to reject her upon seeing her attire and company. Instead, he reached for her hand and pulled her into a tight embrace inside the hut. A small sound of relief came from her, and Faythe closed her eyes to savor his tenderness.

"Faythe?"

At the chirp of Marlowe's voice, Faythe snapped her eyes open to land on the ocean-blue orbs emerging from the bedroom. Marlowe's smile was warm, and Faythe's nerves about seeing her after their last somber conversation eased when they embraced.

"How did you get here?" she asked when they broke apart.

Faythe glanced behind her at the two fae who remained outside. She quickly beckoned them in, and they obliged as they all shuffled farther into the hut. The small front room was hardly large enough to accommodate them all.

"Well, you know Nik. This is Tauria." Faythe introduced them.

"I've heard so much about you both," the ward said. Then she

47

looked at Marlowe specifically. "You sound like quite the impressive woman."

The blacksmith blushed deep crimson and flashed Faythe an accusatory glance. She simply shrugged sheepishly. It was true Faythe had gushed about Marlowe's many talents and extensive knowledge.

"I've heard a lot about you too," Marlowe said timidly, having never been in front of a fae female before, let alone a princess. "I'll make some tea. I'd love to hear more. Faythe is a little sparse with the details."

The two of them went over to the dainty kitchen, and Faythe's heart warmed at the sight of everyone in the room—her unbreakable circle of friends. Family. She looked to Jakon and found him observing her royal blue formal attire, she shifted anxiously, glancing down.

"A condition of getting to come here." She felt the need to explain herself at his unspoken judgment.

Her friend smiled sadly. "I always thought red or green suited you best, but I suppose the blue works," he mused playfully, and Faythe relaxed, relieved he didn't hold any resentment toward her for it. "I wish you didn't have to be tethered to that bastard." Jakon paused, shooting a look at Nik and muttering a quick apology.

The prince's jaw flexed, but he said nothing to scold him for insulting his father, their king.

Faythe reached out and squeezed Jakon's upper arm. "It's only a job. I'm treated well," she reassured him even though downplaying what she was really used for twisted in her gut.

Jakon knew everything, but she was glad he never brought it up or made her speak of how she was a silent intruder of thoughts. He'd made it clear to her the night of her birthday that no matter what she was forced to do at the king's hand, he would never think of her differently. It was a great relief, but also damning, as she felt his words were preemptive forgiveness should she ever be forced to do something unthinkable.

When they turned to make the few strides to the table, Faythe heard Jakon inhale before catching his hand over his abdomen. His rigid posture was a sure giveaway that he was in pain. Her face wrinkled, but she said nothing.

Faythe and Tauria settled at the small bench in the kitchen across from Marlowe and Jakon. Nik stayed standing, leaning against the countertop behind her—mainly because there wasn't enough room on the already overcrowded bench, but even if he had a side to himself, Faythe knew he would barely get his legs under the feeble table anyway.

For nearly an hour, the five of them chatted and caught up on each other's lives, and Faythe relished in the normalcy. It warmed her heart to see both sides of her friends, fae and humans, getting along so well. It was easy to forget everything that made them different: wealth, status, strength, poise. Right here in the hut, everyone was equal, and it gave her a new beacon of hope for what the lands could be one day.

Faythe was listening to Marlowe tell a story of a particular client she had worked with recently when she heard Nik shift behind her.

"Tauria, what's wrong?" His voice was soft but worried, and he was by her side, peering down at her with a hand on her shoulder, in an instant.

Faythe's eyes fixed on the ward who wore a deep frown.

"Can you not hear that?"

The rest of them exchanged confusion as they looked to each other in question. It was Faythe who said, "Hear what?"

The ward slid her gaze to Faythe. "Like whispering…but I can't make out the words."

Faythe raised her eyes to Nik, whose concern increased. He shrugged, not having any idea what was going on with Tauria either.

"We don't hear anything," he answered for everyone.

Tauria inhaled sharply then, closing her eyes and tilting her head as if trying to tune in to a faraway sound. Nik crouched beside her and took one of her hands. Noting their closeness and the prince's fixation on her, Faythe put effort into ignoring the pinch in her chest. Not of jealousy, but of a sinking loneliness.

It didn't get the chance to take root when Tauria opened her eyes again and the next three words she uttered chilled the temperature in the room. "The Eternal Woods."

Faythe's eyes widened, and she leaned away from Tauria. The ward turned her head to look directly at her—which only rattled her nerves further. She shot a quick look at Marlowe, then Nik, the only others who had been to the Eternal Woods with her before. Somewhere that was once a safe haven to practice swordplay and mind tricks with the prince now shook her very bones since the discovery of the Spirit's dwelling.

Nik looked just as stunned at the mention that only confirmed what Faythe was afraid of. The ward had never been to the woods, so why was she hearing the words now?

Marlowe appeared deep in thought before she cocked her head at Tauria in curiosity. "Faythe mentioned you had elemental gifts," she said as more of a question.

Faythe wasn't sure why it was relevant, but she had learned by now to trust and listen to the blacksmith's strange questions. She was an oracle, and they would all be wise to pay attention however odd her words sometimes seemed.

Tauria nodded. "I'm a Windbreaker primarily, but I have some of my mother's Florakinetic ability."

Marlowe was contemplative for a moment, her eyes boring a hole into the tabletop.

When Faythe couldn't take it anymore, she asked, "What is it, Marlowe?" An unnerving feeling of dread washed over her, making her too antsy where she sat.

The blacksmith's eyes widened a fraction, and in them, while she looked at no one, it was as if some grand puzzle in her brilliant mind had been granted its final piece and become whole. "I get it now," she began quietly with a pause, then her head turned to look at Faythe who balled her fists to keep from trembling. "I had a dream once, about the different magick abilities and where they came from—or *who* they came from."

Faythe's foot tapped nervously on the wooden floor. She knew Marlowe's "dreams" were never innocent anymore. They weren't mindless visions; they were real knowledge, real warnings, from the Spirits themselves, delivered through her gift as an oracle.

"Every ability was given long ago as a blessing from each of the three Spirits, as a means to grant a select few a higher power: the ability to keep the peace," she began to explain with an air of wonder. "Over time, these abilities manifested, spread, and strengthened. But they also weakened through crossed bloodlines. It was the work of the Spirit of Souls, Marvellas, to make sure those of equal power found each other and always kept their abilities thriving.

"When Marvellas left her sacred duty a thousand years ago, those souls wouldn't always find each other, which resulted in diluted power. The fae people came to call those who did connect 'mates.' Even those without an ability have an energy within that longs to be matched. Not just a romantic pairing, not just love— those who connect with their mate, their equal, continue to strengthen their bloodlines as well as each other."

Faythe was wholly engrossed in the fascinating story. Though she dreaded the answer, she asked, "What does all this have to do with Tauria?"

Marlowe took a breath before continuing. "The Elementals were a blessing from Aurialis, the Spirit of Life." Some part of Faythe knew the conclusion Marlowe was about to draw, but it hit her like a ton weight all the same. "I think her temple calls to you."

Only Tauria kept her frown of confusion as the rest of them looked between each other in dawning realization. Faythe's hand went to the pommel of her sword—more specifically, the Riscillius: The Looking Glass. It would be fully charged to see the Spirit of

Life once again since their last encounter was well over twenty-eight days ago, the time period the stone needed to be strong enough to pierce the veil. She had never fully explained to her friends what greeted her the day the light engulfed her inside the Light Temple—the day Aurialis came to form in front of her. The only one who knew was Marlowe. She was too afraid to share the revelations that changed everything.

"What else do you know?" Nik asked.

Marlowe's face creased as she tried to recall more information. "Those with abilities of the mind, the Nightwalkers like you, are supposedly—"

"Marvellas-blessed," Faythe finished for her, not meeting anyone's eye though she knew their stares were all fixed on her. She took a deep breath, straightening, and said to no one in particular, "I think I need to tell you what I learned in the temple that night."

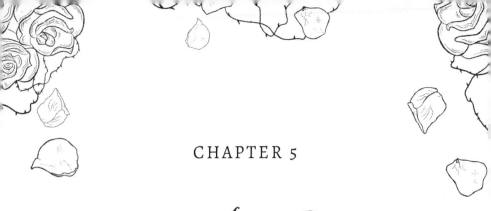

CHAPTER 5

Faythe

"I SAW AURIALIS."

The expressions around the table were a mix of shock, disbelief, and confusion as Faythe dove into her encounter with the Spirit of Life that seemed so distant now. She shifted nervously under the scrutiny of so many eyes. No one spoke, allowing her to recite the details of what the Spirit told her, but Faythe found it difficult to put the experience into words. It all sounded fictitious. Still, she rattled through the brief conversation, which didn't consist of much that even made real sense to her yet.

When it came to the part about her father, Faythe took a long pause before saying, "I'm not sure if I believe what she told me..." —she released a shaky breath—"but she seems to know who my father is."

Jakon's shock was the loudest. "Did you find out who he is?" he asked carefully.

Faythe shook her head. "Not exactly." She gave a nervous laugh, anticipating what she was about to say would be immediately rendered a ridiculous claim. "She implied he was a Night-walker...which would mean he is fae."

The room was silent, and all Faythe could hear was the thundering of her own heart.

"It makes sense." Nik was the first to speak, and she whipped her head to him as it wasn't exactly the dismissal she expected. "Your speed, even your strength, is more than the average woman. It also explains why you're so adept at swordplay. If Aurialis speaks the truth, technically, you're half-fae. Though it's clear you somehow take after your human origins more," he clarified, shaking his head in disbelief. "I should have thought of it sooner, but demi-fae are rare, and I've only ever known them to look like us in appearance." He didn't have to say it—that aside from her rounded ears, her stature and poise were far from that of the fae. "They're often rejected and abandoned by their parents, human mothers who fear being seen bringing up a child with pointed ears, and fae fathers who refuse to tarnish their name with a half-breed."

"That's barbaric," Marlowe snapped.

Faythe was weighed down with horror. Her stomach churned, and she swallowed hard to remove the burn in her throat. A pulse filled her ears. She didn't want to hear anything further. She was a twisted blend of everything that shouldn't exist in the world. Her ability, her blood, her ancient heritage—the more she learned about herself, the more detached she felt, a damning feeling of not belonging anywhere anymore. She looked over to her friends. *Can they see it too?* Everything that was wrong beneath her skin. They said nothing, but their gazes held pity. *Or is it wicked self-pity clouding my mind?*

A warm hand encased her own, and Faythe stared down at her ghostly-pale skin against Tauria's golden-brown tone. It snapped her from her racing thoughts. With the small gesture of comfort and reassurance that there was no judgment around the table, Faythe soothed her rising panic of uncertainty.

"Your mother never told you anything about your father?" Tauria asked.

"No. I mean, maybe it wasn't—I don't know if she…" Faythe tried to get out some of the conclusions she'd pondered when she first found out about her father's fae heritage. The worst of her assumptions was the possibility her conception had been the product of something nonconsensual. It was a thought she couldn't bear. "She never said a word about him. I'm terrified that…that he might not be worth seeking out."

"You don't ever need to find out if you don't want to. It changes nothing about who you are," Jakon said, soft but fierce.

She glanced up to offer him a weak smile. In truth, she hadn't yet made up her mind about whether or not she would attempt to trace her father. Even if she wanted to, she had absolutely no leads to start with.

"Did Aurialis say anything else?" Nik asked.

She was glad for the change of subject the prince knew she needed, but Faythe wasn't sure if she wanted to share the part about her mother. Specifically, her impossible heritage and blood-line connection to Marvellas, the Spirit of Souls. She spared a glance at Marlowe, the only one who knew of the information she withheld. The blacksmith kept her expression neutral, but her slight smile gave Faythe the reassurance she would keep her secret for now.

Faythe shook her head in answer to Nik's question, leaving out the real explanation for her ability and letting them believe it was simply passed down in an obscure way from her long-lost Night-walker father.

A mischievous grin spread across Marlowe's face. "Did you bring your sword?"

Faythe gave a wary nod, and the blacksmith beamed brighter, standing abruptly from the table.

"If the Spirit calls, we should answer."

Of course she would say that. She's practically duty bound. Knowing

55

exactly what she meant, Faythe shook her head wildly. "No way. It's probably nothing. Like you said, Tauria has a link to Aurialis—she would have heard it anytime." She failed to convince herself it was mere coincidence the ward heard the calling tonight.

Marlowe gave her a flat look, knowing as much. "You said so yourself, there's more explanation she owes you, and you're long past the twenty-eight days. You can't hide from it forever."

Faythe glanced at Jakon, her eyes falling to the hand still hovering over his tender old wound. If the Spirit had answers about why his pain was returning, it was reason enough to push aside her cowardice over a confrontation with Aurialis.

She pushed herself up from the bench, casting her gaze to Nik's. "What were you saying about adventure?"

The prince's mouth twitched upward in a devious smile that made her shiver in delight. Jakon and Tauria rose too, and she looked around at her circle of friends. She could almost see as much as feel the bonded line that ran through them all in one way or another.

Faythe said with newfound confidence, "Let's go see what the almighty Spirit has to say."

It was harder to be stealthy with more bodies to consider. The five friends crouched in the shadows of an alleyway, each taking turns to dart across intersections and weave in and out of the maze of streets. There would be other patrol groups besides Caius and Tres that they didn't want to risk crossing paths with if they could help it.

When they scaled the hills and came to the tree line of the Eternal Woods, Faythe paused before it in sudden realization and looked to Nik. He seemed to arrive at the same thought with the look they shared.

Turning to Tauria and Jakon, she said, "The woods are

guarded. If you try to pass, you might see things, horrible things, made of your own fears." She winced at the memory of her worst fears made flesh in front of her by the woods' wicked defenses.

"I'll stay out with Tauria," Nik offered.

The ward shook her head. "No—I can handle it." She walked past them all toward the veil of black.

Nik hooked his hand around her elbow. "You might experience *past traumas* in there," he said, low and careful.

Faythe already knew the prince was caring, but at his tenderness and concern for Tauria, she knew the bond and history between them went deeper than she could comprehend. They had a century together and likely knew each other as much as they knew themselves. It reminded her a lot of herself and Jakon.

The ward smiled gratefully at his obvious worry, putting her hand over his. "I'll be fine," she said with confidence.

He gave her one nod and released her arm.

With a deep inhale, Tauria vanished through the black curtains.

Faythe's attention fell to Jakon. "You don't have to go through. It won't be pleasant," she said, putting it lightly.

Her friend scoffed. "I'm not about to be shown up, fae or not," he replied in playful humor, stepping up to the dark entrance. She didn't try to stop him. "See you on the other side." With those last words, he disappeared into the abyss.

She looked to the remaining pair beside her, already having been through the wood's trials. Faythe blew out a breath. "Shall we?"

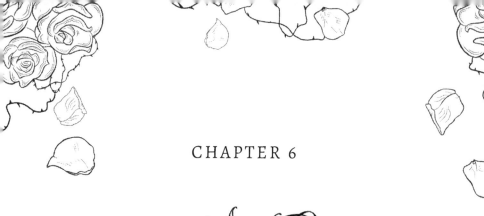

CHAPTER 6

Tauria

TAURIA WAS DOUSED in cold terror the moment she stepped through the impenetrable black veil of the woods and walked straight into the one scene that had haunted her while awake and in sleep for over a century. Though she anticipated it would be the trauma she faced, nothing could have prepared her to revisit the vision of death and devastation.

She watched as the once vibrant green hills of Fenstead burned bright in hues of red and orange, made all the more stark against the dark, smoke-clogged sky that choked the stars. The canopies of beautiful forests that held so many of her childhood memories were also ablaze, carrying the thick black clouds higher, and she could do nothing but watch the inferno wage its destruction on her homeland from her position on the balcony of the castle.

Her ties to nature cried out deep inside. She was helpless to save any of it, and a part of her burned excruciatingly along with the natural world below. Her people's screams filled her ears, and she could do nothing but stand frozen in shock as the scenes of carnage unfolded right in front of her.

"Tauria."

The voice struck her to her core, pooling tears in her eyes as she'd pined to hear it for so long, thinking she never would. He was gone. She couldn't bear to turn and meet the face of her father. She stayed silent as water flowed down her cheeks.

Green banners of the great stag where unlawfully torn down in the streets below, hastily replaced by the black-and-white-fanged serpent of the kingdom brutally dominating hers. Valgard. They had conquered at last with a force too large for Fenstead to defend themselves against. Her once peaceful and prosperous land of thriving green space and wonderful creatures had been defiled into nothing but blood and ash. She didn't deserve to lead these people if she was too weak to protect them.

"What are you afraid of, my child?" Her father's voice was exactly as she remembered from a century past.

"I could have done more," she said, her lip quivering at the sight of the devastation around them.

Fenstead soldiers fought valiantly until their last breath, never letting the oath they swore to protect their kingdom falter. She would commemorate their bravery; take each and every name of the fallen and make them eternal on the lands they died for. This, she promised their souls.

"Tell me," the voice of her father pressed.

She tore her eyes from the bloodbath below, and a small whimper left her at the sight of the King of Fenstead, the dark skin of his usually perfect face now bloodied and marred. An exact replica of the last memory she had of him as he left the battlefield to force her into the arms of the guards who would get her to safety. She'd wanted to stay, was armed to fight, but he convinced her to leave as the kingdom would need a ruler to see it rise again. It was the moment she saw it in his eyes: They were fighting a losing battle. So, she went with them, turning her back on her people in their time of peril.

"I'm afraid I am not enough." Tears continued to fall as she confessed to her father what she was terrified to admit. That when the day came to reclaim her kingdom, she would no longer be fit to rule Fenstead. No longer *worthy.* "I ran when they needed me most."

"They needed you to live."

"No, Father. They need a ruler who will fight for them, stand and protect them. Someone who will give their life for the king-dom." It took everything in her to tear her eyes from him when all she wanted to do was fall into the arms that always encased her in safety. But she wouldn't turn her back on her people—never again. "I ran once… I won't ever run again."

She faced the carnage once more, calling upon every ounce of her strength and courage. Tauria braced both hands on the flat of the stone railing and hauled herself on top in one swift motion.

"You are not strong enough. You are not brave enough," the ghost of her father mocked her.

She blocked him out. It wasn't his voice—not anymore. She had nothing to prove to him, and everything to prove to her people below. Soldiers and innocents, humans and fae—she would fight with them and fall with them.

Tauria shook her head fiercely. "You're wrong."

She held out her arm, feeling her fingers curl around the phantom wood of her staff. When she looked, it was made real against her palm. Facing the carnage, she hardened her expression and her will, summoning the bravery and resilience that left no room for second-guessing she was her father's daughter.

Then Tauria leaped.

Conjuring the will of the wind to break her fall, she landed without injury on the blood-coated stone below, sending the tail blast of her short tornado to knock the enemy back. She straight-ened as the rest of the band of soldiers who remained standing all turned to her at once. Angling her staff between both hands, Tauria raised her chin, determination sedating her fear.

Before they could advance, she felt a gentle hand on her shoulder. She immediately met the brown eyes of her father once more, and she whimpered in relief at the sight. No longer did he wear the fresh scars of war. It took everything she had not to fall into the arms of her mother beside him. Tauria choked on a sob at the sight of her delicate, pale face and soft features.

Her mother smiled with a warmth she would never feel again. A mother's warmth. "Your time to fight will come, my darling. You are ready." Her voice soothed Tauria's aching heart. Only for a moment.

"I miss you both so much," she whimpered. Though she knew it was only a vision of them, she hoped their souls could hear from their place in the Afterlife. She took a deep breath, wiping her tear-stained face. "I won't fail you again. Fenstead will rise and prosper, and I will do everything in my power to restore the lands and make you proud," she said fiercely.

A soft smile spread across the king and queen's faces, pride and love shining in their eyes to fill her with confidence. "We know you will. Now, go, Tauria. Fenstead needs you to live."

Tauria glanced at the many soldiers engaged in combat around her, the clang of steel, the scent of fire and blood. With all her might, she forced herself to turn away, and she ran. Two Fenstead guards covered her as she took off down an alley that was free of lingering bodies. Horses were equipped and waiting. They hurried for them.

Halfway down the alley, the guard on her right let out a shrill cry, and Tauria's head snapped to him. Her blood chilled at seeing the dagger protruding from his throat and his final wide-eyed look of agony before he fell. Her scream was smothered by her other escort's piercing shout of pain before his body also met the ground.

Tauria was wild in panic and angled her staff as she whirled to their assailant.

She was met with a lone figure, cloaked and hooded to shadow their face. Their sword was drawn, the length of dark steel dripping with thick blood. Tauria paled but breathed to focus herself for defense. They didn't advance. Instead, their head tilted faintly, observing. It was then Tauria remembered she was in a memory; she had already lived this moment.

Her assailant spoke—words she would never forget in her lifetime. "If you're smart, you'll get on that horse, ride far, and won't look back for one second."

A feminine voice, as unexpected as the mercy she offered. One of the enemy, yet she chose to spare her life. Whether she knew her to be the princess or not, Tauria would never be sure.

Just then, a single warrior came rushing out from behind her enemy and savior—a Rhyenelle warrior, one of their neighboring allies, Tauria quickly distinguished from the accents of crimson on his black leather armor. He was battle-worn and tired, with loose lengths of brown hair matted to his fierce but striking face. He halted, and the enemy turned to him.

They stared off for a painstakingly long moment. Neither raised their sword. Before they could face off in deadly confrontation, the assailant suddenly turned and moved impossibly fast. The Rhyenelle warrior didn't move as he tracked her with his eyes, both he and Tauria stunned to watch as she scaled the side of the building before disappearing as if she were no more than a shadow.

Tauria looked down at her slain escorts, swallowing the guilt. They'd died protecting her. When she met the eye of the Rhyenelle ally, all he gave was a short nod—a push for her to flee, and he would keep her back clear. Tauria uttered a thank-you in trembling bewilderment. It barely left her lips as a whisper. Turning, she shielded her eyes against the pane of white light that opened up before her.

She would have her time and her revenge. Until then, Tauria took the steps to return to Nik...and High Farrow.

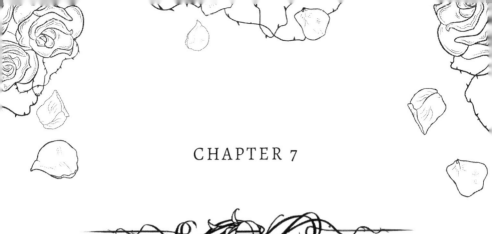

CHAPTER 7

Faythe

THE SOOTHING CASCADE of water in the glade did nothing to ease Faythe's anxiety as she paced the open space near the lake, chewing at her fingernails.

"They'll be okay. Any minute now," Nik said. His words were futile in an attempt to calm her, and he failed to hide his own concern as he stared back through the tree line they had emerged from.

Faythe was afraid of what horrors Jakon and Tauria would endure as they waited, and of the possibility they might not make it past at all. Nik had indicated the woods was selective with who it let enter into its eternal daytime.

Marlowe also stood beside Nik tensely waiting for Jakon, imitating his stance, but she couldn't find it in herself to comfort her friend while her own nerves rattled.

As a distraction, Faythe watched the dance of the glowing yucolites under the water, reminiscing on better memories when it was just her and Nik as a "fae guard."

At the sound of snapping branches, she halted her pacing, her head spinning to the trees where Jakon emerged, paler than before and a little bewildered. But he had made it through. Faythe visibly relaxed. Marlowe ran the few paces to him and threw her arms around his neck. When they parted, she reached up on her toes to kiss him. Faythe averted her gaze from their intimate moment, and just as she did, the king's ward also came into view through the tree trunks. Another wave of relief washed over Faythe.

They had both made it, and now they were all together in the secret cover of the woods.

Nik made the few short strides to Tauria and assessed her quickly. Faythe once again felt the need to look away as the fae talked closely between themselves, deliberately quiet. In her second of loneliness, a stab of sadness hit Faythe's chest. It was gone as quickly as she felt it when she was joined by Jakon and Marlowe, shortly followed by the prince and the ward.

She smiled weakly. "Let's get this over with," she muttered, suddenly wanting nothing more than to be in the quiet confines of her rooms. To brood or to avoid the confrontation with Aurialis, she wasn't sure.

Everyone followed her lead though she had never been to the temple glade without the guidance of the mighty sliver-antlered stag. She only hoped it would reveal itself if she walked in the same direction she recalled from memory, but the array of crooked wooden bodies all looked the same no matter which way she faced. None of her companions talked as they trudged slightly behind. She powered ahead, not really in the mood for conversation anyway. Nik must have noticed, because she felt his presence creep up and fall into pace beside her. His arm brushed hers, and she felt his sideward glance like a brand.

"Are you okay?"

She heard the question as he projected the loud thought. Caught between wanting to confess she hadn't been okay in months and saying what she needed to for him to believe she was, Faythe decided to stay silent.

The temple came into view a few short paces later, the sight bringing both relief and fear in overwhelming amounts. Faythe didn't let it show. Instead, she stormed through the last of the tree line and out into the wide clearing to face the tall ancient structure she dreaded to meet again. As they approached, she drew Lumarias, the cry of steel as it left its scabbard the only sound to disrupt the silence around them. She lifted the pommel that held the Riscillius to her eye and saw the symbols on each of the doors that had erased themselves from her memory through magick. She was about to slice down on her own forearm and draw blood to trace the symbols, but Marlowe's soft hand encased her wrist to stop her.

"I brought this," she said, holding out a shard of chalk.

Faythe gave her a grateful smile, admiring her for always thinking one step ahead. "Thanks," she muttered.

Bounding up the steps, Faythe quickly sketched the first symbol on the right door with the white chalk then hastily drew the second before her recollection of the image could be wiped. As she finished her lazy artwork, the doors groaned open, just as they did the first time she visited with Marlowe all those weeks ago. The sound vibrated through her to rattle her anxiety some more. She had a dizzying sense of déjà vu and wanted desperately to retreat and abandon the temple, never return again if she could help it. But she kept her exterior tame, and as soon as Nik pushed the doors further open for them to follow through, she marched in without hesitation.

It was exactly as she remembered—not that she expected anything different when she held the only key to open the temple in her sword. The musty old scent hit her first. It wasn't comforting like the pages of aged books, but rather dreadful as the smell clung to the ancient bones of the long-forgotten temple. Her eyes were transfixed by the pool of light that beamed down around the center mark like a beacon, calling to her. The symbol of Aurialis.

She felt her hands begin to tremble as the nerves caught up with her, perturbed to find out what the Spirit of Life had to say this time. In that moment, she wished she were alone. The thought made her guilty for wanting to push her friends' love and support away—a self-destructing flaw she didn't think she would ever win her battle against.

"This place is incredible." Tauria's voice was the first to echo through the silence. "It radiates power."

Faythe didn't comment that she couldn't feel it and was pretty sure her companions thought the same. Tauria's bloodline was directly blessed by Aurialis; she had a deeper connection to this temple that none of them would be able to understand.

Marlowe was already scanning the walls of artifacts, just as she did during her last visit. Jakon stayed close to her side, eyes darting cautiously around the great hall, jerking every time the blacksmith reached for something new. Nik remained next to Faythe, and she noted the worried look in his eyes as they flicked between her face and the stone in her sword that would summon the Spirit of Life once again.

"You don't have to face it alone," he said.

She mustered a weak side-smile. "I do."

His look softened in understanding. She would perhaps get answers that would be difficult to hear—answers about her father. And she didn't want an audience for it.

Faythe walked the few short steps to the center and hesitated for a second outside the circle of sunlight before stepping inside and turning to face the doors. The beam of light was already shooting from the Riscillius in the pommel of her sword, still clasped in her hand. The light shook slightly, and she gripped the hilt tighter, cursing the betrayal of her wavering courage.

"We'll be right here for you," Jakon said.

She glanced to the side to find her oldest friend watching her.

His features were laced with concern, but his presence was a sure, comforting sight. Marlowe also gave her a nod of encouragement, and to her other side, Nik and Tauria stood reassuring and calm, like four pillars of support to prevent her from collapsing under the weight of her own cowardice. With that thought, Faythe straightened with new confidence, raising the hilt of her sword between both hands and guiding the laser of light it cast across the room to meet its sister stone on the eye sculpted above the temple's exit.

As they connected, she closed her eyes. The harsh white light that encased her was bright enough to make her flinch even behind closed lids, and she knew when she opened them, she would no longer see her friends.

"You have returned at last."

Though she was expecting it, the Spirit's voice still sent a tremor through her like a ghost's kiss. Faythe peeled her eyes open, blinking to adjust to the change in brightness, then Aurialis's stunning ethereal figure came into clarity. Exactly as Faythe remembered. She was struck as if it were their first encounter, both from her beauty and the fact she was real and in a physical form.

"It hasn't been that long," she grumbled.

"We are running out of time. It has been long enough."

Faythe flexed her fist. "I've been a little...preoccupied," she said, putting *very* lightly the series of events that ended with her castle imprisonment.

"You promised to retrieve something that was stolen long ago from my temple. You have been in the exact location you needed to be to find it."

Faythe huffed an incredulous laugh. "The ruin. Yes, I know." She shifted on her feet under Aurialis's intimidating, impassive gaze. "It may have slipped my mind while I was simply trying to stay alive long enough." It wasn't a complete lie. While the daunting task would often weave its way through her lattice of overwhelming thoughts and emotions, it was always drowned out by Faythe coming to grips with her ability and staying out of the king's line of execution.

"We are running out of time."

Aurialis's urgency brought forth the burning question that had made Faythe desperate enough to venture here tonight rather than hold off for as long as possible. "Jakon's pain—are you behind it?"

Aurialis raised her chin, a sign Faythe knew to anticipate as affirmation or a movement before the fall of hard knowledge. "Where life is granted a second chance, so can that mercy be taken back."

"You've proven your point. I'm here. Tell me you won't threaten his life again."

Aurialis gracefully dipped her head. "You have my word. So long as you find my ruin, the light magick will sustain him for as long as he lives."

The words crushed Faythe with relief. "Thank you."

"But Faythe, in the bargain you struck, your reward was instant. Magick can be impatient even beyond my control. I must warn you that your friend's pain shall only get worse until the ruin is within your grasp."

A wave of ice flushed her skin, but even Aurialis intimated with a hint of sympathy that this was out of her control. Faythe began to feel the choking suffocation of guilt at realizing she'd put Jakon's life on borrowed time until she fulfilled her end of the bargain.

"Why is it within the castle? Why would the king have it?"

"We do not have enough time right now to explain. Find my ruin, and you can summon me at will by connecting the power of the true sun to it through the Riscillius. I'm sorry this task falls to you, Faythe, but it is urgent."

"What is it you're so afraid of that you can't take care of yourself? Aren't you supposed to be the ones watching over *us*?" Faythe ranted in growing frustration, tired of the cryptic messages.

"It was that way for a long time, until Marvellas broke the balance."

Faythe's head rattled at the mention of the Spirit of Souls. "Where is she now?" she asked, unsure if she wanted to know. Until now, she had believed—or rather, *hoped*—the ancient Goddess no longer walked their lands.

"I lost track of her over two hundred years ago. You are not safe as long as she remains in your realm. None of you are."

Faythe swallowed hard at the confirmation Marvellas was very much still alive. "Why?" was all she could ask, dizzy with cold apprehension.

"There is not enough time to explain. Find the ruin within the castle. The princess is powerful with my gift—she may be able to help trace it."

"Why me?" The question was more of an escaped breath of disbelief at her tangled strings of misfortune.

"With every evil born, a way to destroy it is conceived in turn. It can only be you. But you are not alone, Faythe." Aurialis was calm in her tone, a stark contrast to Faythe's wildly rattled nerves at the riddle. The Spirit's image started to fade around the edges.

"Wait!" Faythe called desperately. "I came to know more about my father."

"You will have the answers you seek soon, Heir of Marvellas."

With those last echoing words, Aurialis was gone.

Faythe stood alone within the impenetrable veil of light, completely dumbstruck that she had once again been so distracted by the Spirit's own demands she'd received no insight of her own. When the circle around her fell, she made no movement and didn't even register her friends closing in. She stared at the exit in complete exasperation as she took in everything Aurialis had said and how it left her with more questions than answers. This was becoming an infuriating pattern.

"Faythe." Jakon's voice was the first to shake her back from her reeling thoughts.

She didn't look at him—didn't look at any of them—as she stormed out of the temple, sheathing her sword at her hip while descending the stairs. She vaguely heard the series of footsteps following after her and almost felt guilty for her silence, but she needed a moment to calm down.

At the risk of releasing her anguish and indignation on them, she figured it would be easier to apologize for not sharing her feelings at all than seek forgiveness for sharing too much.

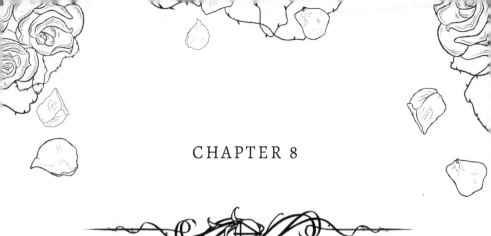

CHAPTER 8

Faythe

FAYTHE STOOD IN awkward silence under the intense gaze of her four companions who waited expectantly for her to explain what she had learned from the Spirit of Life.

They'd returned to the hut after a muted walk back. She was grateful no one had tried to make conversation, as it gave her time to sort through her thoughts and make sense of what Aurialis had said. And to calm her anger over what the Spirit *didn't* tell her.

Her eyes landed on Nik for a moment longer than the rest. She planned to ask him if he knew anything of the ruin the Spirit so desperately wanted her to retrieve, but she found herself doubting whether she could trust him. Not because she thought he would turn her in to the king for seeking out a treasured possession, but because he was his son. While she knew they didn't have the most loving bond, she was afraid to test where his loyalty would lie if it came to making a choice.

"I made a bargain when I needed the yucolites to heal you." She glanced at Jakon, wincing at his stiffened posture as he tried miserably to disguise the fact his wound was bothering him. She averted her gaze out of guilt. "To get them, I had to offer something in return. I didn't know it was Aurialis at the time. I suppose it didn't matter. But she's calling in my end now. More than that, she's threatening to undo the magick that saved your life if I don't find what she seeks soon."

Faythe had to tell them. Her friend deserved an explanation and to know she was once again the cause of his suffering. She couldn't bring herself to look at him out of shame.

The pause of silence in the room was suffocating. Faythe stared at the ground, wishing it could open up and swallow her pitiful existence. Jakon crept up beside her, an arm going around her shoulders in silent comfort.

"What is it she wants?" he asked, folding her into his warmth.

Faythe's brow wrinkled as she looked up at his brown eyes that held nothing but gentle understanding and a fierce protectiveness. He was fully prepared to dive into the damning pits of the Netherworld with her, no matter what. Rejecting his embrace would be an insult to his unconditional love for her—something she didn't deserve after all she'd put him through.

Faythe offered a small smile to shadow her dark, growing remorse. "I'm sure you noticed the missing ruin from the podium in the temple. She wants me to get it back."

"Did she say where it is?" Tauria asked.

Faythe glanced briefly at the emerald orbs of the prince to check if he showed any recognition of the item she mentioned, but he looked at her with the same curiosity as the rest of them. She fixed her eyes on the ward. "Within the castle."

Everyone's eyes widened slightly, their shoulders slumping at the same time. Nik and Tauria looked to each other as if silently communicating their mutual fear and confusion that it was within the walls of their home. Faythe didn't know why the exchange bothered her so much.

"It's my bargain—I'll find it myself," she said, dismissing their assistance in tracking it down before it was even offered.

To her shock, it was Marlowe who snapped. "When are you going to stop trying to do everything yourself?" The sharp tone was completely out of character for the blonde. Faythe opened her mouth to respond, but the blacksmith continued. "We're not going anywhere, so the sooner you accept our help, the quicker we can get this done—and anything else in future since, knowing you, Faythe, there's likely to be more situations you'll wind up needing our assistance with."

Even the others in the room looked to the soft-spoken blonde, taken aback. Anger wasn't an emotion that surfaced in the blacksmith often, and Faythe recoiled, embarrassed at the gibe. Jakon shifted, an arm subtly going over Marlowe's lower back in comfort. The movement stirred something dark and ugly from the depths of Faythe's mind. It raced ahead of all kinds of hideous thoughts.

All she could think when she looked at them was that Jakon didn't need her anymore…

None of them did.

A response so cold and resentful burned in Faythe's throat, and she had to bite down hard, teeth clashing to prevent the sour words from spilling over in her humiliation and worthlessness.

Without her, everyone would be safe. Both pairs in front of her would be *happy*.

A steel guard built around her mind, sealing her emotions before they could recklessly consume her. Instead, Faythe's face fell hard, blank, as she stared back at Marlowe's frown of frustration, so out of place on her usually cheerful, bright face.

At the risk of saying something she might regret, Faythe tore her eyes from the blacksmith without responding and focused her attention on Tauria. "You might be able to feel the ruin like you did tonight if you get close enough."

Tauria's gaze held sympathy, and Faythe could hardly stand to look any of her friends in the eye. The ward gave a nod in response to the knowledge Faythe shared.

73

"We should be getting back," Nik informed them, cutting through the tension that had built.

Faythe kept the sulking off her face, not even knowing how long had passed since they left Caius and Tres.

Nik and Tauria left through the small front door after saying a short goodbye to Jakon and Marlowe. Faythe paused when the fae were out of sight, turning back to her human friends.

"It's time to move on," she said quietly, looking around the worn wooden walls of her old home of ten years. "We all need to let go of this damned hut." She met eyes with Jakon when she couldn't shift her gaze to Marlowe, still picturing that quick look of anger in the ocean of his irises. She couldn't bear it. "Move to the cottage. Live comfortably. There's nothing left here for any of us."

"I miss having you with me every day," Jakon muttered, and she didn't stop him when he pulled her into his embrace.

She had no choice but to catch her gaze on Marlowe at his back, and she wished she hadn't, for something far worse than anger glittered in her irises. Something akin to pain and sadness. Faythe had to swallow the marble of grief and apology that she couldn't form into words.

As the tears pricked her eyes within Jakon's arms, she cowardly closed her eyes and savored the moment wrapped in his woodsy scent.

Faythe loved Marlowe unconditionally. She loved Nik and Tauria. But for just a few seconds of sorrowful reflection, she couldn't help but think back to when it was just herself and Jakon. Without danger or intrigue. Plain routine, but joyous memories. When he needed her as much as she needed him, because all they had…was each other.

Whether he realized it or not, the truth that tore a deep wound within her chest was that Jakon had everything he needed. Faythe was *not* good for him. Not like Marlowe. She clutched him a little tighter with the painful squeeze on her heart at the thought.

"I miss you too, Jak," she whispered.

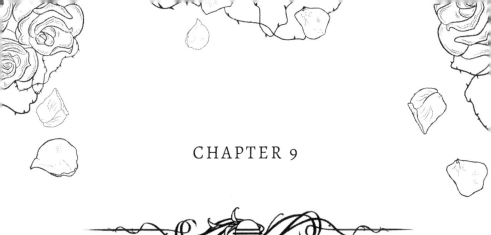

CHAPTER 9

Faythe

"YOU'RE JOKING, RIGHT?"

Faythe stood with arms crossed, staring at the prince from across her room as he kept his distance. If she didn't know any better, she would think he was actually *afraid* of her reaction to the information he'd dropped on her.

The idea was ridiculous, laughable even, but had she really built up such a bad reputation for herself that he expected her to lash out with violence? The thought made her drop her arms and relax her posture. She was angry, but not at Nik, and she decided it was best not to kill the messenger this time.

It was not enough for her to be humiliated standing in the shadows in a guard's uniform; now, the king wanted to parade her right in front of the vultures who would tear her apart simply for being human.

The king's plan made sense. Faythe even wanted to admire the brilliance of it. She would have a lot more opportunity to rummage through the other courts' minds if she was forced to be among them instead of trying to be inconspicuous from a distance. But the thought of having to suffer their judgmental stares and hear them slander her in their minds while she forced a smile with pleasant chat… It would be a new test of wills for Faythe.

"He wants me to make sure you're…prepared."

Faythe chuckled without humor. *"Prepared,"* she mocked. "You mean he sent you to tighten the collar."

Nik sighed and finally came closer to where Faythe stood by the warmth of the fire. It blazed at her back to take away the creeping winter night's chill, a perfect blend of amber since she refused the magick cobalt flames in an attempt to retain some semblance of normality.

"I'm not here to tell you what to do, but to ask you to be smart," he pleaded. "This won't be a simple council meeting with the Lords of High Farrow; these are the powerful courts of Ungardia, and you'd be wise to acknowledge that. Your pride means nothing if you're dead, and it will be too far out of my hands if you decide to piss off the wrong royal."

Faythe heaved a long sigh, but a small, sly smile tugged at the corners of her lips. "Thanks for the warning. I'll behave." She batted her lashes, and he nudged her arm with a chuckle.

"Spirits help us all," he muttered.

Faythe slumped into an armchair by the fire. She thought Nik would announce his departure—he never did stay long—but he strolled over and helped himself to the chair opposite her. While she studied the flames in the pit in quiet contemplation, she felt him studying her.

After a short pause, she pondered, "Has the alliance ever extended to Lakelaria?"

The question clearly took Nik by surprise. His face seemed to fall in understanding, as if he knew her curiosity about the kingdom was fueled by her guilt over her friend Reuben, whom she'd sent there so many months ago. She'd never had closure on his fate.

"No. Their queen has always insisted she wants no part in the mainland kingdoms' alliance since it formed after the Great Battles over a century ago. They vowed to take no side and have remained free of conflict." Nik ran a hand through his black hair. "It's a completely arrogant way of thinking if you ask me, but they're almost untouchable with the defenses of the Black Sea along with their fabled warriors who have all kinds of water abilities. I guess they believe they'll never need our help, so why should they offer theirs?"

"There's strength in unity."

Nik nodded in agreement. "Yes. But some prefer to remain ignorant to conflict."

"If they offered aid, perhaps you all could have come together to fight back by now." It came out as an accusation, and she muttered an apology. Such political matters were outside the prince's sphere of influence. The drop in his expression made her feel guilty for the remark, as if he agreed, but he also knew there was nothing they could do. "Have you ever met her?" Faythe asked instead. "The Queen of Lakelaria…?" Her heart drummed harder, realizing she was hoping to receive some soothing information about the ruler of the kingdom she'd sent her friend to as a stowaway. She prayed every day that Reuben was safe.

Nik nodded, and Faythe shifted forward in her seat, her attention piqued. "Once. Over two hundred years ago, when she came to the mainland. I was fairly young." Nik paused.

Faythe waited and then realized he was finished speaking. "What was she like?" she pressed, not quite believing he planned to drop the topic there.

Nik took a long breath as though trying to scramble for loose memories. His cheeks flushed. "Honestly, I was hardly interested in anything political at that age. I don't remember a lot of that visit as I was usually itching to get back to the training ground or—" He stopped himself, the redness trailing down his neck.

Faythe's lips curled in amusement. "Or what?"

He scratched the back of his neck. "I was young," he felt the need to reiterate.

Faythe's smile stretched to a grin. "Nikalias Silvergriff, what dirty little secrets do *you* have to hide?" she teased.

He huffed a laugh, not forgetting he'd asked her the same thing once the first time they lay on the grass in the Eternal Woods and she allowed him into her subconscious mind. Slipping back into his cool arrogance, he said, "Wouldn't you like to know, Faythe?"

She rolled her eyes, leaning back in her chair and folding her legs under her gown. "I think your younger antics with the ladies would hardly surprise anyone."

Nik sank back in his seat, one ankle crossing over his knee. "I shall not wreck your innocence with my…antics," he drawled with the most devious look.

Faythe quickly extinguished the flames that rose on her face, not wanting to give him the satisfaction of a reaction. She crossed her arms and matched his stare. "Then I shall not wreck yours with mine."

His green irises twinkled in delight. He folded his hands behind his head. "I never did get to 'sample the full-course menu,' as you so eloquently put it."

It was a playful challenge to see who could concede to embarrassment first. Faythe shook her head, knowing when she was outmatched.

"You're insufferable," she muttered.

His grin was devastatingly enticing. "Another time then."

She ground her teeth, muttering a prayer to the Spirits to soothe her chagrin. "The queen. What do you know of her?" Faythe asked flatly, desperate to change the subject.

Nik groaned, clearing not reveling in the subject. "She was kind, if a little dull. Stunning, blonde, blue eyes, large—"

"I'm not interested in the size of her breasts, Nik," Faythe cut in with a deadpan look when he gestured in front of his chest.

His smile turned feline. "Large hands," he finished, flipping his palms around to her.

Fire ignited inside her body. "Hands?"

"You should have seen them—big enough to hold four apples in one."

She held his stare, the emeralds shining as he reveled in her flustered look at the conclusion she'd jumped to. Then he barked a laugh, and Faythe's mouth fell open in incredulity.

"Stupid fae prick," she grumbled. It only added to Nik's rolling laughter.

Faythe sank into her chair with a childish huff. He'd played her for a fool. She had the right mind to cast him out.

"So gullible, Faythe. We'll need to work on that."

She didn't look at him, taming her need to take this to the fighting ring below.

Nik schooled his face before he continued. "The Queen of Lakelaria was exactly like you'd expect of any monarch. It's said she had a daughter who would have been a little older than me. She was conceived out of wedlock with an unknown father, barely past her first century when she died, but no one knows how." Nik blew out a breath. "I couldn't come to care for the queen though— she held an air of self-importance. She's powerful, and she knows it. Her Waterwielding abilities are legendary, and there are those who believe she commands even the most wicked creatures of the Black Sea."

Faythe loosened off her disgruntled posture, her irritation fading in her interest. "Do you believe that?"

"I don't think so. Waterwielding is one thing, but taking command of a creature would be more akin to your ability."

"Mine doesn't work on animals."

"Exactly. And as far as we know, no other of your kind exists either."

Your kind. She hated that the words made her feel isolated. Alone.

"What of the land and people there?"

Nik shrugged. "I've never been. Though in teachings, we were told it's perhaps the most beautiful and scenic of all the kingdoms. The water fae are said to be a peaceful people, but absolutely lethal. Water is so variable, a force that can drown, freeze, flood... I wouldn't want to challenge them, and I'm not surprised Valgard has stayed clear of the great western island."

"No water fae dwell on the mainland?"

"There are some who migrated, but they're not common. Lakelaria is famously named for its water channels that run throughout the kingdom as though they were stone paths, like in High Farrow, along with various snow-capped mountain ranges. It makes sense they'd want to reside there."

"Hmm," was all Faythe responded, turning to the fire in quiet thought. The Kingdom of the Water Dragon sounded remarkable, and the small weight of guilt over Reuben's fate eased slightly as she considered perhaps he was safe and living a whole new life across the sea. She held onto that thought, hoping it was enough to relieve the constant turmoil whenever she wondered if he was even still alive.

She heard Nik lean forward in his seat. "Your friend will have made it. I don't believe they would turn away a desperate citizen if he was proven to be no threat."

"He was never a threat and should never have been made to feel as if his only option were to flee his home." She realized immediately that her bitter words sounded accusatory again and snapped her head to him. "I'm sorry—"

"You're right," he interjected, his face full of understanding. "I can't speak for my father's actions, but they come from a place of wanting to protect the kingdom."

"Reuben did nothing wrong."

"He committed treason."

"He was scared and afraid."

"Isn't everyone?" Nik said in a way that didn't exclude himself.

Even on this side of the great fortification, they were afraid. It made her tremble to think that perhaps the scale of the war was worse than the citizens had been led to believe. She supposed in this case, ignorance was bliss, maybe even a mercy, if the alternative was fear and panic with no sense of ease.

"What is the punishment for treason?"

"Death."

"For all? No matter the scale?"

Nik's eyes narrowed a fraction at her fierce pressing, knowing she already knew the answers. He obliged anyway. "Yes. An act against the crown can't be met with leniency no matter the person. It would show a weak leadership and open the gates for merciless vultures such as Valgard to strike in full force."

"Everyone should have a right to trial, to be heard."

"And they get that chance, but the ruling must be consistent."

"Do you think Reuben should have been killed?"

It was a test, and one he'd walked right into. Nik knew it, his face wrinkled with conflicting emotions.

"Do you forget I was the one who warned him to flee?"

No. She would never forget. Nik's act of mercy had sealed her view of him before they even got the chance to meet. Those emerald orbs she locked eyes with before they spoke—she knew even then that he was different. Nik was good in every sense of the word.

She amended her question. "If you were king…would you have ruled his execution?"

Nik's face looked pained, and for a moment, she regretted the question, knowing it weighed with the burden he would one day carry. Decisions he would be forced to make.

"Why are you asking me this?"

To prove I'm right. To know you're not your father. She didn't voice the words. Faythe didn't envy his position and the fate of a kingdom that would fall to him when he became king. But she also couldn't imagine a more fair and just ruler for High Farrow.

She shook her head. "Never mind."

With the silence that fell, Faythe expected the conversation to be over and for Nik to wordlessly take leave. But then he answered quietly, as though his traitorous confession would be swallowed by the crackles of the burning timber they both stared into.

"No. I don't think I would."

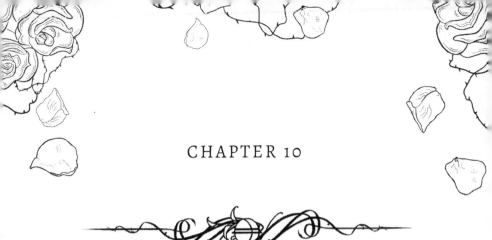

CHAPTER 10

Faythe

THE FOLLOWING EVENING, Faythe dressed in her uniform after the king requested her presence in the throne room. She nervously walked the halls unescorted, her hands slick at her sides as she was not usually summoned on such short notice. She was always briefed—or rather, *warned*—well in advance of the king desiring her talents at his congregations.

"I'm going to enjoy this one."

Faythe's heart leaped up her throat at the sound of the wicked voice that haunted her. Captain Varis fell into step beside her, his face beaming with sadistic delight, which made her whole body tremble at the thought of what awaited her.

She hadn't had many run-ins with the captain since she became a resident of the castle—much to his fury that she wasn't damned to ash instead. She didn't know enough of Varis's routine to purposely avoid him and wondered if Nik had made sure their paths would cross as little as possible.

"Don't you have little girls to go scare?" she replied, hiding her intimidation.

He scoffed. "None as amusing as you."

"The last time you underestimated me, Varis, you ended up on your knees in front of the king," she stated, deliberately leaving out his title, which she knew he liked to hear to assert his rank. It wasn't wise to poke the bear, but she couldn't deny it was mildly entertaining despite the fear he struck within her.

She didn't have to look at him to feel the ripples of his rage.

"Let's see you flaunt your ability once you find out what the king has planned for it tonight," he taunted, his tone playfully dark.

She didn't have time to reply as they rounded the last corner to the throne room. The doors were already wide open, with the usual guards posted outside. They didn't even glance her way as she passed and headed straight inside without a faltering step. Varis steered away from her as she walked a straight line down the great hall.

Her pulse picked up speed as she took in the formal setting. Then a feeling of dread struck her heart still. The king sat proudly on his throne while Nik and Tauria sat at their places on either side. There were only two reasons why the monarchs gathered together: for ceremonial events…and judgments.

Faythe's blood ran cold as she concluded the event's purpose with her first scan of the hall. There were several other fae, both male and female, scattered down the sides near the colonnades. Other court members, she assumed. In front of the dais, on their knees, was a frantic and terrified young human. He was so out of place with his tattered brown clothes and unwashed appearance. Just a boy, likely no older than twelve, and too thin to be from a home where he was properly fed. Faythe's heart broke at the sight. She wanted desperately to go to his aid, but she had to be smart. Causing a scene now would only end badly for both of them, so she passed the human without another glance and came to a stop in front of the king.

"Your Majesty." She reluctantly bowed. While she got away

without it in close quarters, she knew better than to test her lack of respect in front of an audience.

"Everyone out except the guards," the king announced.

Shuffling feet and murmured voices sounded around the great hall. Faythe took the opportunity to cast a glance at Nik to see if she could get any hint of explanation, but he refused to meet her eye. Her panic only surged while he stared off to the side with a tense jaw, and she glanced at his white-knuckle grip against the arm of his chair. She tried Tauria, who was already staring at her with a disturbingly apologetic look that twisted her stomach.

When all that was left were the quiet sobs of the human boy behind, Faythe's ears rang in anticipation. Finally, Orlon spoke again.

"The boy has been accused of consorting with Valgard against his king."

Faythe swallowed to wet her bone-dry throat. "It sounds as if you have already cast your verdict, Your Majesty. Why am I here?" she asked, struggling to keep her words from wavering.

A cruel smile played on the king's lips, and it pierced Faythe with heavy dread. "Did you not say you could make my enemies confess in front of me?"

She knew the king to be wicked and merciless, but she didn't take him as one to enjoy pointless entertainment. No—not like Captain Varis who reveled in such games. She had no choice but to play along, however. It wouldn't be wise to question him.

Faythe kept her mask of impassive confidence. "Very well." She turned, and the prisoner immediately locked eyes with her in a silent, desperate plea to the only other of his kind in the room. His relief was misplaced as he had no idea what she was or what she was about to do, which made her sick with guilt in a damning way she'd never felt before. Faythe pushed her own gods-awful feelings aside and dove into his mind before she could hesitate.

His emotions hit her in an overwhelming dose. She had to fight against letting them physically affect her. There was so much fear

Faythe clamped her fists shut and then clenched her teeth to prevent the tears that pricked her eyes. For once, she wasn't sure if it was her own anger or his terror that made her heart pound faster. She tried to keep focused, to find the information the king was looking for and bring it to the surface, but it was a struggle, as the boy's thoughts and emotions where an erratic mess.

So she took away his fear.

He visibly relaxed, and it soothed his mind enough for her to find her way around clearly.

"I'm not going to hurt you," she said into his mind, and his eyes widened as he heard it. *"Is there anyone else at risk?"* she asked, trying to find something to atone for her actions. If she could save others without the king's knowledge, she could live with the stain on her soul for doing his bidding.

"It wasn't Valgard."

Faythe tried to keep her face placid as she heard his response, but she couldn't disguise the slight frown that creased her forehead in confusion.

"What do you mean?"

"They're looking for some kind of stone and wanted us to find it. But it wasn't Valgard soldiers."

Faythe's breathing turned ragged at the information. She didn't want to believe the item that flashed in her mind. *Some kind of stone.* Suddenly, the Riscillius set in the pommel at her hip weighed heavier. Faythe shook the daunting thought. It couldn't be one and the same.

"Then who?"

"Today, spymaster," the king drawled, bored.

She didn't have much time, but she needed the answer. Faythe trembled with building apprehension.

"They stopped us when we were playing in the forest. Their uniforms were all-black, but…"

"Perhaps I overestimated your ability."

Faythe ground her teeth at Orlon's impatient, mocking tone.

Holding the boy's stare, she forced the words right from his mouth —exactly what the king wanted to hear and a detailed recollection of what he'd been up to since the encounter. As a slight consolation, she also used her ability to fool the king by withholding the information about his friends and not sharing his suspicions that the soldiers weren't from Valgard.

"Very good," he said in playful malice.

Faythe broke the boy's stare to meet the eyes of the king. She had been foolishly naïve to ever hope that was all he wanted—a display of talent and to relish in his control over her, even against her own kind. It wasn't enough, and she heard the command that crushed her spirit and darkened her soul before it was even spoken.

"Now, *kill* him."

The boy sobbed loudly. Without Faythe to help, he was out of his mind with fear as the king gave the order.

The words rang like an echo in her ears, over and over, as time seemed to slow. She wanted to beg, plead, and was prepared to fall to her knees and accept her own execution before she would willingly follow through with such a heinous, evil act. This was a test to see if Orlon held a tight enough leash; the one thing he could ask of her that would solidify her allegiance to him and be a permanent branding on her soul. Faythe knew she had been brought here for a bigger purpose than to show off party tricks and repeat the knowledge he'd likely already gained from another Nightwalker.

As she looked down at the helpless, terrified young boy, fated to die regardless of her involvement…it dawned on her.

She had to be the one to do it.

"Your Majesty, I don't think the task should—" Nik began in an attempt to offer salvation. Faythe wanted to embrace him for trying.

"As you wish," she cut in before he could save her humanity.

She felt the eyes of all three royals in front of her snap in her direction, but she held only those of the king. Not as an obedient servant, but to show he would not break her.

Without another word, she turned back to the boy shaking violently against the cold marble. He began to plead for his life, and she made herself numb to the cries, or she would never be able to carry it through.

"And, Faythe, I don't want it to be painless," the king sang behind her. "The punishment for treason deserves to be felt."

Her nails cut into her palms with how hard she fought against damning all the consequences and killing the king instead. He'd no doubt learned to barricade his mind against her, but he considered her no threat with a sword in a castle of fae and allowed her be armed like the rest of the guards at all times. Unknown to him, she was half-fae, and her reckless, rage-fueled thoughts dared her to attempt the maneuver and plunge her blade through his chest.

The king would meet the end he deserved, but not today.

Faythe didn't waste any time in seizing the boy's mind once again. She immediately switched off his fear and would take his pain too when the time came.

"Who did you see in the woods?" she asked once more, determined to make his life count for something. She could save the others before the king got to them.

"I don't want to die here."

Tears rolled down the boy's cheek, and Faythe fought against her own at the sadness in his voice. She took him out of the cold, strange hall, made the fae disappear, and instead enfolded the scene of his home around him, filling it with the people he loved. The boy instantly calmed, and she felt his mind at peace as she made him forget where he was and that he was about to meet the end of his tragically short life.

As much as it tore apart her heart, she only accepted the role of executioner because she knew she was the only one who could offer him a pain-free death and this last gift of seeing his family. She made a scream tear out his throat, and the boy fell with his back to the ground in an illusion of torture. Next, she made his body contort and wither on the floor with cries that echoed sickeningly around the hall, all for the king's pleasure. In his mind, the boy was exactly where he deserved to be: completely unaware of his true surroundings and without an ounce of hurt or fear.

"Who did you see?" she tried gently once more, now his mind was at peace.

In his head, the boy smiled at her as if he knew the mercy she had given him in place of whatever brutal, agonizing death would have befallen him. *"I recognized one of the soldiers. I'd seen him before,"* the boy said, then he glanced to the vision of a delicate woman. *"I can be with my mother now. She has come for me."*

Faythe looked to the small brunette woman, too young to have had her life taken from her, and realized the boy knew everything he was seeing was an illusion. She had failed to find the detail that gave it away. He was content, happy even, and she supposed her mistake had turned out to be the best comfort she could have given him, showing the boy not who he would lose, but who he would be reunited with.

"It was not Valgard. The fae was a guard from Farrowhold."

Faythe felt struck where she stood, not sure if she had heard him right. It couldn't be true. All the guards of Farrowhold answered to the king. What reason would he have for killing his subjects if he was the one terrorizing them for information within his own kingdom? It didn't make any sense, but she was in the boy's mind and would know if it was a lie.

His eyes met hers once more, and he showed her exactly who he saw that night. Faythe didn't recognize the fae whose hood was pulled down to cover most of his face, but she committed the image to memory while also noting every one of the boy's friends who were with him that night, hoping she wasn't too late to get them to safety.

"Will it hurt?"

Faythe was snapped back from her own thoughts, which reeled at the new information and what it possibly meant, by the boy's question. The final task she had to perform once again dawned.

She could hardly get any words past the painful lump in her throat and shook her head, mustering a small, warm smile in her gut-wrenching sorrow.

"Just like falling asleep," she whispered.

He matched her smile as if in thanks. It only tore her heart deeper.

"I'm ready to go now."

The boy's mother walked over to him, and they joined hands. Blood pounded in Faythe's ears, sending her pulse into a frantic sprint. She begged for forgiveness within herself, but it did little to ease the dark grasp she felt encasing her heart. What she was about to do was irreversible, a permanent branding on her soul, but she couldn't afford to be selfish when the boy's alternative death at the king's hands didn't bear imagining.

Faythe shut out her screaming thoughts, which fought against her movement as she raised an open palm—more for the king's show than anything. She felt the pressure pulsing, building, right there in her fingertips as if she held the essence of his mind in her physical grasp, a fragile sphere of thin glass to shatter at her mercy.

To everyone in the hall, the boy was still rolling and crying out in agony, begging for it to end. But in his mind, he was at peace, in no pain, and staring happily into his lost mother's eyes. Holding that image as the last he would remember, Faythe closed her fist with a sharp twist. She felt his death like a scorching pain in her gut and winced, her teeth clenching so hard she thought they might break. Only for seconds.

The boy and his mother froze still. Then, slowly, their image and the scene broke off into fragments, floating upward before dissipating into nothing, and the throne room came into view around her once more. His body fell limp against the white marble floor. Then silence settled, save for the pounding of her own heart.

Faythe took a moment to breathe consciously, feeling the rapid rise of bile in her throat. She kept her quivering fists clamped tight and reeled back the all-consuming rage that could drive her to do something reckless. She didn't look at the boy, motionless against the cold floor, to preserve the picture of his last moments in his own home with his mother, instead of in a large foreign room surrounded by strangers. She turned to the king, barely able to contain her hatred.

"I'm sure one of your other servants can take it from here."

The king chuckled darkly. "Impressive, spymaster. You're more ruthless than I gave you credit for. My son may come to learn a thing or two from you."

In his twisted mind, it was a compliment.

Faythe had never been more disgusted with herself. She kept her face impassive and refused to look at either of her friends for fear of the judgment and horror in their eyes. To them and every guard in the room, it would have looked as if she truly did mentally torture the helpless boy before mercilessly crushing his mind.

"If that was all, Your Majesty," she said, monotonous, desperate to retreat back to her rooms before her mask of stone-hearted arrogance fell apart completely.

King Orlon waved a lazy hand in dismissal, and she didn't hesitate for a second, spinning on her heel and not daring to glance down.

A young boy, one of her people, whose life she had taken.

Although she gave him the only merciful end and the last gift of seeing his mother…she felt it. With every new thump of the heart in her chest, she felt the darkness beating with it.

CHAPTER 11

Nikalias

T HE ECHOES OF the human boy's screams resonated chillingly
in the prince's ears even after he was granted leave from the
throne room following Faythe's brutal display. He couldn't fault her
—or judge her—for doing what the king had asked. If she refused,
Nik didn't want to think about the repercussions of her disobedi-
ence. She was already walking a thin line with his father, and
perhaps she was starting to come to her senses and see that the only
way to ensure her survival was to do as he asked.

Her agreement still shocked him, however. Nik was fully
prepared to say and do whatever it took to get her out of it. He
knew it would be the one task the king could ask of her that Faythe
would refuse, more likely to surrender her own life before taking
that of another.

Perhaps she had reached breaking point.

Nik found himself almost jogging to her rooms to make sure
she wasn't self-destructing after the horrific execution she was
forced to carry out. He knocked on her door a little more eagerly
than he intended and waited for her invitation to enter. When only

silence came in response, in a surge of panic, he twisted the handle and hastily stepped inside anyway.

The room was intact, so she hadn't destroyed anything physically in an act of rage against herself and the king. But it was her mental state he was worried about, and Nik would gladly let her wreck the place if she needed to.

He started to panic further when he didn't immediately spot Faythe in any of the adjoining rooms—until he felt a breeze from the slightly ajar glass doors leading onto the balcony and spotted a silhouette protruding from one of the pillars on top of the stone rail. He walked out carefully since she could very well fall off the high edge in fright.

Faythe sat with her back against a stone pillar, arms keeping her knees tucked up, while she stared away from him and over the brightly lit city. Night sky surrounded them. It was bitterly cold even with the jacket he wore, but Faythe had removed hers and sat in only a thin shirt and pants with bare feet.

"You'll freeze out here," Nik said quietly, stopping a few paces in front of her. He kept far enough away to give her space, but close enough he was sure he could grab her if she decided to topple herself off the balcony. He couldn't comprehend what effect the events of the night had on her and how sensitive she would still be. Faythe could do the most unexpected things in the heat of her emotions sometimes.

She was silent for a while and didn't turn her head to look at him. He cautiously stepped closer. When he was certain she wasn't going to cast him out or do anything foolish, he hoisted himself onto the flat of the stone rail and twisted around to dangle his legs off the edge and stare out over the inner city with her.

"He never felt any of the pain and fear you saw," she said, achingly quiet. It broke him to see the suffering on her face.

Nik was dumbstruck when her words finally registered. He stared at her with awe and insufferable guilt that he had allowed himself to believe for one moment her golden heart was capable of the brutal murder of an innocent. He realized now that Faythe had given the boy the best possible death with her ability. Though it was a mercy, she would shoulder the burden of that act for the rest of her mortal life. Nik knew this firsthand as he too had been forced to commit such odious acts at the command of the king.

"Then he got a better end than what he would have done without you," he said, but he knew it would do little to console her. It never did for him.

"He was only young. He didn't deserve an end at all."

"No, he didn't."

She turned to look at him then, her gold eyes hard and robbed of all glittering joy. "You shouldn't be here."

He frowned, hurt by her rejection and the coldness in her tone. "Why?"

"Conflict of interest," she said simply, and her emotionless features twisted his stomach.

"I'm here at your side, not his."

"When he allows you to be. Blood is thicker than water, Nik. I'm not a fool to believe you would choose me over him."

"I didn't realize it was a choice."

"Then you are the fool. You can't be on both sides. Your father is wrong and has to be stopped."

The prince shook his head. "You talk of high treason, Faythe, yet you forget where you are; who could quite easily overhear you. I've done what I can to keep you out of trouble, but if you're going to go looking for it, I won't be able to save you this time."

Faythe laughed bitterly. "You've only proven my point, *Prince*. Now, go, like the good little lapdog you are."

Nik knew she didn't mean it—not truly. She was hurting, and he couldn't blame her for wanting to project her feelings onto him for being the son of the king who had forced her to carry out heinous, irreversible acts. Still, he felt a surge of anger at the comment and pain that it had come from her.

He let it simmer before saying, "He wasn't always like this, you know?" Nik didn't look at her again as he spoke. "Everything changed just before the Great Battles. He came back from a kings' trip to Rhyenelle, and he was never the same. Then the battles happened, and my mother was killed shortly after. I always thought it was a collection of things that turned his heart," he admitted, not sure why it was all pouring out of him now. Perhaps this was his campaign to make her understand why he couldn't turn his back on his father despite a century of disagreement and hating his new harsh and merciless ruling. "I guess a part of me hopes the father I knew, the one I have better memories with, still lives on in some tangible way."

Silence fell between them for a long moment. They both sat in each other's company, reflecting on their own sadness and losses while they looked out over the city lit up like a river of floating lanterns.

"I'm sorry," Faythe said quietly.

Nik smiled weakly. "Me too."

"You're the king these people deserve, Nik. If I were granted one wish in this life, it would be to live long enough to see it happen."

His pride swelled, humbled by the comment, but then his heart fell in sadness at the reminder of Faythe's mortality. As he looked upon her face, he knew his one wish was to see her live for far longer than her human body would allow.

Nik held her distant golden eyes and was overcome with a wave of immense guilt. Part of him wanted to embrace her, comfort her, but he was pained with the internal knowledge of how he had taken advantage of her before when she was vulnerable. When she was searching for an outlet; a light in the dark that he wanted to be for her.

He had selfishly given in to his attraction to Faythe even though he'd tried to deny it for her sake. She had become a distraction, an addiction, as he always craved more of her. To know what it felt

95

like to kiss her, to touch her, to know of every strange impossibility that lay within the human.

The bond they shared and the love he felt for her was real—that had never been a question in his mind—and it had only strengthened with time. But the romance he'd led her into...he knew even then that it would never last.

If time didn't tear them apart, his heart would, for it had always belonged to another, and the truth that churned his gut with self-resentment...was that he had *used* Faythe. Used her to feel again when he'd spent decades with a heart so numb.

Before Faythe, he had not wanted nor desired any deeper feelings with the courtiers he occasionally gave in to flirtations with. He used them too, but at least they were knowing and willing.

Faythe was...*different*. In attempting to protect her body, to keep her from the hands of the king—which he'd failed at too—he'd been drawn to her fierceness and resilience, her strong will and need to protect, even when he tried to keep his distance. Now, when she learned the truth, he feared her heart would be damaged as a consequence of his actions.

It was a thought he couldn't bear.

Giving in to his desires for Faythe had also done nothing to ease the deep root of pain he felt from always being so close to the one he longed for but could never have.

Nik never believed Faythe and Tauria would ever cross paths. Even more, that they would forge their own bond of friendship. It warmed him as much as it pained him to see them together.

He'd hurt the princess too. Not that she would ever confess to him through her hardened mask of indifference when it came to any of his *private affairs*. It was better this way. Better for her to think he held no deeper feeling for her. The soul-deep twist he felt every time he caught that flicker of disappointment in her hazel gaze was bearable only in the knowledge it kept her safe.

All he could do was hope that when he did find the courage to bear all to Faythe, she could find it in her heart to forgive him.

Because romantic or not, it pained him horribly to imagine the void that would hollow his chest if she decided he wasn't worth her friendship either.

Faythe would never know that she had saved him. From becoming so ice-cold in his silent misery and torment that he feared he would never feel again.

CHAPTER 12

Faythe

A soft knock sounded at Faythe's door, halting her back-and-forth pacing and silencing her reeling thoughts. In her restless solitude, she'd been wearing down the floorboards near the fire all day. She didn't identify the knock as either of her fae friends or her two handmaidens. Instant curiosity had her striding to answer.

Faythe blinked in surprise to find a familiar head of disheveled brown hair and a bright, boyish smile standing outside. Caius waited patiently while she stared at him in confusion, trying to rack her mind for reasons why he would visit her rooms.

"Can I come inside?" he asked hesitantly.

Faythe realized her pinched face was anything but a warm reception. She relaxed her expression and forced a smile to accompany her nod as she stepped aside for him to enter. Clicking the door shut, Faythe turned to him and crossed her arms.

"There are no meetings today," she stated.

It was near nightfall too, but it was the only conclusion she could draw for him being here.

Caius glanced casually around the room as he walked in

farther, and then he turned to her with a soft half-smile. "That's not why I'm here. May I?" He gestured to one of the armchairs by the fire.

Faythe nodded and dropped her arms, strolling over as he made himself comfortable.

Caius's effortless presence was what had drawn her to him during her first few weeks in the castle. He was warm and kind, and being around him was like being in a constant embrace. Though they had formed a friendship from their posts in the guard together, it was the first time he had come to her directly off-duty.

He looked from her to the vacant chair opposite expectantly. Faythe didn't want to sit. She had barely been able to sit all day with the storm of thoughts and emotions battering her mind. Yet it didn't look as if the fae guard was willing to talk until she did.

With a suppressed huff, she reluctantly forced herself down. Her knee began an irritating bounce in place of her need to pace. Caius seemed to notice her restlessness, and his face fell to understanding.

"I'm sorry for what you were forced to do," he said at last.

Faythe had to look away from him, targeting her hard gaze on the amber flames instead while her lips tightened at the mention of the murder she committed last night. It was the reason she had driven herself from sleep to focus solely on reinforcing the barricade on her emotions that strained painfully to burst. She couldn't afford to break down right now. There was still work to be done, other young lives that could be saved.

Caius went on. "I know you won't want to hear this, but it was brave, what you did."

He was right: It was the last thing she wanted to hear. Nothing about what she did deserved an ounce of praise.

"It's not the act but the intention that separates the good from the evil."

Faythe shook her head, wanting to expel his words from her

mind. She didn't deserve consolation; she didn't deserve for her actions to be justified. Anger made her surge to her feet.

"Did Nik send you?" she accused.

"No," Caius answered calmly.

"Then why are you here?" It was a snap she couldn't bite back, the only way she could get him to see how dark and ugly she felt within.

"You've been distant lately, and you haven't accompanied us on patrol for a while."

Faythe waited for him to expand on it, finding it hard to believe he was here out of his own *concern* for her. Why would he care to notice?

"I'm fine."

He curved a brow, flashing a look at her clenched, vibrating fists. "Really?"

"Really," Faythe echoed through her teeth.

Caius didn't balk at her dismissal. He folded his ankle across his knee casually. Faythe could only stare at him incredulously and with growing ire.

"I want to be alone," she ground out, trying not to release the full force of her frustration on him. He was the least deserving of becoming the target of her indignation.

"No, you don't."

Her nostrils flared at his defiance however well-intentioned it was. She held his brown eyes—so innocent and warm—and her anger diffused the longer she stared at the boyish face that calmed her wrath, wondering why he would extend his kindness to her. Whatever he read on her face curled a small smile on his mouth. Faythe couldn't return it. If she didn't have her anger to over-shadow her guilt and grief, she embraced a cold numbness instead.

"You don't have to check in on me, Caius." It left her lips as a whisper, a hushed plea.

Caius shuffled in his chair, saying casually, "We all need someone."

Her brow flinched at that.

"Besides, it's not like I have anything better to do."

He added a smirk, and Faythe did smile then, even huffing a short laugh at his effortless attempt to get her to forget, just for a moment, the darkness that surrounded her.

With a long breath that felt a little lighter, Faythe once again took up the chair opposite Caius.

For a long moment, neither of them spoke, simply tuning in to the fire's dance in their own quiet thought. Having friendly company *did* help to soothe Faythe's sharp emotions. Even in silence.

She slid her eyes to the fae guard. "Don't you have family waiting for you if you're not on duty?"

A flicker of sadness crossed Caius's expression, but he was quick to wipe it away with his usual quirk of a smile. "It's just me," he answered through a long breath. "It's been that way for a long time, so you don't need to feel bad for me," he added with a knowing look, but the shadow of loss, however long ago, lingered on his face.

Faythe's throat tightened. "What happened?"

Caius unhooked his legs, leaning on his forearms, but he didn't meet her eye as he seemed to travel to the memory she'd stirred. Faythe waited patiently and was about to divert the subject at the dark crease of sorrow on his face. Then Caius spoke.

"I'm not full fae," he confessed.

Faythe's shock hit her like a physical blow. Caius spared her a quick glance to absorb her reaction, and she pictured her own wide-mouthed bewilderment as it triggered faint amusement in him.

His face fell into a frown as he continued. "My father is fae, but I've never met him. My mother was human but died in childbirth. I was lucky enough that the woman who aided her labor had a kind soul and big heart. She took me in rather than abandoning me to the grim fate so many other demi-fae meet.

"Despite everything, my childhood wasn't all that awful. I was housed and fed, albeit isolated. She kept me hidden, and as the years went by, all I could do was watch her age and eventually die, old and frail, while I wasn't even full-grown in the lifespan of a fae.

"From then, I had to carve a path for myself when no sure way was laid. That's when I joined the guard, just old enough to start their basic training. I found friends here, family, and for a while, I thought perhaps life as a demi-fae wouldn't be so bad after all. You see, the woman who brought me up tried to instil in me the hardship I may face from the world outside our small home."

Caius's face was soft and bright as he spoke of the woman who raised him, but when it fell again, Faythe braced for his story to take a sorrowful turn.

His features sharpened as the amber flames highlighted the hard mask he had to wear to get through the next part of his life story.

"There were many for a long time who looked at me as if I were sullied and unworthy of being in their ranks. I was tormented mentally, reading into every sign. I look just like a fae, I have their strength and speed, and I was never behind in training, but it didn't stop me from feeling like I was always *weaker* in comparison. I still do sometimes."

Caius locked onto her gaze, face full of...*understanding.* "Even in friends, I thought I saw things that were never there—hatred and disgust. I was different, and I was almost ready to bow down to that fact and accept it was all I would ever be. Different and unworthy." He took a pause, and hesitation flinched his brow. Faythe kept still and patient though her heart was splintering. "I guess I'm telling you this because I know how it feels...to think you're a burden and unwanted, even to the people who are close to you. It's like we always feel as if we have something to prove—to others, to ourselves—perhaps in a longing that our twisted existence will count for something in this world."

Faythe swallowed, having no words to respond with even if she could get them past the hard lump in her throat. In the way Caius spoke, connecting them as one and the same though their experiences were separate, she felt a new sense of liberation. To have someone who truly *understood*. Every dark and desolate thought she'd ever had about herself, Caius had felt it about himself too.

She never would have known the guard wasn't full fae. That he was like her in a way. Never in the time she had known him did he appear any different on the exterior. But in his mind, he would always harbor that doubt. She knew this because she *felt* this.

"Thank you for sharing that with me," she finally choked out.

Caius's smile turned up on her own face, and she felt a small weight lift from her shoulders.

"Your differences only make you weak if you let them, Faythe. It's when you embrace them that you start to live the life you were meant to lead. Not everyone has that strength." He stood, looking down at her with a hint of challenge. "I believe that you do, but let me tell you, it's easy to push away those who are there for you. It takes strength to accept help and even more to ask for it."

Faythe stood too and felt a new confidence curving her spine and squaring her shoulders as she did. In the flare of Caius's eye, it was as if he saw the change within her too.

"You are the brave one, Caius."

He huffed a laugh at that, and when it ceased and they looked at each other, his arms opened at the same time Faythe took a step to fall into them.

Her brow furrowed as she closed her eyes in his embrace. "Thank you."

His arms tightened a fraction. "Anytime."

When they released each other, Faythe took a long inhale, feeling her mind clear as she began to absorb his encouraging words. They helped her sort through the chaos of thoughts she'd pondered endlessly before he arrived.

The kings' meetings were in just a few days, and Faythe couldn't risk frequent absence to get the boys to safety. It dawned on her there were only two people she could ask, but after their last rocky meeting, Faythe couldn't stand the thought of bringing danger to Jakon and Marlowe's door when it was the exact reason she felt the need to distance herself from them.

But this wasn't a selfish ask, and when she took her own insecurities out of the mix, she knew both her human friends would want to help if the alternative was letting the boys get captured.

"What are you thinking?"

Caius's careful voice cut through her thoughts, and for once, she felt liberated to open up about the storm in her mind.

"If I accompany you on patrol tomorrow night, can you get me to Jakon and Marlowe?"

Diverting from the rest of the patrol group was easier than Faythe anticipated with Caius by her side. The windows of the cottage her friends had moved to glowed with hues of orange and yellow, signaling they were home and still awake.

A head of smooth blonde hair greeted her, and Faythe stiffened as Marlowe's stunned face looked back at her. For the first time, she didn't know how to react in Marlowe's presence, feeling the mild tension from their last encounter still lingering in the air between them. So many words chaotically swirled at the forefront of her mind but became choked in her throat every time she formed any kind of sentence.

Faythe realized what she owed Marlowe…was time. To listen to everything she had bottled up inside since they were torn apart. Amid the chaos of her own life and the guilt of wrecking Marlowe and Jakon's with her mess, Faythe had failed to consider how deeply the events of her capture and their separation might have affected the blacksmith along with losing her father and the burden of her gift.

Staring at her now, Faythe's mouth opened without words to

follow. Before she could try to voice something to alleviate the tension, Jakon calling her name snapped their attention toward the cottage.

Marlowe dropped her gaze, stepping aside. Faythe's stomach hollowed at her blank reception.

Inside, Jakon scanned her from head to toe, taking slow steps toward her. "Is everything okay at the castle?"

Faythe thought she would be able to hold it together. She had hardened herself against the dagger of shame and grief to get here after all. But at his question, knowing she would have to explain her evil act, her mask fell apart instantly, breaking the dam on her emotions, which drowned her completely and all at once. She had to cover her face while she trembled with sobs, unable to look him in the eye. He was unaware of the monster behind her golden eyes.

Jakon's arms went around her tightly and wordlessly. Faythe cried harder and then realized she hadn't allowed herself to release her pent-up anguish yet. She'd made herself numb to it all—until now. Her friend continued to hold her in silence while she ugly cried, smoothing down her hair. She didn't deserve his comfort, but selfishly, she couldn't reject it.

"I had to do it," her voice croaked when she calmed enough to speak. She moved with the expanse of his chest as he inhaled a deep breath.

"I know," Jakon replied softly.

Though he didn't know the specifics of what she'd done, it was as if he'd already prepared for this moment and had long forgiven her for everything that happened beyond the wall. This brought on a whole new round of trembling sobs. Jakon simply held Faythe for as long as it took for her emotions to run dry, leaving her hollow and exhausted. Then he kept her in his arms for a little longer before pulling back and taking her face in his rough palms.

"Listen to me, Faythe. You are far stronger than the king could ever prepare for. He cannot break you. You bow to no one, submit to no one. You are a fighter. You always have been. Remember your golden heart within, because I will. Those who matter will always remember you for who you are, not what you've done."

Faythe's eyebrows knitted together, filled with deep love and admiration for her friend and his words, which were exactly what she needed to hear. No more tears fell. With the new bout of strength and courage she absorbed from Jakon's speech, she raised her chin, wiped her eyes, and felt ready to explain what happened, what she had been made to do, and seek their help to demand justice.

Marlowe fixed them some tea, and they all sat at the small, crooked table so Faythe could dive in deeper and share the reason for her visit. She turned her head and almost did a double-take before beckoning Caius over sheepishly. Though she had forgotten the young fae guard who stood poised by the door, he obliged with a pleasant smile.

"This is Caius, a friend," she reassured Marlowe and Jakon as they cast him a wary look.

The young guard extended an amiable greeting before taking the seat next to Faythe, who took a deep breath and rattled through the events of the previous night just to get it over with.

After her recount of the execution, her role in it, and how she'd only done it to give the boy his only possible mercy, everyone was silent. Faythe couldn't bear it and quickly continued, "I came because I need your help. He wasn't alone, and the king will find and execute them all if we don't seek them first and get them out of Farrowhold."

She noticed her friends casting a cautious look at Caius once again, and Faythe found herself also seeking to gauge his reaction. She hadn't told him what she had come to do, and if the guard was caught with even the knowledge of her intention, he could be executed for treason. She suddenly felt responsible that she had practically forced his hand. Now he knew her plans even if he didn't want to, and his only choice was to risk no one finding out or turning her in immediately.

Caius shifted under everyone's attention. "If I'd known you had a death wish, Faythe, I might have tried to talk you out of it," he said. She was about to beg for his silence when he continued. "I wouldn't like to witness another young death again. I'll help where I can."

Faythe's shoulders sagged with the reassurance he would remain on their side no matter the risk. She gave him a guilty smile and nodded in appreciation at his offer.

Jakon turned to her then, eyes fierce as he said, "How do we find them?"

"I recognized one: the Pierre boy. He lives just a few doors down from the hut. He'll be able to lead you to the others." She paused, deliberating. "Though I have no idea what to do with them from there."

The look on her friends' faces suggested they were at a loss for further actions too. It would not be as easy as when they helped Reuben stow away on a ship to Lakelaria many months ago. Getting half a dozen young boys to safety, and possibly their families too, would require a much larger operation.

To her surprise, it was Caius who offered a solution. "The king has removed the fae soldiers from Galmire. They could be safe there."

Faythe should have thought of it sooner. She was a key hand in getting the king the votes he needed from the lords to make his forces retreat from the bordering town.

"It's worth a shot," Jakon said, giving the fae guard a nod in thanks.

She only expected Caius to keep quiet about his knowledge of her plans. Yet on his face, she could see he *cared* about the fate of the remaining human boys' lives. She was grateful for the burst of warmth in her chest that chased away some of the sadness. In the young guard, there was a glimpse of hope for a united High Farrow, undivided by race.

"There was something else," she began. She wasn't sure if she should share the next piece of information as she didn't know what it meant. "The boy mentioned one of the guards he saw who ambushed them to seek information... He said he recognized him —not as a guard from Valgard, but one from Farrowhold." Faythe cast her gaze to Caius at first, to see if he showed any inkling he might know of any guards under Orlon's command who could be tasked with something unimaginable. Something *secret*. But she felt instant relief as his expression remained just as shocked and confused as her human friends'. Caius was a loyal friend and ally, both to the prince and to her. She had no reason to distrust him.

"I'll see if there's anything I can find out in the guard," he said.

She gave him an appreciative smile. "I know it puts you all at risk to ask, so thank you."

Jakon shook his head. "This is our fight too. I'm glad you came. We'll take it from here on the outside."

Faythe had every confidence in them both, yet it still turned her stomach to implicate them with the risk of such danger.

"I can get information between you both. It might look suspicious if Faythe is absent all the time, especially when the young ones suddenly go missing," Caius said. She could have hugged him for it.

"Thank you—truly. I wasn't trying to force you into it." Words of gratitude didn't seem like enough, but it was all she could offer for now.

Caius waved a dismissive hand, giving her a playful smile. "You didn't. I want to help if I can."

With the plan settled and the rest out of her hands, Faythe stood from the table, knowing they would have to get back to the others on patrol before the length of their absence became suspicious. Everyone around the table copied her movement, and she hated that it signaled another goodbye.

Faythe spared a single look at Marlowe, hating that time was a luxury they did not have for the unspoken issues that had formed as friction between them. Her distant blue eyes almost made Faythe wince.

She looked between her two human friends, alive and happy, and longed for the simpler days when she was a part of their daily lives. Now, it seemed as if their paths had branched off in different directions. Yet Faythe was confident no matter what separated them for days, months, even in death…they would always find their way back to each other.

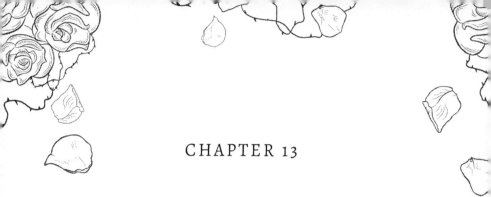

CHAPTER 13

Jakon

J AKON AND MARLOWE stood patiently outside the home a few
doors down from the hut after knocking the front door. They
were cloaked, hooded, and inconspicuous as they carried out
their task to get the first of the boys on the king's list for slaughter
prepared for the trip to Galmire where they could seek refuge.
They couldn't waste any time as it was a race against the King of
High Farrow, so the day after Faythe's grim visit, they jumped
straight into action.

Though he had tried to get her to stay home, Marlowe insisted
on coming along. Jakon hated to admit part of him was glad for
her presence. The soft-spoken blonde would likely be a greater
source of comfort and more able to break the news to the family
inside.

The door timidly creaked open, and a familiar slender brunette
woman came into view. Jakon recognized her as a neighbor, though
he'd had little interaction with both mother and son in all the years
they'd lived on the same street. He and Faythe had a habit of
keeping to themselves and limiting their contact with the townsfolk

—something he felt guilty for now. However, he knew they were the only occupants of the small dwelling that looked even more impoverished than the hut. As far as he could tell, the father had never been in the picture.

"Can we come inside?" Marlowe spoke sweetly.

The woman instantly relaxed as her gaze flicked to the petite blonde beside him. She remained apprehensive in the doorway a little longer then gave one nod before stepping aside to let them pass.

The run-down interior smelled of damp and dust. Jakon passed no judgment on their poor dwelling as he knew firsthand the struggles of life in this part of town. Still, his heart cracked to see an innocent woman and young boy suffer through daily life like this. He noted her son was nowhere to be seen in the small front section of the home.

"We need to talk about your son, Kade Pierre," he said plainly.

At the mention of his name, the woman stiffened, and panic fell over her face.

Jakon added, "We're here to help."

She remained rigid. "He's not here."

He was about to stress the urgency when a clamor sounded from a cupboard to their left. He cast a pointed look at the woman whose eyes widened as her lie was exposed. Seeing she was already trembling in fear, he made no move to advance toward the boy's hiding place and pull him out. Instead, he spoke softly.

"You can trust us. Kade is in danger. I'm sure the news of his friend has reached town by now."

"We need to find the others," Marlowe added gently, "everyone who was involved that night, and get you to safety. We don't have much time."

Hinges creaked and footsteps sounded until a familiar young boy came into view in front of them. He went to his mother's side as she let out a sob, pulling him into her as if she could shield him from the threat. It riled Jakon's rage to think innocent games between young friends in the forest had turned into targets on their lives.

"There was five of us," the boy said in barely more than a timid whisper. "They took Sam—will they take me too?"

Jakon was struck for a moment as the boy, who looked no older than ten, reminded him of a similar scared child he came across over a decade ago. His heart ached at the memory of Faythe, and he saw her golden eyes in place of the boy's hazel ones. He walked over to him in two strides, kneeling to his level and pulling down his hood.

Jakon mustered a smile. "We won't let them." He reached to his side and pulled out a short dagger, holding it out to the boy. "Will you help me protect the others?"

Kade's eyes lit up at the offer, and he reached out his small palm to wrap it around the blade's handle. "Yes, sir," he said with newfound confidence.

Jakon grinned and ruffled the boy's hair. "Good lad." He stood. "Now, before we can begin the quest, we need supplies, don't we?"

The boy grinned wide, nodding enthusiastically.

"Enough for three days' adventure. Do you think you can do that?"

Kade didn't waste a second before running off to the bedroom, believing it was all part of the fun. The sight struck a chord, reminding Jakon of his younger self with Faythe by his side. It had also worked to turn fear into a playful task back then.

With Kade out of earshot, Jakon's face fell serious as he addressed the boy's mother. "We're going to get you all out of here to Galmire. You should be safe there."

The woman nodded solemnly but let out another sob in fear. Marlowe moved past him and put a comforting arm around her.

"It's a chance for a new life—a fresh start," the blacksmith said warmly, trying to perk up her spirits.

It worked as the woman's sobbing ceased, and she gave a grateful smile. Marlowe led her over to the wonky dining table and went about the sparse kitchen, likely looking for what she needed to make tea.

Jakon watched in silent admiration of her calming approach to relieving others' distress.

For the next half hour, they gathered all the information they needed to track down the remaining three boys. They gave Kade and his mother time to gather their provisions for the trip to Galmire they would start the following day and agreed to leave by dusk.

The rest of the night was spent making the necessary stops at the houses of the boys in danger and repeating their plan to meet by Westland Forest. They would have to go on foot as horses and wagons would leave them too exposed in the open. He had no doubt that when the king set out to retrieve the remaining young ones and found them gone, a search patrol would be sent out for the mockery alone. It was a risk, and one he and Marlowe gladly took on to help save the lives of innocents.

When they arrived back at the cottage, Jakon was emotionally exhausted. It was still odd to call the much more comfortable space home. Strangely, he often found himself missing the dreary confines of the hut, but with Faythe's encouragement and Marlowe's persuasion, he reluctantly agreed to abandon the poor wooden structure he'd shared with his dearest friend for so many years.

"I'm so proud of you." Marlowe's soft voice broke through his thoughts as her slender arms went around his waist and her warmth enveloped him from behind.

It was an instant comfort that he eased into, swiveling around to return her embrace. Her petite form fit neatly against his as he rested his chin lightly on her head.

"You were great tonight, love," he mumbled quietly.

She pulled her head back, and he met her ocean-blue eyes. "It was all you. What you did for those boys...you gave them courage."

At the pride in her voice, Jakon's heart swelled. He smiled gratefully, though he didn't believe he'd instilled anything in the young ones, only encouraged what was already there. As he looked over her delicate, innocent face, his anxiety rose.

"Are you sure I can't convince you to stay home tomorrow?"

Marlowe's soft features turned fierce. "I want to help, and I'll only go insane with worry if I stay here." Her warm palm went over his cheek, and he leaned into her touch. "I'm not as fragile as you think I am."

Everything about her stood to be admired. In a surge of passion, Jakon leaned down to press his lips to hers firmly, almost desperately, as if she could be taken from him at any moment. While he knew she was resilient and brave, he couldn't help the need to shield her with everything he had and everything he was.

Their lips moved together in a gentle but claiming kiss, and he felt the urgency in her response. Perhaps it was the lingering threat that would follow them like an eternal rain cloud waiting to break. Even once they got the families to safety, their own minds would never be safe.

Marlowe removed her cloak and swiftly unlatched his too before her nimble fingers set to work on the buttons of his jacket. Their lips didn't break apart even for a second as his hands roamed the contours of her body, and he relished the feel of her smooth, pale skin after unlacing her dress and letting it fall. They parted only for Marlowe to hoist his shirt off over his head, and then they joined again, Jakon's hands going to her thighs to lift her and feel their bodies pressed together.

Pulling her head back, Marlowe cast a pointed look down at Jakon's abdomen. He could hardly feel the tenderness of the old wound while his mind was clouded with thoughts of her. Of her body and her soul. He wanted it all.

"I'm fine," he said, his voice a husky whisper, trailing his lips down her neck. "More than fine." His words vibrated over the hollow spot on her throat, and her legs tightened around his waist. He smiled deviously. "I promise."

Marlowe tipped her head back with a soft noise. His fingers flexed on her thighs desirously at the sound. He would never grow tired of the feel of her, never stop loving the blonde who captured his heart the moment he looked into those wonder-filled eyes. Once, Jakon thought he would never come to feel for anyone other than Faythe. Then Marlowe opened his heart to a whole new, deeper kind of love he would never have had with his dearest friend. This would never truly feel *right* with Faythe.

Faythe was and would always be a different kind of soul mate. To him, to Marlowe, and to many others. He realized that now.

Jakon carried Marlowe into their new shared bedroom. If there was one thing he greatly appreciated about his new accommodation, it was the large, spacious bed. He wouldn't miss the cramped confines of his cot at the hut.

He lay her down on her back gently, but their need to be close to one another pulsed in a frenzy. He wanted to take his time, savor every inch of her, and appreciate each taste and sensation. Jakon kissed over her jaw, down to her collarbone, feeling the curve of her body when his lips met the space between her breasts and she arched her back. He caught one of those glorious round breasts in his palm. Everything about her—he couldn't help but adore how perfectly she fit with him.

He took a moment to pull back, needing to see the pleasure-hazed face that was almost his undoing. When her ocean gaze met his, a faint rose colored her cheeks, and Jakon smiled tenderly at the familiar sight. Her innocent beauty stole his breath with every glance.

Shifting to hover beside her, his fingers traced the blush. "Beautiful," he murmured while his other hand slowly trailed lower, past her navel, dipping under the band of her underwear.

Marlowe's lips parted, and he claimed them before she could make a sound.

There was nothing gentle in the kiss, not when her hips moved against his and she began fumbling for the buttons on his pants, which had become painfully tight. When they lay bare against each other, skin to skin, it was the single most treasured feeling in the world. Every physical and emotional barrier was released in the moments they were alone and free to indulge in their pleasure until they tired themselves out. What Jakon delighted in the most was getting to see a side to Marlowe no one else would see. To see the usually composed and quiet blonde completely unleashed. It was often enough to tip his own release over the edge without any other effort.

Tonight, he planned to push the boundaries of pleasure and endurance, knowing the path they would take by morning left no time for nights like this, and he couldn't be sure when they would return.

"I need you now," Marlowe pleaded breathlessly.

Those words brought on a new surge of abandon, but he breathed deeply and took his time positioning himself weightlessly above her. He had every intention of making the night span beyond measurable hours. To forget time and everything else except her.

"You have me," he whispered against the tender spot below her ear. "Until the last star in the sky winks out, you have all of me."

CHAPTER 14

Faythe

AYTHE'S HEART WAS already thundering in her chest, and she
had yet to leave her rooms. Elise and Ingrid had left her half
an hour ago, and she hadn't moved from staring at the stranger in
the mirror since, scrutinizing her extravagant, over-the-top gown
and styled-back hair. She wanted nothing more than to tear off the
expensive deep blue layers of silk and slip into some more comfortable casual attire. The dress was stunning, she hated to admit, but
she was once again stuffed into the king's colors to stand in front of
the other courts who were due to arrive any minute.

After venturing into town to devise a plan to save the human
boys, she'd spent the rest of the week in her rooms, brooding and
contemplating how else she could be of aid to her friends. But
there was nothing else she could do. By now, they would be starting
their trip to Galmire, if they hadn't gathered the boys and left
already.

Faythe was avoiding Nik and Tauria. It made her feel slightly
guilty when they tried to coax her into talking, and she refused all
their advances to distract or console her. She was still coming to

terms with the new brand on her soul from taking a life; it didn't feel right to accept any friendship or happiness after what she'd done. She didn't deserve it.

Everyone who mattered knew what really happened that day— that the boy's pain was an illusion and she'd granted him peace and comfort before shattering his mind. Still, it didn't make her feel any less like the ruthless silent assassin she had proven herself to be.

Two knocks sounded at the door, making her jump even though she was expecting it. Faythe took one last deep breath to summon the dregs of her confidence as she stared once more at her reflection. Her head sparkled like the sea with the blue-and-white crystals woven through her interlacing braids, and the deep blue layers of her gown flowed like peaceful waves around her as she stalked toward the door. If the color weren't a constant reminder of the king she despised, she would have greatly admired its elegance.

The protocol for the evening was simple: they would greet their guests at the castle entrance before gathering for a grand feast to welcome them. The food was the only part Faythe was looking forward to as there would be no expenses spared tonight. The rest rattled her nerves like nothing else. She had only just gotten used to the fae and royals she was forced to live among, but to be a human in the presence of so many foreign fae...

She had no idea what to expect or how she would be received.

Nik had tried to settle her worries and assure her she would be seated next to Tauria the whole time and would only have to engage in conversation when spoken to. She hoped that would be as little as possible, even though her task was to get talking to as many of the other court members as she could so she could inconspicuously wander their minds. It was what spiked her fear the most and caused many sleepless nights over the past week. If she was caught, there would be no one to rescue her this time. She wouldn't expect Nik to implicate himself to save her neck. It would undoubtedly spell his death too, prince or not.

When she swung her door open, she was greeted by two

guards, one of which she was grateful to see: Caius. A familiar friendly face was exactly what she needed right now. Nik and Tauria would already be with the king and likely making their way to the front doors, just as she was about to be.

Both the guards looked at her wide-eyed for a few seconds, making her shift awkwardly on her feet, then Caius cleared his throat. "We're to escort you down, *milady,*" he said, and she noted the hint of playful mockery in his smile. Caius knew she hated the title imposed upon her to keep up pretenses in the castle. The king had thought of everything, devising a whole series of lies to convince their unwitting guests she'd been a member of the court for most of her life. The idea was as insane as it was brilliant. The other houses would find it strange, unorthodox, but no one would question the word of a king.

She scowled at the young guard but said nothing as she closed the door behind her and they all began their short journey down the hallway. Each step felt quicker than the last although they maintained a steady pace. Before too long, Faythe felt the nip of a cold breeze from down the large grand hall, where straight ahead, the main doors to the castle were already wide open. A young servant girl came up to her, extending a white fur cloak. Faythe smiled gratefully and slung it over shoulders, relieved her shaking hands would be concealed.

Rows of guards in impeccable matching uniforms filed along the hall, all the way out onto the portico, and down the front steps. Faythe had never felt so awkwardly out of place. While she tried to convince herself she didn't care what the foreign royals thought, she would be lying if she said the anticipation of their judgment didn't make her sick to her stomach. Faythe assumed she would be the only set of round ears seated at the table tonight. The only others would be those serving them, which made her feel even more like a lamb at a feast for lions. Still, it was the king's job, not hers, to explain why a simple human girl was a member of his court.

When they at last made it to the doors, several other court members were already organized formally on each side of the portico. Nik and Tauria were nowhere to be seen. Caius led her over to the front edge of the right side, and Faythe wished desperately she could be at the back of the crowd instead. He gave her a small smile and a nod of encouragement even though she begged him with her eyes not to leave. Then he subtly squeezed her arm though her cloak, and she was appreciative of the small gesture of comfort before he retreated to the back with the other guards.

She focused on her breathing, which was sure to give away her nerves as it came out in small, frosted clouds against the bitter-cold air that promised snowfall. She didn't even register the frigid wind that nipped her cheeks while she anxiously fiddled with her skirts under her cloak, staring straight down the immaculate garden path, upon which a royal blue carpet led all the way inside for their esteemed guests. It all seemed a bit excessive and unnecessary to Faythe, but it also made her worry about the expectations of the royal courts of Olmstone and Rhyenelle.

Before she could catch a glimpse of any impending parties, Faythe heard movement from the front entrance and twisted her head to see the king, flanked by the prince and his ward, exiting the castle. She found herself instantly struck by the elegance and poise of her two friends.

Tauria was dressed in Fenstead colors. From the sweetheart neckline of her pine-green gown, tendrils of deep emerald crawled down to the skirts that flowed like a wave around her, complemented by the embellished collar, which curtained sheer green material over her arms and trailed at her back, leaving the bronzed skin of her chest and shoulders shimmering against the fleeting rays of sunlight. Upon her dark brown hair, a crown of woven silver antlers adorned the lattice of braids. She stood confidently, and it would take a fool not to see her for the great queen she would become to Fenstead one day.

Nik was also spectacularly dressed in a tailored royal blue jacket with silver embroidery. Badges of the royal sigil pinned a thick cloak to his shoulders, and his own crown glinted proudly against the bold sunset under his sleek, combed black hair.

The three royals remained in the center, right before the stairs. Tauria was a few short strides from Faythe, and she cast her a delicate smile of encouragement. Faythe returned it and felt her heartbeat slow a little.

There was a short moment of calm before she picked up on the sound of hooves from outside the open castle gates, striking her heart into a gallop once again. The cavalry came into view soon after in the form of several horses and carriages as well as guards on foot. The first to arrive flew banners of deep purple with the sigil of a two-headed wolf. Olmstone.

Faythe didn't know much about the history of the land mostly made of stone, except that it had lots of mountain ranges and little forestry. This, she only knew from maps. She knew nothing of what to expect from its people either. While it was rumored to be a rural and peaceful kingdom, it was also said to be divided, with the western side of Olmstone occupied by the savage Stone Men. She couldn't be sure if their nickname derived from their appearance or internal nature, or which she feared more.

The squeak of the wheels and the clatter of hooves came to an abrupt halt in front of the steps, and Faythe wrung her clammy hands under her cloak. Everyone stood straight and poised in both parties, and she did her best to keep up the same calm, welcoming stature among dozens of immortals naturally graced with perfect posture.

A guard opened the door to the largest carriage and placed down a small footstool for the passenger to step out. Faythe guessed it was the king's carriage as it was far larger and more ornate than the two smaller ones following behind.

A massive figure stepped out first, dressed unmistakably in the royal coat of arms—finery only reserved for the highest in rank: King Varlas Wolverlon of Olmstone. He stopped and turned back once he'd exited the carriage and held out a hand. A moment later, a smaller female fae also stepped out, and at seeing the crown that adorned her beautifully styled blonde hair, Faythe could only assume she was the queen. The carriage behind theirs was swiftly prepared in the same manner for the other high-court members to emerge.

Faythe cursed herself for moping around all week, for if she'd accepted Nik and Tauria's invitation to educate her about the Courts of Ungardia, she would be better clued up on names and who to expect. It was the last thing on her mind after the brutal act she was forced to commit but would have been very helpful as she would now have to pay extra attention to remember everyone.

Two fae stepped out of the second carriage also: one young female—Faythe guessed she was around ten in human years—and a male who looked only a little younger than Nik. They too were dressed in finery fit for royalty, and her common sense picked them out to be the prince and princess.

The four of them joined together and began to walk up the blue carpet, flanked by several guards in ornate armored uniforms with deep purple cloaks.

"Varlas, it has been too long," Orlon spoke loudly, opening his arms as if for an embrace. His cheerful tone was strange to Faythe, but she didn't sense it was by any means forced as he welcomed their guests; for once, he truly seemed like a warm and friendly ally. For a brief moment, Faythe almost saw the man Nik spoke of from his childhood.

The two rulers touched forearms and leaned in for a quick, cheerful embrace.

Varlas beamed. "Indeed it has, old friend."

To hear anyone address Orlon as "friend" was definitely odd to hear. From what Faythe had gathered of her king's nature, he was one to gain following and allegiance by intimidation, not love. She had to wonder if the King of High Farrow disguised his wicked nature in front of those who didn't see him often enough to realize his hidden malice.

"Princess Tauria Stagknight, you look more like your father as the years go by," King Varlas said with a hint of condolence.

"It's good to see you again, Your Majesty," the ward replied with a grateful smile and a small curtsy.

Varlas then turned to Nik. "And Prince Nikalias Silvergriff… You still take after your mother, and thank the Spirits for that," he commented in light humor, but it was also laced with sadness that she was no longer with them.

The King of High Farrow laughed—*genuinely laughed*—and Faythe couldn't hide her bewildered look at the joyful sound she didn't think Orlon was capable of making.

When the foreign king glanced around the rest of the court, she held her breath until his eyes lingered over her in passing and her shoulders fell in deep relief. Perhaps he didn't notice the shape of her ears yet, and there were plenty of human servants both in the castle and Olmstone's entourage to cover her scent.

"You'll remember my wife." Varlas put a hand on her back as she stood politely beside him and gave a small bow.

"Of course. Queen Keira Wolverlon." Orlon gave a warm nod of the head in acknowledgment and looked to their children beside her. "Prince Tarly and Princess Opal, you both are looking well."

The prince, who Faythe gauged to be around the same age as Nik, was handsome, with neatly combed dark blond hair and a boyish, soft face. He barely offered a greeting, looking thoroughly unimpressed to be here. The young princess, adorably cute with ringlets of honey-blonde hair just like her mother's, grinned in response.

Faythe didn't get a moment to settle her racing thoughts and anxiety once the first round of pleasantries was over. The familiar sound of horses' hooves carried across the stone outside the castle gates once again, and when Faythe looked over, she saw the next entourage was far smaller than Olmstone's. There were no carriages this time, only five males on top of impressively large horses. They trotted up the path to greet them. She identified them by their dark crimson coats at first, which rushed like a red flood toward them. Then her eyes traveled up to find the flying banners with the sigil of Rhyenelle: the Phoenix firebird.

Four of the males were dressed in impeccable royal guard uniforms. One of them, however, stood out in a tailored black jacket under his crimson shoulder cloak, also styled differently to those who trailed behind. Logically, Faythe singled him out as their leader. Only, he didn't wear a crown of any kind on top of his silver-white hair, bright even from the moment she fixed eyes on him at the bottom of the stone path.

They came to a stop behind the Olmstone carriages, and all dismounted in unison, either from subconscious training drills or by some perfectly timed accident. Regardless, they moved as one like a thundering red storm toward the awaiting parties on the portico. Something about them sparked Faythe's interest, and unlike the others, she was more in awe than fearful as they approached.

The Court of Olmstone stepped aside, and the leader of the Rhyenelle soldiers ascended a few steps with unwavering confidence. "Your Majesties," he said, bowing low. His voice was firm, with a mild accent she had never heard before. It sounded like gravel but felt featherlight, prickling her skin where she stood. Faythe shivered against the cold. "I have to apologize on behalf of King Agalhor. As you will no doubt have noticed, he is not in our company. He would have sent word earlier of his absence, but it was last-minute urgent business that made him unable to attend. He sent me in his stead."

Faythe flashed a look toward the King of High Farrow, surprised to find he was not in the least bit disappointed. At least, if he was, he kept the discontent off his face. Instead, his smile stretched out to a grin.

"General Reylan Arrowood, famous white lion of the south. Of course Agalhor would only send his best. I don't think I've seen you since the Great Battles that earned you your name."

The general cast a half-smile back at the king, though Faythe gauged it was more as a formality than from any genuine friendliness. Then, as if he knew exactly where she stood, the general's eyes slid sideward to lock directly on her.

Faythe's breath caught in her throat as her eyes connected with irises of mesmerizing sapphire blue. He was beautiful. Dangerously, alluringly beautiful. She thought she caught a hint of assessment in his look when his brow flinched, but she couldn't be sure from his steel expression that yielded nothing.

The few short seconds felt like minutes to Faythe, but he didn't stare at her long enough for anyone to notice the strange exchange.

General Reylan Arrowood appeared to be the same age as Nik, but she could only guess at how many decades or centuries were between them when their immortality drastically slowed their physical aging. He stood slightly taller than the Prince of High Farrow, and she couldn't help but admire his strong physique, which made him look honed for the battlefield. She supposed he was—his title gave away as much. Her cheeks flushed, and she had to avert her gaze from the stunning fae, mentally scolding herself for reacting to his presence. He was just another highly positioned court member whose mind she would have to riffle through.

Reylan didn't look to anyone else but the king and offered a customary bow to the prince and the ward at his sides. It made her uneasy he'd found her eye among the other court members, offering no one else even a flicker of attention. It would have shaken her, but she remembered it was most likely her rounded ears and human scent that caught his curiosity, and she relaxed.

The royals from all courts chatted as they began to make their way into the castle. The two kings and the general led the way while the others, including Nik and Tauria, fell behind a little. Faythe had no idea when to move and stayed rooted to the spot with the other court members. Again, she cursed herself for not seeking out one of her friends to explain the protocol beforehand.

Just as she planned to wait until the others followed or Caius came back to help her, Tauria turned and subtly motioned for Faythe to fall into step beside her.

Faythe stumbled in her haste to catch up and likely looked very unladylike as she hurried her step. She muttered a silent prayer to the Spirits to help her get through the next couple of hours unscathed.

CHAPTER 15

Faythe

IN THE GREAT banquet hall, lords and ladies from all courts were already being seated in clusters of their kingdom colors. Tauria was the sole representative of her tragically captured lands in green, which left the only missing color from the mainland kingdoms to be Dalrune's vibrant amber. As far as anyone knew, the royal court of High Farrow's eastern neighbors were all slaughtered during the Great Battles over a century ago.

Faythe kept herself glued to Tauria's side, observing the crowd and marveling at the beauty in the diversity of the court members from other lands. Aside from the colors, every kingdom had distinguishing features represented in its people's attire and hairstyles. Olmstone had an earthy appeal with their stonelike textures and tunics and dresses with straight-cut lines, while the Rhyenelle soldiers were clean-cut in crimson velvet textures that reminded Faythe of ash and fire, making them a dominant force in the room. High Farrow always favored flowing, light fabrics and detailed embroidery that mimicked the calm sea, and as for Tauria in

Fenstead green, she radiated life and nature with the intricate patterns of her gown.

In her royal blue colors, Faythe felt strangely out of place despite having been a citizen of High Farrow her whole life. It scared her to acknowledge which of the congregations she was most drawn toward. It had nothing to do with the ridiculously striking fae general. No—while she gazed at the Phoenix crest on the shoulder clasp of one of the accompanying Rhyenelle warriors, she saw the bird's wings catching fire in blazing hues of orange and red as it poised to take flight.

A tug on her arm made her eyes snap to the side, and Faythe was met with the ward who gave an encouraging nod for her to follow her around to the other side of the long oak table. Before she did, Faythe felt compelled to glance back once more, but she found the Phoenix emblem to be nothing more than an inanimate carving in solid brass. She blinked and swiftly averted her gaze before it looked as if she was staring. Then she shuffled after Tauria who was already being offered her place next to Orlon's throne.

She had to shake her head to clear it, bewildered by the bizarre vision she conjured most likely out of racing nerves since she was now about to be seated where there was no hiding her heritage, among the table of fae royals and high-born fae. No one sat at either head of the table. Instead, the king was positioned at the center, with Nik on his right and Tauria on his left, and other High Farrow high fae seated alongside them. Faythe had a chair pulled out for her, and she smiled gratefully but awkwardly at the human woman who offered the seat and took her cloak. Even though she knew she was positioned next to Tauria, it still rattled her to be only a chair away from her king. There would be no small amount of speculation from all the foreign fae as to why she had been granted such a position.

Varlas sat directly opposite Orlon, with the queen to his right to engage with Tauria, and his children to his left, leaving the princes to become better acquainted if they weren't already. At seeing

Tarly's bored look, Faythe didn't hold out much hope for the two royals to converse much and wondered if there was a history between them.

Princess Opal sat happily next to her older brother while another lady in Olmstone purple kept her occupied. They were strategically placed, Faythe thought. Tauria and the queen were already chatting away while Faythe was completely in her own head, overwhelmed by the situation and trying to sort through the masses of new faces with pointed ears.

She was snapped from her wandering observations when the chair parallel to hers trailed across the stone floor with a groan. When she turned to see who she'd been landed with, she was instantly hit with a wave of anxiety as she locked eyes with the sapphire gaze she failed to shake from the forefront of her mind. The general's eyes already bore holes through Faythe before he'd fully sat down.

His look was hard to read as he studied her. Curious, likely, at the unexpected human sitting across from him. But there was something else in his gaze that made every hair on Faythe's body stand on end. She shifted in her seat. His eyes narrowed a fraction, and she had to divert her attention, or else she thought she'd turn to stone with how tense he made her.

"It is my pleasure to welcome you all to High Farrow. I look forward to our meetings this week to further secure our defenses and strengthen our alliance. I trust your stay will be comfortable as we have spared no expense or luxury. My home is yours." King Orlon raised his glass, and the other courts followed suit, toasting his words.

As she looked at her king, Faythe's brow raised in a shallow curve at his friendly demeanor. It was completely foreign to her. He was either a spectacular actor, or perhaps Faythe was too quick in her judgment of him.

"Now, we feast in honor of the great houses that have held allegiance for centuries. As one, we will not fall."

A wave of arms went up on each side of the table as everyone lifted their goblets in agreement. "As one, we will not fall," the room echoed in a cheerful cry.

It was touching moment, and Faythe felt privileged to witness firsthand the close alliance that had kept them safe from Valgard for all these years. The fae were painted as arrogant and ruthless, but it was not entirely the truth. They too had children, loved ones, and a fierce passion to protect their people no matter what.

Chatter fell over the table again as people went back to their individual conversations. Faythe kept silent as directed, but Reylan's stare was far louder than words even though she refused to meet it. When food was placed in the center of the table, Faythe found her appetite lacking due to her fluctuating emotions, and the evening had barely begun.

Everyone else started to help themselves, the room a clamor of voices and clanging silverware. To avoid looking more unseemly than she already did, Faythe reached for her fork and speared a piece of meat onto her plate. The feast went on in full swing. She turned her attention to appear as if she were included in Tauria's conversation with the queen. She didn't hear a word of it, and occasionally, when the ward turned her head in an attempt to include her, she would match her emotion, hoping whatever Tauria said wasn't open for verbal input. She couldn't focus on anything except the eyes across from her that felt like a branding. The general cast frequent glances her way, holding his curiosity as if he were figuring out a new clue. Every time she met those deep blue eyes, her body flushed at the odd attention.

After what seemed to be close to an hour, Faythe idly pushed food around her plate, her hunger diminished completely at the tightening knot in her stomach. Varlas's voice carried across the table to grab her interest.

"I've never known you to be so invested in the humans, Orlon. Now, you have one seated at your table."

Her heart picked up in a rapid tempo, and she brought her eyes up to meet the King of Olmstone who peered at her with intrigue.

Orlon cast Faythe a bored look. "She is my personal emissary to the human towns. You'd be surprised how cooperative they can be when you invite one of them into your home and give her a title." He chucked dismissively, and she didn't miss his mocking tone.

They talked about her as if she wasn't even in the room. An object rather than a being. Her grip tightened around her fork, and her teeth ground at the insult. She kept her face calm, however, recalling Nik's warning to be smart, and smiled sweetly at the royals in purple who studied her.

Varlas chuckled. "How interesting. Like a little pet." Echoes of laughter carried down the table.

Faythe tried—*really* tried—to keep quiet and polite. She barely scraped an hour into the feast before she lost her composure.

"If you desire a pet, Your Majesty, might I suggest a hound?"

Silence fell, save for the wild throbbing of her heart and the high-pitched ringing in her ears in anticipation of the tongue-lashing she was about to receive for her fatal error. Or perhaps the lashing would come from steel. Nobody addressed a king in such a way, and she didn't doubt the insult struck tenfold coming from a *human*. In a flash of rage, the words had tumbled out of her mouth faster than vomit—though that too rose in her throat as she waited for the king's command to detain, reprimand, or perhaps even *kill* her.

She was completely taken aback when instead, she was answered with a bellow of laughter from Varlas. Soon, everyone else was laughing along. Torn between staring in wide-eyed bewilderment and joining in with their amusement, Faythe settled on something in-between. Her breathy chuckles felt odd considering her inner turmoil.

"I like this one." Merriment danced in Varlas's eyes as he addressed her directly. "What do they call you?"

Her pulse was an uneven gallop, but she kept her calm demeanor. "Faythe, Your Majesty," she answered with false confidence.

His smile widened. "I hope we can find time to get better acquainted, Lady Faythe. I have a feeling you will be full of interesting stories."

He had no idea, and she almost shook her head at the perfect irony. "I'm sure we will." She gave him a stiff nod and forced a courteous smile, which seemed to satisfy him as he turned his attention back to the King of High Farrow, who was likely itching to rip her throat out at the near conflict.

Faythe knew her relief would be short-lived once he got a hold of her after the feast for stepping out of line. She focused on keeping her breathing regular as she turned back to find Reylan still fixated on her. This time, a smirk tugged at the corners of his lips, disturbing the sternness he usually held. If Faythe wasn't careful, she would end up with another confrontation, as he was starting to irk her and had yet to say a word.

Instead of voicing her dismay, she decided to get a head start on her work. It was the only reason she was here after all. She stared back and gently tested Reylan's mind for entry with extra caution, straightening her back in the seat when she was immediately met with a firm black barrier. She kept her face mild despite her confusion and surprise.

Her first instinct was to assume he was a Nightwalker, but none she'd come across so far had such reinforced mental walls since there was no need for them in the daytime—or so they believed. There were always gaps for her to peer into and get what she needed. In fact, she'd only been met with such an impenetrable block once before, in Nik, who was always fully aware of her ability. But it was impossible for the general to know what Faythe was capable of. This didn't prevent the quickening of her pulse.

She tried once again to access his thoughts with a bit more

pressure. The general's eyes narrowed a twitch, and she recoiled back with cold dread.

Did he know what she was trying to do?

He gave nothing away as his eyes left her at last and he casually reached for his goblet, taking a long drink. Faythe wondered why she had been placed opposite him. Even more daunting was the fact it would have been the King of Rhyenelle himself if he were present. She glanced again at Orlon, looking ever the cheerful host. Varlas had called him an "old friend," and to everyone in the room, they looked as such. She found herself curious to know if the Rhyenelle King would have shown the same bond.

"General Reylan, I hear your armies are something to behold these days," Orlon said across the table.

The general set down his cup. "There's always room for improvement. We never know when the next battle might start."

"Indeed. Your reputation must stand true."

Faythe wondered if anyone else detected the slight awkward tension in their tone. The general was younger, but he certainly wore the coat of authority well and seemed in no way rattled by the ancient kings or the fact he was representative of one.

"I do my best to serve my king."

Orlon hummed. "I fear my own commanders are somewhat lacking. Warriors are left to be lazy. Training is not as often or as brutal as it should be."

Reylan breathed a fake laugh. "Warriors are more inclined to follow out of respect, not fear. An army is only as good as its weakest solider, and I don't mean physically."

Varlas silently nodded his head in agreement while Orlon's smile widened. "It's a shame Agalhor got to you first. If you ever grow tired of the south, I could use a strong commander in my armies." The King of High Farrow let the offer linger.

Faythe couldn't be sure of his motive in trying to enlist the general onto his side. With the alliance, Rhyenelle's great armies would respond to a call of aid anyway.

"I'll keep that in mind, Your Majesty."

She was slightly taken aback that he didn't immediately shoot down the idea. She didn't know him, but she assumed him to be fiercely loyal to his kingdom. It wasn't for her to speculate though. The fae could simply be many centuries old and bored of the same old routine and lifestyle.

The king raised his glass slightly, and the general responded with a short nod of appreciation. Then his eyes were back on her, and Faythe flushed red, realizing she was still staring. His head tilted faintly to the side. She'd had enough and was about to question what his problem was. Then, without warning, she felt a sharp tug in her mind.

Faythe dropped her fork in shock at the foreign feeling, and it clattered off the table, making a lot of eyes snap toward her in disapproval. Flustered, she muttered an apology to no one in particular, but her heart beat frantically. As she scrambled to retrieve her silverware, Faythe's vision swayed, and she realized her mind felt hollow, as if someone had thrown a blanket over her senses. A young servant quickly approached to help while another began swiftly replacing her utensils.

"Is everything all right?" Tauria asked quietly.

Faythe brought her eyes up to meet the ward's, not exactly sure how to respond. She gave a quick nod and mustered a weak smile, straightening back in her seat. She snapped her gaze to Reylan but found him looking away for once, glancing casually around the High Farrow courtiers. She still couldn't figure out what felt *missing* within herself.

Until she met the eye of another Rhyenelle soldier who happened to be looking her way. Everything was quiet—*too* quiet. Then it clicked. She couldn't see or feel anything, even when she tried to brush the surface of his thoughts. Faythe sucked in a subtle breath that cut through her like a spear of ice. There was a time when she wished desperately for this moment; for her ability to suddenly vanish and to go back to being her old mundane, boring self. Now, her ability was the only thing that kept her alive.

She'd despised herself for her invasive talent at first, but had then come to embrace it as a part of her being. Having it gone didn't only panic her because she'd be useless to her king. She felt empty without it.

When Reylan's gaze found hers again, a weight pressed down on her mind, slowly building in pressure. Faythe's eyes widened, and she threw up her own mental block, knowing exactly what the sensation was.

Only, she didn't know *how* he was doing it.

Did he have the same ability? The prospect thrilled her, only in thinking perhaps she wasn't an anomaly in the world. But her excitement was overshadowed by the fear her life hung at his mercy. Did he know about her? It would be her end. He would tell his king or perhaps expose her before his visit was over.

Faythe had to brace a hand on the table to keep from swaying with the waves of anxiety. The temperature in the room rose dramatically, but she knew no one else would feel it. Her dress became painfully restricting, and she wanted nothing more than to rip it off and be free from the scrutiny and false pleasantries of the damned feast. She didn't know much about fae etiquette—or any rules on what was proper, for that matter—but she knew it would be on her head if she left before the end. So she breathed slow and steady, making it her only focus while taking long drinks from her cup. Usually, she would be glad for the wine, but right now, she wished her ability were to turn it to ice water.

Tauria frequently cast worried sideward glances, which Faythe responded to with a smile that would do a lousy job of convincing anyone. When she felt calm enough, she dared to face off with the lion once again.

Reylan didn't waste any time trying his luck in her mind. Faythe felt the familiar impression. While it roused her anger, it was also interesting to know exactly what Nik felt all those times she'd tried. She cringed a little in shame.

The force grew stronger, and before she could think, she snapped. "Stop that," she hissed under her breath.

A few of the nearby fae cast her confused, distasteful looks. Faythe cursed herself for the mistake. The general hadn't uttered a word to her yet, and to everyone else, it would look as if she were scolding him for absolutely no reason. He cocked an eyebrow, and she saw the amusement twinkling like stars in the night sky of his irises.

"Is there something wrong?" His voice stoked that featherlight touch down her spine, blurring Faythe's ire with desire. Her teeth clenched as she failed to form words. At least, none that wouldn't condemn her.

After a careful breath, she forced a smile and answered through tight lips. "Not at all." She was about to rip her gaze from his and not engage for the rest of the evening. Then a heavy weight fell, almost crushing her mentally. She blinked hard to fight the blackness that clouded her vision. Her head throbbed, only for a few impairing seconds, then she straightened as the room stopped titling, hoping no one was paying attention.

To be sure her ability had returned, she caught the eye of the queen across the table who was already staring. When she glimpsed a few thoughts on the edge of her mind—mostly curiosity aimed at the odd human across from her—Faythe breathed a subtle sigh. It was concerning that she was drawing the wrong kind of attention, but at least she could focus again without the lingering panic. She just had to get through the next hour; survive the feast she had already failed to remain silent and hospitable through as she was ordered.

It would be a miracle if she ended the week with her head still fixed on her shoulders.

The excited clamor began to calm, the high fae around the table elated and full-bellied. Faythe, however, was beyond bored and had barely eaten anything thanks to the twist in her stomach from her irritation at Reylan's frequent glances and the fear her ability would go mute again.

She wanted to confront the general, demand what his problem was and settle her giddy need to know if he harnessed a similar ability, but she was at a loss for how to achieve the latter without outing herself. The possibility he already knew terrified her. If he was suspicious, he remained silent, which was always the most deadly sign before the strike of a predator. What she desperately desired, above having her questions about Reylan answered, was complete solitude. A moment of stillness. In her exhaustion, she couldn't even find the strength to block out the loud thoughts of those around her that hummed incoherently in her head like an irritating swarm of wasps.

For the first and likely only time, Orlon's voice was her saving grace.

"The servants will show you all to your quarters and will be at your disposal should you require anything."

The royal parties mercifully began to rise from the table. Faythe let the stiff posture she'd endured falter slightly while they were otherwise occupied.

"My home is yours to wander freely, and I look forward to meeting formally to discuss matters after your day of rest."

Faythe stood too, walking around the table to stand with Tauria while they watched their guests exit with a few short words of gratitude. As the Rhyenelle general bowed in thanks before the king, he cast Faythe one last fleeting look before turning on his heel and leaving behind the sea of purple.

She didn't like him—didn't *want* to like him—yet she cursed the dangerous thrill that caressed her spine at the exchange.

When all their guests were out of the hall, including the High Farrow court members, the three royal hosts and Faythe were left in an awkward silence. The ward was the first to excuse herself, casting Faythe a tight smile before she was dismissed. Faythe didn't ask permission before trying her luck and took the first steps toward the door that beckoned her escape.

"Faythe," Orlon's voice sang behind her.

She closed her eyes, cursing inwardly as she realized she wasn't going to leave unscathed. She turned around to face him.

"You step out of line again, say one thing you shouldn't, and I won't hesitate to cut out your tongue."

His threat was clear, and it was far from empty. The mask of the pleasant, cheerful host had completely dissolved, revealing the cold, dark face of hatred she was all too familiar with. Though she trembled inside, she rallied the remnants of her quickly dissipating bravery to respond.

"King Varlas was not going to be won over by niceties or feminine charm. You told me to get close to them. I saw what would grab his interest, and I did, didn't I?" The lie tumbled out of her so easily she was impressed. She couldn't decide if it was a good or bad thing she was becoming a more efficient liar in the king's court.

Orlon's eyes narrowed slightly, debating whether she spoke true or was playing him for a fool. By some mercy of the Spirits, he decided not to call her bluff and dismissed her with a wave of his hand. Faythe held poise and refrained from sagging forward in relief. She turned and briskly exited the grand dining hall at last.

She was halfway down her second hallway when she heard quiet footsteps catching up to her. She didn't have to turn around to know who it was.

"You didn't really know your audacious words would be well-received with Varlas, did you?" Nik accused playfully.

She was grateful for the familiar voice she hadn't been able to converse with all night but didn't look at him as she answered, still dealing with the mental chaos from the night's events.

"Not in the slightest."

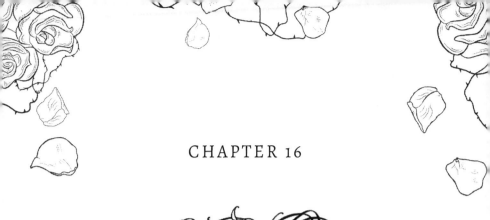

CHAPTER 16

Faythe

FAYTHE HAD TOSSED and turned in her sheets for hours since returning from the feast. She lay in a hot, tangled mess, unable to get her racing mind to settle. Specifically, she worried the Rhyenelle general knew her secret and somehow possessed a similar ability to her own.

She'd declined Nik's offer to stay in her rooms in case she needed someone to talk to. She clearly did a lousy job of convincing him she was absolutely fine. She was anything but and was going out of her mind, wanting to scream out loud with unrest.

Finally giving up, she flung back the covers with a disgruntled huff and walked over to the balcony doors for some fresh air. As she yanked them open, the sharp sting of cold hit her like a wave of ice water in her short silk nightgown. It was long past midnight, but the sleeping city still glowed beautifully below as if she were looking down upon the stars.

After cooling down, she walked back inside and partially closed the doors, not wanting to completely freeze her ass off. Her stomach growled loudly. She barely ate anything at the magnificent feast, and now she was angry with herself for it, and angry at the annoying silver-haired fae general for distracting her so much she didn't enjoy any of it.

Deciding she was unlikely to get any sleep, she stormed into the closet and swiftly changed before stuffing her feet into her boots. She may as well satisfy her hunger while the castle slept. She could ransack the kitchens for leftovers.

She left her rooms cautiously, though it was likely wasted energy in a castle crawling with fae and their heightened senses. Still, she crept as stealthily as she could down the torchlit hallways, darting between the shadows, trying to avoid confrontation with any of the guards should they want to question where she was going. It wasn't as if she was up to no good, but she knew they were under strict orders not to let her out of sight. To their credit, they tried to be subtle, but she always noticed a pair of surreptitious guards trailing nearby wherever she went.

At the sound of quiet chatter and light footsteps, Faythe ducked into a dark alcove and waited for two fae guards to pass before dipping down the stairwell that would take her to the servants' quarters. When she arrived, she winced as the door creaked loudly and slipped inside.

Within the eerie, dark confines of the kitchen, she relaxed, knowing no one would be coming down here anytime soon. She wished she'd thought to swipe one of the torches from the wall, realizing she had little light to maneuver. Weak beams of moonlight shone through the line of high box windows along one wall. She would have to make do, and as her eyes adjusted, she could just about make out the different areas and where she would look for food.

A large bench held various covered platters, and Faythe began to lift the rags, squinting to determine what was underneath. She could already smell the delectable notes of chocolate before a full cake came into view, and her mouth instantly watered. It wasn't exactly what she had in mind for supper, and she didn't remember seeing dessert at the feast tonight, but she started to crave the sickly-sweet pudding as soon as the scent hit her nostrils.

Looking around for something to cut a slice, or even a fork to save the hassle, she spied the utensils hanging along a rack by the sinks. Eagerly skipping over, she grabbed both silverware and a plate before turning back to dive in.

"Straight for dessert?"

Faythe's heart leaped out of her chest as everything loosely held in her arms clattered loudly to the stone floor. The plate shattered, pieces shooting out all the way to a new pair of boots that now occupied the kitchen. Her eyes trailed upward from them, and if it wasn't for his silver-white hair, stark as the moon, she wouldn't recognize the intruder in the dark. Caught between shock and anger, she could only gape at General Reylan.

"Did you follow me?" she asked through a breath of disbelief when she'd calmed enough to speak.

Instead of replying, Reylan raised an open palm, and a second later, a blue flame sparked to life within it. Faythe's mouth popped open in astonishment, awed as she watched the fire dance under his touch without burning. Then he twisted his wrist, and it darted out from his palm, splitting into three before latching onto the torches along the wall and blazing brighter.

It was perhaps the most mesmerizing ability she'd seen so far, close to Tauria's talent for creating life in the form of nature. It also made her stomach drop as the small show answered her question about the general.

He didn't have her ability.

She was disappointed by the fact, even if it was a fool's hope to think another like her existed.

"Our rooms happen to be opposite each other's. Didn't you realize?" he said casually.

In the now decently lit kitchen, she took in his full appearance. It was hard to maintain her composure as his deep blue eyes bore into hers, the assessment in them striking a vulnerability within.

Reylan had abandoned his formal attire and crimson colors and now stood plainly dressed in a loose shirt rolled up to his elbows. Faythe's attention was grabbed by the intricate swirling black markings that traveled up both his forearms, and she wondered if the tattoos held any meaning beyond decoration. She had yet to meet a fae who wasn't immortally alluring, but Reylan was a particular sight to behold. Perhaps it was his obscure hair color paired with dark brows against faintly tanned skin, long lashes that curved around striking sapphires, his challenging poise... All those things added to his sharp facial features, making him intimidatingly beautiful. He stood with arms crossed, watching her, and she realized he was waiting for her to speak.

"I can't say I did," she muttered in her daze and then wondered why the general would care to notice anyway. "You didn't answer my question."

He shrugged, nonchalant. "I heard you leave. I was curious as to what the king's pet would want to get up to at such a late hour."

She lost all reason to be friendly toward him at the remark and clenched her fists in anger. He must have noticed the reaction as he released a shallow chuckle, only adding to her growing ire.

"I don't know what your problem is, but you're wasting your time."

The general's eyes twinkled in amusement. Leaning back against the counter, he reached for something on the surface behind him that glinted when the torchlight caught it. Reylan flipped the dangerously sharp knife mindlessly in his hand.

"I don't have a problem..." He trailed off. Each vertical spin of the blade was one miscalculation of balance away from slicing into his palm. Faythe swallowed hard, gauging it wasn't a simple act of boredom. "But you might." His eyes met hers, and the knife stopped turning. His fingers curled around the handle of the silver blade, ending its carousel to point it directly at her.

The lingering threat made a spear of ice shoot down Faythe's spine, but she stood firm, determined not to give him the satisfaction of rattling her. "I thought you'd have better things to do with your time here than intimidate a harmless human *pet.*" She sneered the last word, using their insult to her strength. She wouldn't let herself be bothered by their snide remarks. The way she saw it, the weaker they thought she was, the less suspicion she would raise. Though it didn't seem as if the general would be so easily swayed.

"You'd like people to believe that's all you are. I'm sure your king hopes so too." He used the knife as a pointer while he spoke. Then, noticing her fixation on it, he smirked and set it aside. This relaxed Faythe slightly, but she was more afraid of the hand that held it than the blade itself. "I think there's far more to you than meets the eye."

She tried to maintain her mask of confidence. "A rose is just a rose no matter which angle you look at it," she remarked, bored.

His head tilted in curiosity. "Even nature has its secrets. Everything is not always as it seems."

"I'm afraid you'll find things here are exactly the way they seem. I'd hate for you to waste your time looking for something only to be thoroughly disappointed."

"I have lots of time. Maybe we'll get the chance to spend some of it together."

"I'm sure there are plenty of other ladies of the court who would be more than delighted to keep you company."

"And if I don't want the company of any *other* ladies?"

Faythe damned the Spirits to burn for the heat that flushed her cheeks and only hoped it wouldn't be noticeable in the dull lighting. "Then the male guards are also at your disposal."

The general flashed a rogue grin. The bastard was enjoying this. He folded his powerful arms, his poise dancing the line between casual and threatening.

"How does a human with such wit keep herself out of trouble in a kingdom such as High Farrow?" It was more an observation than a question, but the answer was easy: She didn't. If only the general knew the half of it, they might actually have a good laugh together.

"It doesn't sound as if you hold the greatest respect for the kingdom that hosts you," she said to divert the attention from herself.

Reylan eyed her. "I'm not the fondest of the north, no," he said carefully.

Faythe wanted to press further, to know exactly what displeased him about High Farrow compared to the mighty kingdom of Rhyenelle. In fact, seeing the warriors in crimson had made her interested to discover more about the south. But the general was already uneasy about her. Pressing for information now would only land her on his radar for the rest of the week.

Reylan pushed off the counter, and his first step toward her stiffened every muscle in Faythe's body. He kept advancing in slow, careful steps that felt awfully like the stalking of a predator. His eyes never left her face, weighing her reaction as he closed the distance.

Faythe was struck still in her frantic thoughts, in a mental tug-of-war over how to react. Instinct told her to flee from his path, but something else, something that tingled every inch of her skin, kept her from the most basic and logical response. Wariness forced her back a single step, though, and that was as far as she got before she met something solid. Her hands gripped the edge of the counter behind her.

Reylan halted just outside of arm's reach.

Her heart pounded, her breathing uneven and shallow, but she didn't stop looking at him, transfixed by the night sky dancing in his irises.

He took another small step, and her pulse skipped.

Slowly, he leaned over, bracing his own hands on the counter-top. Trapping her. His fingers grazed hers, only a few inches of space left between their bodies. He searched her eyes, her face, but she couldn't be sure what he read there while his own expression remained bland. The moonlight from the windows above highlighted every perfect angle of his stern, sculptured face, soft-ened only by the few loose curls of silver that fell down over one side of his forehead. It looked as though he'd ran his hands through his hair several times before coming down here, leaving it more disheveled than Faythe remembered. She shouldn't care to notice such things. What was worse was that she started to imagine *her* hands there; wanted to find out if the thick, cropped locks would feel as silken as they looked woven between her fingers.

All she could hear was the hard pounding in her chest as his proximity flushed her whole body with heat. Not the heat of fear, but something far worse. Longing. She didn't know him and never should have let herself become caged in by his powerful, towering form, unaware of what he was capable of.

Something changed in the darkening of his eyes, a dangerous hunger she knew she should run from. Yet in that moment, she could think of nothing but getting closer to him.

Whatever Reylan read in her reaction made him inch his face farther forward. Her heart beat a frenzy she feared would break her rib cage, her fingers gripping the wood so hard it verged on the edge of pain. Her spine locked. *Wrong.* This was so *wrong.* Scattered words of self-preservation floated into her mind, but not a single protest was strong enough for her to listen.

His head angled and dipped until she felt his breath on her neck below her ear. Reylan paused, inhaling a deep breath as if he would claim her, devour her. A shiver formed at the base of Faythe's spine, shooting through every nerve ending in her body and subconsciously tipping her head back a fraction. He stilled, and his breath stopped caressing her skin for a few long, agonizing seconds. Whatever he pondered seemed to pass when his warmth returned, blowing across her chest and trailing inside her shirt in a long exhale. It shivered over every inch of her and pebbled her breasts. Faythe only hoped he wouldn't glance down far enough to notice it under the loose shirt she wore without undergarments.

"You're not afraid," he said, his voice grating on every cell along her collarbone.

Faythe swallowed, finding it difficult to form words in her dry mouth. "No." Not a whole lie. She *was* afraid, but not for the reasons he expected.

Reylan paused in contemplation. Both of them remained so utterly unmoving it built coils of tension in Faythe's stomach. She wondered if he would make contact as the near touch of his body, his mouth, inspired a thrill that hummed in her blood.

"You should be."

Alarm rang out, and though her mind was clouded with the effects of his closeness, it seemed he too was distracted enough that he didn't pay notice to her hand, which had slowly been inching back, hoping to find the small but sharp carving knife she spotted before. Feeling the cold wood of the handle, her fingers gripped it, and in the same breath, she brought it to his throat.

"So should you."

Reylan didn't so much as flinch. Not a single flex or flicker. His head slowly pulled back to lock onto her gaze. Faythe held her hand firm, applying slight pressure to his skin to stifle her own trembling. It was a reckless move, but as she acknowledged before, she couldn't be sure what he was capable of and figured it was better to be at least somewhat armed.

A slight curl disturbed his straight mouth. "It's not often I'm caught out by something unexpected," he said, blade moving against his throat with every word.

She wasn't sure if it was a compliment. It was clear he was unfazed by her feeble threat, as though she were holding a spoon, not a blade, to his neck. She almost flashed her eyes down to check it wasn't.

"Unexpected. But foolish."

Before she could detect even a slight shift, Reylan moved faster than she could blink. One hand lashed out to grip the hand holding the blade, the other seized her loose wrist, and she was whirled around so fast her vision swayed when she stilled again. Her breathing was hard as she processed the maneuver, her back flush with his front where he pinned her arm across her abdomen. His warm hand encased her fist, resting the cool length of the blade against her own throat.

Realizing she had been so easily compromised flared her humiliation. Faythe clenched her teeth, knowing she was completely at his mercy. A single second was all it took for him to effortlessly overpower her. In a flash of sheer will laced with fear, she attempted to bring her foot up to where she knew she could instantly incapacitate a man. He sensed it too, shifting out of her way before hooking a long leg around both of hers to prevent a second attempt.

"Are you quite done being violent?"

Faythe stilled, knowing her struggle would be wasted energy against his stone grip. Though he didn't move, nothing about his hold on her was even mildly tight or painful.

"Are you quite done being an arrogant prick?"

He snickered a laugh that rumbled faintly through her despite her head just meeting his shoulder. She couldn't decide if she enjoyed the sound or wanted to take the knife to his throat and cut it out.

"I'm going to release you," he said, but he didn't immediately move. "You'd be wise not to try that again." Reylan pulled away from her at once, taking a long step back.

Cold air wrapped around Faythe, snapping her back into her senses. Her face, body, and mind blazed with bewilderment. Flustered, she twisted toward him, the knife still clutched in her grip while she tamed the anger that rushed through her.

"Brave of you. But your close defense could surely use some work if you're going to go pulling knives on those who are leagues above your physical strength." His head tilted as he observed her, studied her, as if she were some foreign object he'd never encountered before. It only strained the tether on her violence further.

"Though I do admire you for trying. You had me worried there for a second." There was nothing condescending in his tone and no arrogance either as his features softened around the edges slightly.

"I doubt that," Faythe ground out. Their stare down only intensified. "You should leave."

Reylan didn't immediately move. Instead, he assessed her for another irritatingly long moment. Her eyes blazed into his, anger rising with each second he spent reading her because she had no idea what he was seeing. Then he turned, nonchalant, as though the close encounter never happened at all.

"As you wish," he said plainly. When he got to the door, he paused in the frame before turning back. "How old are you?"

She wasn't sure why it mattered or would even slightly interest him. Not in the mood to string out another round of questions, she answered, "I just turned twenty."

His eyes narrowed a fraction, but she couldn't read the expression that crossed his face at the knowledge. Then it was gone, replaced by the same impassive calm. "I'm sure we'll be seeing each other again soon, Faythe," he said with a lingering promise before disappearing out the small wooden door he had to duck down to fit through.

She hated her body's reaction to her name rolling off his tongue, smooth as a lover's caress. Alone again and bemused, with a heart still thrumming wildly, Faythe found her appetite completely gone for the second time that night.

CHAPTER 17

Jakon

J AKON HID UNDER the cover of green and brown foliage as he scouted ahead for the fae patrol. The coast was clear, though he wasn't foolish enough to start walking around without caution. The fae could creep up on them a lot faster than any of their human senses were able to detect.

He remained vigilant as he backtracked the few paces to the group where Marlowe waited as a source of calm for the frightened, wary ensemble of four young boys, along with their parents and siblings. Altogether, Jakon and Marlowe had escorted fifteen refugees from their homes in Farrowhold over a day ago. The journey so far had been anything but pleasant. Everyone was on edge, including Jakon. Marlowe worked wonders to soothe the worries of the mothers and calm the scared children. He could only watch in admiration, knowing she wore a mask of her own to appear brave for those around her. He didn't think it was possible to love the woman more, though he found himself falling deeper every day. Marlowe never failed to amaze him.

Her face displayed instant relief when she spotted him, and she walked a few paces away from the group to meet him.

"Everything's clear. We should get to the halfway point by nightfall if we keep moving," he told her.

She nodded and gave a forced smile. He wanted desperately to console her worry, and it pained him he had no idea how to. On the road, everything was uncertain. The days dragged out far longer than they should, and they had two more to go before they reached Galmire. No one could rest for fear of being tracked down or discovered.

Looking over everyone's grim faces, Jakon felt hopeless.

Just then, his ears picked up motion from behind. He looked in panic to Marlowe first, who was already wide-eyed at having also heard the rustling of distant leaves. Jakon held a finger to his mouth as he motioned with his other hand for everyone at her back to stay still. His heart thundered in his chest as he slowly reached for his sword and silently pulled it free of its scabbard, though he knew it would be useless if they were about to be confronted by a band of fae guards—or even one for that matter. Regardless, he vowed to protect every soul behind him with his life if need be.

He took one soundless step forward, then another. The disturbance got closer, louder. The fae had every ability to maneuver undetected. It was a slight relief to think perhaps the intruder didn't know of the humans they were about to run into. They might still maintain the small advantage of surprise.

The bush directly in front of Jakon shook as someone made to pass through the small gap. He brought his sword up, poised to strike, and was about to bring it down in an instant when the assailant moved faster than mortally possible to step completely out of the blade's path. He twisted to switch positions without hesitation but was struck dumb when he came face-to-face with the unexpected guest.

After the two shared a mutual wide-eyed stare, Caius grinned widely. "Sorry I couldn't leave with you. It took a bit of time to convince the guard for some time off."

Jakon blinked, still baffled at the fae in front of him. He supposed now it was obvious his loud approach had been Caius's attempt not to frighten them by creeping up unawares.

"We weren't expecting you at all," he spoke at last.

The young fae guard shrugged. "I figured someone with equal senses might be of help as you're trying to avoid my kind. Even out the playing field, you know?"

It was an unexpectedly kind offer, though his years of always being wary of the fae made Jakon shy to trust him at his word. "Did Faythe send you?"

Caius shook his head. "She doesn't know I'm here."

The fae guard looked no more than seventeen in human years and still held an innocent, boyish appearance with short, curly brunette hair. It baffled Jakon that although he appeared older in looks, Caius was likely multiple times his twenty-three years.

"Why are you here?" Jakon pressed to get all his suspicions out of the way. He felt guilty for the doubts he had about the guard's intentions, but when he had sixteen lives to protect, he couldn't take any chances.

Caius's eyes flicked to his sword, which Jakon still held between both palms, positioned to strike at any moment. "I can understand why it might be hard for you to trust me, but I hope I can prove I'm on your side," he said calmly.

A small gloved hand moved to lower Jakon's sword. "I trust you." Marlowe's voice was warm as she offered Caius an inviting smile.

Jakon wanted to protest, but Marlowe looked at him, her head dipping slightly in a nod of reassurance. It shook him as much as it made him awestruck that sometimes he couldn't be certain if it was Marlowe who spoke or the oracle. Regardless, he knew he could follow her guidance no matter what. He held onto some of his reserves but accepted the fae's presence. For now.

"All right. Well, we'd better get moving." He didn't sheathe his sword but didn't raise it again either. Caius noticed but nodded his appreciation anyway.

Once they made it to Galmire and back, confident the refugees were safe and the guard had not outed their location, Jakon would make an effort to apologize for his lack of initial trust and reception. Though he remained vigilant, he was silently grateful for the fae's presence, feeling the weight of protecting the people behind him shift slightly now another shared the burden.

Pressing forward, Jakon, Marlowe, and Caius led the group for another long stretch. The path was uneven and damp. He knew the humans behind would be suffering with the trek in the midst of winter as even he trembled with frigid, wet feet.

"Thank you for what you're risking to help us." Marlowe broke the silence.

Caius smiled down at her. "You don't have to thank me. We all want the same thing, and that's what friends are for."

The blacksmith beamed at the young guard. Even Jakon felt appreciative of his declaration. It wasn't because of Faythe that he was here, yet he saw a lot of her spirit in him—a dreamer of a better world, a united land. Caius didn't discriminate against them because of the shape of their ears or comparative weakness.

"Was Faythe okay when you left?" It was the only topic they had in common, and a part of Jakon would always want to check up on Faythe whenever he got the chance.

The young guard nodded, but he was a little wary at the mention of her. "The kings' meetings were beginning when I left. She's been tasked with finding out information from the ally kingdoms." Jakon must have looked as horrified as he felt because Caius quickly went on. "I wouldn't have left if I thought she was in danger. Nik has her back for this one should anything happen."

It was a relief to know she had the prince on her side, but he felt nauseous at the thought of Nik being unable to intervene if Faythe was caught in the minds of foreign kings. It angered him to no end to know she was being used like an object by the King of High Farrow with no regard for her life.

As if sensing his unease, Marlowe's hand slipped into his and squeezed once. In response, he pulled her against him, slipping an arm around her waist and savoring the heat as they walked together.

A cry cut the silence they had fallen into, and Jakon paused with Marlowe, turning around to find the source. Behind them, a young boy trailed exhaustedly beside his mother. It broke Jakon to see one so small trudging through rough terrain, forced to endure what no one should have to. He was about to release Marlowe and go to the mother and child to offer help, but Caius moved first. The woman retreated a few steps as the fae guard approached, but the boy stopped sobbing when he kneeled to his level.

"I know what you need." Caius grinned. "A better view."

Jakon watched, stunned, as the young fae twisted in his crouched position and held his arms behind him for the child to hop onto his back. He didn't move at first, and Jakon anticipated his thoughtful gesture would go unaccepted out of wariness of his race. It pleasantly surprised him when instead, the boy beamed and lunged forward eagerly. His mother didn't object, glad to have some relief for a while.

Caius hoisted the boy up with immortal ease and made the few strides to join Jakon and Marlowe at the front again. He didn't realize he was staring with raised eyebrows until the fae passed him to press onward, and Marlowe pulled at his arm to begin the walk once again.

The boy on Caius's back was elated with his new means of transport, and the fae didn't seem at all fazed when he fiddled with the points of his ears in curiosity. Marlowe chuckled softly beside him, witnessing the wonderfully unusual sight up front. A warm grin also spread across Jakon's face.

Hope. The sight offered hope.

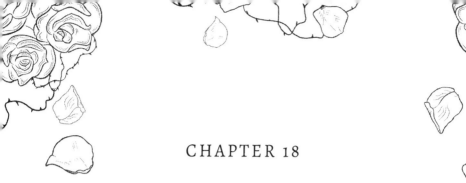

CHAPTER 18

Faythe

THE MORNING AFTER the feast and her rocky encounter with
the Rhyenelle general, Faythe lay in bed, blissfully
submerged in clouds of feather and silk, with no plans to leave
anytime soon. Two knocks sounded at her door, disrupting her
peaceful mood. She groaned internally but chose to ignore them,
pulling the thick cover over her head. It did nothing to muffle the
echo of knuckles against wood when the intruder tried again. She
made no move to answer, hoping they would give up and leave.

Luck wasn't in her favor this morning.

Instead, her door swung open, and she growled out loud,
throwing back her sheets with a childish huff. She only scowled at
the crown prince who smirked at her from the closed doorway he'd
welcomed himself in through.

"I was trying to be polite, but if you're only going to ignore me,
I won't bother next time," he said by way of greeting.

She didn't match his amusement. "What do you want?" she
grumbled in her sleepy state.

After her uneasy conversation with Reylan, she'd hurried back to her rooms without even a taste of the decadent chocolate cake. He had succeeded in rattling her so much she failed to get much sleep and lay awake shaken after being enlightened to his presence mere feet across the hall. She couldn't settle with the knowledge the white lion slept so close by.

"I took the liberty of sending for your handmaidens since you decided to dismiss them earlier this morning and laze in bed." Nik strolled over to the balcony doors. The winter sun sparkled through the glass, making his sleek hair glisten, adorned with a silver crown.

Then she noticed his formal attire, even more ornate than usual. Faythe had long since come to terms with Nik's status, but it still set a strange unease in her at having the *Prince of High Farrow* so casually stroll into her rooms, especially in his royal finery. She dismissed the irrational nerves as quickly as they came.

"I believe the king said this was to be a day of *rest*. I plan to take full advantage." She rolled onto her side and nestled farther into the sinking pillows.

The prince chuckled. "Unfortunately, the term wasn't meant so literally. There won't be any meetings today, but the courts will still be gathering for more casual affairs. It's the perfect opportunity for you to gain their trust and affection." He said the last words with a hint of mockery.

She groaned loudly and sat up against the headboard. "Then Orlon should be more specific with his words. A day of *leisure*, or a day of *forcing reluctant royals to mingle with each other?*"

"Yes, Faythe, you really have an eloquence of speech. Maybe you should run the kingdom," he gibed.

A devious grin spread over her cheeks. "Doesn't seem that hard. Maybe I'll work my way up in status. The Prince of Olmstone seems like a charmer."

Nik turned to her, holding a hand over his heart in mock hurt. "You would really choose Tarly over me?"

She shrugged casually. "At least his father seems to like me already."

Nik shook his head and huffed a laugh, but she saw the flicker of sadness in his eyes. It was a subtle reminder of one of the many reasons there could be nothing romantic between them. King Orlon would accuse her of seducing his son through compulsion of the mind and have her executed. Sharing his son's bed ranked high on the list of life-condemning acts in the eyes of her king.

"I'm flattered you came all this way to get me out of bed. You could have sent a messenger," she teased to change the subject.

An arrogant grin tugged at his lips. "I prefer to entice ladies *into* bed, not out of them."

Faythe gaped at him, though she was glad to see his usual cavalier attitude had returned. As insufferable as it was. She picked up a small decorative cushion and launched it at him. Nik didn't even have to move an inch as her unbalanced throw didn't come close to hitting him. He only chuckled at her, then his look fell serious with a furrowed brow, killing her retort as the shift in mood rallied her anxiety.

"Actually, I came to warn you."

Faythe kept quiet.

"I didn't get the chance to last night, but you need to be wary of General Reylan."

At his mention, Faythe fell cold under the thick blankets, shifting to sit up straight in anticipation. "He seems pretty harmless to me," she muttered, failing to add confidence to her words.

Nik shook his head. "His ability—it's extremely rare and…variable."

Faythe's eyebrows knitted together in confusion. She knew fire could be unpredictable, but the prince's warning seemed too laced with concern for that to be the only danger. She didn't mention she'd already caught a glimpse of his magick during their unexpected late-night encounter in the kitchens for risk of it sounding like a far more scandalous meeting than the slightly hostile run-in it was.

"I'm sure it's nothing I can't handle." It was false arrogance, and she only said it in an attempt to settle the prince's worries.

Nik smiled, but he was far from convinced. "He has a mind gift...of sorts."

Faythe's heart increased in tempo, and she had to draw back her covers, feeling her body flush in fear. What Nik implied didn't make any sense; she *saw* the general conjure bright blue flame right in front of her eyes.

"There are other abilities of the mind?" she dreaded to ask, hating that her voice dropped.

He nodded. "Nightwalkers are the most common. Reylan's ability is more like yours in a conscious sense." Nik stopped his pacing in front of her bed, and she gripped the sheets beneath her a little tighter. "Truthfully, I don't know the specifics of how it works, but he's able to sense others' abilities around him...and take some of them for himself. Temporarily, I believe."

Faythe blanched, but the prince didn't seem to notice.

"When I saw him arrive, I was worried he would find you out immediately. But I've been watching him closely, and so far, he hasn't appeared at all suspicious—thankfully. I can only guess that by some mercy of the Spirits, he can't sense it in a human," Nik finished with a breath of relief.

Faythe, on the other hand, was overcome with apprehension and had to force down the nausea that stung her throat. Her mind reeled and her gut twisted as she recalled what happened at the feast. The momentary loss of her ability, and if what Nik said was true...

She put effort into keeping her face placid. She wouldn't tell the prince she was almost certain Reylan already *did* know about her, deciding she had to confront him for herself first to find out the extent of what he knew—or assumed. The killer question, the one that speared her chest with more dread than relief: Why had he kept quiet and not turned her in already? Outing her ability would gain him favor with Olmstone and grant him great merit with his own king for the rare discovery of a human spy. She trembled with fear to think he might be holding onto the knowledge for some greater unveiling.

"Well, I'm sure I'd be hanging by the gallows by now if he did, so I think I'm safe," she lied. She was anything but and had long forgotten what safety truly felt like, walking a thin tightrope over the Netherworld since she first set foot inside the castle.

Nik didn't seem convinced either, but before they could say another word, a knock sounded at her door. The prince made the few strides over to invite Elise and Ingrid into the rooms and kept the door open to take his leave.

"Just remember, Faythe, you are a *lady* of the court. Please try to act like one."

She darted for another cushion, lifting it in a feeble threat. Nik's rumbling laughter was the last thing she heard before he swiftly maneuvered out of range then out of sight completely as the door clicked shut behind him.

Elise and Ingrid stood together wearing Cheshire cat grins. Faythe flushed hotter as their giddy looks of excitement spoke of romanticized thoughts. They went about the room as usual, falling into idle chatter.

"Did you see the general from Rhyenelle?" Elise asked with a squeal of delight.

"Of course she's seen him—she was sat across from him!" Ingrid turned to her with an envious, dreamy stare. "What was he like?"

Faythe rolled her eyes, rising from the bed and heading into the closet. She was desperate for them to drop the subject that filled her gut with anxious knots. "Irritating," she mumbled. "Arrogant." Faythe filtered through the racks of garments with building frustration. "Infuriating."

"Beautiful, mesmerizing, charming," Elise gushed from behind.

Faythe scoffed. "Certainly not charming."

"Tell us everything!" Ingrid squeaked.

When she turned from her sifting, she beckoned both hand-maidens into the confines of the closet, beaming bright with girlish excitement. "I brought you both chocolate cake," she diverted quickly, needing a moment to calm her flushed body from their playful jesting. "From the feast last night. It's in the dining room."

Both their eyes lit up, and Faythe shooed them away to change despite their protests to help and listen to her gossip.

In solitude, she tried to extinguish the flames on her face at the thought of Reylan. She wanted to hate him, or better, not pay him any mind at all, but all that clouded her mind was their encounter and how she'd naïvely allowed him to get so close when he posed more than one threat. Banishing him from her thoughts was near impossible if she was still to find out what he knew of her ability. That thought erased any foolish desire to make way for fear and dread.

Faythe strolled down the hall escorted by a guard. She had no complaints about who she was paired with, as Tres was one of the friendlier toward her, but she felt ridiculous for being assigned a guard at all. It was part of keeping up appearances that she was high enough in the king's court to warrant one, and thus, the royals might be more inclined to engage with her.

She found herself a reluctant key player in the courtiers' game. She had tried and failed to brace herself for the long week ahead of maintaining the guise she *belonged* here and wasn't just a peasant girl in fancy clothing. Layers of blue and white floated behind her as she walked, consciously trying to keep her posture straight and poised as Tauria had taught her during her months in the castle. Apparently, it was the most blatantly obvious thing that gave away her human nature—aside from the rounded ears. If she was to convince everyone she was a lady of standing, Faythe's gait was the first thing the ward claimed would require work. It still didn't stop the glares and disapproving looks from other high fae ladies of the court.

Rounding the next corner, Faythe breathed a sigh of relief at the sight of Tauria heading toward her. The ward smiled warmly and stopped right in front of Faythe.

"I'm heading out to meet King Varlas and his court for a walk in the gardens. Care to join us?"

Faythe was immensely grateful for the invitation as she had no idea where else she would be headed otherwise. Looping her arm through Tauria's, she turned back the way she came and let the ward lead the way while their guards flanked them.

It wasn't exactly the court she was hoping to run into this morning, but she didn't want to rouse questions by seeking out the Rhyenelle general specifically. Her heartbeat seemed to be on a constant sprint in anticipation of his next move.

At the doors to the gardens, two human servants waited with cloaks in hand. Faythe took her white fur garment gratefully and fastened it around herself. Winter had chased away the blossoms, and she would have declined the offer to trail the dreary, frozen pathways if she had a better excuse to occupy her time.

Out in the courtyard, the deep purple colors of Olmstone were vibrant against the faded winter grass and dull browns coated in light frost. Varlas and his family were admiring one of the great sculptures of an ancient High Farrow ruler when they approached.

"I trust you found your first night with us comfortable?" Tauria spoke with perfect eloquence as they approached the entourage.

The royals all turned to them. The king beamed widely at the ward, taking her hand in his and planting a tender kiss on it by way of greeting.

"Indeed we did. High Farrow never fails to disappoint. Though there is one presence that is always greatly missed when these events take place," Varlas said with a hint of sadness.

Tauria squeezed his hand that still held hers. "My father would be proud of the alliance we have all worked hard to maintain. Peace was always his greatest desire."

Varlas gave a knowing nod. "And he will be proud when we take back Fenstead and crown you as its queen, Lady Tauria," he answered with a father's warmth.

Faythe didn't know much about the history of the kingdoms and their relationships, but it was clear Olmstone and Fenstead must have been close allies even before the Great Battles as the grief and loss were evident on both their faces.

Then the king's eyes flicked to Faythe for the first time, sending her heart leaping up her throat. "I am glad you could join us, Lady Faythe. I'm intrigued to hear more about you."

Faythe mustered a sweet smile through her inner turmoil. "Of course, Your Majesty. I could not pass up the opportunity to learn more about the land of wolves and Stone Men."

Varlas grinned, and it loosened off her nerves slightly. "I'm sure we'll have plenty of stories to exchange."

Faythe smiled kindly, reining back the seed of disgust that grew at knowing her mundane and impossible stories were completely warped with falsehoods. A past with no merit, no excitement, and worst of all, no *truth* was all she could relay to him.

Tauria fell back to walk with Tarly, and Faythe internally cursed the ward for handing the role of engaging the king in pleasant discussion to her. She kept silent as she'd been warned. *Speak only when spoken to.* Faythe didn't get to enjoy the pause for long.

"How do you find living in the castle? In such prestige, away from your kind in the town, that is," Varlas asked.

Faythe supposed he was too imperious and entitled to see insult in the question. Her gloved hands clasped tighter in front of her. "I have never known any different," she lied through her teeth, feeling slick with oily hatred for it. Toward Orlon, toward herself—she couldn't be sure who she resented more.

Varlas hummed. "Unfortunate about the passing of your parents. You are lucky to have such a merciful king."

It took great will not to retort, and she was even impressed with herself that she refrained from damning her guise and letting loose what she really thought of her far from *merciful* king.

"Lucky indeed," she muttered.

They came to the fountains, and everyone stopped to admire the glistening waters, which leaped and flowed in their own magickal dance. Faythe looked around the ensemble. Everyone was conversing among themselves, occupied, and her heart picked up tempo. It was the perfect opportunity to pry into their ally court's minds while they were preoccupied.

Tauria spared her a quick glance, and Faythe almost missed the subtle nod of her head while she engaged the royals in a story. She hadn't the faintest idea what the ward spoke of as her own thoughts were in a frenzy at what she was about to do. Tauria knew it and was helping by keeping them distracted. A small relief, but it wouldn't save her if any of the court happened to feel her probe into their minds.

She moved inconspicuously, to be in a better position to catch the eye of her targets, and tried the guards first, in turn catching a glimpse into their thoughts, which were solely laced with disinterest at all things political. They offered no insight, and she was confident none of them were high enough to be confided in about any sensitive affairs.

Faythe tried the queen next. Her pulse was erratic as she made quick work of maneuvering through her surface thoughts. She found nothing. In fact, it was possible Keira was involved even less than the guards in the politics of their kingdom. While she thought it strange, Faythe didn't waste any time dwelling on it.

In Tarly's mind, her cheeks flushed at having to sift through enraptured thoughts of the Fenstead Princess he kept his gaze locked upon. While his adoration for Tauria was sweet, Faythe felt horribly guilty for trespassing on those private feelings. She dove in deeper, searching for any information on his kingdom, and found various council meetings and suchlike, similar to the ones she was forced to attend in High Farrow, but nothing to indicate any ill will or out-of-the-ordinary defense strategies she thought would be alarming to Orlon. She retreated from his mind with a small frown.

Her face quickly fell when she went to catch the eye of her final and most daunting subject, only to find Varlas already looking at her. Faythe went rigid to her core to stifle her trembling. She didn't have a choice: she had to do this. When he looked away, she stepped into his mind, remaining there while his eyes left her. She had to focus and stay calm, or she risked her own emotions giving away her mental presence.

In the void of Varlas's mind, Faythe felt…strange. Unlike everyone else, his thoughts were organized, easy for her to find what she was looking for. There were no loose feelings, no passing notions. She had never come across a mind so collected and tranquil, but she was not eager to spend a moment longer than necessary pondering it.

She filed through any memories that featured battle plans, fortification defense, ally relations, and everything else so painstakingly dull. Nothing revealed itself as malevolent or false. Varlas was good, honest, and had the best intentions for his kingdom and allies.

Faythe pulled herself from his mind with a drop of guilt that she had been made to riffle through the thoughts of such an innocent and kind-hearted court. Then she felt angry it was her own king's paranoia and thirst for dominance that demanded she stoop to such levels.

Laughter broke her from her slump, and she mustered a weak smile to act as if she was involved. The attention dissolved away from Tauria as everyone started to walk off and head indoors.

Faythe fell behind everyone, watching the coats of vibrant purple with shameful moral regret.

The more she used her ability for the king's bidding, the more she grew to resent herself.

For the next hour, Faythe, Tauria, and the royals of Olmstone completed the tour of the gardens and trailed around a few halls and guest areas even she had never seen before. She had to put effort into maintaining her gawking and admiration of the art and architecture to avoid giving herself away.

Varlas devoured every lie she fed him. She had spent the whole time conversing with him while Tauria engaged the handsome Tarly. The once brooding and sulking fae prince had completely fallen for the charms of the ward and now seemed elated with his company.

Faythe almost felt bad for her deceit as Varlas turned out to be a very passionate and kind man. In getting to know their neighboring kingdom, she couldn't understand why Orlon would have any reason to doubt their loyalty in defense against Valgard.

Now, they were all gathered in the great dining hall for a small luncheon—a lot more humble than last night's grand feast. Faythe followed the flow of her companions and noticed everyone being seated in the same positions as the night before. She followed suit, smiling her gratitude as her chair was pulled out and her cloak taken by a petite servant girl. Faythe would never become accustomed to the human service no matter how routine it became.

Upon noting the empty chair opposite and the lack of crimson altogether, Faythe couldn't be sure if it was relief or panic that pulsed through her. Nik was also missing, and she dreaded for one second the general had approached the Prince of High Farrow or the king himself with the knowledge of her ability.

Perhaps they were dealing with it this very moment.

Faythe was never one for paranoia, so she hated that Reylan brought the ugly side out in her. The thought of him exposing her was enough to make her tremble where she sat, and she found no appetite for the selection of cold meats and cheese on the table.

Tauria must have noted her nerves because she turned to her. "Everything okay?"

Faythe forced a smile. "I'm fine," she said a little too quickly. Then she added casually, "Will Nik and the others be joining us?"

The ward's eyes briefly flashed to the door as if she would see them there. "They should be. Must be running late doing whatever males like to get up to in their spare time." She rolled her eyes.

Faythe huffed a small laugh as Tauria went back to engaging with the royals of Olmstone. But she couldn't find the attention to tune in, let alone offer any input in their conversation. She picked at her food while nervously casting her gaze between her current company and the main door where the others might walk through at any moment.

She didn't need fae hearing to pick up on the clamor of voices before they reached the inside of the hall, however. Faythe straightened as the Prince of High Farrow strolled through the door, laughing and conversing with the Rhyenelle general, the other coats of crimson in tow. For a moment, she was struck by the sight of the two immersed in effortless conversation as if they were lifelong friends. Perhaps they were, though Nik had failed to express his relationship with Reylan when he spoke of him briefly in her chambers that morning.

The general's eyes flashed to her directly, and her cheeks flamed as he caught her already staring. Nik left him to come around the opposite side of the table and take his usual seat. King Orlon had still not made an appearance, and she wondered if he had any plans to. She certainly had no complaints if he didn't.

When Reylan's seat was offered to him, he took it gracefully, keeping his eyes fixed on her like a lion stalking its prey. She swallowed hard, hating that he had the influence to rouse such trepidation in her. She had a feeling he'd be keeping her on edge all week if he didn't take the opportunity to fold the hand that would seal her fate. Perhaps he found some sick satisfaction in watching her squirm at his mercy.

"You missed out on an entertaining hunt. General Reylan showed us all up with his impressive long shot with a bow." Nik's voice sounded over her thoughts as he spoke to Varlas.

The king cast the general a look of approval. "Is that so? I hope we get another chance to come along before week's end."

Reylan's only response was a nod of promise and a pleasant— if forced—smile. She wondered if any of the others recognized his lack of want to be here. In fact, she found him to be even worse at subduing his true feelings than she was. Only, his life didn't depend on mastering the façade, she supposed.

Faythe had no idea how she would get the general alone to confront him as he seemed to be in quite high demand.

"I am sad to have missed it also," Faythe blurted before she had the time to think it over. "Or is it not something us ladies can find sport in?"

All eyes landed on her, and she had to resist the urge to shrink back in her seat.

The King of Olmstone curved a curious eyebrow. "Not traditionally, no."

"Hmm," Faythe said, reaching for her cup as a casual gesture to hide her stage fright. "Traditions need to change, or we shall always be stuck in the past." She dared to lock eyes with Reylan while she drank. He watched her intently, a hint of wicked amusement fighting to disturb his stern poker face. Inviting herself to the hunt wasn't exactly alone time—quite the opposite—but it was another opportunity to keep a close eye on him.

King Varlas nodded respectfully. "Wisely said. I look forward to seeing you in action then."

When everyone's attention had dispersed, the thought dawned

on her. She was an awful hunter. What was worse, she had hopeless aim with a bow and had never even ridden on horseback before.

Faythe tuned out of all conversation after her impulsive statement, eager for the gathering to be over so she could retreat back to solitude and work out the mess in her head.

The most concerning thought...was that the week had barely begun.

CHAPTER 19

Tauria

"LADY TAURIA?"

The king's ward snapped her head back to the Prince of Olmstone. Her cheeks heated as she realized she had missed what Tarly said completely. Even more embarrassing was that he followed her line of sight and caught on to exactly who had distracted her.

Prince Nikalias sat across the room, engaged in conversation with the Rhyenelle general and his companions at a table farther down the games hall. She had more than once caught his glance in her direction while she sat alone with the Olmstone prince. Every time their eyes locked, she felt her stomach flutter and cursed herself for paying him any attention at all.

"Forgive me—it's getting a bit stuffy in here. Care to accompany me on a walk in the gardens?" It was the best excuse she could come up with, and she knew the prince would appreciate her offer of alone time.

He nodded with a smile, and they rose from the chaise longues. Tauria took the arm he extended in offering, and the pair strolled from the hall. She dared one last look at Nik and quickly averted her gaze, lifting her chin when she found him to be tracking them as they left.

Prince Tarly was more pretty than handsome, with his blond hair and brown eyes that made him look elegant and delicate. He was charming, if a little boring. Tauria could imagine a happy, content life with him. It would be a suitable match for their kingdoms' alliance after all. Yet even at the mere prospect, she couldn't help but feel her stomach drop as if her heart already belonged to another.

Tauria sat in an armchair by the fire in her rooms after a delirious day of talking politics with Tarly. She felt guilty because her boredom had less to do with the prince's company and more to do with her brooding need for solitude. To occupy her mind, she retrieved a book about the Spirits from the library and splayed the pages over her knees, becoming quickly lost in reading. She had been alone in her rooms for over an hour since supper with the Prince of Olmstone, and she was glad for the peace.

Since their guests' arrival, Tauria had not resisted any offer to spend time with Tarly. She knew it was in her own best interests to explore the possibility of the match that was obviously favorable with his father and King Orlon. Love—well, she supposed that was always destined to come second to duty with the role she was born into. Her parents were not mates but had learned to find deeper feelings. All Tauria could hope for was the blessing of the same when the day came for her to sacrifice her hand for the good of her kingdom. She tried not to dwell on the idea, feeling her mood grow somber every time she did.

As much as she was grateful to the King of High Farrow for opening his home to her in a time of desperation, she didn't like that it now seemed as if he held her fate in his hands. As if her choices weren't always entirely hers to make, and this was only now coming to light as the price of his refuge all that time ago. She refused to be anyone's property and only explored the union with Tarly for herself with her own kingdom's future in mind.

Five knocks sounded at her door in a specific short sequence. She pictured the familiar face and head of inky black hair before he twisted the handle and welcomed himself in.

After over a century of living in the same castle, Nik and Tauria had settled into a natural routine with each other and quickly abandoned all formalities and etiquette when it came to visiting each other's rooms. She'd arrived a broken female, having lost everything. Nik was the single thing that kept her together and brought back her will to keep on living. Then, when the prince lost his own mother, she was right there for him as he had been for her. They were undeniably bonded.

"What are you reading?" he asked by way of greeting.

She knew he wasn't really interested in the pages on her lap as he took up the armchair opposite. "A volume on the Spirits, to see if there's anything I can find out about the ruin," she answered anyway.

"Hmm." Nik braced his forearms over his knees. "Good idea."

Tauria waited patiently, watching while he stared at the cobalt flames in silent thought. When he didn't explain his visit, she asked plainly, "Why are you here?"

His emerald orbs turned back to her. "Do I need a reason?" he countered, and she caught the note of hurt in his tone.

She took a long breath. "We have guests. You know it's not proper for—"

Nik cut her off with a single dry laugh. "Is this about Tarly?" It was horribly out of character for him, but her temper flared at the insinuation.

"That is none of your business," she said firmly.

He straightened. "He's only interested in you for the prospect of gaining a foothold in your kingdom."

Tauria slammed her book shut, also sitting upright. "I don't need you to look out for me. I know what I'm doing."

"Do you? Flaunting yourself around him like some possession to be won?"

She shot to her feet and cast her arm toward the door. "Get out."

Nik rose from his chair but made no move to do as she commanded. "I only came to warn you."

"Is it really so inconceivable that someone might actually like me for me and not just for political gain?"

Nik scoffed. "In the game we play, I'd expect you not to be so naïve."

He may as well have struck her as his words and bitter tone stung far more than a physical blow. Her eyes burned, but she would not let a single tear pool to the surface.

"You really are an asshole, Nik. You can bed as many court ladies as you like, yet when I get the slightest bit of attention, I'm being reckless. It's a new low, especially for you."

The prince's expression shifted from quiet agitation to guilt that she was right. She was unpleasantly surprised when his sour side took precedence.

"Just don't come knocking on my door when the realization sets in." With that, Nik stormed out of her rooms, closing the door with more force than necessary.

Tauria remained where she stood, completely stunned by his outburst that was so unlike the gentle prince she knew. When his last words sank in, within the arms of solitude, she allowed the tears to form and fall.

Her heart ached as she climbed into bed, where she finally gave in to the sadness and frustration that had been crushing her, just for one night. With the new dawn, she would rise and put on her mask of contentment once again.

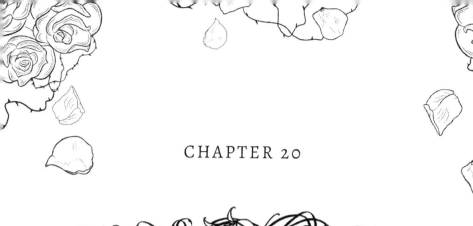

CHAPTER 20

Faythe

FAYTHE WAS AS stealthy and alert as a hawk as she left her rooms after midnight while the rest of the castle slept. She was too aware of the general who dwelled in the rooms opposite and was mindful of his fae hearing when she snuck out. Though she expected most to be soundly in bed by now, it hadn't stopped him from following her on his first night here, and she didn't want another encounter like that where she was headed.

It was coming up to the fourth day of High Farrow playing host to the other kingdoms, and her self-invitation to join the royal courts in a final hunt had not been forgotten. They scheduled it for the last day of their stay, and Varlas had indicated his excitement over her presence more than once in the couple of days she'd spent with him.

This left Faythe only three days to familiarize herself with a horse and a bow. It would be to her eternal humiliation if she couldn't even mount a horse, never mind ride one, so her destination for the night was the stables. She figured now was the perfect time. Even though her body and mind longed for restful sleep after endless days of court chatter and pleasantries, she knew no one would be around to notice her obvious inexperience with the large beasts.

Faythe was jittery even thinking about trying to mount a horse when it could easily trample her or throw her a mile if it felt like it. She had been a fool to include herself in the event in the first place, but she couldn't back out now.

She made it through the castle and out of the servants' quarters without being seen by a single guard and kept the hood of her black cloak up as she scurried through the grounds toward the stables. The night was eerily dark and bitterly cold. A torch would be an obvious giveaway, but she longed for the light and warmth of one.

The moon was bright, however, illuminating enough of the space that she could make out the individual horses as they shuffled around in their stables. They were magnificent creatures. Huge and dominating, yet beautiful and calm. One in particular poked its giant head over the wooden gate at her approach. She was struck by its dark perfection, allured as it stared back at her, stark black all over that blended into the darkness of the night. Except it stood out with eyes of glacier blue, and Faythe felt herself drawn to the fantastic beast.

She walked over slowly, cautiously, knowing one wrong movement could spook a horse and terrify *her* if they started restlessly shifting. A few other horses turned to gaze at her, but the black beauty remained the most inquisitive. When she reached out a hand, it pushed its large snout out farther as if to meet her touch. Its hair was like glossy satin under her fingertips, and she marveled at the smooth luxury of its coat.

Faythe had seen horses before but had never gotten the chance to experience such an intimate moment with one. The thought of riding on the back of such an impressive species made her giddy with a thrill but also terrified.

"She doesn't usually take to strangers."

Faythe jumped back in fright, whirling toward the voice that had disturbed her moment of quiet thought. At the sight of Reylan, she gaped in disbelief. How had he managed to follow her once again?

"*Gods*, do you ever sleep?" She scowled angrily.

His hair rivaled the moon as it seemed to shine brighter in the dark, all hues of gray and silver turned to chalk white. "I happened to be here already. Your weak human senses simply failed to notice." He stood with arms crossed, looking over at her with stern inquisition.

Faythe shifted restlessly, no excuse for why she was in the stables in the middle of the night. Though she supposed she wasn't the only one who needed to explain why they were here in the late hour. Neither of them asked the direct question. Instead, Reylan's head tilted, and his eyes flashed between her and the mare at her side.

"Do your little mind tricks extend to animals too?"

Faythe's stomach dropped. There it was: the confirmation she'd been waiting to hear for days, refusing to be the first to mention it in the fool's hope she was wrong. Reylan *did* know about her ability.

"So, you do know," she stated.

He didn't respond and instead conjured a bright blue flame before lighting the four surrounding torches.

"You have quite the mind talent yourself," she commented, trying to keep her calm.

"There is a High Farrow guard who is conveniently a Firewielder. He won't even miss the kernel of power I borrowed," Reylan said as he admired the dancing flames. It filled Faythe with questions about how his ability worked as she'd felt the complete loss of hers the first night.

As if knowing what floated in her mind, Reylan continued. "Your particular ability was quite fun, if a little heavy. Having all that power to reach into a person's mind and take whatever you want, to be able to kill with one thought..." He took a subtle step toward her.

Faythe couldn't be sure if intimidation was his game or if this was his attempt to better gauge her reaction. She remained impassive externally.

"Why haven't you told anyone?" she dared to ask.

A cruel smile curled at the corner of his lips. "Who do you expect me to tell?"

It was a taunt. He delighted in having the upper hand, believing Faythe was a mouse in his trap. It made her fists curl to consider herself as such.

"The king? I don't suppose it matters which one."

Reylan huffed a single laugh, eyes twinkling in amusement. "What would be the fun in that?"

Faythe turned even colder and was glad for her cloak to hide her slight tremble. Something in the gleam of his look made her fear the general's idea of *fun* more than the repercussions of being turned in.

"Why didn't you tell me you knew sooner?"

Reylan shrugged casually. "You didn't tell me of your ability— why would I expose mine?"

She didn't answer.

"I assume the prince warned you. He does seem to have a particular affection for you."

It wasn't a question, and Faythe noticed his eyes flash to her chest where Nik's gift—the necklace—lay even though it was concealed under her cloak. She didn't want to ask how he knew of it.

"What do you want?" she asked, temper rising at his arrogance. He had her, and he knew it.

His eyes hardened then, amusement disappearing in an instant. "I want to know how a human girl comes to be the King of High Farrow's spy."

"I'm not a *girl*," she snapped. "And I'm no one's spy."

Reylan's eyes narrowed, and he took a step forward to close the distance between them. Faythe held firm against the white lion who promised a swift death if he found her to be even a slight threat. He assessed her with a fixed stare for a moment longer before speaking again.

"What if I said you could trust me?"

Faythe blinked in surprise, her brow creasing in confusion as he skipped from foe to friend, the contrasting twist almost giving her whiplash. "I'd say you wouldn't trust a lion with a lamb."

"I think you're hardly as feeble as a lamb—despite being human."

"You're wrong."

"Am I?"

They stared off in challenge, the intensity growing electric between them. When Faythe could no longer stand the hum of the phantom current, she broke first.

"King Orlon will vow to have no knowledge of my ability. You can out me. I suppose it might win you some favor with your king for a rare find. Either way, I'm already dead."

The general hummed, unfazed. "I didn't take you for one to give up so easily."

"If you expect me to grovel at your feet for my life, you'll be greatly disappointed."

"Now, that would be a sight, but no." He took a few more steps forward, reaching a hand up to stroke the great black beauty's mane.

Faythe tried not to pay his closeness any attention, but she couldn't ignore the shallow fire inside at his proximity.

"I expect you to own what you are and fight for yourself. So far, all I've seen is a submissive pet to the king who holds her leash, cowering at the slightest threat." His eyes met hers again, stars dancing in them from the infusion of moonlight and flickering flame.

Faythe frowned, taken aback. It was not what she expected

from the Rhyenelle general—someone who held her life in his hands should he choose to share her deadly secret with those with the power to put her down. Yet instead, it was almost as if he was *helping* her.

"I don't have a choice," she said lamely.

Reylan clicked his tongue. "How disappointing."

Her anger flared, and when he didn't continue, she snapped, "What?"

He deliberately left another pause of silence, fighting an amused smile at her obvious impatience. *Arrogant pain in my a—*

"Such a weak excuse. I guess I was wrong." He continued his lazy strokes of the horse's head and didn't meet her eye again. "You really are just as pathetic as you appear."

Faythe hated that the comment stung. "You don't know anything," she hissed defensively.

"Care to enlighten me?"

Her eyes narrowed on the general, and she backed up a step, crossing her arms over her chest. She looked at him accusingly. "If you're trying to turn the tables to get information, I'd rather you kill me. I may not have love for the king, but I won't betray High Farrow."

Reylan grinned, flashing a perfect set of white teeth at getting the entertainment he sought from riling her up. She cursed internally for allowing herself to react to his bait.

"You're sharp, I'll give you that. And your loyalty is admirable."

She waited for the catch.

"What reason would Orlon have to want you poking around the minds of his allies?"

If Faythe was honest, she'd admit to him she had the same burning question. Instead, she dropped her arms, appearing bored of the conversation. "He only wants to be sure no one is working against him. Royals can be *very* insecure."

Reylan was far from convinced. "You'll understand my

concerns for my kingdom," he said as if it would coax her to realize his motives.

"I'm already walking a fine line to the gallows. I won't get involved on two sides."

"I'm not asking you to. I simply want to be certain your king doesn't pose a threat to mine."

"Royals change their minds faster than clothing. Neither you nor I can be certain what they're thinking from one minute to the next. I say we let them figure it out for their damned selves."

If she didn't know any better, she'd interpret his look as agreement laced with a hint of approval. Reylan said nothing. Instead, he wordlessly reached out a hand to the lock of the stable, and it came loose with a *click*. Faythe backed up a few long strides when he swung open the only protection they had against one of the beast's powerful hooves.

"What are you doing?" she asked, her voice dropping in fear.

The black mare took a few steps out, rays of the white moonlight glistening against its sleek body. It stood impressively tall. Faythe balked, feeling silly for thinking the beast inferior to her.

"Don't you want to do what you came down here for?" he asked casually as he smoothed down the horse's mane. "You've never ridden a horse before, have you?" It was more an observation than a question.

Her cheeks flamed. "How did you know?"

The general smirked. "I didn't."

Faythe ground her teeth, angry at herself for falling naïvely for his verbal sleight.

Reylan grabbed the large saddle and reins hanging over the horse's stall and maneuvered his way around the beast with expert precision. He was unflinching as he equipped the horse for riding in a few impressively quick minutes. Meanwhile, every huff or step of the horse had Faythe shifting around the space anxiously, keeping her distance. He must have noticed her unease because he flashed her an arrogant side-smile, which she responded to with a scowl. When Reylan was finished, he dragged a small stepping stool over and straightened before looking at her expectantly. Faythe didn't move.

"Go on then," he challenged with a flick of his head.

Faythe gaped from him to the massive creature. "I only came to admire them from this level. I'm good," she rambled quickly as every shred of confidence left her completely.

Reylan rolled his eyes. "A horse can sense your fear. If you don't overcome that first, you'll have no chance of getting up there." He jerked his head again for her to come closer.

She swallowed hard but took a few tentative steps around to the side of the beast. Hesitantly, she reached out her hand again, and when the horse didn't buckle in response, she slowly stroked its sleek, toned body.

"Good. Now, use the step, one foot in the stirrup, and you'll have to use your strength to pull yourself up," he instructed.

Faythe looked to him, feeling like a child as she had no idea what he was talking about.

Reylan sighed, pointing to a metal half-hoop that dangled from the horse's side. It clicked, and when she realized what he expected her to do, she took a step back again, shaking her head vigorously.

"You had to pick the biggest horse in the stables?" She blanched at the thought of being so high that one wrong fall would be fatal.

He chuckled. "Kali is my horse. She seemed to take a liking to you, so I thought she'd be a good teacher."

Faythe scoffed at the implication of having the horse direct her rather than the other way around. It didn't help as it was exactly what Faythe was afraid of.

"Are we going to be here all night?" Reylan drawled, bored.

She glared at him and mustered all her bravery to step up to Kali once again. She got up onto the stool, near to leveling in height with the general. His goading look had her bracing her hands on the side of the saddle and slipping one foot into the stirrup. It was false confidence as she really just wanted to wipe the smirk off Reylan's face.

"I've seen children with more conviction than this," he gibed at her pause.

Faythe knew it was his tactic to rouse her into committing to the mount. It worked. She pushed her foot down while simultaneously using her arms to pull herself up. She strained with the strength it required, but when she slung her other leg around and found herself finally on top, she was both shocked and stunned. The new height and vantage point made her slightly dizzy. The horse took a few steps where it stood, and she moved with each dip and shift, holding onto the reins tightly until her knuckles turned white. But when she adjusted to her new position on Kali's back, she marveled at the powerful feeling.

"Not so hard now, is it?" Reylan quipped.

She ignored him, running a hand over Kali's neck in silent thanks the mare hadn't immediately launched her from the saddle.

"It does make me wonder…why invite yourself to a hunt you have no interest or experience in?"

Though he said it with casual curiosity, Faythe detected a hint of suspicion and accusation in his tone. "Who said I have no interest? You fae males get to have all the fun," she answered loosely. She didn't think it satisfied his inquiry, but he said nothing more about it.

"Going for your first ride in the dark is probably not the best idea," he said instead.

Faythe didn't even expect to get on top of a horse, never mind ride one out for a canter. "At least I know which way to face."

He released a short laugh, and she found herself also smiling with him as she looked down. She couldn't figure out what it was about Reylan that made her torn between wanting to run from him, far and fast, or gravitate so much dangerously closer.

"I have a rather dull territory meeting to attend tomorrow

morning, but I should have the afternoon free if you'd like an escort for the ride."

The offer was tempting. Not only would it make Faythe feel at ease having someone experienced to guide her, it would also give her the perfect opportunity to get to know more about the mysterious general. Both for her own curiosity and to erase any doubt about his intentions in High Farrow.

"Why are you helping me at all?"

Reylan's sapphire eyes were bright against the moon as they locked on her, and she resisted the urge to flinch at their shift in intensity. "Don't make the mistake of believing everyone who offers you kindness isn't only doing so for personal gain."

Faythe's heart skipped at the obscure warning. "I think I have that covered with my particular talents," she said warily.

"Not with me."

Her eyes narrowed a fraction. "Are you trying to tell me of your ill intentions toward me?"

"I'm trying to tell you not to be so reliant on your ability. Even you can be tricked into false truths inside a person's mind."

A twisted feeling settled in her stomach. She hadn't considered the possibility that those who knew of her ability could alter their own minds to mislead her. There was no reason for her to be concerned about it as no one in the know had cause for her to use her talent anyway. Yet the warning in the general's words was clear. Who he meant for it to be about, Faythe couldn't be sure...

CHAPTER 21

Faythe

THE FOLLOWING MORNING, Faythe was on edge. Sleeplessness
had returned like an old friend as her wild thoughts kept her
alert and awake. This time, it was Reylan's subtle warning to be
vigilant with who she trusted. It was ironic she would pay his
warning any notice considering he was first on her list of those to
be wary of. It was completely illogical and brash that she should
trust him in the slightest, but in her gut, the twisted feeling he'd left
her with wouldn't subside.

Elise and Ingrid had left hours ago. Faythe was fully dressed for
the day, opting for riding leathers for her afternoon with Reylan
later. She'd spent hours pondering the possibilities of who had
cause to alter their thoughts specifically to elude her. If it wasn't
Rhyenelle, there was only one party left—one she didn't want to
believe harbored a sinister side considering their warm reception.

Olmstone.

Suffocating between the walls of her rooms, she found her way
to the castle library. A few of the scholars cast disgruntled looks at
her invading presence in their ambient space, but she ignored

them. She wasn't even sure what exactly she was looking for. She strolled aimlessly through row after row of impossibly tall book-shelves. The scent of old books, like chocolate and musk, filled her nostrils, and she breathed deeply, savoring the safe and comforting smell.

Then one set of books caught her eye. They stood out for their size and gold-embossed spines. *Royal Histories and Lineage.* She stopped before them, running her fingers along the titles on the sides. Pulling one free, Faythe walked over to a table before placing the large volume down and opening it onto no page in particular. Dust caught in her throat, and she coughed, fanning the air around her to catch a clean breath. It was obvious no one had touched the book in a very long time.

Faythe haphazardly skipped through the pages, finding it was mostly a scripture on the noble houses in all kingdoms. Flicking forward some more, she paused. She had no reason to suspect King Varlas of anything—he had been nothing but kind and welcoming since his arrival and seemed completely harmless—yet she couldn't shake the unsettling feeling no one was exempt from suspicion.

Tracing a finger along the elegant swirled inscription about the royal families, she finally found the lineage of Olmstone. Her eyes widened slightly to discover Varlas was over eight hundred years old, the same as Orlon, while King Agalhor of Rhyenelle was older by a century. It made Faythe feel insignificant with her twenty years' existence and the knowledge she wouldn't even come close to a quarter of their current lifespan. The kings barely looked middle-aged, so to discover they were likely only halfway through their years… It was an inconceivable thought for a mortal.

She read over the rest of the Olmstone lineage before her finger halted, brow furrowing. Two separate branches stemmed from Varlas's name on either side. Her gaze widened as she read them. The current queen, Keira Wolverlon, was not the first. No—before her, another wore the crown: Queen *Freya* Wolverlon.

It wouldn't have been surprising, except two things written

above the previous queen's name made Faythe's heart shatter for the King of Olmstone.

Mate—Deceased.

Queen Freya's death was dated back to the Great Battles. Faythe assumed her life was collateral damage in the war. She didn't want to imagine the pain of losing a soul-bonded mate, and she felt even more guilty for thinking ill of Varlas at all considering everything he had suffered, yet he hadn't lost his kindness and heart completely.

The last piece of information she gathered was that Tarly was Varlas's heir from Freya, while Opal was Keira's child. The prince's lack of warm reception and general sour mood felt all the more justified now she knew the truth.

Faythe slammed the book shut, angry at herself for not taking the time to become educated on the Courts of Ungardia. She had allowed herself to remain ignorant, sheltered. Not anymore. Now, she wanted to know everything.

About to turn back for another book, Faythe halted at the quick gust of wind that blew past her. Loose strands from her lattice of braids danced across her vision, and a chill rattled her spine. When she turned her head, there was nothing but a long, dark hallway with no door or window in sight. She held still, wanting to believe it was simply a draft drifting through the rows of bookcases from the front entrance, but her skin pricked all over, her senses set on a razor's edge.

Then she heard a whisper.

Faythe jerked back a step. Still, she saw nothing, but she stiffened with fear. Logic deduced it was a mere whistle in the wind, or perhaps her own loose thoughts. However, reckless compulsion urged her to investigate the dark, beckoning stretch of passage.

Her hearing was on high alert to pick up even the slightest shift of sound while her eyes adjusted to the creeping darkness. Halfway down, Faythe reached for the final torch on the wall as the rest of the slim hallway was cloaked in blackness. The blue wisps of flame were also soundless as it illuminated everything around her.

The silence was deafening.

The end of the hallway was a dead end, but to her left, it widened, and she discovered a deep hidden alcove with a few modest bookshelves, a table, and some lounge seats. It was a quaint space for private study, though it looked to have been neglected for years, perhaps even decades, everything coated in a thick layer of dust and cobwebs. The smell of damp and mold was pungent, and Faythe stuffed her nose into the crook of her elbow while casting her torchlight around the area.

Three tapestries lined the back wall, and she walked closer to glimpse the wonderfully intricate pieces of art. It made her wonder why they were left to be forgotten in a cold, dark corner of the library.

The center tapestry made her breath catch as she instantly recognized the moon-white hair and ice-blue eyes of Aurialis. It chilled her to see the Spirit in woven form. She could only guess the age of the tapestry. Whoever crafted it must have had contact with the Goddess of the Sun at some point in time. But Aurialis wasn't the only character in the scene. She stood proudly with another female on each side. Faythe didn't need Marlowe's oracle talent to guess they were her sister Spirits, the Spirit of Death and the Spirit of Souls. One had hair of raven black that matched her eyes, while the other...

Faythe lifted a hand to trace her fingers over Marvellas's face. She knew it was the Spirit of Souls for her eyes burned a bright gold, complementing her striking amber-red hair.

Faythe's direct ancestor.

It was an impossible thought, yet it was her reality. Part of her wanted to remain in denial of the fact, but now, seeing the ethereal beauty with eyes almost identical to her own, she couldn't deny her ancient heritage anymore. As much as the picture fascinated her, it also shook her to her core at the coincidence of seeing them here, seeing them now, when she was tasked with finding the Spirit of Life's ruin.

Behind them, their symbols were woven in gold over the solar setting they represented, Marvellas against a striking eight-point star, Aurialis against a beautiful wavy-rayed sun, and Dakodas against a flawless half-moon. As she continued tracing the lines in awe, a flicker of movement caught Faythe's eye. She turned her head to the edge of the tapestry, but everything was perfectly still.

Just as she was about to tear her gaze away, the cloth rippled again. so fast she would have missed it if she blinked. Hesitant, Faythe raised a hand to grab at the corner, and before she could lose her nerve, she whipped the tapestry back. Bringing the torch around, her eyes widened.

It was solid stone. Then she found a deep line that ran vertically before cutting horizontal halfway up.

A door!

Perhaps hidden for good reason, she thought as she braced a palm against it but made no effort to push. Her heart picked up into a gallop as she deliberated the possibility of what lay beyond. The fact someone had made an effort to conceal it screamed volumes, but Faythe's curiosity sang above everything else. She strained against the door, and the sound of scraping stone snapped her senses awake. Her rational, cautious side hoped it wouldn't open at all.

Not wanting to cower out, she pushed again until it opened inward enough for her to peek inside. She listened first.

Silence.

A good sign, she hoped.

She transferred the torch into her right hand and eased it into the forgotten passageway. Nothing revealed itself aside from a long void of black. Anything could be down there; it would be reckless and foolish to wander a seemingly abandoned passageway in a castle she had only vague knowledge about.

Yet it was as if something coaxed her into the obsidian unknown.

Faythe threw all caution to the wind and slid through the small gap she'd opened, letting the tapestry fall behind. She remained vigilant as she took tentative steps forward, straining her hearing so she might pick up on the slightest hint of movement that would alert her to any impending danger. But as a silent assassin herself, she knew stillness could also be deadly.

Both the path backward and the way forward were cloaked in darkness with only the blue flame casting an orb of light around her. Her mind screamed at her to turn back, but her feet pressed forward almost of their own accord.

After a short while, Faythe came to a junction. In front of her were two separate hallways. She was about to decide on the right-hand path out of unexplainable intuition…until she heard a faint echo from the left.

Alert chose for her in her need to discover the source of the traveling murmur. As she inched toward the sound, she knew exactly what she heard. Voices. She was relieved it wasn't some foul, lurking creature, but it made her panic surge to think she could be close to getting caught. The king had warned her thoroughly about wandering anywhere she wasn't permitted.

Her steps were silent, and she pressed her body closer to the wall, ready to abandon the torch and retreat at the first sign of anyone approaching. She came up to the end of the hallway that turned off to the left, seeing no flickers of light except from the flames she held. Not taking any chances, she set the torch on the ground before reaching the corner and pressing her back flush to the wall. She held her breath, slowly dipping her head around enough to catch a glimpse of the voices that grew louder.

To her shock, no one was there.

Instead, a small rectangular window flooded a pool of warm light halfway down the passageway. Faythe ducked out of hiding and walked tentatively toward it. The gap in the stone was covered with ornate brass, but she could squint through the gaps.

What she saw made her eyes bulge.

She was in the council chamber. Or above it, so to speak, as she looked down on the gathered royals and nobles.

The territory meeting Reylan mentioned was fully underway. She could hear everything clearly even with her human senses but was too stunned by the existence of the passageway to spy on the king's council.

"Olmstone has stayed quiet for long enough. Fenher was taken from us—we want it back." Varlas was firm as he addressed the Rhyenelle general sitting opposite. It was unlike him to use such an aggressive tone.

Faythe supposed she still knew little about him, and Reylan's words from the previous night rattled in her mind louder than before. The longer she remained in the castle, the more she came to realize kindness was often self-serving. Court was a game, and its players were smart, cunning, and masterfully deceitful. She'd seen a glowing example of the excellent charade before, with her own king able to switch between his true malicious nature to wear a mask of pleasantry when it was called for. Perhaps Varlas wasn't so different to his lifelong friend.

As much as she wanted to deny it, Faythe was already sadly disappointed she had been misled by Varlas's niceties. The only question that remained: Why bother with her?

Reylan's stern look was intimidating. "Fenher has been under Rhyenelle jurisdiction longer than you've been king. It will remain so long past your reign."

Even Faythe recoiled at the way the general replied to the King of Olmstone. As if he wasn't likely twice Reylan's age and superior in status. Presumably, acting in place of King Agalhor granted him equal rank during his stay.

"Olmstone grows smaller with the Stone Men occupying the

passes. There is simply not enough territory for my people. Rhyenelle has no right to that land."

"What you do with your land and who you let run it is none of our concern. The borders remain. We will not surrender Fenher for nothing in return."

Finishing his indisputable statement, Reylan's eyes flashed upward. Faythe jerked back as they landed directly on her. She would have passed it off as coincidence, a simple bored gaze around the room, except his look lingered specifically on the vent she peered out of for a second too long. She felt doused in ice. It was irrational to believe he was able to hear her. She had put effort into being as still as the dead and was far enough away from the metal lattice that visibility was near impossible. Even for a fae.

She shook the thought as Reylan's eyes returned to the king in front of him. Faythe could *feel* the tension rising in the room.

Orlon's voice sounded next. "I think it remains to be negotiated," he interjected as if to calm both sides.

"There is nothing to negotiate," Reylan said coolly.

Faythe's eyes widened at his misplaced courage. Going head-to-head with powerful royals was never a smart choice. Then again, Faythe supposed it was hypocritical of her to scold him for it.

Varlas slammed a fist on the table, rocking the few goblets of water as he seethed. "You have no authority to say that!"

It was a side to the king Faythe had never seen. She was a fool to think he could be any different, his sudden short temper reminding her a lot of her own cruel king.

Reylan didn't balk. "I speak for Rhyenelle."

She didn't know if she wanted to admire his boldness or cringe at it.

The King of Olmstone braced his hands on the oak table and rose from his seat to stare the general down. Reylan remained unfazed by his attempt to assert dominance. Instead, he leaned back casually in his chair, and Faythe imagined his cool demeanor riled the royal even further.

"Agalhor cannot be too concerned with current affairs if he sends his *dogs* to speak for him," Varlas hissed.

Reylan took the insult, rising slowly from his seat to level with the king in a deadly stare-off. Faythe's heart was erratic in her chest at the growing suspense. She had no love for anyone in that room, yet she found herself rooting for the Phoenix against the two-headed wolf.

The general's voice was lethally calm as he said, "I'll ignore the disrespect just this once, King Varlas, and I don't mean toward myself." He stood proud in his colors of crimson, black, and gold, and Faythe could see exactly why the King of Rhyenelle entrusted him to act in his place. Even she felt mildly intimidated by the white lion despite not being part of the congregation below. Reylan went on, "So far, you have made demands but no offerings. The borders will remain." His closing statement left no room for argument.

Varlas flinched as if to retort, but it was Orlon who cut in. "Perhaps we shall save such matters for when Agalhor himself can be present. As I'm sure you can respect, General Reylan."

She didn't expect her own king to be the voice of reason, but it seemed to work, for Varlas straightened and decided against pushing the matter. The general gave one short nod at the decision to postpone the obvious conflict—something it seemed was a long-standing negotiation between Olmstone and Rhyenelle.

"Then we are done here for today," Orlon concluded.

The Phoenix and the wolf stared off for a moment longer as everyone else started to rise from their seats. Then, for a brief second, Reylan's eyes once again drifted upward to land on Faythe's inconspicuous position. She recoiled, pulse racing at the possibility he knew she was there the whole time. It would only add to his suspicions about her as he would no doubt assume it was by Orlon's command.

When his eyes fell back down, he moved from behind his seat to take leave. Faythe held back her small gasp, knowing exactly where he would be headed next: to the stables, where they had agreed to meet yesterday.

Like a rodent outrunning a flood, she scurried back down the passageway. She swiped the discarded torch that still burned a bright blue and ran, not bothering to even try being quiet as it was clear now the passageways were long-forgotten and unused. She passed the intersection and hesitated for a brief second at the alternative route she didn't have the chance to explore. Considering the hideout she'd found, she could only imagine what else might be down there that could be useful.

It would have to remain to be discovered...for now.

"You're too tense."

Faythe couldn't argue with the Rhyenelle general's observations as she sat on top of a large brown-and-white stallion. She must have looked as rigid as she felt.

They were the first words either of them had spoken since leaving the stables five minutes ago to stroll around the horse fields near the castle. They went at a painstakingly slow pace thanks to Faythe's unease.

Next to her, Reylan rode effortlessly on his great black mare, Kali. His silver-white hair was stark against the obsidian of the horse's coat, making them an alluring pair of darkness and light. A semblance of the lunar night sky. He sat lazily, his body partially turned to observe Faythe, holding the reins loosely in one hand.

Although she had raced to beat him to the stables after the council meeting ceased, she was baffled to find the general was the one waiting for *her* when she approached. He had even stopped to ditch the heavy formal attire he wore to the meeting. Mercifully, he didn't seem apprehensive when she turned up. She felt confident he didn't really catch her in her hiding place as she would expect him to call her out and solidify his claim that she was Orlon's cunning spy.

"Riding requires trust on both ends," he continued coolly.

She hated to admit Reylan's calm voice worked wonders to slow her racing heart. A voice that could both inspire strength and invoke fear given the situation. She relaxed her shoulders and loosened her viselike grip on the reins. After another minute, realizing she wasn't about to be thrown from the saddle, a small, triumphant smile tugged at her lips. She actually *enjoyed* riding. Sitting high above another walking creature—it was a powerful notion.

Faythe looked to Reylan. "Why do they call you the white lion of the south?" she asked, more as a distraction than anything else.

He huffed a laugh. "You don't miss much, do you?"

Faythe didn't respond.

"During the Great Battles, I borrowed the ability of a Shapeshifter for long enough to turn myself into an abnormally large white lion and take out a significant portion of an enemy legion."

Though he passed the story off nonchalantly, Faythe gaped a little. She had never seen a Shapeshifter before and blanched at the thought of the fae beside her having the ability to switch forms into something *that* powerful and terrifying. It brought forth another burning question.

"How does your ability work, exactly? I mean, you said the Firewielder wouldn't notice the power you took, but the first night at the feast, you took all of mine, didn't you?"

He cast her a sideward glance, and she could see he was deliberating how much he could trust her to share. "I can sense an individual's ability from across a room—what it is, how powerful they are—and I can take as much as I like. Temporarily, of course."

Faythe stayed silent, soaking in the information.

"You can imagine my surprise at sensing you, a human, with more power than anyone in the castle and you don't even realize." Their eyes met, and Faythe swallowed hard at the intensity in the general's look. "I've never come across anything like it in my four hundred years. So, I took it all, just to experience it fully. I've taken complete abilities before and been able to hold them for days, but yours...it was draining. I don't think I could have harnessed it for even a day. Not all of it anyway."

Faythe broke the stare to look ahead. She felt herself sway a little and couldn't be sure if it was from all the revelations or the horse's uneven trot. First of all, Reylan's age surprised her. A century may not be much in the lifespan of a fae, but considering he appeared no older than Nik, Faythe didn't expect the age difference. Second, it unnerved her greatly to hear him speak of her ability. He *sensed* its full extent when she barely knew what that was.

She took a deep breath to calm her mind. "Can you only use one ability at a time?"

"I can hold several in smaller strengths. My record is four, during the Great Battles and others. It comes in useful to have so many options to call upon. But the more I have, the quicker I burn out. All magick has its limits. If it didn't, I'm sure we would have all destroyed each other by now."

"We're not far off."

"No, we're not."

Before the heavy mood could settle, Faythe said, "So, you're a magick thief?"

Reylan chuckled, deep and genuine, and Faythe cursed herself for delighting in the sound. "A Mindseer," he corrected her. "I've only come across a handful of others in my lifetime."

At least he had a term to describe what he was. Faythe couldn't decide if it was liberating not to be categorized or if it made her feel even more alienated from the world.

"People must fear you," she wondered, "being able to strip them of their abilities."

Reylan studied her as if gauging whether she spoke of her own fear for what he was capable of. She didn't know why it pained her that he seemed to expect her to fear him, but not out of want.

"Those who don't know how it works or aren't strong enough to block me—yes, they can be...unreceptive of my kind."

For a moment, Faythe felt connected to the general in some despairing way, as if they both understood what it was like to be outcast, different from any conformity that left people no choice but to bow to fear of the unknown.

He seemed to read the thought in her expression, adding, "There are usually two types of people: those who fear power, and those who *want* power. We're often judged by *what* we are rather than *who* we are."

Faythe said nothing though his words struck a chord. What she had come to discover about the general was that he was a puzzle of broken pieces, but it was on purpose, for even if one attempted to figure him out, he held the missing shards buried deep. He didn't care what people perceived him as without those pieces. Faythe found herself admiring him, maybe even envying him, for that trait.

At risk of allowing her guard to slip, she diverted the topic. "How does someone block you?"

Again, Reylan took a deliberate pause but seemed to decide she wasn't much of a threat. "Abilities like ours, like the Nightwalkers', can always be blocked. We don't attack physically; we go for the mind, the most powerful weapon of all. It has the capacity to defy us from taking what isn't ours if the host is aware," he explained, holding her stare. "I guess it all comes down to who is the strongest."

"You've bypassed a block before," Faythe stated.

Reylan gave a short nod. "Yes. But challenging someone to take their ability can harm them greatly. I've only ever had cause to in the face of an enemy."

So, he isn't devoid of morals. A soothing thought at last. Faythe doubled back to something that grabbed her curiosity. "How do you know when you're close to your limit?"

His eyes narrowed a fraction, and for a moment, she worried

she'd pushed too far for knowledge and exposed her lack of it. While she could *feel* his swirling essence of suspicion, her tension eased slightly when he continued to answer.

"It takes time and practice to recognize it. Those of us with abilities can push our physical bodies past their limit of harnessing power, and it can kill us. Think of it as nature's fail-safe to stop us from destroying others or the world. Use too much of the power you've been blessed with, and it will consume you. There is no switch-off, no plug to pull to make you unable to call upon your magick anymore; you have to recognize when you've depleted your well, reached your own limit—and know when to stop."

Faythe shuddered involuntarily at the notion. It made sense, and part of her was relieved to discover her magick wasn't limitless or unchallenged. But it also terrified her that she didn't have a clue about her own restrictions and might one day push herself beyond capacity without realizing. She didn't respond, staring directly ahead, pale-faced in her cold dread.

Reylan pulled at his reins, and Kali came to a stop. Faythe's horse walked a few more paces before she mimicked his action and halted in the same manor. Her heartbeat spiked as she waited in giddy anticipation for his reason to stop.

The general walked Kali a few more paces until he stood horizontal in her path. "Who are you really, Faythe?"

She shifted in her saddle at the question. Despite the cold winter air and her fear, her body flushed with sticky heat under his interrogation. "I was raised in the castle with—"

"Yes, so I've heard." He immediately cut off the false tale of her upbringing. "But that's not the truth now, is it?"

She swallowed hard, coming up short of convincing ways to back up the story of her childhood. When she didn't respond, he continued.

"A human girl raised in a court of fae in High Farrow, yet she can't ride a horse, doesn't have the etiquette of a lady, seems to have every guard around her on edge, lives within the guest quarters, and has no idea about her own ability's extents and limits."

Faythe could only stare in panic as he called her out on every detail that discredited her story. While she thought she had done a commendable job of blending in and remaining inconspicuous, Reylan's eagle-eye observations had picked up on everything.

He knew the lies, but not the truth.

"Who I am is none of your concern," she said coldly.

"It is if you're a threat."

Her lips curled up in amusement. "Careful, Reylan. You wouldn't want people finding out the great Rhyenelle general is quaking in his boots over a mere *human girl.*"

"You're not just any *mere human girl* though, are you?"

"Am I not?" she challenged.

His eyes flashed, and she couldn't be sure if it was in delight or warning. "It's not I who should be careful, Faythe."

She dismissed him with her eyes. "If you want to be the one to end my life, you can join the damn line."

His amusement faltered, yet he said nothing further.

Tired of the teasing, Faythe tugged on one side of the reins, a little surprised but glad when the horse turned around and started walking back toward the stables. She got all of a few feet before Kali once again crept up like a midnight shadow beside her. She made no effort to turn to the black beauty's rider.

"Where did you really grow up?" Reylan asked, his voice unusually soft.

While she wasn't in the mood, she appreciated his efforts at a civil conversation. Her cover was blown—or, she supposed, had never really existed with him. He could hand her in for glory and prize any moment he felt like it, and sharing some of the truth would do nothing to change that.

"In the human town of Farrowhold," she said, which felt liberating to admit. She had no reason to pretend she was something she wasn't in front of Reylan anymore.

"Parents?"

Faythe winced. "My mother died when I was nine. I've never known my father."

The general was silent. It was a long enough pause that she turned to glimpse his reaction, surprised to find his brow creased in his own deep thoughts.

Thinking perhaps she'd triggered dark memories of his own past, she said, "What about you?"

He met her eye then, and she detected his suppressed sadness. Before she could think anything of it, he wiped his expression blank. "They died around the start of the war," was all he said, in a way that didn't feel right to press further.

But Faythe was quick to asses the timeline. The war began over five hundred years ago, and Reylan was four centuries old. She wondered how young he was when he was abandoned in the world, and it emitted a pinch in her chest.

"It seems we've both suffered at the hands of Valgard," she said quietly.

Reylan nodded. "Us and many others."

"Do you think it'll ever end?" Faythe didn't expect a realistic answer. Rather, she hoped for some insight from someone who was constantly on the front lines.

"Everything has an end. It is both the most feared and most anticipated part. Variable, uncertain, unpredictable. There are two sides: those who are fighting to live, and those who are fighting to conquer. But who wants it more? Whoever can answer that has already lost the war."

A heavy weight settled over her. "It doesn't sound as if you hold encouraging odds for us."

"If you want the truth, Faythe, count yourself lucky if we hold out long enough that you're not alive when the beginning of the end falls upon us."

The beginning of the end. All too familiar words. Faythe's hands trembled on the reins. Even though he spoke as if it wasn't her fight, simply a waiting game to see if she would die before the worst came to pass, Faythe didn't see it as such. She was human, inferior in almost everything when it came to the front lines of battle, yet she had never felt such a burning *need* to do everything in her power to fight back. While she could, while she was still alive, she knew she would give everything she had to stand up against the forces that threatened the balance of her world.

"Maybe it's time to strike back instead of waiting like sheep for slaughter." It came out as a bitter accusation, but it was not Reylan she directed it toward. She knew nothing about the tactics of war or the alliance, nor the formation and numbers of the kingdoms' armies, but she felt a sudden rush of frustration that nothing was being done to counter the threat. In her lifetime, there had been no retaliation, no uprising, no talk of avenging the centuries' worth of death and destruction at the hands of the enemy.

"We will, when the time is right."

"And if that's too late?"

Reylan looked at her, studied her, but she didn't shrink back from his assessment. His eyes were filled with conflicting emotions. She couldn't be sure what he was thinking. But nothing about the look felt condescending to her as a human who knew nothing and should have no input on the movements of war.

"All we can do is never surrender. Never bow to fear, never yield to odds, and always be ready. Until the end comes. I can't soothe your worries with falsehoods. Hope is a sedation of fear; fairness is delusion against wrongdoing. Both make those on the right side feel as if they have the upper hand. Always see the enemy as equal as they have just as much desire to conquer as we do to survive."

"Hope stops the spread of panic."

"Yes, and for the people, it's a wonderful thing. The heart of a warrior knows how much hope to hold to lift the spirit, but it makes room for the fear that will strike it in the fight to survive."

Faythe looked away from him, over the city and beyond, as if she could picture the horizon as the front lines of the battlefield. As if Valgard lay in wait this very moment.

War wouldn't come, because it had never left.

Reylan called it *luck* for her mortal lifespan to spare her from witnessing the pinnacle of death and carnage. For once, Faythe didn't want that luck; she wanted to fight back.

Even if it meant her end and the war's end became one and the same.

CHAPTER 22

Jakon

THE NIGHT WAS still as Jakon sat on watch while the others slept. He was not alone, for the fae guard Caius insisted he stay awake too. Jakon felt guilty for not trusting him enough to take watch alone despite his offer. It had been tempting as his eyes protested the late hour, but he didn't know the fae well enough to feel right about placing not only his own life in his hands—that didn't matter—but that of the people behind him. They were his responsibility. Yet he was still grateful for Caius as he would alert them to any oncoming danger far sooner than Jakon's human senses could detect.

They didn't risk a fire. Jakon trembled slightly under the thick cloak he pulled tightly around him. He cursed the winter season as every breath became visible in the bitter air. The others huddled together for warmth, and he longed desperately to take the chill away from Marlowe who was using her whole body to shield a young girl. The sight brought a smile to his face and filled his heart with warmth.

"She has a fighting spirit," Caius commented from opposite him, his eyes following Jakon's to fix on the blonde.

He gave a subconscious nod in agreement. He already knew that about her, but it was nice to have others see it too. Jakon turned to the fae guard. A large part of him wanted to crush his thoughts of doubt toward Caius, but he gave in to the seed of wariness.

"Why are you here?" he said. Not in accusation or resentment, but in genuine curiosity as he wondered what the fae guard could possibly gain from helping them.

The young fae smiled sadly. "I was there when Faythe was summoned to the throne room that day," he began. He didn't meet Jakon's eye as he spoke, frowning intently at the ground instead. "She offered him a mercy, I know that now, but what the king asked of her...to a young boy..." Caius struggled to form sentences as the memories clearly haunted him.

Jakon shuddered to imagine the scene Faythe created for the king. His fists balled with anger, both for what his friend had to endure and the short life that was taken by the ruler of High Farrow.

"I may be a king's guard, but it doesn't mean I agree with everything he stands for. There are a lot of us who hope, dream, of a fairer High Farrow."

Jakon was silent. As he looked to the fae, he knew his words were genuine. He had spent his life believing all fae species were the same: power-hungry and uncaring of human lives. Yet here was Caius, in a position of power and influence, choosing to fight on the side that defended the weaker race.

"Do you think that day will come?"

The fae guard met his eye, determined as he said, "I do. And I've always believed Prince Nikalias will be the one to bring it about. I know he will restore the values of High Farrow. But the world calls for a different kind of savior. Someone with resilience and a strong mind. Someone with enough power to challenge, yet with a heart true enough not to be consumed by its darkness."

"You sound as if you know of such a person."

Caius's smile widened as he said, "I think we both do."

Jakon wasn't sure if he was trembling from the cold or the realization of who Caius was referring to. He wanted to laugh at the idea that someone like Caius—or any of the fae for that matter—would place their faith in a human. Yet even Faythe's name stood for exactly what the people needed.

"You can't expect the fate of the world to depend on one girl alone," he said quickly, almost defensively. Though she was now a woman and no longer lived by his side, he would always feel an overwhelming need to protect his dearest friend.

"She's not alone."

Jakon was about to respond when the fae guard snapped his head to the side, tuning in to something his human ears couldn't hear. Jakon's hand went for his sword, but Caius raised a hand for him to be still. He obeyed though his heart thundered as he waited for the guard's next signal. It bothered him to depend on another for guidance, but considering Caius might save their lives with the early warning of any impending threat, he tried to be grateful.

"Fae patrol," he whispered. Caius's eyes shifted to the pile of soundly sleeping humans, and Jakon saw the panic in them. Though he still couldn't hear a sound, the fae's reaction made his blood turn cold. He had no idea how close they were or if they would be able to get everyone into hiding before the patrol sensed them.

His voice dropped low as he turned to Jakon. "You need to get everyone off the main route. You'll have to head north. It will add a day or two onto the journey, but they won't bother checking the long way through Springhill. Wake them. Make sure everyone is silent. If I can hear them, they may very well hear us too."

"What about you?"

"I'm going to try to divert them."

"And if they suspect you?"

Caius shrugged casually, but his grin was confident. "Make sure my heroism is remembered, will you?"

Jakon didn't have time to protest before the guard darted into the forest with feline precision. Though Caius said it in humor, Jakon muttered a silent prayer to the Spirits to keep him safe. Then, not wasting a second, he stealthily went to wake Marlowe first.

CHAPTER 23

Faythe

EVERYTHING WAS STILL. Everyone was quiet. All Faythe could hear was the hard beat of her heart and the faint array of woodland murmurs.

The fae picked up on something she didn't, and the general beside her knocked an arrow into place with expert stealth and laser focus. She held her breath, watching intently and following his fixed line of sight. Nothing revealed itself to her human senses. Instead, she admired Reylan's powerful, unwavering hold. His calculated breaths frosted clouds along the length of the arrow in perfect intervals. His eyes were wide and still, tracking without a single blink.

Then he let his arrow fly.

It soared impossibly fast, and Faythe lost track of it in an instant. He relaxed then, lowering his longbow, and Faythe released her tense poise, letting out a long exhale.

His gaze slid to her. "Did you only come here to sit pretty, or are you going to contribute at some point?"

She scowled at him. He knew exactly why she had yet to

attempt her shot. It would be to her eternal embarrassment if she couldn't match her words to her skill. She wanted to try, but fear got the better of her every time she thought to shoot down the occasional bird or rabbit. She was unfairly disadvantaged against the rest of the hunting party who had naturally heightened senses.

"Did you even hit anything?" she shot back. She knew he did, and the weak retort was merely to divert the attention from herself.

His grin creased his eyes. "Let's go see."

With a kick of his feet, Kali jerked forward. Faythe mimicked him to follow. She found herself implicitly, and perhaps foolishly, following the general's lead when it came to anything related to the hunt and horseback riding, and she hated herself for being glad of his presence.

They kept walking forward, and Faythe glanced back the way they came in disbelief that he'd sent his arrow so far. After another short minute, she finally spied the white fletching protruding from its mark: perfectly through the eye of a black sparrow. It was pinned to a tree trunk almost as dark as the bird itself.

It should have been an impossible shot, especially from such a distance, even for a fae. Faythe brought her horse to a stop and gaped at it. Reylan chuckled lightly at her reaction.

She snapped her mouth shut. "Show-off," she muttered.

Branches cracked behind them, and Faythe flinched in fright, which only added to the general's amusement. The rest of the hunting party crept up to them.

Varlas whistled low. "Impressive," he remarked.

Reylan only nodded in appreciation at the comment.

The King of Olmstone straightened. "We should go by foot from here to have a chance of hunting larger game."

Everyone seemed to agree with his plan and didn't waste any time before starting to dismount. Tarly helped Tauria down from her brown mare. Faythe was glad for the ward's decision to join them that morning, thinking she would at least have some female company in the sport that was predominantly for male enjoyment, but she hadn't had the chance to converse with her friend once in the hour since they'd left as the Olmstone prince eagerly stole all her attention.

Faythe didn't mind as Reylan had remained by her side for most of the hunt, at least while Nik was engaged with Varlas. The general was becoming masterful at rousing her irritation with little effort, but she was begrudgingly grateful for his company as he was the only one who knew of her complete lack of experience. Even Nik and Tauria believed she was at least competent from hunting in the outer town.

Reylan had tried his best to teach her the basics, such as how to properly hold a bow and nock an arrow, but she'd yet to put any of those teachings into practice. Mercifully, he didn't taunt or judge her for it, and she was surprised by his patience. He didn't owe her anything, and it worried her that after it was all said and done…she would owe *him*.

Faythe was the last one still atop her brown-and-white stallion. Getting down unnerved her more than mounting. She inhaled a shaky breath and willed her trembling hands to release the reins. When she glanced to the side to gauge the distance to the ground, Reylan was already there, positioned to help. There was nothing teasing on his face as he waited patiently. She smiled a little, immensely grateful for his offer to save her the humiliation of an ungraceful dismount.

With new confidence that he was there to catch her, she slung her leg over to one side. His hands went to her waist then, and she braced against his firm shoulders. She couldn't be sure if her thundering heart and the flush of her body were from her nerves or Reylan's touch. Heat rose up her spine to color her cheeks. She used little effort as he took most of her weight to guide her down. His hands didn't linger when her feet met the ground, but he took a moment longer than she expected to step back.

Sapphire blazed with gold for long enough the two colors were at risk of fusing to forge something…

"Perhaps in pairs, we will have better luck scouting some-thing...larger."

Varlas's loud voice stole their attention, and Faythe felt Reylan's stare break like something physical. He moved to put a few feet of distance between them as the Olmstone king's eyes flicked up to the speared bird. Then they fell to pin Faythe directly, and her heart skipped a beat.

"Faythe, care to join me?"

She didn't know why he'd singled her out of the group of highly skilled hunters. It rattled her awfully, but declining his offer would be a grave insult.

Reluctant, she smiled sweetly. "As you wish, Your Majesty."

A slow grin curled on his face. Instead of encouraging her with warmth, it inspired a sense of trepidation. Her eyes flashed to Reylan, then Nik, then Tauria, none of whom expressed the alarm she felt. She followed after the King of Olmstone who was already making haste away from the group and didn't glance back at her friends or the general.

CHAPTER 24

Nikalias

NIK ALL BUT stormed through the forest, uncaring of the branches that cracked beneath his feet or the foliage he rustled in his wake. His mind was reeling, a loop of tormenting thoughts infusing with his anger from no justified cause.

"If you're attempting to scare off the wildlife instead, I'd say you're doing a fantastic job," Reylan remarked.

Nik paused in his tracks, in no mood for humor. They'd walked in silence for so long that he'd almost forgotten he wasn't alone while he battled with the chaos in his head.

After Varlas paired off with Faythe for the rest of the hunt, Tarly was swift to attach himself to Tauria's side and eagerly steal her away. The unease Nik felt at seeing the king disappear with Faythe was completely overshadowed by—

Gods. He didn't even want to acknowledge the dark feeling that coiled in his gut and flared his ire when he saw the beaming smile on the princess's face at the chance of some alone time with Tarly.

Jealousy.

He was jealous. Of seeing the flicker of excitement dance

across her eyes, the warm rose color of her tan cheeks from the attention, and the adorable shyness that slightly weakened her stiff posture. Spirits be *damned*. It was an ugly, long-dormant feeling he wasn't accustomed to.

Nik tried to convince himself his sour mood and anxious edge were simply in consideration of her well-being. They didn't know Tarly well or what his intentions were in pining irritatingly after Tauria's every move. He should never have let him lead her away.

His gloved hands tightened into fists, and the thought of taking a swing at the delicate prince was a darkly pleasing desire.

"Something on your mind?" Reylan went on, stopping beside him. A longbow dangled in his grasp. "A certain Fenstead princess, perhaps?"

Nik whipped his head toward the general, quick to rally a defense.

"You've always had a keen intuition, but your observations are wholly off the mark this time."

It came out with an edge of bitterness, but even if he'd managed to maintain a cool composure, Nik knew Reylan would not be so easily swayed.

The general's curved brow called out the lie. He said nothing, but a hint of amusement twitched on his straight mouth.

"Are you even going to attempt to shoot anything with that?" Nik all but snapped in his frustration, casting a hand out to the weapon Reylan held loosely.

He had no right to any thought or feeling on what Tauria explored with Tarly. It wasn't his business. Yet it was. As her friend, he would always care and look out for her. But even as he thought of the word—*friend*—it didn't seem appropriate for what they shared. What they had was so much more. It was everything but what he could surrender to.

It had to be this way.

It was entirely selfish of him to interfere with something that could make her happy and someone who could offer her everything he couldn't.

Reylan's voice once again snapped him from his torturous, miserable thoughts. "I would try, but I think you've alerted every creature within a mile radius of our presence with your angry footing."

"My footing isn't *angry*."

"You're right—more like furious."

Nik ground his teeth, failing to bite out a retort because the general was right.

Diverting, he said, "Should I be concerned the king chose Faythe's company just now?"

He watched something flex over the still impassiveness of Reylan's face. If Nik didn't know him any better—know of his lack of feeling toward anyone and anything but duty—he might have interpreted the look as shared worry. The general's eyes flashed, just for a second, as though he could see the pair they spoke of.

"It is odd," he muttered carefully. The glaze in his eyes made it look as if he was mulling over various conclusions about Varlas's intentions. "Perhaps we should have broken off in groups of three instead."

They exchanged a look, and the lingering offer was as much a subtle hint for Nik to curb his desire to intrude on Tarly and Tauria's *alone time* as it was for Reylan to check up on Faythe.

Nik shifted, eying the general and contemplating. Agreeing would all but seal Reylan's observation that he itched to go after Tauria. But he rationalized the itch with the thought that should anything threatening appear, he doubted the pompous prince would be capable of protecting her.

It was a grasp in the dark over the real reason he wanted to impose on them. The coils of his jealousy laughed and taunted his attempt to justify his need.

Nik nodded, adding, "If someone gets injured, one should be able to stay while the other gets help."

Reylan smirked, quirking an amused brow. "That would be smart," he humored him. "So, shall I go to Faythe, or Tauria and the prince?"

Nik cast him a flat look.

The general chuckled. "Just making sure."

Reylan fit the bow over his back, and they retraced their steps to where they had parted with the others. When Nik picked up on Tauria's scent, he bid the general a quick farewell before taking off in their direction while Reylan went after Faythe and the king.

Conscious of Reylan's comment, Nik put effort into being mindful of his footsteps. He knew how to maneuver through woodland with the stealth and silence of any predator, but his teetering temper and irrational frustration made it difficult to focus on the task. As Tauria's scent got stronger, so did Tarly's. Expecting it didn't soothe the dark beast inside him.

Nik slowed his steps as he picked up on the sound of their voices—not exactly low and discreet for hunting. He spotted the flicker of movement, and he couldn't stop himself when he halted and kept cover behind a thick trunk.

Observing them felt wrong, but he didn't care in that moment. Not when his anger completely diffused into something that wrenched in his chest instead. A sharp pain, then a hollow, tunneling void.

The princess leaned against the trunk of a tree, and the prince stood over her, a hand braced by her head. Tauria chuckled at something Tarly said, and the brightness on her face, caused by *him*, twisted the phantom dagger that pierced Nik's chest at the sight. Yet he couldn't look away, even though a voice begged him to turn around, to relieve his sinking pain and let her have this moment of happiness she deserved. That he couldn't give to her.

Tarly's other hand lifted to her waist, and even from this distance, Nik imagined the faint blush that would bloom on Tauria's cheeks at the contact. He was about to tear his eyes from them, overcome with guilt for imposing on a mildly intimate moment. He shouldn't have come.

But as he twisted to leave, his slumped posture straightened when Tauria moved. Not closer to the prince, but in an attempt to maneuver out of his cage. She politely removed his hand from her waist and made to step around him. Tarly turned as she did, his hand catching her wrist instead.

When Tauria attempted to gently pull free and his hold didn't release, a white rage flashed across Nik's vision.

He didn't care for his *furious* footsteps then, and Tauria startled with a faint gasp as he crossed the distance toward them faster than intended. Nik's face was livid, and Tarly stared with surprise in his raised brow, his fingers still curled around Tauria's wrist.

"I advise you to remove your hand as she wishes," Nik said, his tone as cold as the air that clouded his breath as he spoke.

Both princes stared off with dangerous tension. Tarly's fingers loosened from Tauria slowly, and as he tuned to face Nik fully, the challenge for dominance almost palpable. Neither looked close to backing down.

Before either prince could break, in violence or words, Tauria's stunned voice cut through the thick air. "What are you doing here, Nik?"

His nostrils flared at the bitter accusation in her tone—she was irritated at his intrusion—when it was clear she hadn't been enjoying the *alone time* with Tarly. His eyes didn't leave the Olmstone prince.

"Reylan advised it would be safer to travel in groups of three." He passed the blame on to the general so he wouldn't seem like the whelp he was for being there.

Tarly smirked, his mockery subconsciously flexing Nik's fingers as he restrained himself from violence. "Did he now?" he drawled, folding his arms.

The casual gesture was far more than that—it was a subtle way to try to level with Nik. Tarly was a few inches shorter and slightly less built than he. The movement squared his shoulders, expended his chest, and firmed his posture.

Nik wasn't arrogant enough to believe his physical advantages tipped the odds of him winning a fight against Tarly. He didn't know the prince well enough, but something in the gleam of his eye made him cautious and wary that the seemingly innocent and charming *prince* could harbor a cunning wild side.

"You are not needed," Tarly went on dismissively. "Or wanted."

Nik's jaw ticked as he ground his teeth. "From what I saw, I think you speak for yourself."

He didn't have to advance as Tarly did. Nik's hand darted for his sword at the threat, but before either prince could draw their blades even a fraction, a powerful gust of wind stirred before pushing between them. Both princes were forced back a step, frost and brown leaves swirling angrily around them, and they had to shield their eyes. When the quick tornado ceased, Tauria's face was quietly furious as he looked at her.

"That's enough!" She seethed and flashed her glare at Tarly. Much to his pleasure. "Right now, neither of you is *wanted*. And I can take care of myself just fine."

With a final scowl in Nik's direction, the princess stormed to him, then right past him, near brushing his shoulder.

On instinct, Nik was about to go after her, but he detected a movement from Tarly that had him whirling back with a dark look of warning. He took a moment to assess the Olmstone prince. Cooling, Nik decided to diffuse his protective flare.

"Go to her," Nik offered, even stepping out of his way.

Tarly's hard eyes narrowed, gaze shifting between him and where Tauria had marched off to as though it were a trick. Nik's jaw flexed at his hesitation.

"Just know she isn't pleasant and content all the time like the front she's forced this past week. While you have yet to see it, she is not idle, and she is certainly not silent."

213

"Am I supposed to be afraid of her?" Tarly sneered.

Nik's fist twitched tighter. That pretty face wouldn't be so if he got his way.

"No. Not afraid. But she is a queen, while you are still a prince. Don't forget that. Even when you one day take your father's throne, your crown and hers will never weigh the same."

He saw a flash of something akin to dark rage in Tarly's eyes. Admittedly, it took Nik by surprise. It was gone before he could think anything of it, replaced by the usual disgruntled reception as he backed down.

Nik turned to go to Tauria, but Tarly called at his back, "And you think your crown will?"

He stilled, irritation and disappointment stirring a chaos of emotion he wanted to unleash on the prince behind him. Because if that was all he had to say, Nik didn't believe he would ever be worthy of her.

"If it were me who was entertaining the prospect of ruling by her side, I would not be thinking of her crown and mine as different."

Tarly scoffed. "That is a fool's romantic idealism."

"*That*," Nik corrected calmly, "is how equal and fair leadership is formed." He didn't wait to hear if Tarly would respond to his condescension. Nik took off after Tauria without another thought.

He didn't know why he said those words. It wasn't his place nor concern to have an opinion on their match. But at seeing Tarly had yet to glimpse the surface of Tauria's anger and was already cowering, it made him flare with wariness over the prospect.

Nik loved her anger. Loved when she fought him, and when she defied him. When she didn't hold back any emotion. He would always weather her storm no matter how destructive it could become.

His steps quickened to catch up with her. Though he had no doubt she *could* take care of herself, the thought of her wandering the woods alone flared his protectiveness and had him jogging until he spied the brown waves of her hair over her emerald velvet cloak.

When he reached her, Nik's hand caught her elbow. Tauria whirled to him, yanking her arm free and taking a step away. Nik didn't have a second to react as in the short minute she'd stormed off it seemed her anger had boiled to rage and targeted him all at once. A raw emotion he so rarely saw on the cool, collected princess.

"Why would you do that?" Despite the wrath that shook her voice, her eyes glittered with pain.

Nik blinked, dumbfounded. When he didn't respond, he saw the tightening of her jaw and the shift in her stance and knew exactly what she was about to do. Yet he didn't move to avoid it or defend himself.

Tauria pushed him—not with any physical touch, but with the will of the wind she commanded as her arms cast out in a fluid movement. Nik yielded a step from the force.

"Why did you come to me?" she yelled, sending another blast his way.

Nik braced for it and might have been able to withstand the force of the wind, but she needed this. Needed to see his submission and let out the frustration and anger he'd caused.

"Why care who I'm with?" Another gust; another step back. "Why bother to think of me at all when all you do is push me away!"

She was right. And this was her way of pushing back.

Why? Why? Why?

Tauria moved as weightlessly as the wind she conjured, a dance so elegant and free. Many times, he had watched her perform the various sequences of moves that made her a master of her Windbreaker ability—both with her bare hands and with a staff in her clutch—and turned her into a whole new force to be reckoned with. Tauria homed in like a warrior in battle with the grace of a dancer on stage. A storm against her own silent song.

Often, he would watch her when she didn't know he was there, just to be sure she didn't lose herself when indignation and grief overcame her. Nik had been there—would always be there—to pick up the pieces when she broke, help her forget the cracks that would never be filled for one who had lost so much, and remind her every damn time that she was a warrior who had defied the odds to be here.

Nik had to shield his eyes from the debris and slashes of air forcing him back and back. He accepted every blow, deserving of it, and kept retreating until his back met the harsh bark of a trunk. Tauria didn't relent. Nik tensed to absorb each impact that barely winded him. She was powerful, and she was holding back the strength of her blasts significantly. She didn't want to harm him. This…it was a barreling of so much pent-up frustration. A release of indignation. Against him. So, he took everything she could throw at him until she began to tire. He knew the moment her wind weakened that her anger was subsiding to something far more gut-wrenching.

Defeat.

Before her next attack, Nik reached out, an arm hooking around her waist while his other hand cupped her nape as he twisted with her. Nik held her between his body and the tree while she thrashed. Only for a few seconds, until he attempted to reach her from within—tried projecting a sense of calm and an apology that seemed to be heard as she stilled against him. He'd done it before, when heartbreak and helplessness threatened to consume her around the anniversary of her parents' death each year. It calmed her then as it did now. Some invisible, unspoken language they had formed between them.

He couldn't be sure how many seconds or minutes or hours passed as he simply held her while she curled into his chest. Both of them breathed hard, allowing their pulses to steady and giving them time to collect their thoughts before they could speak. Nik idly stroked her hair, not even aware of it as he tuned in to her quickened heartbeat against the faint murmurs of the winter woodland. He didn't know what to say to the questions she'd thrown at him. Nothing sounded justifiable. He should have let her be.

"I'm sorry." It was a pathetic response, but it was all he could find in him.

Tauria's answering voice was weak and muffled. "I know."

His arms loosened as she began to pull back, but he didn't let go, and she didn't try to step away. Her brown eyes glittered with a pain he'd seen before—one he felt so deep it was a wound that would never be healed. Because it was a pain he had only ever seen caused by himself.

Nik's hand raised, unable to stop himself as he took her cheek in his palm. Her eyes closed briefly as he did, and she leaned into his touch. His heart squeezed and squeezed so tightly he thought it might erupt. It didn't make sense, how life could be so cruel and twisted. He would always put her first—her *safety* first. And for that reason, despite the hard thrumming of his blood and the flash of his eyes to her lips that made him want to feel them against his so desperately in their closeness...

"Let's get you back," he all but whispered, letting his hand drop.

Tauria nodded, but her expression was solemn, and the fall of her disappointment was a weight he would never get used to carrying. Their hands brushed, and he couldn't help it when his palm slid into hers, their fingers intertwining so naturally it didn't feel wrong to want to have this moment. This one small piece of closeness that held no expectation.

Both of them stared down at their joined hands, and he planned to keep a hold of her for as long as he could before they inevitably found company when they reached the castle grounds. But he didn't even get that short amount of time he desperately craved.

Branches snapping had Tauria ripping her hand from his, which Nik felt in his chest as though she had clutched and torn his heart instead. He detected exactly who the invading force was by the stiffening of rage that curved his spine. As he turned, the Olmstone prince came into view, stopping a few paces away.

"Wind tantrums over for now?" he remarked in poor condescending humor.

Nik took half a step but didn't get to strike the bastard when a hand curled around his bicep.

"Nik, don't," Tauria warned.

His eyes snapped back to her, and she flinched. Actually *flinched.* Immediately, his wrath cooled completely at the flash of fear in her eyes. Fear...of him.

Her face steeled quickly as she straightened and stepped away from him. In contrast, Nik was close to buckling where he stood, unable to get that split second of emotion from his mind.

Tarly's irritating voice rang through him once more. "I don't know what your problem is, Nik, but you need to cool down."

It was so gods-damned far from what he needed to hear in that moment. Nik targeted his gaze of cold anger at the prince and took the few steps slowly to close the distance, almost going to pass him.

But Nik halted at his shoulder, and his voice dropped low.

"I may not be able to hurt you here, but when you sleep...well, who will know? I can find out everything that makes you weak— every fear, every transgression—without you ever knowing I was there. I can bring forth your most tormenting thoughts, nightmares so vivid you'll awake in your own piss."

To his satisfaction, Tarly's throat bobbed, and Nik caught the scent of fear he tried to suppress. He was about to walk away and leave them, as he should have from the start. He'd only made everything worse by coming. Between the two of them, but worst of all, between himself and Tauria.

Yet he couldn't fight his need to turn back to her. Their gazes locked, and he thought he saw the flicker of sympathy cross her glittering eyes.

"I would *never* hurt you."

As he took his first steps away, three answering words chanted in his mind, but he kept walking. His feet guided his numb body, which had nothing to do with the winter chill. Nik picked up pace until he was certain he was so far away from them it would be impossible for him to still hear her voice. But those words echoed loud and clear. Over and over. He couldn't be sure if they were ever spoken out loud, but it was her voice. Her quiet, broken voice. Three words he would always carry the burden of. Because spoken or silent, they were true all the same.

"You already have."

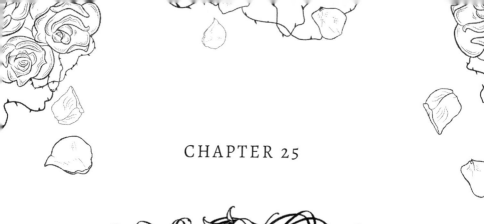

CHAPTER 25

Faythe

THE SPYMASTER AND the wolf king walked in silence for a long
stretch. Faythe's anxiety built as she cast frequent glances
back, trying to keep a mental calculation of how many steps away
from the hunting party they'd ventured, until she considered them
too deep into the woods for it to matter. Her senses were balanced
on a sharp edge, and it shook her to think it had nothing to do with
the wildlife they were trying to be stealthy for.

Finally, Varlas halted, motioning for her to do the same while
he slowly dropped to a crouch behind a tall bush. Faythe saw it
then: a striking stag with powerful antlers. For a quick second, her
breath caught as she envisioned the eerily similar mythical beast of
the Eternal Woods. Except it was clear the stag ahead was perfectly
mortal and *real.*

"This one is yours," the king barely whispered. He held out a
longbow and an iron-tipped arrow.

Faythe's heart began to hammer in her chest, eyes widening
with the knowledge he was passing the kill to her. Varlas looked to
her expectantly, and she had no choice but to take his offering.

It wasn't the embarrassment of missing she was afraid of this time. As she looked to the beast, peacefully unaware of the predators who lay in the shadows as it fed on the frost-tipped grass, she didn't want to be the one to take its life. The king watched her closely, and she swore she saw a wicked gleam flash quickly in his eye as she nocked the arrow into place. She didn't look at him again, raising her arm to aim while the other strained to pull back the string that would launch the fatal dart. Her arms trembled under the strength it took to hold poise. The beast was large enough that she was confident she could hit it without accuracy.

Just as she prepared herself to let the arrow fly, the stag twisted its head to look directly at her. If it knew how close death was, it made no move to save itself.

In its eyes, she saw the silver-antlered stag of the Eternal Woods —the one that helped her gain the yucolites and guided her, the guardian of the Temple of Light.

She couldn't do it.

In a split-second decision, she tilted her aim upward and let the arrow sing free. It soared over the top of the stag, alerting it to the danger. It leaped back in fright but didn't immediately sprint to safety. It held her stare for one second longer, as if in silent thanks, before scurrying off in a delayed reaction.

Faythe shot to her feet, walking a few paces into the flat clearing to stare after it in awe. When it was long out of sight, she heard Varlas come out of hiding to stand a few paces behind her.

"Just as I thought. Spineless, cowardly *human.*"

The king's switch of tone shot a spear of ice through her. Faythe didn't expect it, but she wasn't surprised either. She'd wanted to hold onto the notion he was a ruler to be loved and respected as he'd led her to believe over the week, yet a part of her had always held reserves about him as much as she tried to ignore it. She turned to him slowly. Gone was his mask of warmth and kindness, replaced by the cruel loathing that simmered beneath the surface.

"Your talents are impressive, I'll admit, but Orlon is a fool to trust you in his court."

Faythe straightened in cold terror but tried to remain calm at the bold declaration. She mustered every ounce of courage to force the words from her mouth. "If you know about me, you'll know what I'm capable of."

It wasn't a direct threat, but Varlas's eyes flashed in rage at the implication. "I'm not afraid of a *human*," he spat bitterly. Then he composed himself to stand intimidatingly tall. His cruel smile rattled her very bones. "We both know you can't harm or kill me without signing your own death warrant, Faythe."

She clenched her teeth in anger. One move on him, through mind compulsion or otherwise, was a sure death sentence. But then she supposed he could have her convicted without any action at all. So, the question remained: What did he stand to gain from exposing his knowledge of her?

"What do you want?"

His grin turned predatory. "Straight to the point. I like that," he drawled, beginning a short pace. Every step he took toward her made her heart skip a beat, and she became all too aware of the mighty blade at his hip. She highly doubted her death by his hand would be challenged with the lies he could conjure about this encounter. "That insufferable bastard Agalhor had to find an excuse not to be here," he went on without looking at her, more as a rant to himself than to Faythe directly. "Though it seems it might not all be wasted time." His eyes met hers. "I see the general has taking a liking to you."

Faythe tightened her gloved fists at the mention. His observations about their relationship were wholly misjudged. At least Reylan had never tried to hide his distaste and suspicions.

"You're playing your role well at least. Secret encounters, late-night meets, opposite rooms... Tell me, has he been warming your bed during his stay too?"

Her cheeks flamed at the insinuation she'd reduced herself to being a *courtesan*. Clearly, the king before her knew every detail of Orlon's plans to use her. Only, it struck Faythe with immense fear to realize the week, the meetings, had been planned as a collusion between Olmstone and High Farrow against Rhyenelle, and Agalhor was their target all along. It was supposed to be him sitting across from her at the start, during that first evening at the great feast, and then every time after. Instead, she was herded toward the general. His position across the hall wasn't a mere coincidence. No —they *expected* her to get close to him, whatever it took.

She couldn't settle on what filled her with dread more: the thought of an internal conflict between allies, or the danger Reylan was in if he stood unwitting in enemy terrain. His safety shouldn't bother her, yet as much as he riled her to no end, she didn't want to see him harmed. Not when she had the chance to prevent it with her newfound knowledge.

"I really hope you managed to coax some useful information out of him, however you went about it," he continued to degrade her. Though it was all false speculation and he only used the taunts to goad her, she hated that she let herself feel belittled by it.

He was still dancing around the answer to her question.

"I don't know anything," she ground out.

Varlas cocked his head. "I do hope that's not true. What a waste of talent it would be to end you without any insight. Orlon may trust you, but I do not. An ability such as yours, if left unchecked, could work gravely against my plans."

She knew then exactly why he lured her here alone. It was a test—of both her loyalty and ruthlessness. She'd wholly failed, though it seemed he was expecting that. Varlas was a man of little patience and sought answers from her without the need to involve Orlon. Then he'd dispose of his *spymaster* out of paranoia she could be used against him.

"What do you want from me?" Faythe kept her voice calm,

taking a step back as he slowly closed in. She didn't expect a real answer, but she fought to keep him talking while she figured out an escape plan. The others would be too far to hear—Varlas had made sure of that. It dawned on her the stag had always been safe as she was the intended prey all along. She'd allowed herself to be herded into the perfect moment for the wolf to strike.

Varlas reached for the hilt of his sword. "You're going to tell me everything you know about Rhyenelle." Steel sang, glinting with dangerous beauty against the flickers of sunlight through the canopy. "Then I may have to inform everyone of your tragic hunting accident."

She blanched, pulse picking up in a frantic sprint. She was running out of time. Faythe was unarmed, having foolishly forgotten to retrieve her sword. It remained strapped to her horse, and she cursed herself for the amateur mistake. Even if she wouldn't hold out against Varlas in combat, it might cause enough commotion for her companions to hear. It could buy her precious time.

He took a step forward, but she didn't retreat once this time despite everything screaming at her to run. She held firm.

"If you kill me, you'll get nothing." Her voice wavered.

He stepped forward again, slowly, deliberately, relishing her fear. "Oh, Faythe, I will have *everything*. You're merely a plan to get it faster. Nevertheless, I will conquer Rhyenelle. The general will be next to die. Orlon doesn't think it wise to kill him yet and risk retaliation, but with him right within my grasp here, it's too perfect an opportunity to pass up. To remove the strongest commander in Rhyenelle's forces…"

"You won't get the chance," Faythe snapped, feeling her anger rise to crush her panic.

His eyes twinkled in delight. "Have you come to care for him, Faythe?" he sang mockingly. "Silly, pathetic *girl.*"

"Why would you seek to destroy the alliance when it is all that keeps us safe?" She seethed.

His irises darkened, and he took another step. "You know nothing. Rhyenelle has taken land in greed, hidden behind high walls, and forced their ideals on us for centuries. I only seek to take back what is rightfully mine yet have been undermined and made to feel a fool by that insufferable bastard and his dogs. I will stand it no longer!" Spit flew from his mouth, his voice unrecognizable as he spoke with unhinged wrath. He stopped advancing, and his chest heaved as he took a few breaths to calm himself. Then he rolled his head, squaring his shoulders, and poised his sword. "I did like you, Faythe, and thought you would make a fantastic ally. But I was right: your heart is too soft. You don't see that we stand to be stronger with Agalhor removed and Rhyenelle under our command." He braced both hands around the hilt, lifting higher.

Faythe's eyes remained on his even though she trembled, wanting to track the looming steel.

"I'm sorry it had to come to this, truly, but I cannot have you running off to warn the general, and I won't risk you siding with him now you have inevitably discovered my plans." Varlas raised his arms a fraction higher, poised to take her life in one swift movement.

Faythe cursed the spirits, cursed the world, cursed all the damn kings to burn in the Nether for eternity. Reaching into his mind, she shattered his weak mental barrier and seized control.

The fall of the blade halted.

His fury knocked into her like a physical blow. She gasped and swayed, adjusting her footing before she could straighten from the impact. She commanded him to drop his sword, then his arms. His face contorted in savage rage and disbelief. She tried to maintain her composure, but her mind became a chaos of clashing emotions. His and hers. The nerves and fear, they were her own, from having no plan for how she would keep her life after committing the worse crime possible: high treason.

"You're going to die painfully for this." His voice rattled menacingly

in her mind, and she resisted the urge to retreat at the ripples of hatred and malice that flowed through her.

Faythe fought to keep herself separate from his erratic emotions. She couldn't kill him—there would be no coming back from that. But with his overwhelming want to kill *her*, it was a tough mental battle not to give in to impulse. She threw up walls around herself in his mind, needing a moment to calm and gather focus before she did something irreversible. Taking long, physical breaths, she felt herself regaining her control, remembering who she was and what she was doing. As soon as she dropped her shield, she took away his anger.

Faythe soothed the wicked storm of hatred into a tranquil river of peace. It was reflected on his face as his creased tan skin smoothed his furrowed brow. Quickly sifting through his memories, she brought to the surface something to offset his animosity. It was not his wife or even his children she found in the depths of Varlas's happiest memories; it was someone else entirely. Someone Faythe had never seen before.

She was impeccably beautiful with auburn hair, and her image did exactly what she needed it to. It brought light to the darkness of Varlas's mind and eased his melancholic heart. It elated his spirit and joined together the cracks of his broken soul. Faythe knew who she was then.

Varlas's mate.

Not the current queen; not the female he arrived with. Faythe was stunned, struck stupid at the realization. Varlas's loathing and coldheartedness had nothing to do with land nor anything as trivial as power.

It was fueled by his eternal heartbreak.

The scene changed, and she fought against the suffocating weight of pain and grief. Varlas kneeled on blood-soaked grass, cradling a limp body while he rocked and trembled. His mate's body. Faythe could have blocked the emotion from herself, but she felt the need to experience it, to *understand* it. Varlas snapped his head up. She didn't know him well, but the utter devastation on his tear-stained face pierced her heart and pricked her eyes. His gaze burned with grief-stricken fury, and she followed his line of sight. Faythe almost buckled at who she found.

Reylan. Only, his silver hair was longer, and he appeared slightly younger in age.

"This is your fault!" Varlas cried.

Faythe couldn't take her eyes off Reylan's desolate face. He also looked doused in grief and agony, so much crushing sadness in one memory. Faythe felt the wetness on her cheeks as she refused to shield herself from the flood of emotion. Seeing the suffering on Reylan's face stabbed her with a different kind of pain. Her own pain.

"It is not, Varlas," another voice echoed in the vision.

She peeled her eyes from the general, and they landed on a tall, striking male. He too looked battle-scarred and torn with sorrow over the events.

"We did all we could, but it seems we were misled by Valgard this time. I am sorry. I know no measure of time nor words can fix this, but it was not our fault, and we cannot let them win by making enemies of each other."

It was Agalhor, King of Rhyenelle, who spoke. Somehow, Faythe didn't need Varlas's confirmation to conclude as much.

"You said she would be safe here. It is your fault!"

It was a strange feeling, seeing a broken king on his knees. Faythe wanted to hate him for his ill intentions toward Reylan and Rhyenelle, for misleading her this past week, and ultimately, for trying to kill her. Yet she understood and *pitied* him instead. Though she was in his mind, she didn't want to comprehend the full extent of his misery in that moment. Those who were lucky enough to find their mate, their equal, one to complete their soul and strengthen the other…it brought immeasurable pain to sever that bond.

Though his vengeance was wrong, Faythe didn't blame him.

In the vision, Reylan straightened suddenly, a look of the coldest fear blanking his expression. He turned to his king who gave him a nod of understanding laced with his own concern. Then Reylan twisted on his heel and took off running.

Faythe couldn't take anymore. She pulled herself from the memory, bringing them both consciously back to their woodland surroundings once more. She kept control of Varlas's movements to keep him still, but she faltered as her dull headache manifested to a throb that began to pepper her vision.

"I'm sorry that happened to you," she said in barely more than a whisper.

"I'm going to kill you." He seethed.

She shook her head. "Waging war won't bring her back. If you attack Rhyenelle, they win. Valgard wins." It came out as a plea as she was desperate for him to see reason.

"Agalhor was too invested in protecting himself, his own kingdom. He left them as good as undefended there with an incapable general. Reylan allowed himself to be distracted by a small force of soldiers, leaving my mate and others without enough protection in Fenher. He failed to disperse his forces accordingly and see the ambush, the trap, that was laid for them to be pulled away from the town of innocents. They were slaughtered, every one of them, including my Freya. He deserves to pay for what he did. And Agalhor will pay too for being unfit to lead. Rhyenelle will thank me for removing him from power."

"I can't let you hurt him. I can't let you start an internal war."

Varlas chuckled darkly. "How dare you speak to me as if I require permission from a cowardly *human?* You cannot stop me, Faythe. It is already in place, and you were simply a means to speed up my intent to strike. As soon as Orlon finds whatever it is he claims we need to make it swift, Rhyenelle will fall to me."

There was no reasoning with him. The king's course of action was set, and there was no dissuading him from it. She couldn't unchain the reaction set in stone the moment Varlas lost Freya and cast the blame on Rhyenelle.

In the present, she had a choice to make. Varlas wouldn't let her live—not with everything she knew. Faythe remained in control of his mind, but not for long. Reylan's caution on limits rang chillingly through her head: *Recognize when you've depleted your well, reached your own limit—and know when to stop.*

The void she tunneled into with her ability was depthless, and she felt the talons of that oblivion reaching for her, eager to swallow her whole. Magick as an entity was thrilled to claim her life for the boundaries she pushed. And pushed. And pushed. Every second she extended her ability to grapple the mind of another was one second closer to her end.

But the moment she let go, Varlas would kill her, and she couldn't kill *him* without condemning her life. Every solution her mind frantically drew arrived at the same grim ending. But perhaps she didn't have to surrender in vain. If it meant stopping him and preventing a war…

Faythe's pulse drummed in her ears, sharpening her breathing. She could sacrifice her life if it meant the safety of innocents. Killing Varlas could stop the perilous series of events that was set to unfold if she released him.

"This is not the way, Faythe."

She inhaled in fright at the unexpected voice that joined them. It was almost enough for her to lose focus and let her control on the king slip. Reylan's presence lingered at her back, slowly closing in. The lick of relief at his being here was drowned out by the sickening pulse in her head that started to heat down her neck, veins catching fire as if the Netherworld had already staked its claim on her.

"It's the only way," she rasped. Sweat beaded on her forehead, her trembles turning into a dizzy vibration she felt in her bones. She had to make her choice now.

"Not at the cost of your life." She swore the general's voice dipped with a hint of fear.

"He'll kill me anyway."

"Take his memory."

Faythe's eyes widened as she pondered it. Erasing thoughts was not something she had attempted before or was even certain she was capable of. "I don't know if I can," she admitted weakly.

"You have to try, and you have to do it now, before you burn yourself out." Reylan's words were a command that wavered with shadowy desperation.

"I could end it."

"That's a fight for another day. It is not your role to prevent it."

He was right. This wasn't her. She wasn't a cold-blooded killer. As much as it terrified her to think of the path of destruction Varlas was Nether-bent on in his grief and vengeance, she had no right to claim his life.

With the remains of her ability that had reached a new high—the climax before the final plummet she would not emerge from—Faythe mustered all her strength to focus on the task that taunted her with failure. Reylan kept a foot away, but through the cracks of her own reservation, a slither of his belief wove into her doubt, and it was enough to straighten her spine in a flare of defiance. She would not be weak. She would not cower.

Faythe latched onto the event in the woods from the moment she was led away from the rest of the hunting party and crouched low with the king behind the bush cover. She gripped it with her whole mental being, straining as she felt the resistance; felt Varlas's own rebellion against Faythe for taking what wasn't hers. Darkness closed in on her vision, and before she could pass out, she sunk her claws deeper and tore herself from his mind all at once.

Leaving his mind was not like the gentle slip Faythe was accustomed to. In taking his memory, the link snapped like rope in a strenuous tug-of-war. She stumbled back, her vision cloudy, but her fumbling steps didn't get the chance to trip her before she was caught by a firm force. Reylan steadied her. When he helped her to straighten, his hands lingered on her arms until she was confident in her stability.

She would have thanked him, but her uneven breaths and dizzy bewilderment left no room for coherent thought. Faythe used all her shredded strength not to give in to the need to double over and retch.

Reylan's hands dropped, deeming her steady enough, before Varlas could regain full consciousness. They both stood in front of the king who stared back with a blank expression. Faythe focused on her deep breathing, trying unsuccessfully to disguise the violent tremble of her body while they waited in cold anticipation for his reaction.

The murmurs of the woods were completely masked by her erratic heartbeat as she tracked Varlas's every flicker of expression, looking for the slightest sign she had failed. After an agonizingly slow half-minute, the king blinked once. Twice. Three times. Then he looked between Reylan and Faythe who fought painfully against the rising acidic burn in her throat. She couldn't speak with the hard lump constricting her airways and was awash with gratitude when the general broke the deafening silence.

"We were just heading back, Your Majesty. It seems the hunt turned out to be something of a disappointment with the lack of game this time," Reylan said casually, as if they were in the midst of a conversation before.

Varlas's eyebrows knitted together in confusion. He glanced around the forest then down at his drawn sword. "Yes. I suppose we should head back," he mumbled, still dazed.

Faythe's relief drowned her like a flood.

The king turned and started to walk back. Faythe didn't immediately follow, struck with too many contrasting emotions to make any move.

"Keep it together. You're safe. Now, let's go."

With Reylan's words in her mind, she felt his hand on her lower back give a gentle nudge forward. It struck her back to consciousness like a bolt of electricity. She looked at him but couldn't even muster the energy to utter her appreciation. Instead, she urged her feet to press forward, desperate for solitude so she could give in to the darkness that beckoned at the exertion of her ability.

CHAPTER 26

Faythe

BURSTING THROUGH THE door to her chamber, Faythe didn't have the energy to cast out Reylan when she felt him follow her in. She wanted to be alone, to rest as her mind and body called for, but the events in the woods with the King of Olmstone rattled in her mind, and she knew the general would demand answers to what happened before he arrived as her savior.

"You have to leave," she said before he could ask anything.

"What is Varlas planning?"

On her retreat back from the forest, Faythe had started to put together the pieces to help her make sense of the chaotic week. Everyone seemed to have their own agenda, and Reylan was no different. His fixation with her, his unexpected appearances—it was all a ploy to point her in the right direction. All this time, he'd had his own silent suspicions—not about her, but about the King of Olmstone. She hated that it stung to think he was using her all along.

"You knew Varlas wanted to get me alone, that he would threaten me for information he thought I would get from you. You knew all this time and were playing both sides." Faythe kept her voice low, but she let her building rage seep into her words.

Reylan didn't bother to deny the fact or try to apologize.

"You used me," she laughed bitterly. "You're just as cunning and deceitful as the royals. You wanted me to get inside his head, get whatever knowledge you thought I could gain, with no regard for my life—"

"That's not true," he cut in sharply. Then he straightened, his face sympathetic but not remorseful. "We have long known Varlas is holding a grudge, only I didn't realize the true extent of what he was willing to do. I need you to tell me, Faythe. Everything you found out."

She shook her head in disbelief. "You're just like them, you know? The position suits you well."

His jaw flexed with impatience. "You have to recognize, we are on the same side, you and I."

"There is no *you and I!*" she shouted in exasperation. She wanted to trust him, believe he could be different from the kings, but he was no better than them when it came to manipulating her for his personal gain. She felt the deceit like a twist in her chest, but she pushed it to the side, smoothing the sharp edges of her fury to say, "I can't help you, Reylan."

She wouldn't be the catalyst for this war. If Rhyenelle knew of the impending danger, they might move to strike first. No—she had to figure out a way to stop it at its source. Perhaps Nik could help dissuade his father from aiding Varlas's path of vengeance. Olmstone wouldn't strike out on their own.

Disappointment and ire flashed in the general's eyes. She was about to retreat from the threatening change in his demeanor, but before she could move a step, he advanced faster than she could blink. Her back crashed against the wall while Reylan held her firm, pinning her arms to her sides, making movement impossible. She didn't have the chance to make a sound or attempt to maneuver free because a sharp pull on her mind made her cry out loud. A hollowness settled in, and she immediately knew exactly what he had done.

He had taken her ability—all of it.

She couldn't throw up her mental walls in her state of shock, and she gasped when she felt him invade her mind, swiftly taking control to halt her so she couldn't move physically or throw him out mentally either. It was a sickening, helpless feeling as she remained paralyzed within herself while Reylan took what he wanted. She was completely at his mercy.

Less than a minute felt like a lifetime.

He retreated from her mind all at once, taking a long step back. Faythe gasped, doubling over and spluttering as she tried to process the quick ordeal. She had her physical free will back, but there was still something missing. He had yet to return her ability.

Faythe snapped her head up, eyes livid. She would have shattered through his mental walls no matter what it took if he'd given it back. But she was useless against him without it, and he could very easily stop her in a million possible ways before she tried to attack. Her hands trembled in unhinged fury at the violation.

"How *dare* you!" She seethed, her voice as sharp as a knife's edge.

Reylan didn't flinch at her tone, which only enraged her further. "I only saw what I had to—nothing else," he said calmly, as if he hadn't infringed upon her thoughts and memories, crossing the one line there was no coming back from.

"You're as wicked as the rest of them, General Reylan."

"Faythe—"

"The king will kill you for this, though I'd very much like to do the honors myself."

"You wouldn't get two steps to the door before I stopped you." He meant by means of taking her life. Her hands twitched in a wrath with no end as she realized he was right. Without her ability, she was exactly the weak, feeble, *useless* human she appeared to be.

"You got what you wanted. Go ahead," she challenged.

Reylan's eyes twitched in conflict, and it was enough to fill her with confidence that for whatever reason, he wouldn't kill her.

Without warning, a crushing weight fell back on her mind. It completed her as much as it crushed her, and she braced a hand against the wall while she adjusted to the return of her ability. She was incapacitated long enough that Reylan could have certainly made a swift exit before she struck his mind.

"I'm not your enemy," he said quickly, anticipating her intent.

Faythe hesitated. A destructive hurricane wrecked her thoughts. The reckless, unhinged part of her wanted to screw the damned consequences and retaliate. But she felt the chaos calm as she took a breath that allowed her to deliberate and see reason. Harming Reylan would only satisfy her selfish desire for petty revenge, and it seemed inconsequential in the face of all this. His methods were wholly wrong, but his intentions were for the good of his kingdom. Reylan was many things, but he was not self-serving.

Her anger diffused, leaving only exhaustion and sadness. "You don't even deserve the energy it would take to be considered my enemy. You are nothing to me," she said coldly. "I hope you're praised for your deception, turning the suspicion from yourself to get what you want. Your king will be proud."

"It wasn't my intention to deceive you, Faythe. This is bigger than us and much worse than I thought."

"You're right. It is bigger than us. Knowledge is power, General. I only hope you know what to do with it." She knew the condescending remark should have earned her a swift death, but though she saw his eyes flash, he didn't threaten her. "Leave High Farrow. Tonight. And don't come back. Orlon will be expecting information from me. I won't hesitate to spill everything about you if I see you again."

Reylan looked as if he wanted to argue but decided against it as he turned to take his leave. Just before he reached the door, he turned back to her. "Many more innocents could have died without your help," he offered quietly. It wasn't to justify his actions, but rather to console her worry about the possibility of an impending war.

"It's not enough," she muttered.

His look was grave. He said nothing more. The click of the door behind him echoed in her ears and was felt in the pit of her stomach.

She wanted to despise him for what he'd done. But instead, all she felt was hollow.

CHAPTER 27

Faythe

FAYTHE STOOD ON the balcony in her rooms staring at the sun-kissed sky that rained glittering rays over the city below, but she didn't bask in its beauty. Instead, her mind was elsewhere. She looked beyond the stone buildings as if she could see the duo of lunar night riding off in the distance, yet she knew the general would be long outside of Farrowhold by now. She didn't know why she cared. Perhaps it was the building anticipation that in a few short weeks, Reylan would tell his king of the impending threat, and then Rhyenelle would respond… Faythe felt heavy with dread at the thought.

Behind her, she heard footsteps and knew Nik was being deliberately loud to alert her to his presence before he came outside to join her. She didn't speak or turn to face him.

"He said there was an urgent message from Agalhor and he needed to return immediately," Nik said. She didn't know how the prince knew who was on her mind, but she didn't bother trying to deny it. "I didn't believe him for a second."

Faythe closed her eyes for a moment, taking a deep breath. She had spent the whole night awake, pondering what to do with the information on her end while Reylan rode off to make counter-plans within his own kingdom. She knew what she had to do.

Turning to face the crown prince, the only person whose powers of persuasion could possibly alter the king's movements, she said, "There's something I need to tell you."

Faythe told him everything, starting from how Reylan knew about her from day one, and ending with what she knew about the King of Olmstone. At the mention of his father's involvement, Nik's face was unreadable. Faythe felt guilty for dropping the burden of knowledge on the prince, but he deserved to know and was perhaps their only chance at getting the king to see sense.

"It can't be," were the first words he spoke in response. "What reason would my father have to help Olmstone? We have no quarrel with Rhyenelle."

Faythe didn't want to add insult to injury, so she refrained from voicing her own hatred toward the fae ruler of their kingdom. "They have an agreement. High Farrow aids Olmstone, and in return, Varlas will answer to Orlon. No matter the ask, no matter the reason. He gains power."

Nik shook his head. "I don't understand. Power...it has never been his goal. Never. Loyalty and courage have always been our values. To abandon the alliance now..." His hands clenched into fists, and she could tell he was desperate to hit something. Not wanting to be in the way, she shifted a step. Nik calmed in response, realizing his rising temper.

Faythe sighed at his broken look and approached him, taking his hand. "You can help to stop this."

The prince held a look of defeat. "I don't know if I can," he admitted.

"Together," she promised.

His emerald eyes met hers, and she longed to take the pain from them. The betrayal he felt from his own father. He forced a smile, though he likely knew there was even less she could do to stop the events than he.

"Varlas and my father are meeting as we speak, privately."

It should have made her tremble to think of the two kings possibly detailing plans of an attack, but at the spark of an idea, a cunning smile tugged at Faythe's lips instead. Nik's brow furrowed at her response to the news.

She grinned wider. "Fancy a bit of eavesdropping?"

The prince and the spymaster were as silent as mice creeping down the dark secret passageway in the library. It solidified Faythe's assumptions it was long-forgotten when Nik was equally awed at the discovery of the hidden labyrinth. When they made it to the fork in the path, Nik paused to examine the hallway she had yet to venture down.

Faythe was taking steps toward the other when Nik snapped his attention back the way they came. Her heart battered her chest at his sudden alarm, and she too spun around to follow his gaze but couldn't hear what his fae senses picked up. She was about to toss the torch she held and duck into hiding, but Nik raised a hand, and she paused. He visibly relaxed then huffed. Faythe kept her sharp edge of caution, still unaware of what he had heard.

Her rigidness loosened off in relief as soon as a familiar face emerged into the blue light of her torch. She could only stare wide-eyed at Tauria.

"How did you follow us?" Faythe asked.

The ward shrugged. "I picked up on your scents in the library, which is a strange place for Nik to be at the best of times." Her eyes only flashed to the prince for a second, and as they did, Faythe noticed Nik barely spared her a glance back, averting his attention without acknowledging the remark. It was unlike him. While they had yet to say a word to each other directly, the tension between them made Faythe shift awkwardly in the silence. It didn't feel right to pry about the friction.

She cleared her throat, saying to Tauria, "I suppose I should fill you in."

They continued the walk through the eerie darkness, Nik trailing a distance behind, and Faythe briefed the ward on everything she relayed to the prince earlier that morning. When they approached the last hallway that held the vent to the council chamber, they all halted before it. Nik drifted past them both to look first. As faint light illuminated his features from the room below, she saw his face plastered with shock. When he looked at her again, her mind caught the projection of his thoughts.

"How did you find this place?"

Faythe trembled to think the kings really could hear them if they dared to speak out loud. She was one too-loud footstep away from being discovered by everyone below when she came alone, and she'd clearly underestimated their fae senses. At the look of horror on Nik's face, she knew it was certainly possible. Her only answer was a weak shrug. She didn't have it in her to explain in that moment.

"Do you think he knows?" Varlas spoke below.

Faythe huddled close to Nik to catch a glimpse of the scene, their faces mere inches apart. Tauria crammed in just as close on her other side, and the three of them tuned in to the private meeting between kings.

"I will admit, when he mentioned his need to suddenly depart last night, I did have my suspicions," Orlon replied.

Faythe's heart was erratic as she watched the two rulers ponder over Reylan.

"Your spymaster has not revealed anything?"

At her mention, Faythe recoiled a fraction. Even though she had discovered everything about their plans, about Varlas, it still shocked her that all this time she had been played a fool. It made her question herself, her ability, if it was so easy for him to hide his true nature the few times she'd glimpsed into his thoughts. She was begrudgingly grateful to Reylan for his obscure warnings, which had kept her on the edge of caution around Varlas, easing the blow when he finally revealed himself to her in the woods.

"Not yet. Though without Agalhor, we may not get the information we need."

"The general is a close second."

The King of High Farrow sat lazily at the head of the table. Varlas, on the other hand, was pacing to his side, looking scarily aggravated. His usual cheerful smile was wiped away by harsh lines that aged his face, turning his exterior cold and ruthless. She was a fool for not seeing it before, for letting herself be swayed by his false intents and niceties. Her hands curled into fists, and she wasn't proud of the violent thought that crossed her mind to seek retribution. Not for his lies, but for his intention to have innocent blood pay the price for his revenge.

"How can you put your trust in a *human girl?*" Varlas seethed.

"She would be dead if I found her to be disloyal. Her skills are invaluable," Orlon defended coolly. Not out of care for her life, but for his choices.

"What if she is the reason for the general's unexpected departure?"

Faythe sucked in a sharp breath. The heat was rising, and she wasn't sure if it was from her own rattled fear or the close proximity of Nik and Tauria. She felt the prince's sideward stare but didn't look at him, her eyes remaining fixed on the two kings in anxious anticipation.

Orlon stood from his throne, seeming bored and irritated by the Olmstone king's doubts. "Trust me, Varlas, I will find out everything from the girl. I will get what we need to overthrow Rhyenelle, and when we do, I expect your fealty."

"Forgive me if I do not so easily place my faith in a human and a *stone* to take down a great kingdom."

She saw Orlon's face twitch at the insult. "It is not what the stone can do, but the door it can open that will be Rhyenelle's undoing."

Faythe almost swayed with the information, hot with dread over what she thought they spoke of. Then Orlon's next words fell like a physical weight on her shoulders.

"The Riscillius is within High Farrow and will be in my possession if I have to use and dispose of every human to get my hands on it."

Faythe straightened in cold horror. The boy had been right. The king was terrorizing his own citizens, using them as pawns to scour the town for the very stone Faythe held in the hilt of her sword. Her side felt heavy, and she refrained from reaching to where the pommel usually sat at her hip as she was currently unarmed. She couldn't begin to fathom what the king would want with the Spirits—with Aurialis. And suddenly, she had the overwhelming fear that perhaps she had been played for a fool by more than one evil if the Goddess was on the king's side of destruction all along.

Varlas hummed. "This great power you speak of had better be worth the wait."

The wicked grin that spread across Orlon's face twisted Faythe's stomach. "Oh, it will be."

She couldn't take any more. She stepped away from the small viewing vent and hastily made her way back, not glancing behind her to see if Nik and Tauria stayed to hear anything else. She felt dizzy, and the stone walls seemed to close in around her, making the passageway smaller. Her quick steps turned into a jog. When the narrow passage opened at the junction, Faythe paused to breathe, bracing her hands on her thighs. Her mind reeled and her heart thundered as she tried to process the information, though she failed to make sense of or accept any of it.

"What would my father want with the Riscillius?"

At the sound of Nik's voice, she turned to face him. "You tell me. What would the King of High Farrow want with access to an all-powerful being?" She said it sarcastically, incredulously, but instantly felt guilty when the prince's face fell.

The answer was almost obvious, except what she couldn't figure out was what Aurialis could do to aid him. She didn't know what the Spirit was capable of from her position. Faythe blanched at the thought, the possibilities. An unearthly weapon might be just what the kings needed—not only to tip the scales, but for full annihilation.

"We'd better go. They'll be preparing for Olmstone's send-off soon," Nik said quietly.

Faythe didn't think she could stand to face either king right now, but she nodded and turned to make her way out.

"Wait." Tauria's voice halted her movement.

Faythe jerked in fright, forgetting the ward was even present in her panic. She and Nik turned to her expectantly as she frowned but didn't meet either set of eyes.

"Do you feel that?"

Faythe would have thought nothing of it, except the last time the ward sensed something, it led them right to the being she now dreaded to even think about.

"I don't feel anything," Nik said for the both of them.

Tauria looked to him then. Her expression was conflicted, as if she wanted to confide in the prince, but for some reason, she decided to turn her attention to Faythe instead.

"It's weak, but...it was like that night at the hut. I can't explain it."

Faythe shuddered. Staring down the black depths of the unexplored second passageway, a dark feeling settled over her. "Another time. Nik's right—we need to go."

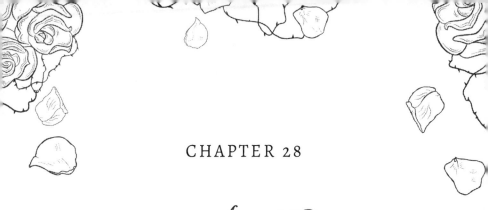

CHAPTER 28

Reylan

T HE GENERAL RODE like a midnight storm, making the trip back to Rhyenelle in ten days rather than the minimal fourteen it usually took. He would have felt bad for pushing his companion soldiers to keep his rapid pace were the news not so urgent. In fact, he'd wanted to abandon all the petty meetings the first day he arrived in High Farrow, for the news that weighed on him so heavily came long before the discovery of their impending attack.

Rhyenelle had suspected the attack already, and confirming it was Reylan's main task during his week with the ally kingdoms— though he supposed the term was no longer appropriate as they sought to overthrow his homeland. It wasn't a surprise, and he knew it wouldn't be to his king either, but at least now they could strengthen their defenses according to the information he got through Faythe's thoughts.

The woman struck a chord of familiarity within him. He had been unable to get the bright gold eyes out of his mind since he first set his own upon them. Their likeness he assumed he would never see again.

Reylan didn't falter a single step as he dismounted Kali and stormed his way into the castle. The crimson tapestries brought comfort and pride; he had grown sick of the royal blue of the north. Guards opened the doors long before he approached, and none dared to stop him for idle chat, which he was sure his face warned against. Every fae soldier and guard in the kingdom answered to Reylan as there were none he didn't outrank, but the respect and loyalty was mutual. It was how it always had been, and he was confident their armies were stronger for it.

While twilight diffused the sky, there was usually only one place he would expect to find his king. No guards were posted outside the doors to the Glass Garden. Through their transparency, he spotted the king at the far end by a cluster of white rosebushes. Reylan slowed his pace and entered gently, still making enough noise for the king to detect his presence. He stayed silent as he approached. One of his large hands held a small bloomed rose still attached to its vine, and Reylan knew the symbolism. It represented a different form of delicate flower that was once his world. The Glass Garden remained thriving even long after its original owner abandoned it.

"You're back earlier than expected," Agalhor said at last. "I trust your trip was fruitful." His brown eyes shifted from the rose he let fall and landed on the general.

It wasn't often Reylan lost his nerve, but he cursed his own cowardice in that moment. "It is worse than we feared. Orlon and Varlas have allied together, and I fear they are working on something bigger than we anticipated to try to take us down." He stared with the news the king was expecting, mostly to delay the harder conversation he had spent the whole journey going over in his head.

The Phoenix king hummed, not appearing the least bit concerned as he turned back to the rosebushes. A lot of the time, Reylan admired the ruler for his cool indifference toward difficult situations. However, centuries by his side had taught him that while the king's exterior remained calm and collected, inside, the wheels to his brilliant mind were working overtime with information.

After a short pause, the king said, "I assume they bought into the story of my unforeseen absence?" A cunning smile twitched his lips.

Reylan huffed a laugh. "They were not best pleased. You would have enjoyed the look on Varlas's face at the news."

Agalhor Ashfyre was no fool. He had spies in all corners of the three ally kingdoms. The discovery of the King of High Farrow's new *spymaster* had not come as a surprise to Reylan when he arrived, as part of his mission was to snuff them out and dispose of them. Orlon couldn't have such a weapon at his disposal. Agalhor was not about to risk exposure to an ability like that.

Yet nothing could have prepared Reylan for *who* he was sent to execute.

"And you took care of the situation?"

Reylan shifted, and for the first time in centuries, he feared the king's reaction to his more imminent news. He took a deep breath, ignoring Agalhor's words to say, "We need to talk about Lilianna." There was no answering his question without it.

The new rosebud under the king's fingers crushed together as his fist enclosed around it. Reylan swallowed hard.

"I told you never to speak her name again." Agalhor's voice was low, lethal.

It was rare Reylan heard that tone, and certainly not directed at him. But the king's response was expected and justified in his heartbreak, so Reylan didn't balk.

"You know I would not if it wasn't important," he responded calmly.

The king met his eye, and the sorrow in them made him feel awfully guilty for being the one to open an old wound. It would crush him to reveal the part that would really damage the king's spirit.

Agalhor hesitated as if he didn't want to ask but needed the answer. "Did you…did you find her?"

At the slight flicker of hope on his face, Reylan's answering look became solemn. He shook his head.

Agalhor's expression fell, and he was about to turn away when Reylan blurted, "But I think I found her daughter."

The king halted but didn't meet his eye again. "She married then. Good." His words rang with heartbreak.

"No, I don't think she did."

His forehead creased in a hard frown, eyes glassy as he waited for Reylan to explain further.

The general took a long breath as he tried to recall the mental conversation he'd conjured on his way here. It was wasted energy as every bastard word on the subject deserted his mind. He grasped frantically at loose sentences to form some kind of explanation.

"It was her eyes at first. The brightest gold—there was no mistaking them."

The king's face twitched in sadness at the stirring-up of old memories.

"Then, when I got close enough, Lilianna's scent was there. Her daughter lives in the castle." Reylan paused to gauge the king's reaction, but he gave nothing away as he stared blankly.

"And her mother?"

It pained him that his king couldn't even bear to use her name. He had hated it for a long time and swore never to mention the human woman again—the one who stole his king's heart and took it with her when she left in the dead of night without warning or explanation, only a note telling him not to seek her out. Agalhor didn't obey her wish at first, spending five years sending out bands of soldiers to search the kingdoms for her. When she heard of it, she sent him another warning that she didn't want to be found. Reylan greatly admired his king for remaining strong and focused for his kingdom though his heart was clearly in pieces. He knew firsthand the ache of losing one who was as good as a mate.

Although Agalhor's falling in love with a human had caused a political stir, he couldn't blame the king's heart for it when he watched how passionately they cared for each other and how equal they were in power. Her mortality was simply a cruel twist of nature in an otherwise perfect match.

He couldn't look Agalhor in the face as he said, "I didn't learn much about her and didn't know her well enough to press further, but...she claimed her mother died eleven years ago."

When he dared a look, the king was emotionless. Reylan took that as a worse sign than any outburst of anger or sadness.

"Why are you telling me all this?" Agalhor's calm tone shook his very bones.

Not wanting to delay the inevitable drop of staggering information, he said, "When I got close enough to detect Lilianna's scent, another scent was there. It was faint. Nobody else would sense it if they weren't looking."

The king's eyes alone pressed him to continue. Reylan paused, looking him dead in the eye as he delivered his final blow.

"It was yours, Your Majesty. I believe you have a daughter, alive and in High Farrow."

CHAPTER 29

Faythe

B EING REQUESTED IN the council chamber rattled Faythe's nerves to new extents, as if she always had something to fear or hide from the King of High Farrow and was one summons away from it being her last. She had every reason to be on edge today. The king was even more unpredictable than she could have possibly imagined. He had many secret plans she doubted anyone in the castle suspected. As much as she didn't like the arrogance of the other lords and councilmembers of High Farrow, she knew they were not merciless killers and would not submit to such a plan as to wage war on an ally kingdom. It was blasphemous, unlawful, and immoral. It shouldn't have shocked her that her king was capable of such an act, but admittedly, a part of her longed to believe the prince—that perhaps Orlon still held love and mercy in small doses.

She entered the council chamber without hesitating, mustering every ounce of confidence she could although internally she trembled horribly. Faythe expected this meeting. The king would want to know everything she was able to find out from their guests who left over two weeks ago. Faythe had been painfully on edge for the confrontation ever since.

What she feared most was not that she had next to no information to give the king; it was that she now knew the ruler standing in front of her hid the true extent of his evil behind a mask of impassiveness. It sickened her to be standing in the same room as him, and even more so to be in his service.

Faythe stood confidently at the end of the table. The king had yet to meet her eye. The doors groaned shut behind her, and she quickly noted they were completely alone in the room. Not a single guard remained like there usually was. She swallowed hard.

Orlon pondered over a map spread at the far end of the wide table in quiet contemplation. "I like to think we have an understanding, you and I."

At the king's opening sentence, Faythe shuddered. He still didn't look at her as he continued.

"Your ability could not only serve High Farrow. It could be used to better the world."

Her heart thundered as she thought perhaps the king foolishly trusted her enough to reveal his plan to overthrow a great kingdom. Finally, he looked up, black eyes swirling with shadows.

"Yet you still resist. Why?"

The knot in her stomach clenched, but she kept her face placid. "Have I not done everything you asked, Your Majesty?"

His eyes narrowed on her, and he stalked toward her slowly. It took everything in Faythe not to cower from the demon who radiated power and evil. He stopped a few seats away, yet even from this distance, she felt him loom over her, his shadow like the gentle caress of death.

"There was a group of human boys to be brought in for questioning—friends of the one you executed."

Faythe's teeth ground at the comment. She knew he purposely mentioned her role to pin the blame for the boy's death on her—

and to gauge her reaction. She didn't give him the satisfaction of one and kept her face emotionless.

"Yet on the day I sent out guards to seize them, they happened to vanish."

His lingering accusation wasn't subtle. She feigned a bored look. "So, they caught wind of what happened to their friend and fled. They'll likely die on the run anyway." She tried not to think of her two friends and if they'd even made it to Galmire as planned, alive and safe. They had to be. She wouldn't accept any alternative.

"Perhaps," was all he said, and it surprised Faythe he didn't press the matter further since it was clear his suspicions were far from curbed.

He turned and strolled back to the top of the table. Faythe visibly relaxed with his back to her, but her spine stiffened again when he turned and stared down at the map once more. His hand came to rest on it, and she didn't fail to notice his fingers lingered over the south: Rhyenelle.

"The general's departure was quite sudden after the meetings… I don't suppose you learned anything that might shed light on what was so urgent?"

It was a test as he went straight in for the targeted kingdom. Faythe had spent the whole of the previous night coming up with lies she would spin to not only keep the damned general safe, but herself too, as the king would expect something of use from her. She held no love for Reylan, yet she didn't want to see him with a target on his back if the king found out what he was up to: getting his own information from his short visit.

"His mind wasn't easy to get into. A forewarning about his ability would have been appreciated," she said, leveling with his cruel tone. "Luckily, he didn't detect mine. I assume my being human had something to do with it," she lied smoothly. "I managed to get in eventually, of course, but I'm afraid you'll be disappointed with the boring details. Their armies are strong, but that's common knowledge. The general's reasons for leaving were true. There's unrest in Callune, a town bordering with Fenstead, over fears of an impending attack from Valgard. General Reylan is their best commander—it makes sense for them to want him back immediately."

It all came tumbling out as if she spoke the truth. It made Faythe sick to think she was becoming a master deceiver. Yet the king didn't look convinced, and she trembled to think the question was a trick all along, that perhaps he already knew there were no urgent matters in Rhyenelle. She counted her breaths as she waited for him to out her lies. Instead, he looked away and seemed to drop the subject. Her shoulders relaxed with relief, but she didn't let herself believe for one second she was safe. Her turn on the game board was simply over—for now.

The more conflicts that arose, Faythe found herself not standing on any one side. High Farrow was her home, but her heart was divided with longing not to fight for a kingdom but for the people, no matter what color they wore, no matter the shape of their ears, no matter their race or gender. She longed to liberate all of Ungardia from tyrants like the king before her.

"You may go," he said in dismissal.

She turned immediately, not wanting to linger for even a second.

His voice drifted to her quietly right before she met the door. "If I find out you have lied to me, Faythe, your death will be a kindness."

CHAPTER 30

Jakon

J AKON AND THE group pressed on for the final stretch of their
journey. They would reach Galmire by nightfall. Jakon had
resisted every urge to stop and turn back for the fae guard
who left them over three days ago to divert a band of fae patrol. It
would be a futile effort anyway, risking the mission and the people
in their company. Still, it didn't ease his guilt that Caius had offered
himself as a distraction knowing his life could be on the line if he
was suspected of being party to their escape.

A hand went around his own, pulling him out of deep thought,
and he smiled down at Marlowe. He longed to remove the gloves
they wore against the cold and feel her soft skin. She had been the
one to lift everyone's morale through their weeklong trip—over a
day longer than anticipated thanks to the diversion. He didn't hate
himself to admit he couldn't have done it without her. He needed
her—they all did. Not for her strength or skills with a weapon, but
for her wonderfully calming and upbeat nature no matter the
situation.

They walked the last few hours with little conversation. When they at last spied the signs of civilization, faint flickers of amber against the twilight sky, Jakon could have collapsed with relief. The burden of ensuring so many lives would make it here alive lifted as they neared the town alight with glowing torches. Everyone was immensely tired, but he pushed them to make the final journey over the stretch of hills.

When they reached the solid stone path that led right into Galmire, Jakon gaped at the person standing at the end of it. Caius's smile was wide as they approached.

"Thank the Spirits," Marlowe muttered, not hesitating to embrace the fae. It took him by surprise, but Caius returned the hug.

Jakon was stunned with a mix of relief and disbelief that the fae guard was alive and had beaten them to their destination. "How?" was all he could manage as they embraced forearms, all wariness of him dissolved by knowing he was okay.

The fae guard's eyes danced with mischief. "They were headed here to scout for the fugitives, so I joined them. We got here a day before you by taking the main route, and when they didn't find who they were looking for, they left. The humans should be safe."

He didn't know how to respond. A simple thanks didn't seem sufficient for what the guard had risked for them to ensure the town was safe from the others for their arrival.

"You stayed?"

Caius nodded. "Thought I would let you know the coast is clear and accompany you two on your journey back. If you don't mind, that is." The young fae was surprisingly polite, and Jakon felt immensely guilty for the preconceived notion he had toward his kind.

He smiled warmly, giving him a small nod in appreciation.

They walked together through the town, the ensemble of refugees trailing behind in need of a proper bed and a good night's rest in safe quarters. When they came across an inn, Jakon went inside with Marlowe while Caius stayed with the group outside.

The place was quiet and dreary, with only a few men seated at lone tables who looked to be drinking away their sorrows. They paid the two foreigners no attention as Jakon walked right up to the barkeep.

"Do you have any rooms?"

The short, rotund man barely lifted his eyes to greet him, his face that of a man who had long given up living for any kind of joy. "How many?" was all he grumbled in response.

"Over a dozen."

"How long?"

"As long as they need."

Sooner or later, they would have to find their own accommodation and work to become permanent residents of Galmire. There was only so much help Jakon and Marlowe could extend to them.

Before the man could protest, Jakon reached into his pocket and lay five gold coins on the counter. They were from Faythe's winnings at the Cave. Neither he nor Marlowe had touched the money, instead putting it aside in case his friend should need it one day, possibly to escape the king. But he knew she would be more than happy with where her earnings were going now, *who* they would be helping, so he didn't feel the need to ask if he could use them.

The barkeep's eyes widened, and he quickly swiped the coin. With a wary glance around, he said, "I don't want any trouble."

"There won't be any. They come from Farrowhold and will earn their keep to stay in Galmire when they are well-rested and ready."

The man shook his head with a grim look. "I'm afraid they'll find Galmire isn't what it used to be," he said quietly, leaning a forearm on the ale-soaked counter. "Whatever they've run from in Farrowhold, coming here is no better."

It was a bold statement considering the man had no idea of the threat on the lives of those outside. Jakon's brow furrowed deeply. "What do you mean?"

Marlowe was stiff beside him, and he drew her closer with an arm around her waist in silent comfort, giving her a gentle squeeze. It eased his own tensions to feel her relax from the movement.

The barkeep trailed his eyes around the gloomy establishment before he spoke despite there only being a few drunk humans in the vicinity. "People have been going missing," he said under his breath as if the shadows were listening.

Cold seeped under his skin. "Valgard?" A dark feeling settled over Jakon at the thought he had led the band of innocents to worse doors.

The man shrugged but kept his solemn look. "No one knows. Sometimes, they vanish for good, but…" He paused, and Jakon's heart thundered as he noticed the man's face blanch at recalling whatever events had caused him to be on edge. "Sometimes, the bodies turn up near the edge of the town, close to the Mortus Mountains."

He knew there was more to the story and found himself snapping a little harsher than intended in anticipation. "What of them?"

"Most of the time, they're left in one piece, only the bodies are completely drained of blood, no wounds except neat puncture wounds." As the man tapped his neck, Jakon recoiled at the grim detail. "Ain't never seen a creature that kills so…clean."

What he didn't understand was, if there was immediate danger to Galmire and the humans were being targeted…why would the king remove the small protection they had? There was nowhere else to lead the group of humans, and the dawning fear he had escorted them from one danger straight into the arms of another was almost enough to buckle him.

"Have any of them been women or children?" Marlowe asked when Jakon couldn't.

His heart ached at her distress, and he wished desperately to at least be able to console her. But there was nothing he could do or say against the horrifying revelation.

The barkeep shook his head. "Mostly, it's been the men of the town. Strapping lads at first, though now, there doesn't seem to be a pattern. A few women, yes, but mostly men," he confirmed.

Marlowe turned to him then. "We can't take them back. We can't destroy the hope of a new life for them. It's a risk, but it's far better than living a life in fear of who might come to their door next in Farrowhold."

He could see the terror in her eyes—that they would be responsible should something happen to them in Galmire. But she was right: going back was not an option. He pulled her into him as if it would help ease her nerves. It did nothing for his, but it was a necessary comfort.

"Maybe Faythe can speak with Nik and persuade his father to reconsider the protection needed in Galmire. They've already searched the town for the boys—they should be safe from the King's Guard at least," Marlowe mumbled.

They both knew it was a long shot. Even if the king was aware of the threat to the humans of this town, Jakon doubted it would rank high on his list of priorities.

Jakon felt the overwhelming need to get back to Farrowhold as soon as possible. There was only one person who would be able to find out more information and possibly help keep the humans of Galmire safe. For the first time, he was actually glad for Faythe's position in the castle. But he and Marlowe had already decided they would stay for a week to ensure the fugitives would be able to build lives and be safe here, as well as resting themselves before the grueling journey back to Farrowhold on foot.

It took over an hour to huddle the band of humans into the inn and divide them between the few rooms on offer in the sparse establishment. When everyone was as content as they could be and had been given a questionable but hot meal, Jakon finally allowed himself to breathe a full, relaxed breath.

When he got to his own allocated room down the hall, he creaked the door open slowly, hopeful Marlowe would have surrendered to her exhaustion. Instead, he found her perched on the edge of the small, feeble cot, grasping a cup of hot tea between both palms under the warmth of a blanket. His shoulders loosened off the moment she flashed him a smile in greeting. The sight filled his chest with warmth despite his freezing body from the trek.

"You didn't have to wait up for me," he said, beginning to strip out of his damp clothes. Jakon shivered against the cold, swiftly changing into his spare dry shirt and pants.

Marlowe set her cup on the wonky nightstand and stood to walk over to him. Removing the blanket from her shoulders, she reached up on her tiptoes to drape it around his. Jakon's heart fluttered at the tender and selfless act, arms going around her so they were both in the warmth of the comforter—and each other.

She leaned the side of her face against his chest. "We made it," she whispered, her words laced with relief as if she'd had great doubts before.

His arms tightened around her, a subconscious action at the thought of the alternative—of ever being without her.

When her head left his chest to peer up at him, whatever she read on his face had her reaching up to curl her fingers in his hair, bringing his mouth to hers in a surge of need. A relief and a reward now they were both safe and had succeeded in their task to get everyone here.

Marlowe took the lead, twisting them, and with a gentle hand she guided him backward until his legs felt the low edge of the wooden cot. The small size of it didn't matter as he had no intention of leaving an inch of space between them all night. As he lowered to sit on the edge, he held in a groan of pain from his stomach—not successfully enough that Marlowe failed to notice. Her face creased in concern, but he slinked his arms around her waist and coaxed her down too until she straddled him.

"Faythe has been in that castle for months," Marlowe muttered, a hint of rare anger seeping into her hushed tone. "She could have found the ruin by now."

Jakon's brow furrowed as he tucked a strand of honey hair behind her ear to prevent it from shielding her expression from him. Marlowe's jaw was tight as she stared down at his old wound, her delicate touch tracing over the raised scar under his shirt.

"It's not her fault—"

Marlowe shook her head with a loose huff, and her abrupt retreat from his lap cut off his words.

Jakon remained still, watching her pace a few steps away. When she turned back to him, her face was desolate, dropping a nauseating weight in his stomach. Jakon braced himself for the outpour of emotion that seemed to surface in her all at once.

"She could have tried harder," Marlowe said through an exasperated breath. Even as she spoke it, Jakon could see it pained her to say what she truly thought. "Faythe could have fought harder." Her voice broke, and Jakon stood, heart clenching at the noise. But Marlowe held out a hand to halt him when he tried to go to her. "For months, she's been in that castle. I lost my father, you were hurting—we needed her—and she wasn't there."

"When are you going to stop defending her every action?" Marlowe's tone took on a harsh edge, her heartbreak and anger fusing to form something Jakon had never experienced from her before. They had spoken of Faythe, voiced their concerns and upsets since the events that tore them apart from her, but he had been a fool not to see just how deeply Marlowe was hurting. The emotions she had been bottling up all this time...

When he said nothing in response, she continued. "I understand that you grew up together. That you and Faythe have a bond I will never glimpse. But Faythe has a life of her own now and seems to have accepted that although you haven't."

Jakon felt her bitter words like the twist of a blade in his chest. "Where is this anger coming from?"

"I'm not angry—I'm *hurting!*" Her lip quivered, and Jakon almost went to his knees before her. "I have this *gift* that I can never turn off, and I am *tired*, Jak." Her voice broke as tears fell, months of pent-up anguish he had missed completely. Perhaps she was right and his concern for Faythe had clouded his senses too much to realize Marlowe was suffering in silence. The emotion that choked his throat was agony.

"I love her, Jak, I really do. I know what Faythe sacrificed for me, but she was also the reason we were torn apart. Maybe this makes me selfish, but I lost my father, and she wasn't *there*. I found out about being an oracle not long after she *left*. It doesn't stop— the visions, the knowledge. I am just so, so *tired*, Jakon. And Faythe, the only one who can understand what I'm going through, wasn't *there* for me."

"I'm here for you," he all but pleaded.

Her face fell along with the note in her voice. "Don't you see? In some ways, it's like I lost both of you that day, because your mind lingers in that castle with her."

Marlowe paused to gather a shaky breath. "I kept silent because I thought you were right. How could I blame her when she was there not out of her own choosing? But I realize you're wrong. We can change nothing about the events that unfolded, but she could have tried harder to *fight back*. To fight for *us*, for more than just our physical safety. Instead, she submitted and was content to never see us again."

"That's not true," Jakon felt the need to interject.

It was the wrong thing to say, as her expression hardened once again, defeat etched in her brow.

"You won't ever stop defending her, will you?"

Jakon swallowed hard, but it did nothing to relieve the marble of grief that constricted his airway.

"Why does it feel like you're making me choose?"

Marlowe's disappointment, folded with shock, hit him like a punch to the gut. Her shoulders lifted and fell weakly.

"I shouldn't ever have to." She turned away from him.

Jakon took tentative steps toward her, watching her shoulders tremble lightly with quiet sobs. Wordlessly, his arms went around her from behind, drawing her flush to his front. Marlowe cried harder, and he held her silently, letting her release the emotions she had been selflessly holding in. Feelings he should have known she harbored sooner.

While he held her, Jakon sorted through his own thoughts, considering every word she'd uttered and every event that had happened between the three of them. He didn't know how long had passed, but her crying slowly eased then stopped. Neither of them moved. He couldn't let her go.

"You're right," he said at last. His hands took her shoulders, guiding her around to look at him. His jaw flexed at the broken look on her face, and his palm met her cheek, thumb brushing away the wetness there. "I'm sorry I haven't seen you, Marlowe. Not like you deserve after all you've been through. Perhaps I did allow myself to be distracted and clouded in my concern for Faythe, and that's no excuse. You're right—she does have a life without me now, and I'll admit—" He had to pause, resenting himself for the words he was about to speak. "Sometimes, I also wish she had done more somehow. That she would have fought to find a way back to us sooner. But I also cannot begin to fathom what she's been through and is still going through in that castle.

"I held resentment for a while—toward the king, the fae—but some of it was directed toward Faythe. I kept silent because I can't fault her when I haven't tried to get to her either despite my many thoughts of it. I have failed both of you." He pressed his lips to her forehead. "I'm so sorry, Marlowe. Can you forgive me?"

Her expression wrinkled, but she nodded before curling into his embrace. He released a breath of relief as she accepted his comfort.

"I'm sorry too."

"Don't be." Jakon took slow steps backward until he felt the bed behind him. He lowered himself down slowly, not taking his arms from around her until her thighs were spread on either side of him once more. "Don't be sorry for one second about voicing your mind."

Marlowe's face pulled back to lock eyes with him. Pain still swirled in the oceans of her irises. "You should know that I don't resent her, or you, I just—"

Jakon's mouth met hers. "I know," he said against her lips. Pulling back a fraction, he ran his fingers from her temple to her mouth. "I'm here to listen to you, Marlowe. Everything that burdens that wondrous head of yours. But I think you and Faythe need to air your thoughts. You may find your minds align more than you think."

Marlowe nodded. "If we get a moment in between fugitives, Spirits, and evil kings," she mused lightly.

The small smile she offered lifted the darkness that had coiled in Jakon's chest, and he huffed a laugh.

He hooked an arm around her, and a small squeal of surprise left her as he twisted, pinning her beneath him on the bed. She broke out in a grin then, and it was enough to take his breath. He brought his mouth to hers firmly, and Marlowe's legs parted wider before she pressed herself tighter to him. He stifled a groan as she undulated her hips.

His lips went to her neck. "These walls are far from...sound-proof," he ground out while his mind turned to a haze.

Her hands trailed under his untucked shirt, running along his tensed abdomen before her nails scraped down his lower back as she arched into him, a silent longing for *more*.

They needed this. The distraction and closeness.

"You'll just have to be *very* quiet," she said in a lust-filled whisper.

His lips crashed back to hers. There was nothing soft or tender about what pulsed between them. It was anguish and need. Longing and forgiveness.

Jakon's hands trailed up her thighs, lifting until his fingers hooked under the waistband of her leggings, and he swiftly freed her glorious slender legs while she removed her own top. He took a second to pull back and marvel over every perfect curve and angle of her body, eyes drinking in every inch of her hungrily.

Marlowe propped herself up on her elbows, her palm reaching down to stroke the length of him through his pants. He hissed, jerking into her touch. Then he took her wrist before she could do it again, and she caught his eye. The heat and desire in her blue eyes made him want to fall before her. And it was exactly what he planned to do tonight.

His lips met her collarbone, and Marlowe's head fell back with a shallow sound.

"It's not me who needs to be mindful of making a sound," he said huskily, trailing his lips south. His hand enclosed around one breast while he took the other in his mouth. Marlowe bit her lip, suppressing a cry. Jakon smiled against her skin, relishing in her reaction.

He continued down her body. "You matter, Marlowe," he said fiercely, kissing her chest. "Every thought you have, every feeling you bear." His breath caressed her navel as his knees met the ground, cushioned by her discarded clothes. Jakon hooked his hands around her thighs. "Your mind, your heart, your soul. I love every damn piece of you, Marlowe Connaise." He pulled her to the edge of the bed, and she let out a breath of surprise as he locked his gaze between her legs.

He kissed the inside of her thigh, not taking his eyes from hers. "Tell me you won't keep your thoughts or feelings from me again, no matter how hard they are to hear," he mumbled against her skin.

Marlowe's chest rose and fell with uneven, sharp breaths, her scattered thoughts written on her face.

Jakon smiled deviously. His lips pressed to her thigh again, closer to where he refrained from devouring her until he heard her words.

Her head tipped back.

"Tell me, Marlowe."

"I will tell you everything," she panted.

"Always?"

"Yes."

"Look at me, Marlowe," he commanded.

When her head dragged back up and her gaze met his once more, the lust in her eyes, on her face, demanding he sate the desire pooling right in front of him, was almost enough to make his own release surge.

"I want you to see as much as feel just how much you matter to me."

The following day, Jakon strolled the dire streets of Galmire alongside Caius. They had decided to rise early, letting the fugitives and Marlowe rest in while they got up at dawn to scout the area. Mostly to be sure it was safe from the Farrowhold guards, but also with one specific destination in mind: the Dark Woods.

The very name riddled him with fear. It was woodland that had become the foundation of many horror stories whispered among the children and adults of Farrowhold. It was also where Reuben claimed Valgard soldiers had ambushed him and then recruited him for information about their home kingdom—something Jakon had horrible reservations about after Faythe's warning at what she obtained in the captured boy's mind. But the Dark Woods was where the barkeep of the inn claimed most of the bodies had turned up, so they decided they would check out the threat with their own eyes to better gauge what they could be dealing with before they left the humans here.

He was grateful for the guard's presence, mostly for his fae advantages should they run into any real danger. He hated that he felt inferior and incapable in comparison, but Jakon was armed to the teeth and highly confident in his combat abilities. He had

Faythe to thank for her constant pestering to practice swordplay relentlessly while growing up together, finding scrolls on various maneuvers and combinations as though it were a lethal dance with endless steps; a choreography to be mastered. He likely wouldn't have an interest in the sport otherwise.

The barkeep didn't exaggerate. The sparse amount of bodies in the inn the night previous was an accurate representation of the town's current population. As they walked the uneven, dusty paths, it was almost *too* quiet. Jakon was used to the bustling, full streets of Farrowhold, and this was a stark contrast. Only the occasional human could be found outdoors, and every face he saw was pale and hopeless. It set a deep unease in him to think of abandoning the humans who had entrusted and followed him here to a bleak, joyless town.

But he couldn't afford to think like that. They were safe and far out of the king's reach. Luxury was never on offer for those on the run with their lives.

As they passed out of the dreary town, Jakon spied the edge of the dark tree line and was instantly hit with cold fear. It was irrational to pay mind to scary stories and obscured truths about a simple woods, but as they approached, it was as if Jakon could feel the ripples of sinister darkness emanating from the timbers. Caius, on the other hand, didn't seem at all fazed. If he knew of any gruesome tales prior to what they were headed in to find, he gave nothing away on his cool, collected face.

Upon entering the woods, they found it truly lived up to its name. Visibility was restricted with the gray canopy and misted floor. It was eerie, prickling Jakon's skin and setting all his senses on high alert. Why anyone would wander through of their own volition, he couldn't comprehend. It was far from inviting and didn't show any signs of wildlife for hunting.

"This way."

Caius's voice made him jolt as it cut through the stillness. He felt foolish for being so on edge.

The young guard followed something Jakon hadn't yet caught onto. He didn't argue and figured it would be wise to trust him on this one. Caius had more than proven himself on their journey. He could have outed their location or apprehended them on more than one occasion. Jakon trusted him without trying. Perhaps he always did.

His human ears picked up on the sound of running water just before a long river came into view. It was not nearly as pure and ethereal as the river in the Eternal Woods. In fact, everything about the Dark Woods was in blatant contrast to it.

"Dear Gods." The fear that seeped from Caius's words was enough to set the emotion in him too. Jakon followed his line of sight, and the spear of ice that shot down his spine had nothing to do with chill of the winter air.

Just a few meters to their right, a body lay by the water's edge. Still—dead. Though it didn't seem to be far into the stages of decomposition yet.

Jakon had only ever seen death once before—his parents'. He was so young, only nine years old, when he watched them deteriorate from a killer illness that swept the town and ultimately left him orphaned and alone. Until he met Faythe, another lonely and afraid soul he felt bonded to from the first day he laid eyes on her on the streets of Farrowhold.

The death before him now struck him with the ghostly image of his long-passed mother and father whom he had buried deep for so long. His hands trembled at his sides, but he couldn't peel his eyes away from the body, fighting against fully shrinking into his terrified nine-year-old self. When a hand landed on his shoulder, he snapped his eyes to meet Caius's. The guard looked back in concern.

"You don't have to get any closer. I'll check it out," he said, no hint of mockery or irritation at his reaction, only understanding.

Jakon took a deep breath to calm his racing heart. He smiled gratefully but shook his head. "I'm okay," he reassured Caius.

Caius gave a nod then stalked toward the body. Jakon followed suit, trailing a little slower as he focused on reeling in his growing panic and stopping the nightmare flashbacks that surfaced. When he got close enough to take in the full scene, he had to turn away, forcing back the vomit that rose in his throat at the horrific sight. Taking a few steady breaths, he reluctantly twisted to face it again, finding Caius crouched and examining the body intently without touching it. He covered Jakon's view of the most gruesome part: the gaping cavity in his chest. It was a man who had died in clouded, wide-eyed terror. His eyelids were still open along with his mouth, and Jakon could almost hear the last scream that would have torn up the deceased's throat while he stared into the eyes of his murderer.

Jakon kept his distance, letting Caius and his fine-tuned senses deduce what he could from the body. After a moment, he finally straightened and hummed.

"What do you notice about the forest ground—the foliage?" Caius quizzed.

Jakon observed it but found nothing out of the ordinary.

"Frost." The guard answered his own question. "It's the dead of winter. The body is pale and cold, but not enough to have been here long."

The detail and what it meant had Jakon whirling around, not trusting he could leave his back exposed if there was a chance the killer still lurked in the woods. He drew his sword.

"We should go," he said, not wanting to become the next target.

"He's not drained of blood either. The barkeep said they were almost always drained of blood. And his heart is torn out, but it's still here," Caius went on in confusion.

Jakon couldn't be sure if the grim detail was a relief or if it filled him with even more dread. If whatever it was killed for blood, at least it had a purpose. If it simply killed for sport, it was a far more sinister creature than he initially suspected. It meant it had a mind, a conscience, and there were very few animals that would kill so ruthlessly, so *specifically*, to target the heart and leave the rest. It was an unsolvable puzzle that daunted Jakon with questions he didn't know how to answer.

As he stared and stared through the black curtain of the forest and the ghosts of mist, every flicker of movement set him on edge. A slow chill crawled up his spine as he felt…felt as if they were being *watched* that very moment.

"I don't detect anything nearby. Whatever it is, I think it's long since moved on."

Jakon wasn't convinced despite the fae guard's senses. Then, straight through the warped, staggered trees in front, he swore he caught a movement that could have been mistaken for wind passing through the tree canopy. Except all he could think of were…*wings*. Wings, and a vibrant flicker of amethyst that pierced through the dark veil of gray and black. He blinked, and it was gone, and he couldn't help but wonder if his mind was conjuring its own visions out of his rising fear. A painful tremor shook him to his core.

"We should go," he repeated, quieter than the last time in his cold apprehension.

CHAPTER 31

Tauria

"H E'S JUST A complete ass sometimes."
Tauria couldn't help the rant that flooded from her
when Faythe questioned the friction between her and the prince.
Her friend lay sprawled across her bed as she released all the
emotion that had built inside her since the night of her argument
with Nik over three weeks ago. They hadn't addressed it since, even
after their awkward encounter in the secret passageway the day
they bid farewell to the King of Olmstone. It saddened her as
much as it infuriated her that perhaps Nik was avoiding confrontation. She felt his absence more than she cared to admit.

"In fact, all of the time," she amended as she paced the space
in front of the fire.

Faythe rolled onto her stomach and propped herself up on her
elbows. "I think he's jealous."

Tauria gaped at the human as her cheeks heated. "Nik? No
way," she said quickly. She thought she would feel awkward for
bringing the conversation up to Faythe given their short history, yet
her friend showed no sign of discomfort or sadness, which relived

Tauria immensely as she initially felt guilty for mentioning Nik at all. There were feelings between Faythe and Nik still, that was clear, though it was not romance she saw when she looked at the pair together. Love, but not lust. But Tauria knew she had been the same way with Nik once upon a time, and she hated the ugly pinch of jealousy in her chest at the fact.

Faythe rolled her eyes. "I'm sure he'll come around. He's a stubborn prick, but he knows when he's in the wrong."

It relieved her that she wasn't alone in thinking Nik was out of line with his confrontation. She was also grateful to have a friend to confide in after all her lonely years in the castle. When she had arguments with the prince in the past, the other ladies of the court were like mosquitoes, sucking gossip and any sensitive information she shared and spreading it around like a plague. Tauria quickly learned to keep things private even when the secrets ate away at her. However, with Faythe, it was like a new wave of freedom to be able to speak so openly and know the news would go no further. She never would have imagined she would confide in a *human* and come to consider one her closest companion.

Faythe got to her feet. "There's a council meeting I'm going to be late for if I don't go," she muttered begrudgingly.

Tauria winced. She couldn't imagine being used for her ability in the way Faythe was. She had to admit, a part of her resented the king for it. Reluctantly, she nodded in understanding, wanting nothing more than to be able to spend the day with her friend, if only to distract herself from a certain fae prince.

Faythe left with a weak goodbye as neither of them were in particularly high spirits. Along with their own personal conflicts, there was the weight of the impending war between the supposed allies. Tauria was still in shock at the revelation.

She had known Varlas since she was a child. Her father considered him a good friend, and now she questioned everything she knew about the King of Olmstone. Her heart tugged at the thought of the prince she'd spent the week getting close to. She didn't want to believe perhaps Tarly knew of his father's intentions and she had been a part of his ploy all along. A marriage to her would gain them even more power as they would have great control over Fenstead too when she reclaimed her throne.

Tauria shook the thoughts. Needing to clear her head, she decided to leave her rooms for the first time that day. The hallways were quiet, and she didn't bother to tell anyone where she was going, wanting to remain unescorted. In truth, she didn't have a particular destination in mind and strolled through the halls with her mind elsewhere. When she came to stand in front of the great doors to the library, her heart picked up tempo. Ever since that night in the passageway with Nik and Faythe, the ward had felt a strange pull to go back and find out what called to her at the end of the unventured passage.

She was about to push through the door when an invading voice made her whirl.

"I hope you're not planning to go back there alone." Nik's words were laced with worry more than scolding. Still, she couldn't hold back her glare.

"I don't need your permission. Or protection," she added, pushing through the doors with more force than was necessary. She didn't need her fae senses to know he had followed her into the library.

Tauria didn't pause as she stormed down the rows of book-shelves toward her dark, forgotten destination. Nik didn't speak as he followed on her tail, and it irked her more than she cared to admit.

When she couldn't take the silence anymore, she stopped abruptly, spinning around to face him. "Isn't there a council meeting you should be attending?" It came out harsh with the echo of their last encounter.

The prince frowned and halted a few paces away. "There are no meetings today."

Tauria straightened, and her eyebrows creased together to

mirror his expression as the prince and the ward stood in equal confusion. "Faythe said..." She didn't have to finish her sentence as realization dawned on both their faces. She twisted to stare down the dark stretch of passage toward the forgotten alcove as if she would find the human standing there.

Nik swore and passed Tauria in a few quick strides. She followed closely behind, her heart already thundering at the thought of Faythe walking into danger alone.

As much as Tauria admired Faythe for her bravery, she also thought it was a miracle the human was still alive with her reckless impulses sometimes. If there was anything of threatening origin down that second passage, she doubted Faythe's mind ability would be of much use. It was easy to forget her fragile mortality when the human lived as if death could never touch her.

She let Nik lead the way as they both bustled through the dark. Neither of them stopped to swipe a torch—with their fae eyesight, they didn't need one to maneuver through. They didn't pause to contemplate when they came to the junction and hastily took the route they were yet to venture down.

It rattled Tauria's reserves that not even the prince was aware of such a passage existing within the castle walls. It was both incredulous and unsurprising that Faythe was the one to come across such a place. If danger didn't find her, the human had a sure way of seeking it out for herself.

They came to a descending stairway and halted. Nik cast her a glance as they both stood deathly still, straining their senses to pick up on any hint of threat. The prince looked back at her and opened his mouth to speak.

"Don't you dare ask me to stay behind," she cut in before he could voice the suggestion on his face.

At her firm look, Nik reluctantly backed down, though she could see he was struggling to accept it. Without a word, he turned to begin the eerie descent into the unknown void below. Tauria kept close behind.

Straight ahead, they came across a thick steel door, already open. It was then Tauria picked up on Faythe's scent. There was no mistaking she was down here now as it was all over the door in front of them. Nik would have sensed it too, and even in the dark, she saw him stiffen and his strides become wider.

Halfway through the hallway past the door, Nik halted, and Tauria nearly went careening into his back. Then she felt it. A gods-awful pull. Except not in beckoning like she felt before. This…it felt as if it drained her with its tug.

"What in the rutting damn is that?" she said in careful horror.

Nik shook his head. "It can't be what I think it is."

At his tone, Tauria trembled where she stood. The prince pressed forward again, slower this time as he took each step with extra caution. They came to another steel door that was also ajar. Before they could slip through, they heard a shift from beyond it.

Tauria was about to leap back in fright until the scent hit her stronger than before. She sagged with relief. Nik too loosened his shoulders and eagerly entered the next passage. They spotted Faythe immediately through the metal bars of the cell she was crouched inside. She had her back to them, examining something on the ground, her weak hearing yet to pick up on their presence.

Gods, it was a miracle she'd managed to stay alive without something or *someone* getting a hold of her if it was this easy to sneak up on a human.

Tauria was too distracted to speak. Everything inside her screamed to run from this place as the glistening, iridescent black walls of the lone cell suffocated her even from her position outside of it.

"This place…" Nik trailed off.

Faythe shot to her feet and whirled to see them, halfway to drawing her sword until she took in the two fae. Her expression was bewildered until it fell into an irritated frown at the fright.

"Did you two follow me?" she accused.

Tauria responded with her own allegation. "You lied to me."

She couldn't help but feel a little hurt she didn't trust her enough to tell her where she really planned to go that afternoon.

Faythe's face fell in apology. "I didn't want to put you at risk until I knew what was down here."

Tauria wanted to laugh at the absurdity, yet she refrained from pointing out Faythe's mortality and weak senses made her far more fragile than she. Even if she wanted to argue, she was too distracted by the sickening feeling that settled, and her head, which started to form a dull ache.

One look at the prince's blanched face told her he too was feeling the negative effects of the long forgotten underground dungeon. It reeked of death and radiated evil. Nik scanned every inch of the cell in horror and disbelief. Then he muttered one word that made everything in her recoil.

"Magestone."

Tauria had only ever heard legend of the fae-incapacitating stone and matched his terror as she looked over the cell walls that sparkled with polished black. It was inconceivable to think she was standing in a cell lined with the fatal stone, which had been right under their feet all this time. She instinctively backed up a step, not wanting to get any closer to the mineral to find out if its full effects were true.

"Gods above…" Nik breathed, daring a step closer to Faythe who stood fully inside it.

"Care to find out what it feels like to be human?" Faythe taunted playfully. The prince didn't match her humor. As he stared at her wide-eyed from outside the open cage door, she added, "If it makes you feel any better, it takes away my ability too in this amount. Only, it has no physical effects. I'm just as weak and *human* as ever." She caressed the distorted black wall.

The material was lethal and alluring. Tauria even dared to call it beautiful despite its promise of torture. It wasn't only her ability and her fae advantages she was afraid of temporarily losing—even as she kept her distance from coming into direct contact with the stone, she could *feel* its deadly beckoning, and her head throbbed at the mere sight of it. Though she didn't know much about Mage-stone, it was obvious it had a more detrimental effect than being simply incapacitating. At least in this quantity.

"Do you think Orlon knows?" A dangerous question, and Tauria slid her gaze to Nik as she asked it.

The prince was pale when he turned to her. "It doesn't look as if anyone's been down here in centuries."

It wasn't a direct answer, and she didn't press for more as she saw the dread that perhaps his father knew such a place, such a *weapon*, existed in his own castle. What use he would have for it was a fear not worth visiting now.

Something else caught the ward's attention, and she turned her head to stare down the end of the cellblock. She only found another steel door, except this one was yet to be ventured through.

"What's down there?" she asked, though she didn't expect a real answer.

Faythe and Nik followed her gaze, and the human shrugged. "Let's find out."

The prince caught her elbow as she stepped past him outside the cell. "Do you ever stop to think anything through?" he scolded.

"What is there to think through?" she challenged. Tauria didn't know if she admired or feared Faythe's heedless bravery sometimes.

After a short stare-off, Nik didn't form a counterargument, but the protest remained on his face. Faythe pulled her arm free and stalked for the end door. Tauria didn't hesitate to follow. Something called to her beyond that door, and if there was a slight chance it was the ruin they sought, she had to find out.

Faythe unlatched the series of bolts that locked it, and Tauria noted there were far more security measures on this one than on any of the previous doors they had passed. A dark, unnerving feeling settled in her stomach, and her heart galloped with antici-pation. The human strained against the final large latch sealing the steel door. Tauria was about to offer to help when the prince stepped past her. He put a hand over Faythe's, and they exchanged a quick look. Tauria couldn't read it, but it dropped her stomach for a second. Then Faythe backed away and let the prince undo the final lock that protected them from whatever was behind the door.

Nik pulled it open, taking a peek inside before either female could glimpse what lay beyond. He inhaled a subtle breath, audible enough that Tauria picked up on it, and her heart skipped a beat. There couldn't be any immediate danger as Nik slowly slid himself through the small gap. Faythe quickly followed, and Tauria joined with heightened caution.

She took a long breath, and her mouth popped open at the large, cavernous dwelling that opened up in front of them. They stood on a ledge that had no railing or barrier to protect them against the fatal fall into the pitch-black, bottomless pit. Scanning around, she saw several levels and gaps in the stone that led off in various directions.

An underground labyrinth. Mercifully, there was no Magestone to be seen or felt in the cave. Yet it gave off a different kind of ethereal feeling.

"It's here," she said in realization. When her companions looked to her expectantly, she added, "The ruin—I can feel it."

Faythe's eyes widened. "Do you think you can find it?" she asked eagerly.

It was faint. The uncanny similar power she felt from the Light Temple. It quietly called to her, and she was confident, given enough time to scour the various passages, she would be able to track it down.

"I think so, but I'll need time."

Tauria's senses spiked on high alert, but she couldn't place what it was about the dark dwelling that screamed at her to run.

She heard it just as the prince straightened to tune in too. The whoosh of air—climbing, beating louder. Wings, she concluded, sounding down below. And with them, a terrible scent of death and decay rose from the pit.

Nik drew his sword, and at his obvious alarm, Faythe mirrored his movement. The slice of steel echoed through the otherwise soundless dwelling. Everyone braced in anticipation.

Then, shooting upward to their level, death greeted them in the form of wings and flesh.

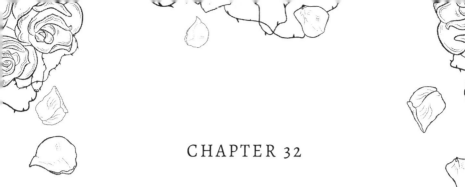

CHAPTER 32

Faythe

"R UN!"

Faythe didn't argue as the prince barked the command, but two prominent thoughts surfaced in her split second of deductive thinking.

The first was that even if they attempted to outrun the beast back into the castle library, they would only unleash damning chaos on the unwitting occupants above. The guard might be able to take care of the problem before it caused too much destruction, but it would ultimately give away the passages they'd found.

The second was that if the temple ruin was down here, they had to at least *try* to locate it. And that meant eradicating the threat standing in their way.

Neither problem offered a desirable outcome nor held confident odds for their survival. Perhaps she'd gone utterly insane in her quest for the Spirit Ruin.

While she knew Nik meant to retreat back the way they came, back to the only confirmed exit…

Faythe darted right instead.

Her recklessly impulsive maneuver put enough distance between her and the fae that the winged creature, reeking of blood and decay, landed in that space to separate them.

And chose to face her.

She trembled at the ghastly sight of it but held her blade firm. The creature hissed as it beheld Lumarias, and Faythe's eyes narrowed at the reaction. She didn't expect a simple sword to be of much use against the creature, but its reaction told her it somewhat feared the steel in her palm.

Faythe took all of one moment to gauge the monster in front of her, and she was almost struck. The first thing she noticed was its ears. One was half-torn off, but the other was pointed, just like the fae. Its face was horribly disfigured and rotting with old wounds. Despite the neglect, Faythe could still make out features that would have once been just like Nik or Tauria's, or even *hers*. It shook Faythe to her core to think of what could have happened to it to turn it into such a gruesome creature.

"I rather hoped you would hear my beckoning." Its voice was distorted in a wicked croak that washed nausea through her. Faythe was surprised to find it could speak at all.

A chill slid over every notch of her spine as its words registered. Her first day in the library, she thought she could *feel* something. Which led her to the discovery of the hidden passageway.

Her throat turned bone-dry, but she choked out a response. "Who did this to you?"

The creature was beyond human or fae recognition. She wanted to test if its mind had been twisted beyond salvation too. It flayed its black, batlike wings, which were so shredded it was a miracle it could still take flight with them. The top and bottom tips were razor-sharp, and Faythe tracked them, knowing one swipe of the mighty wings could kill her.

The fae-like being took a step closer, and she retreated in response. Its eyes danced with a predator's delight, and she saw the hunger in them. She'd been lured down here all along. Though she could find it in herself to forgive her own foolishness and naïvety if it led her to find what she sought: the temple ruin.

As if only now remembering she wasn't alone in the cavernous dwelling, her eyes caught the emerald of Nik's already staring at her in wide-eyed terror. She could see he was deliberating every possible strategy to get past the creature of death and rescue her. It wouldn't be possible, and it wasn't what she needed from him either.

"You need to find the ruin," she said into his mind.

His answering voice was near desperate. *"I won't leave you here with that thing."*

She didn't have time to argue and couldn't avert her focus from the monster for long. *"You have to, Nik. Go now!"*

Before he could respond, Faythe twisted and ran. She darted into a side passage and clumsily sprinted through the dark. Chilling laughter echoed through the hallways like a haunting caress over her skin, setting every hair on end. It had no direction, and she had no way of knowing how much distance she'd managed to put between them.

"You can imagine my delight when I caught the scent of a *human* above," the voice sang. "It's been so long since I tasted *warm* blood."

She didn't let the horror settle that it intended for her to be dinner. Something that once would have looked as normal as Nik or Tauria, despite its wings, wanted to *feed* on her.

Hurling around the next corner, she skidded to a halt in cold terror to find the creature already at the end of the passage. Even in the poor lighting, she could see its sly grin as it stalked toward her with predatory slowness. She stumbled back then stopped to angle her sword. Its smile faltered again at the sight of it, giving her slight confidence, and she straightened to strike. When it was close enough, she reluctantly tried its mind.

Faythe cautiously slipped inside but immediately retreated,

physically spluttering at the nauseating dark feeling that rippled into her own body. She lost focus for a second.

It was enough.

Faster than any fae she'd seen, the thing was upon her, and she was slammed into the wall in a heartbeat. The force knocked the breath out of her, and Lumarias clattered to the ground as it clamped down hard on her wrist. She cried out in pain. She would have doubled over at the stench of rotting flesh if she weren't pinned upright. It leaned its face of gore into her, inhaling deeply as it savored her scent. Faythe recoiled and gagged, struggling to keep herself together to find a way out of her compromised position.

Her left hand was free enough for Faythe to reach to her side. Pulling free her dagger, she plunged it into the creature's stomach, and it released her with a blood-curdling shriek that stung her ears.

She didn't hesitate. Pushing off the wall, she swiped Lumarias but only got a step away before a searing pain tore across her back. Crying out, Faythe fell to the ground, twisting to find the thing standing over her. But its eyes were transfixed on its own claws, which were coated in her blood. Slowly, it raised those spindly, decaying fingers to its mouth and licked the crimson liquid with a guttural moan. Faythe clumsily shuffled backward while it was distracted, battling against the searing pain as her wounds scraped the stone, loose debris catching in the open flesh.

Upon seeing her distance herself, the creature locked onto her with a look that was beyond human or fae—utterly monstrous and savage. It lunged for her, and with a cry, Faythe instinctivley swiped her blade.

She felt it connect and slice right across its abdomen. Black blood sprayed out and coated her, the stench so foul it made her eyes water and stomach churn. Its scream shot pain through her ears and mind, but the adrenaline coursing through her veins at the extra seconds she'd bought for herself had her twisting and stumbling back to her feet.

Her pain numbed enough in her instinct to survive that she threw herself down the winding paths. She had no idea where she was going. Each distorted hall she turned into looked the same, and dizziness made her sway into the sharp, unbudging stone walls. She was lost in the obsidian labyrinth. Breathing became difficult in her panic, and the waves of lethargy began to weigh down her steps.

At the end of the next passageway, she saw light—a beacon of hope that snapped her wide-awake. Faythe raced for it, crying out as she nearly met air below her feet and clawed desperately at the wall beside her to regain her balance.

A dead end.

She was one reckless step away from plunging herself deep into the abyss below.

Terror doused her as she heard the creature's playful taunts catching up with her again.

Across from her was another opening in the stone. On a normal day, she would have judged it too far for her to make the leap safely. With her life on the line, however, her flight mode kicked in, and without thinking, she took a few backward strides then launched herself with everything she had.

Midair, she knew she wasn't going to make it. At least, not completely. Her fingers caught the edge, tearing in agony, while her body slammed against the stone. She gripped onto the jagged ledge for dear life, struggling against the wave of dancing stars that threatened to pull her under. Her arms wouldn't hold her for long though, and as she tried to shift her weight in desperation, she couldn't get the angle that would give her the strength to haul herself over the edge. If the creature didn't kill her, the fall to its lair below would surely be her death sentence.

She felt utterly helpless and out of options.

Faythe then heard the fast approach of feet clapping down the hallway she sought to gain a foothold into. It wasn't the creature—it still called chilling chants from behind. She tried—*really* tried—to hold on for as long as she could, but her grip faltered, and she let

283

out a cry as she began her quick plummet into the dark pit, catching the horrified looks of Nik and Tauria above her, seconds too late to prevent her fall. While Nik looked fully prepared to jump after her, the last thing she saw before she was swallowed by the darkness was Tauria's controlled arm motions.

Her body cut through the air, faster and faster, toward a certain death. Her fall was short, but her bones didn't get a chance to shatter against the ground when the air around her stirred, encasing her from below to slow her down and break the impact.

Tauria's wind! Gods above.

It still hurt awfully. She landed on the sharp, uneven floor of the pit, but she was alive.

Faythe took all of one second to breathe and thank the Spirits she had narrowly escaped a tragic end. She rolled, hissing as her hands cut on the razor-sharp sticks that surrounded her.

No, not sticks—*bones.*

Faythe shrieked, fumbling around to try to get her balance to stand. There were so many remains, piled so high she couldn't find any footing on solid ground. When she twisted her head to the side, her blood ran cold and her heart stopped dead.

The small form she spied mere meters away had his back to her and was the only body that still had its flesh. She knew the human boy. She'd been the one to end his life.

Too horrified to make a sound, and too struck with nausea to move, all Faythe could do was remain paralyzed, unable to tear her eyes from the young boy's form. She couldn't even cry in her shock despite the remorse that froze her. She'd killed him, and his body had been heinously thrown down here, discarded like trash to be devoured by that beast. It was an immeasurably guilty feeling and something she didn't think she'd ever feel atonement for in her short life.

A dark shadow appeared above. She knew it was the creature's wings cutting off the small light source as the Grim Reaper incarnate swooped down to claim her. But she couldn't bring herself to make any move to attempt to run from it. She deserved to meet her end here; for her body to be left alongside the innocent life she took.

Before the fae-mutant could land, Faythe felt hands hook under her arms, hauling her clumsily from the pit of bones. She stumbled frantically, snapping back into her fighting senses. When she finally felt firm ground, she almost collapsed in relief and gratitude and spun around to meet the emerald eyes of her savior.

She would have embraced the prince in that moment if the loud snarl behind, followed by the crashing and snapping of bones, didn't force her into flight mode.

"*Go!*" Nik barked.

She didn't have to be told twice, and she twisted, once again on a frenzied sprint from the demon. The prince grabbed her hand as he passed her, and she almost felt as if she were flying as his immortal speed accelerated her steps immensely.

It was still not fast enough. The creature closed in behind them. They weren't going to make it out by attempting to outrun the thing.

Before she could lose her nerve, she tore her hand from Nik's and spun around, blade poised as she spotted the unhinged beast savagely charging toward her. To her surprise, it stopped a few paces away, its face contorted in animalistic fury as it beheld her sword.

Her head tilted when its eyes darted between her and Lumarias. "Niltain steel," Faythe mumbled, realization dawning. She shifted the blade in her hand and stepped forward.

The creature hissed at her and flinched slightly in response. Faythe wasn't foolish enough to think she could kill the immortal monster, but its reaction to her steel made her believe it was entirely possible. It was now clear the doors that held the creature in were also crafted in Niltain steel. She was sure it would have been able to rip them off their hinges despite the series of dead-bolts otherwise.

Nik was beside her, his own blade angled, but his was perfectly ordinary, bright, silver steel. "Remind me to get an upgrade, will you?" he commented, not taking his eyes off the fae-mutant in front.

While his jest was made in humor, she appreciated the promise in his words. They would both be walking out of this cave alive.

The creature lunged without warning. Nik moved first, stepping in front of Faythe and bringing his sword up to strike.

Faythe had seen the prince in action many times, had even parried against him both with and without her ability. His skills in combat were second to none thanks to his centuries of honing them. Yet Faythe dared to say he was outmatched against the uncharted threat.

It was a creation with one purpose, one goal only: to kill. The prince struck the creature several times, but it showed absolutely no reaction to the slices in its already torn up skin. It didn't feel pain. At least, not from any regular mortal weapon.

The pair became a blur with their impossible speed in the dark, and she struggled to keep track. She couldn't find a way to intervene though she held the only weapon that could offer victory. Nik had his back to her, and she saw he was faltering.

An idea suddenly sprang to mind. Another impulsive, reckless, completely insane idea. She didn't have time to think it over as it would be Nik's life if she didn't act soon.

Angling her sword, she sliced quick and fast, hissing at the sting that trailed like fire up her forearm. Faythe felt the warmth of her own blood soaking through her sleeve, and instantly, the creature's eyes twisted to lock onto it. It threw Nik roughly to the side without a second's warning and then darted for her, impossibly fast.

The prince was on his feet in a flash despite the hard blow against the wall.

Just before the thing reached her, Faythe's eyes locked on Nik's, which were filled with horror as death approached her, too quick for him to intervene this time. She tossed her blade to him as the mutant fae grabbed her and sunk its rotting teeth into her neck.

The pain was excruciating. But this was her only option. She wouldn't have been quick enough to make a killing strike before it stepped out of her sword's path.

Flames tore through the veins in her neck, spreading to paralyze her while the creature drank her blood. Then it was gone. Lumarias protruded from its abdomen as it gurgled, and black blood spurted from its mouth. The scorching pain in Faythe's neck raged like fire deep under her skin, and she couldn't hear sound anymore as her ears filled with a loud thrum. Her vision lost focus, vague as she caught the final blow Nik dealt, and the creature's head went tumbling from its shoulders.

Faythe fell to her knees, feeling sleep numb the throbbing pain and lift her away from the foul stench of the thing's black blood. She thought she heard her name but couldn't be sure as agony drowned out all her senses. She swayed and fell into the form that pulled her from the ground, holding tight when her legs failed to withstand any weight. Nik, she realized, as his close scent filled her nostrils. She forgot where she was for a moment as the comforting smell stole her away to better memories.

She was floating and melted into the warmth of the body that carried her. Her head fell back, and the glimmer of emerald was the last thing she saw before darkness claimed her.

CHAPTER 33

Faythe

F AYTHE STIRRED, FEELING horribly dizzy before she even opened her eyes. She could hear voices, but they were distorted as if she were underwater. She took a sharp breath in panic, relieved to feel the cool air rush down her dry throat. It cleared her head but stabbed her chest. Then, in stark contrast, she registered sickly heat and felt suffocated by the blankets that weighed her down.

With a jolt, she snapped her eyes open in a surge of anxiety, blinking rapidly as the new light stung her eyes and caused her head to pound.

"Not too fast."

Her eyes met those of Tauria beside her when they came into focus, and Faythe stared at her, blank with bewilderment as she tried to rack her memory for information.

Then it all came flooding back at once.

The cave, the fae-mutant, the young boy. *Oh, Gods!*

Nik was the other presence in the room, and he made quick strides over to her side as she adjusted to her surroundings. Faythe was in her chambers. Horror overcame her as she looked to the prince and said, "The thing down there, is it——?"

"Dead," he answered before she could choke out the word.

Her mind reeled as memories of the horrific ordeal flooded back to her. "What the rutting damn was it?" She could barely whisper as her throat was too painfully dry. It made her wonder just how long it had been since she passed out from the creature's bite. Her body ached awfully, but she found the strength to sit up. Tauria helped and brought a cool glass to Faythe's palm. She took it gratefully, greedily throwing back the water. It brought clarity to her head and vision as well as soothed her aching throat.

"We don't know yet," was all Nik could offer, and she saw he was just as disturbed by what they encountered in the caves below his home. It came second to his look of fear and concern as he looked down at her though, and Faythe figured she must look as hideous as she felt.

"How long have I been out?" she croaked.

The prince's face fell, and she braced herself. "Three days."

She blanched. Her hand reached to her neck and found it bandaged. Over her shoulder, she felt the dressings on her back under her loose shirt. She shuddered as the feeling of the creature's foul mouth on her neck pulsed through the spot where its teeth pierced her flesh.

"Gods, Faythe..." Nik paused, looking as if he couldn't bring himself to finish what he wanted to say. Tauria cast him a look of understanding. "We didn't know if you were going to pull through. The thing must have injected you with some kind of venom—it took you out almost immediately, and being human, your body couldn't fight it faster than it spread."

Faythe only stared wide-eyed at Nik as he relayed the events. She had been obliviously near to her end and felt a wave of dizziness pass as she asked, "Then how am I alive?" as the prince's grim look told her she should be a corpse instead.

"Yucolites," Tauria answered simply.

Faythe blinked. She had come to love the tiny orbs of light magick that once saved the life of her friend, Jakon. But she knew they came with a price.

"It was Nik's quick, brilliant thinking, actually," Tauria added.

Faythe could tell he knew what fear lay in her mind at the mention of the yucolites.

"I really hope we find the damned ruin. I don't fancy spending eternity with you in those woods in the Afterlife," he said with a smirk.

She relaxed at knowing there wasn't some other impossible task the Spirit of Life demanded to save *her* life this time. Then her face fell.

"You mean you didn't find it in the cave?" It was the only reason she'd risked her life in the first place. Now, it all felt like squandered energy and a wasted visit to death's door.

Tauria shook her head. "I think it's down there somewhere. But we weren't about to leave you to that *thing*, and we didn't know if there might be others."

Nik cut the tension. "You'll need another few days to rest. I managed to get you out of the last meeting without too much suspicion." He turned slightly, indicating his intention to leave, but didn't remove his hand from Tauria's in silent invitation for her to go with him.

The ward looked reluctant. Faythe gave her a weak smile and a nod to confirm she was okay and didn't need coddling. In fact, she would be grateful for the solitude to wrap her mind around the terrifying ordeal and could already feel the comings of sleep despite her three-day rest. Whatever the thing in the cave was, it was unnaturally powerful and absolutely lethal. She could only pray to the Spirits there would be no more from where that creature came.

Tauria slid out the door Nik held open, but he stopped and turned to Faythe. "You try anything like that again, and I'll kill you myself." The ghost of a smile caressed his lips in his attempt at humor, but worry and relief drowned it out.

Faythe picked it up for him as it was the best communication she knew with Nik. "Don't worry, Prince. I don't plan to challenge dark immortal beings again anytime soon." She nestled back down into the sinking sheets.

He chuckled a little and gave her one last longing look as if she might still die in front of him any moment. Then he quietly left.

Tauria

Tauria headed straight for her rooms, perfectly aware of the prince trailing behind her even though they passed the hallway that led to his quarters. He didn't speak, and she didn't care to ask why he followed. She opened her door and was about to close it behind herself when a powerful hand connected with the wood to prevent her from doing so. She scowled at Nik, meeting his eye for the first time since they left Faythe.

"Can we talk?" he said quietly.

Her heart cracked at the pain laced in his voice that she very seldom heard. The last time was when he lost his mother. He needed her then, and it was clear he needed her now. She couldn't turn her back on him no matter what friction lay between them.

She nodded once, stepping into her rooms and letting him follow her in. She went straight for the fire, which blazed eternally in harmless blue flames to take the chill off the winter night.

"You know, I wish it were me instead of her—"

"Don't say that." The prince cut her off in a low, dark tone.

She turned her head to look at him. His eyes were lit with coldness against the cobalt flames. "I would have healed quicker. Perhaps I could have outrun it faster—"

Again, her words were halted as Nik took a step toward her. "If anything happened to you down there..." His face softened, and the pain returned to it. He averted his gaze to the fire, slipping his hands into his pockets as he paced over to her. "There was a split second when Faythe disappeared and that monster along with her that I had a choice." The contours of his face were made all the more prominent in the flickering light, and his jaw twitched as he ground his teeth together. "Faythe was in immediate danger of her life, but there was no guaranteeing that creature was the only one of its kind down there. She means a great deal to me—she always will—and losing her would have broken me in a whole new way."

Tauria almost looked away from Nik as he poured his feelings for the human right out in front of her. Then the emerald of his eyes connected with something inside of her.

"But in that moment, I chose you, Tauria. For everything you've done for me, everything you are to me. I wanted desperately to aid Faythe, but I couldn't until I knew you were safe. I couldn't leave you. If I lost you, I don't think I would survive it. I wouldn't *want* to survive it."

She felt her heart stop. Never in her century of being close with Nik had she seen such a vulnerability within him. It broke her as much as it lifted her. She didn't know how to respond. As much as she wanted to be elated by his declaration, she didn't know what it meant.

She asked in barely a whisper, "What do you want from me, Nik?"

"I don't expect anything—"

"That's not what I asked. What do you *want?*"

"I want you to be safe."

Tauria took a step toward him. "I am safe. With you, I couldn't be safer."

Nik shook his head. "You're wrong."

She ground her teeth, feeling frustration rile her up at his contrasting words. The prince's face was pained. A plea lay in his features for her not to press the matter further. She couldn't understand him even after all this time of Nik pulling her in only to push her away when she came too close to breaking past his steel barrier.

It hurt right down to the depths of her being. It hurt that he kept his deepest feelings reserved.

Tauria held those sparkling emeralds that soothed her pain as much as they caused it. She couldn't push with him, or she risked losing him completely. Swallowing her disappointment, she straightened, her face falling into her mastered mask of cool indifference.

"I poured my heart out to you once, decades ago, and you left me alone in bed by morning as if I were just another one of your courtesans. I won't make that mistake again." She knew it was a low blow to open an old wound they had long since moved past, but it seemed relevant to remind the prince it was he who never saw anything romantic between them. He opened his mouth to counter, but she continued before he could. "Gods above, I couldn't bear anything happening to you either, Nik, but you don't get to put me down for seeking out the company of another when you've paraded your lovers around here and I've said nothing." She tried to keep her tone calm, but she couldn't help the bite in her voice after weeks of pent-up anger since their conversation about the Olmstone prince.

He flinched, and she could see he was deliberating whether to back down or match her indignation. Nik eventually sighed, and his expression softened.

"I don't want there to be any more bad feelings between us," he said. She hated the sinking disappointment, realizing it wasn't the response she was hoping for. "I'm sorry. It was none of my business, and I won't get in the way of you wanting to pursue other relationships again."

He may as well have torn her heart out instead, but Tauria didn't let it show. After all this time, she thought she would have hardened herself against the pain of the prince's rejection. But it hurt as much as the first time he made it clear he wanted nothing from her in that way.

Still, she treasured his friendship, and to protect that, she smiled with all the warmth she could muster to accompany her next words.

"Then there is nothing more to be said."

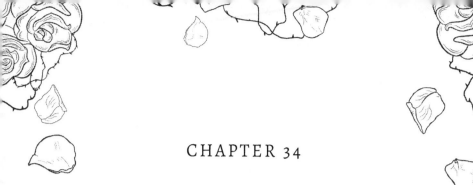

CHAPTER 34

Faythe

AFTER ANOTHER FIVE days' bed rest and a visit from a healer who was paid highly for their silence, Faythe almost felt normal again. The after-fever from the creature's venom was a deathlike experience in itself. She had barely left her bed and hardly stayed conscious for more than the time it took to be force-fed by Nik or Tauria. It was embarrassing to say the least, and she was more than glad when she found the strength to get up and dressed that morning. Her muscles still ached, but it was bearable.

She sat by the fire—perfectly ordinary glowing amber embers as she requested. Flames that could burn; a warmth that was real. Yet she was drawn to it for far more than that, transfixed by the dance of fire and ash as if it could take flight at any moment and free itself from the confines of its stone pit.

Her deep thought was broken by a knocking at her door. She breathed deeply as she tore her eyes away from the mesmerizing waltz of fire. Her voice croaked as she called for the person to enter, having little energy to move to the door. Faythe didn't turn to see who it was, figuring it was likely Tauria or her handmaidens.

Nik was ruled out as he rarely paused long enough after knocking before welcoming himself in.

"You look terrible."

She whipped her head around with a wince of pain to see Caius looking down at her. He held a smile, but his face fell in concern as he beheld the state of her. Faythe tried to stand, but the young guard motioned for her to stay seated and occupied the chair opposite.

"I've been better," she admitted.

His conflicted frown dropped her stomach, thinking perhaps he had news about her two friends. It had been long enough now for them to have returned to High Farrow. Just as the suspense grew too much for her to bare, Caius spoke.

"I went with Jakon and Marlowe to Galmire."

Faythe's eyebrows rose in surprise. She had never asked it of the fae guard and wouldn't have thought to, as it was a great risk should the king ever find out one of his own was party to the fugitives' escape. "Are they safe?" she asked quickly. She wanted the details, every last one, but wouldn't be able to take in anything else until it was confirmed.

Caius nodded, and she slumped back in relief, but he kept a grim look. An unease settled, and her pulse quickened as she waited for him to delve into the journey.

"Jakon and Marlowe are back in Farrowhold. They're safe," he began. "But I fear we've perhaps led those innocents to a worse fate if we don't do something." The guard looked pale, and it stirred a dark dread in Faythe.

"What do you mean?"

He leaned forward to brace his forearms on his knees, shaking his head as if he didn't know how to explain himself. "People are going missing in Galmire. The town is hardly half the population it used to be." He frowned into the fire as he tried to recall what he knew and make sense of it. "It gets worse. Those who do turn up... their bodies are left sloppily, always by the edge of town, and they say they're often drained of blood." His eyes met hers again, and Faythe fell utterly cold.

Her mind raced and even started to throb as she replayed his words. *Blood.* It was the one thing the creature down in the cave wanted most—had even gotten itself killed by dropping its attention in such a frenzy at the sight of it.

Her blood—*human* blood.

She didn't want to believe the pieces that fell almost too perfectly into place. She couldn't ignore the possibility, but she stored it in the back of her mind to look into later.

"Thank you, Caius. You didn't have to risk yourself to go with them." Her gratitude to him was endless.

The selfless guard smiled. "I wanted to."

Week's end marked a month and a half since the kings' meetings with Olmstone and Rhyenelle. Faythe tried not to keep count of the days, but in anticipation of what Reylan would do with the information he took from her—what the King of Rhyenelle would do in retaliation—she was on edge that any day now, one might move to strike first.

So far, it was quiet in all kingdoms. Nik had been keeping close watch on his father's movements and even dared to spy on private affairs he was not invited to in the secret passage overlooking the council chamber. Nothing alerted him to any plans to carry out the king's desire to conquer Rhyenelle. It was a relief, but Faythe knew better than to let hope settle that perhaps both kings had decided against such a brutal, ruthless act, knowing they could be treading water in the calm before the storm.

Walking through the gardens with the king's ward, she almost felt guilty as their footprints disturbed the peaceful sheet of purest white. The first snowfall of the season had brought the clouds to the ground, and she marveled over the thick, glittering crystal blanket. Innocent snowflakes flurried down in a beautiful cascade after the tantrum of ice and wind the previous night. Faythe deliberately left the hood of her cloak down to feel the cold nip her cheeks. The child in her longed to roll the icy sheets into compact spheres and make a snow creature. Even beyond childhood, it was something she and Jakon had found laughter and joy in. She smiled at her memories, which seemed so distant, the serenely quiet and colorless surroundings almost taking her away from the troubles that plagued her mind. Her once carefree, mundane life was now packed with horror and uncertainty in a court of nightmares.

"I really wish you could attend the Yulemas Ball. It will be deliriously dull without you." Tauria's voice cut through the peaceful silence.

Faythe rolled her eyes at the ward. She didn't let it show that she was glad for not being permitted to attend the extravagant event in three weeks' time given her human heritage. It was a grand ball of splendor and prestige she was far too lowly on the social hierarchy to be granted an invite to. Faythe was relieved more than insulted to be spared a night of distasteful slander and judgmental stares.

"You've survived plenty of them just fine without me."

"I don't want to just *survive* them anymore. You might have actually brought some enjoyment to the night."

Faythe would have appreciated the flattery if it weren't completely ridiculous and exaggerated. She had other plans anyway. While she had been specifically warned not to leave the castle, as most of the guards would be granted leave for the event, she had little intention of abiding by the king's rules. She decided weeks ago she would sneak out to the outer town to spend Yulemas on the hills with Jakon and Marlowe, where she'd spent it every other year.

Faythe and Tauria headed to the stables to seek out the warmth within. The ward rubbed her gloved hands together as she went over to one of the brown mares. Faythe shuddered for heat too now the snow had melted and her wet face was starting to grow numb. She looked around the horses, marveling at their beauty while she blew into her cupped hands in an attempt to warm her cheeks.

Then she dropped her arms, the ice that froze her having nothing to do with the weather, as she caught a glimpse of the horse occupying the end stall. Its black beauty and stark, contrasting glacier-blue eyes were like no other she'd seen before. There was no mistaking the mare, and she knew it was an impossible coincidence, a chance in a million, for there to be a horse identical to Kali here.

She slowly willed herself to walk toward the beast, her suspicions only confirmed when the horse stared unflinching at her the whole way. Even though it was foolish, she couldn't help but think the mare recognized her too. It bowed its head low when she stood in front of its stable, and Faythe raised a hand to stroke her muzzle.

"She's a beauty," Tauria admired as she came up beside her.

Snapping out of her reeling thoughts, Faythe turned to Tauria. The ward appeared oblivious to who owned the midnight mare. At the thought of Reylan, she instantly felt anxious, sick to her stomach.

Why would the Rhyenelle general return?

Every motion set her on edge as Faythe walked the halls of the castle. Tauria left her to go to her own rooms, seeking warmth by the fire and wanting to change out of her damp dress from being outdoors. Faythe couldn't feel the cold anymore in her nervous state. She wasn't sure why she was so rigid at the prospect of running into Reylan at any given turn. Perhaps it was the thought that whatever his intentions were for being here, they were likely not in good faith. Not with the threat the King of High Farrow posed to his own kingdom.

She was about to head back to her own rooms after a futile

effort to scout for him, beginning to believe maybe he wasn't in the castle after all. Then she halted abruptly in the wide hallway, almost jumping out of her skin, when the throne room doors were loudly hauled open.

The silver-white of Reylan's hair was the first thing to catch her attention. The sight gave her the conflicted emotion of thrill laced with fear. She tuned in to the end of his conversation with the king who followed him out.

"I look forward to seeing the results of your labor, General. I'm glad you decided to take up my offer even as a temporary position," King Orlon finished.

Her eyes locked on their joined forearms, incredulous.

"It's my pleasure, Your Majesty. I hope I can make a difference in High Farrow. We are allies after all." With this, Reylan turned to fix his sapphire orbs directly on Faythe. A sharp tremor ran through her at their knowing gleam. When the king's eyes followed, they dropped the handshake, and he turned to her.

"Ah, Lady Faythe, I was rather hoping to catch you. Will you join me?" Orlon's tone was unnaturally tame and even held a forced kindness as he addressed her in front of the general. He held out an arm, silently beckoning her to enter the throne room behind him.

Faythe paled at his deadly stare, knowing the threat of his wrath if she declined. So, nodding sweetly, she gave a small bow of her head, much to her reluctance, before strolling up to the pair and making her way inside. Reylan's eyes never left her, and she tried not to stare back in response. She had so many questions for him, but right now, she had to dine with a demon.

When she was fully inside the great hall, she didn't immediately turn upon hearing the large doors groan shut once again. The king passed by her and twisted around just before the dais.

"I want you to keep a close eye on him," he said plainly but quietly. He didn't have to clarify who he referred to, casting a look behind her as if the general were still behind the doors.

"You don't trust him, Your Majesty?"

His eyes narrowed at the ghost of Reylan's presence, and he raised his chin in contemplation. "Why should Agalhor's best and most loyal general leave him if they face threats, as you say?"

Faythe trembled, realizing this was as much an interrogation as it was a command to spy on Reylan. Nevertheless, she stood firm. "Perhaps there turned out to be no threat after all."

The king hummed, far from convinced. "I'll be having his every move watched, and I expect you to get close enough to him to know his every thought too. I don't care what it takes." It was a command, and she didn't fail to pick up on the hidden meaning. It wasn't enough for her to be the king's executioner or spymaster; he saw an opportunity to degrade her further by expecting her to be his courtesan too.

Her fingers twitched, but she fought the urge to clench her fists in fury at the suggestion. Her teeth ground together instead, and it took all her willpower to force a nod in understanding and agreement. It still boiled her blood to have the king suggest she be used in such a way, as if no part of her remained her own anymore.

She would never let that happen.

Faythe stood outside her rooms after her short meeting with the king, staring directly at the door opposite. She didn't even know if Reylan occupied the same chambers as his last visit now his position was to be extended in the castle, yet she couldn't bring herself to retire for the evening until she found out. She was glad there was no one around to notice her nervous pacing as she'd been deliberating knocking for the past five minutes.

Without giving herself a chance to back out, she stormed the short distance and rapped twice upon the door. Her heart thundered. She wanted to take it back, silently praying no one would answer.

Luck wasn't in her favor.

A heartbeat later, the door swung open, and Reylan wore a smirk as he stepped forward, crossed his arms, and leaned casually against the frame. "I was wondering how long you would stand out here for," he said with a wicked grin. "You far surpassed my expectations."

She only gaped, caught between wanting to abandon the confrontation completely and whack the smug look off his face. "I told you not to come back to High Farrow," she hissed with all the intimidation of a mouse in the face of the white lion.

"Unfortunately, I don't take orders from you," he said dismissively.

She itched to respond in the best way she knew how. Her hand curled around the phantom hilt of her sword, and she longed to swing it at the general in front of her. "I could tell the king everything."

His eyes danced in challenge. "You could. I would love to watch you explain *how* I came to the knowledge of the kings' plans."

She couldn't out him without exposing herself and what she did to Varlas to obtain the information.

"What are you doing here, Reylan?" she demanded with no small amount of accusation.

His head tilted in amusement. "Now who's the suspicious one? A rose is just a rose, Faythe."

She didn't react to his regurgitation of her own words. She lifted her chin instead, determined not to yield victory. "A rose is too pretty for you. You're more like a blossomless thornbush," she sneered.

His smile grew wider. "Because you think I'm dangerous?"

"Because you're a prick."

He straightened and stepped forward so fast she stumbled all the way back until she met the cold wood of her own door. When he stopped, she saw the flash of his extended canines right before he leaned in close and let his breath caress her neck. His hand beside her head trapped her. There were only two reasons for a fae to bare their fangs: in threat, or in lust.

Her throat bobbed, turning bone-dry at knowing it could only be a deadly warning. She was too frozen in shock to think or move. Her pulse became a prominent throb in the veins his teeth would puncture. His mouth never made the connection, but the lingering threat rattled the heart in her chest, and his proximity was electrifying.

"It would be so easy to end you," he said quietly in a deep, gravelly tone. Faythe shivered, but not in fear. "So many ways your life could be gone in less than a second." The vibrations from each word rippled over her skin, and she almost forgot where she was. Her fingers flexed and clenched against the wood as if it were a material that could be grasped in response to the tension flushing her body.

Faythe felt the hum of his touch just before his fingers grazed over her neck above her collarbone, where she knew the unruly scar of her bite wound from the foul beast would remain a permanent marking.

"Who did this to you?" His voice turned surprisingly dark, and she thought she detected anger in it. But she could barely register his words when all she could think about was the cool gap that remained between them and how she didn't want it to exist.

Her heart beat wildly, and she tilted her head subconsciously, feeling his breath become hotter, his mouth closer. She *wanted* him make contact. Her blood roared, eyes almost falling closed.

But then something snapped her sense, and she internally recoiled in horror. Bracing her hands on his solid chest, she pushed with everything she had, and Reylan stepped back, though she knew it wasn't from any feat of strength on her part. He wasn't grinning anymore as he stared back at her, seeming to return to his own right mind. His gaze held shock as he took a step away from her.

"Stay out of my way," she hissed, feeling the fury rise in her with the warning. "You're not here to play general to a foreign kingdom, one you can't even stand to be in. You're up to something, and I don't care what happens to me—I won't hesitate to turn you in if I find reason." Not giving him a chance to belittle her statement or authority, she spun away from him, throwing her door open and slamming it shut behind her.

Her pulse raced, and her thoughts were erratic. She despised more than anything that she'd allowed herself to be foolishly affected by him like some weak, flustered girl! It angered her, bewildered her, but most of all…it terrified her. Not because she feared him, but because she *enjoyed* the completely new, unexplainable thrill of such a dangerous desire.

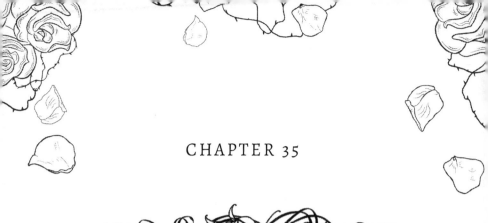

CHAPTER 35

Faythe

T HE FOLLOWING MORNING, Faythe awoke earlier than usual without getting much sleep. She cursed Reylan for being the annoying force that rattled her thoughts too much to get any decent rest. Knowing he was a few steps across the hall, she dressed in her fighting suit and headed straight for the training room to release the frustration and anger he'd succeeded in riling up. What made it worse was that he'd barely even tried to invoke such a reaction.

Nik and Tauria joined her a little later, and she was grateful for a sparring partner to use as moving target practice. She faced off with the ward while the prince observed casually from the side of the large, raised training ring. They used long staffs as Tauria's weapon of choice, and Faythe relished the opportunity to advance her skills and knowledge of the unusual tools of attack and defense. Every time the two females came down here, their time was spent mostly on teaching as Tauria carefully demonstrated her maneuvers and balance with the long stick of wood. Faythe had gotten enough practice during her months in the castle that she was actually becoming quite good at it.

She threw everything she had into the session, releasing all her indignation, and even had Tauria retreating instead for once. When the ward was forced off the slightly elevated platform, Faythe stopped, panting heavily. Even Tauria looked out of breath, but not nearly as much as she. In a castle full of fae, Faythe was starting to hate the physical inferiority that came with being human.

"What's got you so worked up this morning?" Tauria commented with a hint of concern.

Faythe turned away from her, walking back into the center and taking up stance to start again. "Nothing," she muttered through a long breath of exertion.

Tauria didn't move, much to her irritation. Her body protested, but her mind was still wild with thoughts, and she felt the burning need to release the pent-up emotions through the swinging of *something*.

"Perhaps you should take a break," Nik chimed in knowingly. He had been on the receiving end of her sword many times when she was unhinged in anger. She winced at the memories, not proud of herself for those outbursts, and took a few calming breaths. Nik was right. Running her energy into the ground wouldn't do her any favors.

"Humans and their erratic emotions…"

At the voice that joined them in the room, Faythe managed all of five seconds before her fire was sparked again. She had yet to even glimpse the general.

"Or is that just you, Faythe?"

She didn't need to move as he came to stand next to Nik and Tauria in front of her with a crooked, taunting smile. She glared at him with the force of her anger as if it could turn him to ash where he stood.

Nik shifted at the tension, his eyes darting between her and Reylan. "What are you doing here?" he asked the general—and he didn't mean in the training room.

Reylan turned to him. "I think you know why I'm here."

The prince's eyes narrowed as he folded his arms. "Are you on orders from Agalhor?"

She knew they held some kind of friendship. It was clear from the way they engaged at the kings' meetings. However, she wasn't confident it was strong enough for Nik to trust him so easily with the rising conflict between their kingdoms.

"I'm not your enemy, Nik. We've fought side by side in battle against those we should all be focusing our attention on." He spoke to the prince as both a commander and a friend. "I'll be damned if I do nothing to prevent us from standing on opposite sides instead." Reylan was fierce in his words, and her dislike for him wavered slightly in appreciation that his loyalty wasn't mindless to the king he served.

The prince nodded in agreement and understanding. They had a common goal of trying to stop the Kings of High Farrow and Olmstone in their quest for power. She knew it would be hard for Nik to silently work against his own father. It frustrated her that all of this could be avoided were Nik on the throne instead.

With their concerns addressed, Reylan turned his attention to Faythe once again. His smile was goading as he drew his sword. She watched the dark gray blade sing free from its scabbard. Niltain steel. It shouldn't be surprising considering the Niltain Isles lay within Rhyenelle. In fact, she was sure it was more unusual that she owned such a precious metal.

"What are you doing?" She frowned in annoyance as he stepped up and into the ring.

"Wood or steel?"

Her teeth ground as he got closer. "You really want to face off against me right now?"

He grinned wildly. "Why so angry, Faythe?"

It was deliberate; he was trying to rouse a reaction. It worked, and she met Tauria's eye at the same time as she tossed the staff she held back to her. Tauria caught it effortlessly. Nik was already holding Lumarias. He copied her, and Faythe's hand molded around the hilt as she caught it, the sword becoming an extension of her own arm. She flexed it in her wrist, savoring the feel as it awakened a dormant passion, rattled her senses, and honed her mind for combat.

Now, it was her turn to smile with feline delight as she felt her confidence rise with each twist of her blade.

"Are you sure this is a good idea?" Nik said warily from the sidelines.

Faythe's grin was arrogant. "Don't worry—I won't go too hard on him."

She wasn't really foolish enough to think she would win in a sparring match against a centuries-old fae war general. Her pleasure lay in shaking the feathers of the Phoenix.

Reylan barked a laugh. "I've taken down fae thrice your size with little effort."

"I don't doubt it. Though you misjudge my flaws, General."

"You can't get inside my head."

"Are you afraid it'll even the playing field? Or perhaps besting those who are physically inferior is what inflates your ego so much."

His eyes danced in amusement. "All right, I'll let you in. Just the surface."

She didn't let her triumph show as she stepped into a defensive position. Reylan assessed her from head to toe. She thought it was to size her up as the opposition, but a dark look of recognition and then appreciation crossed his face before he composed himself. That was when she realized exactly what had caught his attention.

"How does a human from High Farrow come to possess fae fighting attire from Rhyenelle?" he pondered curiously.

Though he didn't expect an answer, she said, "It was a gift." Not entirely a lie, but she had fully paid her friend Ferris back for the garment after she fought in the notorious underworld of the Cave.

She waited for him to mock her, to say she wasn't worthy of it.

"It suits you," he said, and she was surprised at the sincerity in his words. "Though it's a little outdated. If you win, perhaps I'll see to it you get an upgrade to the latest model."

She didn't let it curb her focus. Instead, she angled her blade in silent invitation for a dance of swords. He didn't take a counter stance, as if he thought he didn't need to brace himself against her. He was about to be proven *very* wrong.

She moved fast. Seeing his intention to step out of her way, she switched her maneuver at the last second. Reylan caught her blade with his own before it could tear the flesh of his thigh, and the sound of kissing steel echoed through the training hall. The vibrations of the blow crawled delightfully up Faythe's arms, and she smiled deviously at his raised eyebrows.

Retreating, she twisted Lumarias once before angling it again in a soundless taunt.

Reylan looked quietly taken aback by her swiftness. She almost dared to believe it was approval in his eyes.

"Okay, Faythe, I see you."

She raised her chin, taking a breath to channel deeper and deeper into the well of lethal tranquility that focused her in combat. On her exhale, she said, "Good. Now, I want you to hear me."

Faythe became spellbound by sapphire orbs, lost in the stormy sea as she captured Reylan's premeditated movements. She struck again and again, forcing him into his defensive stance while she shot out a round of offense attacks. She knew he could switch the order anytime he liked, but he allowed her to lead.

He was impossibly fast. It took every drop of mental focus to strike as quickly as he could deflect. Faythe reveled in the challenge, not registering the rising burn in her lungs nor the pulsing in her head as they darted around the sparring ring. She twisted, thrusting her sword forward. It would have gone straight through his abdomen, but Reylan's blade clanged loudly against it, batting it out of the way before it could. Faythe backed up a step to regroup, panting hard. They circled each other slowly. It riled her to no end that while she used significant physical energy, Reylan remained unfazed by the exercise.

"If you want me to go easy on you, just ask," he said to vex her, as if reading her thoughts.

She rolled her shoulders back, already stiff and sore from the parry of steel. "I'd rather you struck me than insulted me like that."

His lips curled up, but he gave her a slight nod of respect, and she felt strangely proud that it came from a highly regarded fae general. Then she remembered that general was also an arrogant, stuck-up ass.

In her short pause, she failed to catch Reylan's intention to move first. She ducked, narrowly avoiding the blur of steel over her head. But his second maneuver was too quick, and she didn't hold the connection to his mind any longer. Before she could turn and reposition, he was behind her in a heartbeat, his sword resting horizontally against her throat. The cool breath of metal was a chilling warning that one swipe of pressure would spell her end.

In conflict with his actions, however, the warmth of Reylan's body against her back felt like a force of safety. His hand encased her forearm, pinning it across her abdomen so she had no way out of the compromised position. The threat of his sword became insignificant as her mind reeled at the stance, at his calloused fingers over her soft skin.

She was broken from her trance when he stepped away from her abruptly, the ghost of his embrace sending a chill down every notch of her spine, snapping her back to her senses. Her cheeks flamed, and she whirled to him with a deadly glare, anger flaring. Though, admittedly, it was more at herself than at Reylan, for allowing herself to be distracted like a novice.

"Had enough yet?" he drawled, bored.

Her hand tightened around the hilt of Lumarias, and he noted the response, smirking down at her painfully clenched fist.

"Faythe, maybe it's time to—" Nik didn't get a chance to finish his sentence when the clash of swords became a melody in the room once again.

Faythe didn't drop eye contact and pushed herself harder than she had in months. Reylan looked just as focused as she was, and it brought her slight satisfaction knowing he at least had to use *some* effort against her. Her pulse raced and blood pumped faster with every harsh vibration of her sword hitting its target, cancelling out everything else around her. The room became an indistinguishable blur, until she could see nothing but sapphire and steel.

Their blades locked inches from her face, and Reylan smiled down at her in amusement. "Not bad...for a human girl."

Her breathing was ragged, each inhale like spears of ice down her throat. Clenching her teeth in frustration at the comment, she pushed off from his blade with everything she had and didn't pause for a second before moving on instinct, desperate to wipe the victorious look from his face. Not with words, but with one landed strike of her sword.

She wouldn't feel guilty for it; he would heal before the day was up. She couldn't explain what made the desire so prominent in that moment, as if she had something to prove to him.

"Stop," he said, his voice a hard command.

Faythe didn't. She couldn't. It sang in her veins to continue even if it wore her out completely. And soon, it would. Her bones ached, but it was her mind that throbbed worse, almost blinding her. It screamed at her to stop as much as it compelled her to push on.

Reylan backed up a long step, and she was about to lunge forward with another attack when her blade met another's in the ring. There was nothing kind on her face when she snapped toward the person who stopped her, about to direct her unhinged rage at them until the familiar emerald eyes brought her world back into focus.

She breathed hard, and everything caught up with her all at once. Her head pounded sickeningly, and she had to drop to her knees, not trusting her stability now the urge of combat had dwindled. She felt Nik kneel with her. He took Lumarias gently from her grip and set it on the ground.

Then Reylan approached, his large form casting a shadow over her. "Even the best warriors know when it's time to stop fighting," he said, but there was no lecture in the words. "Recognize your limits, learn to disperse your energy, or you'll burn yourself out before you last five minutes on a battlefield."

She raised her eyes to him and found him staring down at her intently, assessing her. To know he wouldn't count her out completely in the face of battle made her humbly proud. And grateful Reylan chose not to condescend her in sharing his commander's advice.

It was then she realized all his taunting and teasing about her mortality was really a test to see if she would submit…or rise above it.

"Now, your sword skills are impressive, I'll give you that," he went on casually, letting one last longing look linger. She thought she detected curiosity tied with awe. Reylan turned away before she saw any more of the rare softer side he didn't like others to know he harbored. "Take a moment to gather yourself. Then let's work on those lackluster close defense skills."

CHAPTER 36

Faythe

B Y NIGHTFALL, FAYTHE couldn't sleep. It wasn't because of the Rhyenelle general this time. Instead, a certain unearthly Spirit dwelled on her mind.

She planned to revisit the cave below the castle with Nik and Tauria to find the ruin, and now she was fully well again, there was no reason to delay. They had made arrangements to meet by midnight tomorrow, fully equipped and armed should they meet any other ghastly, unexpected creatures.

Yet with the discovery of the King of High Farrow seeking out the Riscillius she needed for the Spirit Temples, Faythe felt filled with dread. They could be aiding the king's cause if she found Aurialis's ruin. Perhaps it was lost even to the king, and he had no idea it lay beneath his very feet. Whatever power it held, it could be what they needed to gain the upper hand and follow through on their plans for war.

She didn't make it to the underground labyrinth that led to the outer town without being completely undetected, but she used her ability brazenly to withdraw the short-term memory of the odd single guard who caught her. Doing this, she was able to divert them before they even realized she was there at all. Even though it worked with Varlas, it was a risk, and one she wasn't entirely certain she would succeed in taking. But so far, none had made any move to come after her. All she could do was pray to the Spirits it stayed that way—at least until she made it back.

In the outer town, she was about to pass the hut without a thought, but she felt the quiet beckoning to visit an old friend and found herself compelled to make a swift stop at the abandoned structure.

The hut was somber in its silence and lonely in its emptiness. It brought her both joy and sadness to reminisce in the confines of the small space she once shared with Jakon. At the thought of her friend, and Marlowe too, her heart ached. She longed to see them and find out about their journey to Galmire. It would have to wait, as she was well into the unsociable hours of the night.

The back door into the bedroom creaked loudly on its hinges. The bare cots were a sorry sight robbed of all personal possessions. Faythe was glad her friends had moved to a more comfortable living space, but it was bittersweet to find her home of ten years neglected.

She sat on her old bed, finding the mattress far more uneven and uncomfortable than she remembered. She simply stared at the empty one opposite, smiling sadly as she pictured the ghost of Jakon's long form hanging half-off the too-small bed, deep in slumber. The more she imagined it, the more vivid it became, and she could almost hear his soft snores in the dead silence.

She was snapped out of her memories when the front door to the hut groaned open slowly. Faythe got to her feet, heart racing, and pressed herself against the wall next to the bedroom door. She strained her ears, only making out that the intruder walked casually around the front room, making no effort to be stealthy. Drawing Lumarias slowly, silently, Faythe took one long breath to brace herself then barged through the bedroom door with unfaltering confidence to face the nighttime bandit.

It was not the burly, hooded thief she was expecting. Rather, the bandit's hair rivaled the luminance of a full moon, and his eyes sparkled like the night sky as they bore into her, unfazed by her outburst. She still held her blade poised at the sight of Reylan— from shock or relief, likely both.

"What in the rutting damn are you doing here?" she demanded, finally lowering her blade.

"I could ask you the same thing," was all he said as he scanned the small hut.

She wanted to be angry with him for intruding, for thinking it was okay to follow her in the first place, but the emotion failed her as she took in their surroundings. "This was my home," she admitted quietly, not sure why she felt the need to explain.

Reylan looked at her with curiosity, and she had to avert her gaze in slight embarrassment. "You lived alone?" he asked.

She shook her head. "My friend, Jakon—he lived with me here."

The general took a few steps around the place, picking up discarded items that held no personal value. "You were together?" Again, his statement held a question as he left it open for her to correct.

"Not in the way you think."

She saw him hesitate before he continued. "Where is he now?"

Feeling no need to hide anything from him, she continued to oblige. "Safe. He lives on the east side of town with my friend, Marlowe." She couldn't fathom why it interested him in the slightest, but Reylan seemed deep in thought as he took everything in.

She watched him move around the hut, his tall form eclipsing the place. Then he hit with the question that made her flinch.

"What happened to your mother?" His eyes met hers, and for a split second, she thought she saw sadness in them.

"I think Valgard took her." It was all she could offer as she didn't truly know how her mother met her end after that day in the forest.

"I'm sorry." The sincerity in his voice made him sound as if he wasn't only sorry for her loss, but for his own.

"Me too."

For a rare moment, she found herself and the general on mutual ground. She connected with him and embraced the kindness in place of his hostility.

"You didn't really think you could sneak out of a city crawling with royal fae guards unnoticed, did you? Your ability is impressive, but you could do with a bit more practice at wiping memory." A small, teasing smile turned up one corner of his mouth when Reylan looked at her. "We should thank the Spirits it actually worked on Varlas. Half the guards you tried to elude were on their way to rat you out before I stopped them."

Faythe's cheeks flamed. She saved herself the embarrassment of admitting she really did believe she was stealthy and competent enough in getting here. Though she was irked not to be alone in her quest, she reluctantly had the general to thank, or she would be in deep waters with unwanted questions from the king by morning were it not for his influence. She realized the general likely outranked all the guards in the castle.

Crossing her arms, she asked, "What exactly are you doing in High Farrow?" Not in accusation, but because she genuinely wondered what his intentions were and how he thought his presence here could help.

His shoulders shifted. "Keep your friends close, and your enemies closer."

Faythe rolled her eyes at the vague response.

"What are *you* doing wandering the town in the middle of the night?"

She didn't answer immediately. The general knew everything about the king's plan, but he knew nothing of the Spirit entity who may be an even greater threat than any man or fae on the land.

"I, uh…I have somewhere to be," she said lamely, turning up blank on convincing excuses. Even the truth was likely to be taken as a lie if she tried to explain the absurdity of what she set out to do that night.

Reylan gave her a look that told her he wasn't going to let it go.

Faythe huffed with mild humor. "Follow me if you want. It seems to be your favorite sport." Pushing past him, she exited the hut and joined the shadows.

It wasn't a surprise when she felt Reylan close behind her in the alley. She didn't glance back at him as she said, "I hope you're good with the strange and impossible."

Faythe waited by the waterfall, watching the yucolites chase each other in an eternal dance. She had warned Reylan multiple times of the horrors he might face upon entering the woods and figured the general had many of those from his time in battle for the Spirit of Life to call upon. She shuddered to think what the worst of them would be, but there was no dissuading him from passing through.

She heard his deliberately loud footsteps behind her and turned to him. His face was blank. Unreadable. It scared her more than she thought it would.

"Everything okay?" It was a pathetic question, and not one she really expected an answer to.

His sapphire eyes bore into her, and she swallowed hard at the vacancy in them. Ghostly, haunted, they locked on her for a few painfully long seconds.

Then he looked away, face falling into his usual steely indifference as he said, "Whatever you have to show me, it'd better be worth it."

Faythe huffed, relaxing from the rigid posture his disturbed expression had caused. A hint of a smile tugged at her lips as she turned and started the walk through the tree line in the opposite direction.

"You didn't have to come," she drawled. "In fact, you weren't even invited."

The crunch of his footsteps against the woodland floor caught up as he fell into step beside her. "The streets aren't a safe place for a young woman to be alone at such an hour."

"If you're looking for damsels to save, General, you'll be greatly disappointed tonight."

"You never seem to disappoint." It wasn't a compliment. Rather, he was stating the obvious that she was a walking contradiction and a magnet for danger.

When Faythe stepped into the temple glade, she stopped to turn to him. "Let's keep one thing clear between us. Our goals align to keep our kingdoms from destroying each other, but that's where it ends. We're not friends. You don't have to pretend as if you care for my well-being."

Confliction crossed his face, but it was gone a second later, and he straightened, his powerful arms crossing over his chest. "You still don't trust me?"

She laughed sarcastically. "You stripped me of my ability and used it against me. I trust your intentions are true, but I'm not a fool to believe you won't turn on us all when the time comes."

"It sounds as if you're already preparing for a war."

"Aren't we all, in one way or another?"

He was silent in quiet contemplation for a few seconds, and she was about to continue the walk to the temple when he spoke again. "And if the time does come, where do you stand?"

The question terrified her because she could see in his eye that somehow, he knew she would be conflicted in her answer before he even asked. High Farrow was her home, her place of birth, but she wasn't willing to fight mindlessly for a ruler who was wrong.

"I hope to stand on the right side," she said. "It doesn't have only one color or house emblem, nor a single race or gender. It can be made up of the most unexpected array of those things, all brought together with a common goal."

The answer seemed to satisfy him enough, and Faythe saw the steely edges of his expression soften slightly. Without another word, she stalked to the temple, drawing Lumarias so she could use the Riscillius. Before Reylan could ask, she held her sword out to him and at seeing his cocked eyebrow bounded up the steps to draw the first symbol with the chalk she'd brought along. She bit her lip to suppress a giggle when she turned back to the sight of the great general squinting awkwardly through the small rock.

"How in the Spirit's name did you come across this?" he asked, passing the sword back to her.

Looking through the pommel, she said, "It's a long story." And once again, she rushed to finish the last sketch before the symbol disappeared from memory.

The doors groaned inward a fraction after a short pause, and she looked to Reylan expectantly. When he didn't immediately move, she jerked her head toward the stone doors.

"You can't very well expect me to push them open while you stand pretty."

While he was here, she may as well make use of his strength.

Reylan gave her a faint scowl, and she couldn't hide her light amusement this time. He wordlessly stepped forward, pushing the doors in with little strain. She didn't pay him any attention as she passed to go inside, but now she was here, she was starting to lose her nerve.

"Dare I ask, what is this place, and why are we here?" Reylan commented, scanning the open temple with an edge of caution.

She too looked around, growing bored of the recurring sight. "It's the Light Temple," she answered simply as if it were a mere market stall. "I happen to have dealings with the great Spirit of Life."

The general looked at her as if she'd lost her mind. She smirked at his response. It was exactly what she expected, and she didn't blame him for thinking it insane. Little did he know, she had barely scraped the surface of the impossible yet.

Faythe stepped into the dreaded pool of light and held the pommel of her sword firm between both hands until the beam shot through the Riscillius.

"What are you doing?" Reylan stepped closer. Before he could decide whether to enter the sunlit circle, she gave a crooked smile.

"See you on the other side."

The light met its mirrored stone target, and the glare of its encasing cast out the image of the general's wide-eyed look. Faythe lowered her sword and used it to prop herself up casually as she waited for the Spirit to appear.

But it was not Aurialis who materialized to greet her this time.

Faythe straightened instantly, staring in shock at the glowing form that appeared in front of her. She trembled as instead of the white-haired beauty…

Her mother stood before her with a warm smile.

"Is it really you?" she asked in disbelief, her voice barely more than a whisper.

Her mother's ghost nodded, and a small sound left Faythe's lips. "My dear girl," she said sadly. "We don't have long."

Faythe had so many questions, so many things she wanted to tell her, and so many words that had been left unspoken since the day her mother was cruelly taken. All of it circled in her mind at once, and she almost swayed with the surge of thought.

"I'm so proud of the woman you've become," her mother continued.

A silent tear rolled down Faythe's cheek. "I don't know what I'm doing," she admitted, overwhelmed with emotion and wishing so desperately to release all the worries she would have brought to her mother over the years if she were still alive.

Her mother stepped forward, and it took everything in Faythe not to fall into the arms of her ghost. "You're exactly where you need to be," she reassured her softly.

Faythe whimpered. "I miss you so much… I'm so sorry—"

"You have nothing to be sorry for. I was wrong. I should never have kept you from your destiny. The world needs you, Faythe, but you are not alone. Never alone."

Faythe shook her head. "I can't save anyone."

"I'm sorry this fate falls on you. I tried to prevent it, but I fear I only hurt you more. I denied you the chance to know the other half of your lineage. I will never forgive myself for the relationship you lost. Both of you."

Faythe's stomach dropped at the mention. "My father?" she breathed, unable to brace herself for the knowledge she was about to receive.

Her mother's face fell. "He is good and honorable, and we loved each other fiercely. It was my own selfishness and misjudgment that tore us apart and ultimately ruined the bond you could have had. My only wish here in the Afterlife is to see you have a chance to rebuild it now."

Faythe's breaths came harder at the new information. He was alive, that much was confirmed, and it calmed a raging, gut-wrenching thought that perhaps he was the opposite of how her mother described him.

"Where is he?" she dared to ask.

The ghost smiled. "You may have been born in High Farrow, but you will always fly with the Phoenix."

Faythe frowned deeply, about to question the riddle. She didn't get the chance though as her mother continued.

"I wish we had more time, Faythe. You came here because you have doubts about the Spirit of Life, as did I. I'm here to tell you she is on our side. Trust her guidance as much as you trust those closest to you. Find the temple ruin."

Her mother's form started to dissipate into the light behind. Faythe's panic surged.

"Wait! That's not enough time!" she pleaded, desperate for even a few seconds longer with her.

"I am always with you. Do not be afraid."

"I am afraid," she choked out through the painful tightness in her throat.

Her mother smiled sadly. "You are brave, Faythe."

With those last echoing words, her image faded.

And faded.

And was gone.

A tear slid down Faythe's cheek without a blink. She kept her eyes fixed on where her mother stood, her mind clinging to the vision even once she was gone completely. Faythe imagined her soft features, her brown, wavy hair, her slim figure. Even when the circle of light fell and her eyes burned in the contrasting dark, Faythe didn't blink.

Gold eyes turned to the deepest blue. Reylan stared back with shock and concern outside of Aurialis's symbol. But Faythe wasn't present, didn't even register the general taking wordless, tentative steps toward her. She was her nine-year-old self again. Around her was not the gray stone walls of the temple; Faythe was in a forest so dark and frightening. Silence filled her mind. Silence in anticipation of her mother's scream. She had been taken from Faythe then just as she was now.

Before that chilling sound she would never forget could pierce through her mind...

Calloused palms took her face, and Faythe snapped her head up.

"What happened, Faythe?" Reylan's voice came into focus, his expression alarmed by whatever he read scanning every inch of her face.

Faythe stumbled back a step, and his hands fell. She held in her whimper at being brought back to her real surroundings. Her hand subconsciously rubbed her chest at the tightening pain that constricted her, as though the seams of an old, deep wound were straining to burst with a new wave of world-shattering grief.

It made it real. Seeing her mother. She was in the Afterlife. It was both the liberating closure she so desperately needed and an agonizing realization. There had been a hideous, hopeful part of Faythe that believed in a chance her mother was alive, having never seen her death—never in the final sense of the word.

While trying to gather the words to respond to Reylan, she turned around, and upon spying the podium behind him, she slowly walked toward it. Trembling fingers came up to graze the hollow shape of the ruin she was tasked with finding. Reylan followed but said nothing as he observed her.

She took a deep breath. In through her nose, and out through her mouth. She repeated the motion until she felt collected enough to explain what she could to the general who waited patiently.

"She's gone." Faythe's brow pinched together. "She's really gone."

Somehow, Reylan knew exactly who she meant. "You saw your mother," he said, so tenderly soft.

All she could muster was a tight nod, unable to look at him while she fixed her eyes on the sad, dark stone, focusing on its gritty texture under her fingers to distract from the tears she fought against. Reylan moved around the podium, and Faythe wiped her wet cheeks. He stopped behind her, and she felt his hand gently come to rest on her shoulder. She felt the touch beneath her skin like a pulse of strength and comfort. He said nothing. He didn't need to. She appreciated his silent consolation—savored it. And with a new breath, she straightened, determination returning to her for what she needed to do.

Reylan's hand left her as she turned to him. "You should walk away now, save yourself from becoming tangled in a web of answerless questions, impossible notions, and dangerous propositions," she warned. Yet she knew. Even before his mouth curled with faint humor, she knew his answer.

"I've faced worse monsters, Faythe," he said with an unexpected but soothing warmth. "Let me help with yours."

CHAPTER 37

Faythe

THE THREE FRIENDS stood armed to the teeth within the hidden alcove in the library. Though two of them had the added advantage of immortal senses, Faythe tried not to see herself as the weaker in comparison.

They waited patiently as there was only one last-minute addition to the ensemble to arrive. Reylan had been adamant to know everything, and whether she trusted him or not, she could only see the advantage of informing him about everything she knew of the Spirits and ruins thus far in case he could add any insight. He couldn't, and she had confused him more than educated him on the matter. Still, he listened, focused and attentive, and not once did he condescend or doubt any of her claims. It was refreshing to speak so freely without judgment or question, and she actually treasured the few tender hours they spent on the front steps of the temple, forgetful of time, fear, and worry. There was only one fact that remained confined in her mind as even she was still uncertain of what it meant: that she was an Heir of Marvellas.

Reylan's silver-white hair was like a beacon as she spotted him approaching down the dark hall. There was no dissuading him from accompanying them to the forgotten cave below the castle when she told him where they planned to go looking for the temple ruin. Especially once she mentioned it was once home to a mutated, ghastly creature they'd narrowly escaped. She trembled where she stood to think they could face another like it tonight. But they were ready this time, with both wits and steel.

He came to a stop before them, acknowledging Nik and Tauria but letting his gaze linger on Faythe, offering the most subtle reassurance in the faint dip of his head. He read her emotions so easily it was unnerving, yet she thought she had done a commendable job of maintaining a hardened exterior to mask her great fear.

"All right, demon slayers united. Let's go," Nik said, stealing her attention. When she twisted to him, he was already pulling back the tapestry to reveal the hidden door.

Tauria was close behind as they walked the passageway, and behind Faythe, Reylan became an obvious presence she tried to push to the back of her mind—unsuccessfully.

They came to the Magestone-lined cell. Nik and Tauria hastily walked straight past, but she noted Reylan wasn't so close behind anymore and paused to turn to him. He stared with a furrowed brow into the cells. Faythe didn't say anything and didn't know why she felt the need to hang back for him when her friends had pressed forward.

"This is worse than I thought," he mumbled quietly.

She wasn't sure if he expected a response, but she felt riddled with dread at Reylan's deep concern. "I don't think it's been used in a long time," she commented anyway.

The general stepped inside one of the cells, and Faythe sucked in a sharp breath, lunging forward a step. He hissed in pain, face contorting as he fought against some phantom effects of the stone she couldn't comprehend. He raised a hand to his head but made no move to step back out. Without another thought, she grabbed his arm and pulled with all her might to drag the brute of a warrior the few steps back out of the cell.

Reylan released a quick gasp of air, blinking as if he couldn't believe a full-grown fae could be rendered almost immobile in a room lined with the mineral. He turned to her with raised eyebrows.

"An amount like that…it's not only to take away our ability and strength. It's a means of torture," he said with no small amount of disbelief.

She didn't care what his reasons were for testing it as she hissed, "Don't do that again."

An amused smile tugged at one corner of his mouth. "Were you worried about me, Faythe?"

She scowled in response, spinning on her heel to go catch up with the others. "Should have left you in there," she mumbled under her breath, though he heard her clearly, and his quiet chuckle echoed behind her. She resisted the urge to take her dagger to his chest and cut off the sound.

They walked out into the large, open, cavernous dwelling, and Faythe shuddered with the haunting memory of their last visit, straining her ears to hear the echoing boom of the creature's wings as it rose from the pit below. Her companions were alerted to nothing, but she couldn't relax. Feeling her neck faintly throb around the two small puncture wounds, she lifted a hand to rub the tender spot.

Though there was no immediate danger, Faythe's breathing hitched in her throat, and her vision swayed a little. She stopped in her tracks, bracing a hand against a stone pillar, unable to take her eyes off the black, depthless void below. Her breathing quickened with the flashes of grim memory, still so fresh. She pinched her eyes closed, focusing on convincing her mind she was safe from another attack by the foul creature Nik had slain.

A hand fell on her back, and she jolted violently, pulling her dagger free and spinning around. That same touch curled around her wrist to prevent her blade from plunging upward through Reylan's neck. A strong arm hooked around her waist, drawing her flush against a warm force and saving her from another plummet into the lair below. She breathed hard, staring up into familiar sapphires in wide-eyed horror over what she'd mistakenly attempted in her flash-back of terror. Reylan only looked back at her with deep concern.

"Sorry," she muttered through a short breath.

He released her wrist slowly. "Are you okay?" His voice was gentle, worried.

All she could muster was a vacant nod while he tried to soothe her panic.

"Nothing will get the chance to hurt you down here."

Holding his stare, she nodded again, appreciating the promise in his statement. She pressed her body to his, the pressure and warmth folding a sense of security around her, enough that she could reel in her racing thoughts. Reylan backed up a long stride from the ledge, taking her with him. Then his arm fell, and he put a step of distance between them.

Faythe relaxed, rolling her shoulders back, and breathed consciously. She would have thanked him. Admittedly, she found great comfort and protection with Reylan guarding her back, but her thundering heart still choked her words.

When she turned, Nik and Tauria stood a few meters away at the first gap in the stone, silently observing her embarrassing encounter with Reylan. Her cheeks flamed, and she stormed toward them, determined to forget her outburst of fear-triggered paranoia.

"You went through a great trauma—it's only natural to have that kind of response. We shouldn't have come back here so soon," Nik said gently.

"I'm fine," she snapped and immediately felt guilty for deflecting her irritation at appearing weak. "Sorry, I—"

"This way," Tauria called, not bothering to wait for them as she followed a silent beckoning none of them could hear.

Nik and Faythe exchanged a small smile of understanding before they all rushed to chase after the ward who disappeared around another bend. After a few twists and turns, Faythe's fae companions contorted their faces in disgust, covering half their faces. Then the smell hit her human senses a delayed half-minute later. She flinched and almost gagged at the nauseatingly foul and familiar stench. It was even more pungent than the last time she was here.

The black heap came into view around the next bend, and they all stopped to behold the mass of wings and gore.

"*That's* what bit you?" Reylan said.

She was about to ask how he knew about the bite, but then she remembered the first night he returned. He'd seen the faint scars on her neck when he got close enough in his act of intimidation. She shuddered as if she felt his fingers tracing along the permanent marking.

Reylan moved past her, covering his nose as he went to kneel in front of the thing. He examined it for a quick minute before straightening and saying nothing. His brow furrowed in deep concentration before he turned his head to her, and she almost recoiled at the anger in his look—though it wasn't aimed at her. His eyes were fixed on her neck.

Faythe shifted on her feet, ridiculously nervous under his gaze. Then Reylan wordlessly stepped away from the decomposing heap. She wanted to question what he made of the creature, but Tauria skipped past him, Nik hot on her heel.

Faythe and Reylan exchanged a last grim look before chasing after the prince and the ward who were already around the next turn. The few minutes they walked in deafening silence felt far longer to Faythe who was still painfully on edge. Everyone had their swords drawn, and no one dared to speak in case it delayed their alert to any impending danger.

Faythe was lost in a pool of her own thoughts and would have crashed right into Nik's back when he halted were it not for the hand that hooked around her elbow. She only scowled at Reylan who smirked at her clumsiness. Her question of why they'd stopped was answered the moment she turned back and beheld the iridescent obsidian rock that lined the walls along the rest of the path ahead.

"It's down there. I can feel it," Tauria said in frustration.

The end of the passage held a door, yet none of her fae companions could make it across with the amount of Magestone along the walls. Faythe stepped forward, about to push past the prince without giving her nerves a chance to hold her back, when Reylan's hand caught her arm once again.

"Don't even think about it," he warned.

She would have snapped at the gesture, but she found herself amused instead as she looked down at his hand that was yet to release her. "Are you *worried* about me, Reylan?"

He failed to see the humor and held his look firm.

She rolled her eyes, pulling her arm from his grasp. "It's not as if any of you can go down there." She looked around briefly. "Yep, only human here. Guess I'm shit out of luck." She turned to go forward but was met by Nik's tall figure blocking her way.

"We don't know what's down there," he said, his voice laced with concern. Yet in his eyes, he knew they had no other option.

"I'll come with you."

At Reylan's offer, gold met sapphire, and her retort died in her throat at the unexpected worry on his face.

Her look softened. "You could barely move when you stepped into that cell. You'd be weaker than me down there."

His jaw flexed as if he wanted to protest, but ultimately, he knew she was right.

"It's strong here. I don't think it's far past that door. We'll be able to hear if there's any danger, and she'll make it back to us before anything can happen to her," Tauria said to curb the worry of the overprotective fae males. It was in their nature, even more so than humans. They were annoyingly territorial, dominant, and protective.

Faythe smiled at Tauria in thanks. Reylan looked the most reluctant to agree but gave a forced nod of acceptance anyway. Without giving her mind a chance to submit to her own rising fear about what lay beyond the door, Faythe stepped through the second half of the hallway. She only prayed the damned ruin would be there for the taking and she wouldn't have to face anything nightmarish.

Likely wishful thinking.

"Don't let your guard down for a second," Reylan's voice called out as she met the door.

Faythe would have been irked at his excessive concern, but a small, mischevious smile crept along her face. She would find a way to tease him with his worry later.

She unlatched the four bolts on the door, not giving herself time to dread why there were so many to seal the thick steel, then stepped inside and let her companions fade away behind her the deeper she went through the black hallway. She made one turn. Then there was nowhere to go except forward when she spied a room at the end of the hall. Edging closer with caution, Faythe faintly made out a pool of light that hit the center from a source directly above.

Inside the compass of light...sat a small box.

It was too perfect. Too obvious.

She made it to the entrance and gasped, taking in the sight of a hundred mirrors. With her first steps into the room, her own reflection bounced back at her at every imaginable angle through the distorted cuts of glass. The illusion was spooky. Her heart leaped with each direction she glanced to find a figure staring back before her mind registered her own face.

Faythe stepped up to the box and crouched down low to examine it, not immediately going to touch it. It had strange markings she had never seen before, but there was no keyhole or obvious way to open it. She couldn't even be sure if the ruin was inside, or if it was just some other ancient artifact.

She reached out with both palms to lift the box. Then a gust of wind blew around her, sending wisps of unbound hair over her face. Faythe went cold as ice. Shooting upright, her hand was halfway to drawing her sword when a voice spoke.

"You come for the light temple ruin," it said from no direction in particular, bouncing around like her reflection in the mirrors.

A sharp chill shot down Faythe's spine, heart erratic from an invisible threat, and she whirled frantically to catch a glimpse of the intruder. No other form joined her in the hall of mirrors. When she went to twist again, she froze.

One of her reflections didn't move with her this time.

It smiled wickedly, knowing she'd figured it out. But when she blinked, it was back to her own horrified expression that copied her every flicker.

Whatever it was, it lived in the mirrors, using its prey's own image to terrorize.

"A clever one," it sang.

Faythe's eyes darted from each misshapen shard of glass. "Face me." Her voice wavered with the command, giving away her lost confidence.

Laughter mocked her in the form of her own face. She couldn't stop her eyes from frantically scanning her reflections in anticipation of one not following her next move. Her pulse raced at the haunting concept.

Then she spotted it, angled to look down on her right, an evil grin plastered on its face. *Her* face.

"I am," it said to her. The voice sounded from her left, and she snapped around to catch the out-of-place reflection. "I am your past." Then in front. "I am your present." Then above and behind. "I am your future."

It chilled Faythe to her very bones, and a violent tremor shook her whole body. "I'm not afraid of myself."

Again, its hearty laughter rumbled creepily through the space. *"Liar."*

"What are you?"

Her clone twisted her head in front of her. "I am a Dresair, keeper of knowledge, holder of precious things, and traveler of realms. I can show you if you want." The Dresair extended an open palm, but the cunning curl of its lips gave away its trick.

Faythe shuddered. Getting lured into the depths of the mirrors, leaving no trace of her physical being to explain her disappearance, would be a harrowing fate.

"A Dresair is what you are. What is your name?"

It dropped its arm and assessed her with hair-raising scrutiny. "What a curious little creature you are," it said. "A name can be a dangerous and powerful thing. If you tell me yours, I shall tell you mine."

Faythe furrowed a cautious brow. "You know my name."

The Dresair's grin was feline. "I should like to hear it."

Not in the mood to string out games, she answered, "Faythe Aklin."

Laughter bounced around the mirrors. In every one of the reflections, her own face mocked her. Faythe was torn between fear and frustration at its unhinged merriment.

When its chuckling ceased, it stood straight once more, gold eyes sparkling with dark delight and wonder. "What a fate has been sculpted around you, child. Millennia come and go without such a soul coming into the world—one with the power to challenge evil, the spirit to change hearts, and the heart to move mountains. If you only dare to take the leap and trust you will fly with the Phoenix, of course."

"What does that mean?" Faythe snapped, a chill seeping over her skin.

"It means there is so much for you to learn, golden-eyed child. One born with wings is never destined to remain caged."

Faythe stared into those eyes. Her eyes. Transfixed.

"I do not have a name, Faythe. I simply…am. Do not be so quick to offer what cannot be returned."

For a second, Faythe's guard slipped to welcome the wisdom. Perhaps it made her a fool for giving the Dresair an ounce of merit, but as it spoke through her image, she felt the words as though they were a product of her own conscience. She shook her head from the trancelike state she was slowly being reeled into, unsure whether it was a trick of the Dresair or her own spiraling thoughts, remembering she came here for a purpose.

"Tell me where the ruin is."

The Dresair stepped forward, pointing at the ground. "You know where it is. I hold many items within my mirrors. That which is revealed to those who dare wander is not what they *want*, but what they *need*. Though nothing is given without challenge. Everything has a price, as you very well know."

"What do you want?" Faythe demanded, anticipation stirring her exasperation.

The Dresair kept her face, wicked playfulness returning to its expression. "It is not what you can give to me. It is what I must give to you."

Faythe stiffened in dreadful apprehension. "Give me…what?"

The Dresair tilted its head in amusement as it observed her. "The only way to walk out with the ruin is to accept my knowledge. A dark piece of the future yet to pass."

Faythe blinked. It didn't seem like too harsh a trade. Though the demon's cruel gleam remained.

"I accept," she said before logic or reason could dissuade her.

The corners of its mouth curled in feline delight. "You should not be in such a hurry to agree, Heir of Marvellas. Man and fae have driven themselves to madness, some to their own deaths, at having such knowledge."

It shook her awfully at the thought of what could be so grim to warrant such extreme measures. But she didn't have a choice and couldn't leave without the temple ruin. "Tell me," she pressed, anxious to get it over with.

It looked away from her and paced the length of the mirror's edge. "Very well."

Gold met gold, and her mirror-self straightened, her grin vanishing. Faythe thought she was prepared to hear whatever ill fate might fall on her; thought she could handle the curse of knowledge no matter how damning it was.

Nothing could have braced her for the Dresair's next words.

"In your quest to stop the King of High Farrow, one of those close to you will forfeit their life."

She swayed with the weight of the declaration and stumbled back a step. Coldness embraced her, and the air restricted her throat while the words replayed hauntingly, inconceivably, in her mind. Indelible knowledge that crushed her spirit like a physical pain in her chest. She would have accepted anything else. Any pain, any torture, any misfortune—as long as it wasn't one of her friends.

Faythe shook her head slowly. "No future is certain," she breathed in denial.

"The path can change, but to alter fate would have dire consequences."

"You're wrong," Faythe hissed, refusing to believe there was no escape from the worst of her fears. Her eyes pooled as her retort failed to convince even herself. Tears fell as she thought of each and every one of her friends. Even Reylan. She couldn't let him in, and pushing him away would be one less person close to her. One less at risk from the foretold doom.

She was physically trembling when she looked around the mirrors again. All the reflections followed her now as she dared to ask, "Who?"

"That, I cannot tell you."

The Dresair refused to take her form again, and Faythe screamed in anguish at every one of her reflections. She asked instead, "Will it be my fault?" A sob left her.

At the Dresair's pause of silence, Faythe felt a new scream climbing her throat. Then it answered.

"There will be many to blame."

The statement didn't rule her out completely, and Faythe came apart. She fell to her knees in front of the box and took it in her hands, catching the glimpse of her reflection. It stayed standing.

In a surge of anger, she shot to her feet and hurled the box at the glass with a cry of defeat, pain, and grief. It shattered, the shards cascading to the ground like a glistening waterfall.

Her breathing was heavy with rage that she could not stop the unstoppable. Faythe stared at the fragments of the broken mirror. She jerked as she caught them vibrating against the stone then backed up a step when the pieces began to move, floating upward through the air as if time were reversing itself. In a matter of seconds, the mirror in front of her became whole again.

Faythe stared wide-eyed in disbelief, but not at the magick that brought the glass back together.

At Reylan.

He stood behind her, staring at her through the reflection. He was pale, breathing heavily in exertion while he braced against the stone archway, no doubt feeling the effects of the Magestone passage he emerged from. Faythe believed it to be another of the Dresair's tricks, until he spoke quietly.

"I heard you scream."

CHAPTER 38

Nikalias

THE PRINCE OF High Farrow shook the strange, small box between his palms. It rattled but offered no clues as to how it could be opened. The foreign markings etched into the wood were unknown to him and the other fae in the room even with their combined centuries of knowledge.

They had retreated to Faythe's rooms after their eerie expedition to the passages below the castle, his *home* for over three hundred years, yet he never knew what dwelled beneath his feet. He refused to visit the thoughts his father could have known about them…about the *thing* that lived there and almost ended Faythe's life. Looking away from the box in his hands, he tried to gauge the thoughts of his companions. Tauria was frowning at the item in silent contemplation, but the general watched Faythe.

She'd barely spoken since they returned and was now perched on the arm of the chair by the fire, staring intently at the golden flames as if they spoke back to her. He'd tried to coax something out of her, but even witty remarks failed to gain a reaction, and he dreaded to think what greeted her beyond the steel door none of them could pass.

Well, anyone except Reylan, it seemed.

At the sound of Faythe's scream, *Gods,* he'd tried to force through the pain himself, but the stone rendered him completely incapacitated, and Tauria had swiftly pulled him back. It was obvious the general felt the harsh effects too, but Nik had to admire his strength as he pushed through it regardless to get to Faythe's aid.

"What do we do with it?" Tauria wondered out loud.

It was the question on all of their minds. The box was sealed without any obvious lock or side that could be opened.

Nik shrugged. "Break it?" he suggested. But he knew it wasn't a plausible plan. Something as well-guarded and hidden as the temple ruin was likely not going to be sealed in a destructible container.

"There may be one person who can shed some light on the markings." Faythe's voice was quiet, distant, and he hated that there was nothing he could do to bring the joy back into it. She finally looked away from the flames to meet his eye as she said, "Marlowe."

Nik blinked, feeling foolish he didn't think of her sooner. She was not just a human, not just a blacksmith—Marlowe was an oracle, something that was almost as inconceivable as Faythe's ability. Yet Nik was beyond being stunned by impossible revelations. It made sense that if there was one person with knowledge of the item he held, it would be the one with a direct spiritual connection to the owner of the ruin within.

The following morning, Nik, Tauria, Reylan, and Faythe crowded into Jakon and Marlowe's small cottage in the outer town. It was a relief to see Faythe perk up a little at seeing her friends, though something still tugged on her mind. Before they could ask about the box, the three humans and Tauria sat around the dining table while Jakon caught them up on the trip to Galmire—a trip Nik was only now learning about.

"Caius told me what you discovered. Are the boys and their families safe?" Faythe questioned with worry.

Jakon looked grim. "For now. But we don't know what the threat is exactly, and they have no protection there with the fae soldiers gone." His eyes flashed to Nik for a second, but the prince didn't take offense. He was the son of the king who ordered the town to be left defenseless, yet this was the first Nik was hearing of the threat.

"I'll talk to the king," he said to offer some consolation, though he wasn't exactly a great influence on his father's decisions recently. He was against the movement of the soldiers in the first place.

"You say the bodies are completely drained of blood?" the general asked. Nik looked to Reylan, he wore a deep frown as he calculated the details.

Jakon nodded. "They say they hear the air stir even when the nights are still, and some swear they've caught a glimpse of crea-tures in the sky. Likened to bats, but something far larger."

Reylan looked as if he was putting clues together, but it was Faythe who questioned it.

"Do you know what it could be?"

The general looked at her with an unreadable expression. "It's impossible, but...everything you've described, from the sightings in Galmire to the creature in the castle passageway, winged, blood-thirsty..." His eyes met Nik's then, and the slight fear in them was enough to set the emotion in him too. "There was only one species that existed like that...a *very* long time ago. One that history told us was wiped out during the Dark Age."

Nik's face blanched, his eyes widening slightly in dawning. "The dark fae," he said to no one in particular.

It filled him with cold dread to think of them, and he wanted to pass it off as ridiculous—impossible, as the general said. Yet when he recalled the thing in the passageway, mauled beyond recognition, it fit the description of the dark subspecies long believed to be extinct.

"There are *dark* fae?" Faythe said in disbelief.

Nik looked to her as he tried to call up an old history lesson. "Millennia ago, there existed only two prominent species: humans and demons. The fae were created to be superior to their human origins, and the dark fae to their demon origins, through the blessings of the Spirits. Except, it didn't take long for the dark fae to completely annihilate their weaker ancestors." Nik tried to continue, but his mind reeled with the horrifying notion history could be repeating itself.

Reylan picked up on his explanation. "After that, the fae, the humans, and the dark fae lived together throughout the seven kingdoms. Three races mixed with little conflict." He took a pause, and his face fell grim. "Until the dark fae developed a taste for human blood. They found it gave them a strength and speed that could surpass even our kind, but only temporarily. They had to keep up the feed to keep the effects. When humans started to become targets, killed for their blood, harming them became outlawed in every kingdom...except one."

Nobody needed to say it, but Faythe whispered in fear, "Valgard."

Reylan nodded solemnly. "It was the one kingdom with a dark fae king, Mordecai. So, he went to war against the rest of Ungardia. It was the darkest age the realms had ever seen, and rightly named as such in history."

Everyone's eyes were fixed on Reylan as he told the story, and Nik could feel the fear around the room.

The general continued. "They could have won. With human blood in their system, they could take out an army even outnumbered five to one. But word of the carnage got to Salenhaven, and amid fears it wouldn't stop with Ungardia, they joined the cause. Together, two great continents wiped out the dark fae for good."

Faythe didn't waste any time in saying, "So, how the rutting damn does such a thing rise from the dead?"

It wasn't what Nik thought was happening—or Faythe for that matter, as it seemed merely a comment made out of fear and disbelief for what could really be at large.

"They were created once; maybe they were again and some of the outcomes didn't quite go to plan." Reylan let the explanation linger. The creature in the cave was far beyond any human or fae recognition. And now, it was beginning to make sense that it was perhaps the product of an experiment gone wrong, too savage for purpose.

"You say the Spirits were needed to create you and them..." Faythe's eyes flashed to Nik. "We need to get that box open—now."

He understood, as she had told him it was possible to summon the Spirit of Life with her ruin and the Riscillius without the need to be in the temple. Nik took the few strides over to the table while Marlowe and Jakon frowned at him in question. Placing the small box in front of the blacksmith, he said, "Faythe thought you might know what these mean. They might offer a clue as to how to open it."

Marlowe took the box in her hands and flipped it around in curiosity.

Faythe added, "The temple ruin is inside."

Marlowe's brow curved, and she pored over the box with more scrutiny. Wordlessly, she stood, going over to a tall bookcase in the corner. Every pair of eyes in the room stalked her movement in anticipation.

Nik glanced around the cottage, scattered with open volumes on every possible surface. Most people would glimpse the blacksmith and fear her for the deadly blades she could craft from blunt steel. Nik knew the real weapons that made her a force to be reckoned with were the books she absorbed, the knowledge she tucked away in every corner of her arsenal. Words, when crafted artfully, could cut deeper than any blade and imprint on one's soul for eternity. To inspire or to torment—that depended on the will of the speaker.

Finding the tome she was searching for, Marlowe came back with it, not taking a seat as she thumped the heavy book onto the table. They all stood in silence, letting the rustle of old, stiff paper fill the room as they observed Marlowe filtering haphazardly through the pages.

In front of him, Nik noticed Tauria clasping her hands together tight to keep from trembling. His stomach dropped at the sight, at the thought of her fear. Before he could stop himself, he put a hand on her shoulder in quiet comfort. It was a relief when she didn't immediately shrug him off. Instead, she shot him a quick smile in gratitude. After everything she'd been through, he always thought of her as the bravest and most resilient fae he knew.

"I knew I'd seen the likeness before!" Marlowe's voice snapped him from his thoughts, and his heart thundered as she sounded confident she'd cracked the code. Nik really had to admire the brilliance of the human and the convenience of her gift.

Reylan stepped closer, coming to stand behind Faythe as they all leaned in to glimpse what caught the blacksmith's attention.

"It appears to be a Blood Box."

Across the aged, yellow pages were several delicate drawings depicting the same marks etched into the wood of the box. Marlowe was deep in concentration as she slid into her seat, eyes scanning over the information with a look that glazed her eyes.

"What in the rutting damn is a *Blood Box?*" Faythe asked.

Marlowe inhaled deeply as she peeled her face from the pages. "It's exactly what you'd expect it to be: a container sealed with the blood of its owner," she explained. "And this appears to be a spell to accompany it, both to seal and undo. It's worded in the old language, blood magick in its most basic form. If mastered, the symbols could be etched onto bigger containers for one with enough power to bind the spell on a larger scale."

Nik soaked in the blacksmith's knowledge, tucking it away in the depths of his own internal trove of useful information. He knew very little of spell magick as it was a highly outdated practice reserved for the ancient fae mages who crafted words to call on the weak, diluted power some harbored that never translated into a proper ability. Over time, the practice of such spells had become insignificant and forgotten about the more the abilities manifested. Blood magick in particular was highly frowned upon and even outlawed in some territories long before the kingdoms were established as they were now.

"So, if the owner happens to be the King of High Farrow..." Faythe trailed off.

Marlowe nodded grimly. "You'll need his blood to open it."

She straightened in her seat. "Well then, who's up for challenging the king to a duel?" she asked around sarcastically before huffing in defeat.

"Nobody has to."

Everyone's eyes shot to the general as he spoke, and when Nik did too, he recoiled, catching Reylan looking directly at him.

"We already have his blood."

Nik realized what he was implying immediately. It was a genius thought, and one he should have had first. Yet it was still perhaps a long shot.

Marlowe followed Reylan's gaze to him. "You're not the pure blood source, but it might recognize you as his kin."

Nik took a long breath, reaching for the dagger at his side. He curled his hand around the sharp blade but paused. His heart raced, and a selfish part of him prayed his blood wouldn't open the box, if only so he might hold onto the small shred of hope his father had no knowledge of the temple ruin and didn't seek its power for unlawful political gain.

He ground his teeth at the thought and pulled the dagger from his palm, slicing through it with a quick lick of pain. Before the drops of his blood could fall, he walked around the small table and held his closed palm over the wooden box. Then he clenched his fist and watched three drops fall across the delicate circular marking on its surface.

At the same time, Marlowe began to quietly recite the words on the page with near perfect eloquence. Nik knew some words from old teachings, but not enough to decipher the whole phrase. He wondered if Marlowe found it intriguing to learn the old language, or if she had simply picked up on the pronunciation through her various readings.

She finished her last words in barely a whisper. Nik's wound had already clotted to stop the blood flow. He stepped back.

Then they all waited in painful silence.

Each tick of the clock on the mantel rang in his ears, and everyone's breathing turned shallow.

Nothing happened.

Then the centerpiece lit up like a glowing seal. Those around the table sat back as the circle suddenly caved inward an inch and spun halfway, fixing the symbol upside down instead. There was a dull *click*, and then nothing.

Nobody immediately moved to touch the box. Nik heard Faythe's heart the loudest, and she was the first to reach out both hands toward it. The suspense was torture as they all waited for her to test it. Her small fingers gripped the top edges, and when she lifted upward, the top slab came away from the rest of the container. She looked to him, only briefly, as she believed both their souls were bound to the lost ruin inside. Nik gave her a small nod of encouragement, and she returned her focus to the box, removing the lid and setting it aside.

Then he felt it. Waves of ethereal power emitting a faint hum from within. There was no doubt they had found the Spirit's ruin.

It was confirmed in image when Faythe reached in and pulled the broken slab from its wooden cage. She sucked in a sharp breath as she weighed it in one hand. "Gods above…" she muttered, eyes transfixed on the thick gray arrow slate marked with Aurialis's symbol on its point.

"What does it feel like?" he questioned. It radiated power to where he stood, and he could only imagine what it felt like within her grasp.

She didn't look at him as she said, "It's like…it's like a current of pure energy through every vein in my body. I feel…powerful." Faythe breathed the last word as she held her eyes to it, completely hypnotized by whatever unearthly power was embedded in the stone.

Reylan leaned over her and took the ruin from her hands, placing it quickly on the table in front. Faythe seemed to snap out of a dream and looked to him wide-eyed, as if returning to her own senses instead of whatever Spirit's power channeled into her from the ruin.

"In the wrong hands…" The general trailed off. He didn't have to finish his sentence as everyone in the room arrived at the same conclusion having seen the effects it had on someone as good-hearted as *Faythe.*

Marlowe reached across the table. Jakon jerked to stop her from picking up the ruin, but he wasn't quick enough, and the black-smith held up the stone in curiosity.

"It certainly radiates spiritual power, but I don't feel any altering effects," she pondered out loud, admiring it from all angles.

Jakon added, "I don't feel anything."

Nik frowned inquisitively. "We can only assume it's either because you're human or don't have an ability. Marlowe is linked to the Spirits, being an oracle, but her gift isn't anything that can be heightened or changed physically."

Faythe chimed in, "I'm human, and the king doesn't have an ability. What would he want with it if he can't wield its power?"

Both valid points. Then he remembered.

"You're half-fae."

Faythe cast a quick glance behind her, and he realized the general didn't know that piece of information about her. Yet he didn't appear the least bit surprised by the revelation.

Reylan instead looked mildly confused, stating, "I thought you didn't know who your father was."

Faythe shifted uncomfortably. "I don't. But the Spirit of Life seems to think he was a Nightwalker. Explains my ability," she said quickly.

Nik's brow twitched, feeling there was perhaps something missing from the story she was yet to disclose. It didn't feel right to probe in that moment.

The general dropped his eyes from her oddly and said nothing else.

"Speaking of the entity herself, I think she has a lot of explaining to do." Faythe bounded to her feet before anyone could protest. She drew Lumarias from her hip and paused for a moment, looking to no one in particular to help ease her nerves.

Everyone stood in a disorganized circle around the pool of light by the window. Reylan moved to stand by Faythe. Nik was grateful as he felt compelled to stay by Tauria while she stood in nervous anticipation. Everyone was on edge, and he longed for the confrontation to be over and done with.

Marlowe came forward with the ruin, placing it gently on the ground in the center of the sunlight. Faythe took a deep breath before she steadied the sword between both palms. It would not be new to her to see the Goddess of the Sun, but everyone else in the small room stood in utter silence, knowing the impossible was about to appear before them.

When Faythe connected the light shining through the Riscillius to the ruin, a searing flash of light had everyone stepping back and wincing. Then it dimmed, and from it appeared a tall, ethereal beauty with the purest white hair. Nik was struck by the glowing form that faced Faythe.

He wasn't alone. Everyone except Faythe stood gawking at the spiritual Goddess as if they didn't really believe Faythe wasn't insane all this time until they experienced it for themselves.

"Hello, Faythe." Aurialis spoke first, her voice like a soothing symphony. Then the Spirit glanced around at the rest of them. "Only darkness and light remains," she observed. What it meant, he was too dumbstruck to question.

Faythe didn't appear at all impressed by the Spirit's presence. She had seen her twice before, but Nik didn't think he would ever get used to the physical manifestation of Aurialis.

"What do you know of the dark fae? Is that the evil in Ungardia you're so afraid of?" She skipped all pleasantries to jump straight to the point.

Aurialis's expression turned grave. "They are an accessory, yes."

Nik shuddered at the confirmation of their fears. The dark fae *had* returned. But if there was something else, something *worse*, they should be more afraid of… Terror shook his body.

The Spirit continued. "They are a great weapon, but not all have turned hearts. They will bring darkness, and they will bring salvation."

The contradictions seemed to confuse everyone as brows furrowed around the circle of friends. Faythe looked close to losing her short temper, and he prayed for them all in that moment.

"If you didn't help make them, who did?" she pressed.

It was odd to see human emotions on a Spirit, but a pained look crossed Aurialis's features as she said, "My sister, Dakodas." It shouldn't have come as a surprise; there were only two remaining Goddesses, and it made sense it would be the Spirit of Death behind such a ploy. The shock came with her next words. "But she acts with the desires of another."

Faythe was quick to question, "The King of High Farrow?"

A pain stabbed Nik's chest at the mention of his father. He held his breath until the Spirit answered. At the shake of her head, he almost relaxed.

"He is but another puppet." She turned to him, and Nik

blanched as Aurialis addressed him directly. "It was not your father who locked away my ruin in a place where it could not be stumbled upon."

His blood pounded.

"It was your mother."

Nik could have collapsed with the weight of the words—of the mention of his long passed gentle mother. He felt a warm hand take his, and he didn't have to look to know it was Tauria who offered him comfort. The only sign of gratitude he could give back was a slight squeeze as he couldn't tear his eyes off the glowing form.

"That doesn't make any sense," Faythe said impatiently.

The Spirit turned back to her. "For you to understand, I must start at the beginning, at least before the Great Battles."

Nobody spoke out to object though they knew they were in for a long story and a lot of emotion to absorb at once. At least, Nik felt so, as both his parents seemed tied to it.

Aurialis raised her chin as she began her tale. "Over a hundred years of your time ago, the High Farrow king journeyed to Rhyenelle with his most trusted advisor and Captain of the Guard."

Nik cast a glance to Faythe at the mention of Captain Varis. Her eyes twitched in a wince, but she remained impassive and attentive.

"He was guided to the Riscillius that had laid untouched in the castle of Rhyenelle for centuries, just as I guided Marlowe to it in High Farrow."

The blacksmith didn't appear in the least bit surprised, and he supposed she might have already been aware of it. Nik became nauseatingly aware that perhaps nothing was left to chance anymore.

"With it, he was also compelled to make the expedition to the Niltain Isles, to—"

"Dakodas's temple," Marlowe cut in with a breath of disbelief.

The Spirit nodded grimly. "He used the Riscillius just as you did, Faythe, and summoned my sister with its power." Aurialis paused, and the shift on her face indicated the story was about to take a dark turn. "She is powerful, and in the time she was released before them, she took away the color in their eyes to bend their will to the command of another. It brought about the dawn of the Great Battles. With High Farrow at his mercy and with no one to suspect him, the king was used to deploy and delay armies to give Valgard more opportunity to conquer. They succeeded in taking the kingdoms of Dalrune and Fenstead, but they could not stand against the might of Rhyenelle who extended their reach to protect Olmstone too. So, they retreated their forces, but the war was far from over. Ever since, they have been growing their army to a far more deadly capacity.

"You asked about the dark fae, and you are right to hold fear, for the High Lord Mordecai lives once again. He holds dominion over Valgard, but he has thus far been successful at remaining hidden."

A creeping chill wove through every one of the gathered friends, piercing their hearts with trepidation. No one could have predicted the height of what they were up against—the impossible, the inconceivable, and the damning, foreboding doom that lurked right at their borders. Nik was too struck with stupor to even feel relief that his father's wicked actions over the decades, his hatred and malice, his lack of mercy...were never him. Not truly.

It suddenly all made sense. He *knew* the king was once a better male. Yet it didn't bring him any comfort.

Nik dared to ask, "Did my mother know?"

Aurialis turned to him once again and gave a solemn nod that brought the world down upon him. "The queen found out through the very escape passages that led you to my ruin. Coming across the knowledge by spying into the king's council chamber, she stole the Riscillius to come to me. She took my ruin and planned to summon me in front of the king so I might reverse the damage that was done."

"She never got that far," Faythe interjected quietly.

The Spirit shook her head. "She had very specific instructions on where the ruin was to be hidden should she fail to carry out her plan. She confided in one young human, her most trusted friend and handmaiden…your grandmother, Faythe."

Nik glanced to Faythe on instinct. Her eyes were wide at the knowledge.

"Which is how the Riscillius came to be in your mother's possession. Your grandmother fled to Rhyenelle with it to get the stone far from the king's reach. The Kingdom of the Phoenix was where your mother was born."

Faythe looked shell-shocked, and Nik had to admit, the fact her mother wasn't born in High Farrow was an unexpected blow. If it held any significance, he couldn't be sure.

"The temple ruins possess great power on their own, but it is the joining of the three that makes up the Tripartite that must never come to pass in the wrong hands."

Nik didn't process any of the last dose of history as his mind rang with one blaring question he was terrified to know the answer to, yet had spent a century searching for: "What happened to my mother?" Tension curled up his spine, turning his whole body rigid as Aurialis slid her gaze to him, eyes filled with apology—the kind that braced a person to receive the world-shattering truth.

"I am sorry for the dire fate that fell on her, Prince, and that I now must be the one to give you the truth you have longed for. The King of High Farrow learned of your mother's intentions and without his right mind, only saw a threat, not the female he loved and was soul-bonded to."

Nik trembled all over. The Spirit's next words felt worse than any physical blow in all his centuries of existence.

"The king had her executed. Privately. And blamed a silent intruder to swiftly divert all suspicion from himself."

A hot rage consumed him as he seethed through his teeth. "You're *lying.*"

"She's not." Tauria's quiet interrupting voice made him snap his head to her. She winced, but he couldn't subside the anger he felt at the implication of his father. "I was there," she barely more than whispered.

Nik ripped his hand from hers in shock, and Tauria whimpered. His eyes were wide, and he couldn't help that he looked at her as if she were a stranger in his disbelief.

"That day, I went to seek him out in his study, finding the door slightly ajar and hearing voices inside. I shouldn't have, but I stayed to listen for just a moment. He spoke of a plan, a tale of an intruder, that I found alarming, so I tried to catch a glimpse inside, and then I saw her. She was already gone. There was so much blood. On her…and on the king.

"I panicked, and I ran. It wasn't long after my arrival in the castle, and if that was what he was capable of doing to his mate…" Tauria's voice choked with grief and terror, but Nik couldn't comfort her or find an ounce of sympathy while his own emotions where overshadowed by her betrayal. She had harbored the secret from him all this time. "I'm so sorry, Nik. I ached to tell you straight away, but you were broken when the news surfaced… If you knew it was your father, I feared what the knowledge would do to you. I feared what *he* would do to you if you knew." Tauria's face was desolate and pleading.

Nik shook his head but couldn't stand to even look at her.

"Nik, please," she sobbed.

"All this time…" He trailed off, unable to finish, not even knowing what to say to her. He wanted to rage, shout, and destroy anything in his path. Tauria's was a different kind of betrayal. She knew what she was doing, what she was keeping from him, despite knowing how much it meant.

But his father…

Nik turned his attention to Aurialis. "You said my mother

thought you could reverse the damage to my father. Can you still?" he asked, low and calm, swallowing the eruption of emotion it prickled his skin to withhold.

The Spirit nodded, but not reassuringly. "I could. It would have been a simple reversal if I had the chance when your mother tried. But after all this time, his spirit would be broken. Everything he's done under the influence would still burden his soul. He may very well beg for death as soon as I gave him his free will back."

There was no silver lining to the grim revelation. Nik wanted to kill his father for what he did to his mother…yet a conflicted part of him had to be sure there was no salvation from the demon that plagued him.

Faythe's voice distracted him from his violent thoughts. "Who commands his will?"

It was the killer question. He'd become too consumed by his own grief and anger to even consider the master evil that held more influence than they could have possibly imagined. Nik assumed it was Valgard, their returned-from-the-dead High Lord Mordecai. But Aurialis came out with a different name—one no one in the room could have come remotely close to uttering.

"Marvellas."

CHAPTER 39

Faythe

F AYTHE STUMBLED BACK a step in ice-cold horror. All this time, she had been connected to the name Marvellas as if it were a blessing, *an honor,* to be called her heir. Now, it took on a whole new meaning with the unfathomable revelation the Spirit of Souls was the evil at large, puppeteering the kingdoms against each other.

With every evil born, a way to destroy it is conceived in turn.

It had been right there in front of her since her last encounter with Aurialis. Faythe felt dizzy at the concept. This was bigger than her—bigger than any of them. To think Aurialis believed she was destined to stop Marvellas because she shared some distant blood-line…it made sense. Yet at the same time, she was just one person, one *human*, with a mind ability she highly doubted would even be a slight threat in the face of its master origin. What she also remembered from her last conversation with Aurialis: the location of Marvellas was completely unknown.

It would be logical to assume she was at the heart of the conflict in Valgard or either of the two conquered kingdoms. Marvellas would be in fae form with unimaginable power. It would

be hard to conceal it from everyone, and with some investigation—
very *dangerous* investigation, probing into enemy territory—perhaps
she could be traced.

"I am afraid I cannot stay in your realm any longer," Aurialis
said through the dismal silence that settled.

Seeing her form becoming more transparent, Faythe asked
desperately, "How do I stop her?"

"First, you must stop the King of High Farrow," Aurialis
answered sadly. "He must never get his hands on the Riscillius,
Faythe. He cannot get to the other ruins, or all will be lost if they
reach Marvellas."

With that last haunting statement, the Spirit was gone.

The light drastically dimmed in the cottage, so much so that it
could have been mistaken for nightfall. She let her eyes adjust
before scanning her companions who all looked to her.

Except Nik. He was staring at the ground in his own internal
hurricane of emotion. After everything he had learned today about
his father and his *mother*... Faythe felt the overwhelming need to
comfort him, and it pained her that she didn't know how.

Tauria was silently distraught but held herself together, and
Faythe knew it was only in consideration of everyone else in the
room.

So much pain, despair, and anger in one room, and it extended
to so many of them and for different reasons. Faythe was struggling
to hold herself together and longed to be alone in the confines of
her rooms, or in the forest where she could scream at the top of her
lungs and listen to her anguish echo back to her. She took a
moment to glance at every grim face around her. Her friends, even
Reylan, who had proven to have her back more than once now.

Aurialis said the king had to be stopped first, and with that
warning, the ringing reminder of the Dresair's words followed.

*In your quest to stop the King of High Farrow, one of those close to you
will forfeit their life...*

She couldn't stand to look at them any longer. She wanted to push them all away, shut them all out, if it meant they would be safe from the inevitable fate. But she knew it would do nothing to stop the chain of events that was already in motion.

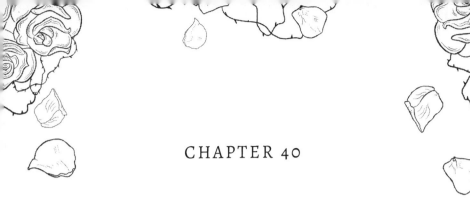

CHAPTER 40

Nikalias

NIK LEANED WITH both hands against the fireplace, watching the blue flames fight against each other like the rage of emotions within him. Above all else, he was heartbroken. With more than one cause.

The first was the thought of his mother and how cruelly she was taken from him by the king she trusted, the mate she loved. It would have been easier to despise the murderer and seek vengeance if it were some faceless assassin like he'd been led to believe.

The next was his father. He'd spent a century by his side, following his orders, yet it was never really him, and Nik hated himself for not seeing it sooner. He always knew his father's heart had turned cold and never thought to question it deeper. He'd let his kingdom be run by a demon and stood by his mother's murderer.

The last and most prominent stab to the heart was Tauria. All this time, she knew what really happened to his mother that night, had *seen* the moment her life was taken, yet she'd watched it torment him for decades without saying a word. It was a betrayal he couldn't bear.

A quiet knock sounded at his door. Tauria hadn't stopped to ask before entering his rooms since the first few years after she arrived in High Farrow. It was a mutual trust they'd fallen into. Until now.

He knew it was the princess—could scent her approach from halfway down the hall. Nik intended to immediately cast her out when the door opened slowly and he heard her slip inside. Yet despite his resentment, his anger dulled in her presence, and he didn't have it in him to shout. His room was scattered with loose parchments and broken fragments of any meaningless item that was in his path when he first returned. He didn't care and didn't move when Tauria took a few tentative steps toward him. He kept his back to her.

"Nik," she said in barely a whisper. She didn't immediately continue with a sentence.

His grip on the mantel tightened. Hearing her voice only made the pain worse.

"I'm so sorry—"

"Don't." He pushed off the fireplace and straightened, but he didn't take his eyes off the dancing flames as he slid his hands into his pockets. "Don't bother, Tauria. I know why you did it. You thought you knew what was best for me." He turned to her then and kept his face calm despite the distraught creases on her golden-brown skin pulling at something painful within him. "You were wrong."

Her face fell even more at his words, but he wasn't sorry. He had trusted her, and she had kept hold of a world-shattering secret this whole time—one he had every right to know.

"I was young and afraid. Your father had just offered me refuge from my own nightmare. I was scared of what he would do if he found out I knew. But I was even more terrified of what the knowledge would do to you, Nik. I only wanted to protect you from that burden," she said, her voice wavering with each sentence.

Nik had only ever seen the princess cry once, over the loss of her parents and her kingdom. Once. Then never again. She was resilient, strong, and brave. It broke him to see her grief now and to know he was the root cause of it.

"You should have told me," he said in defeat, a plea made far too late.

"We weren't close then. I didn't know if you would believe me. You were angry, emotional, and you would have tried to find a way to kill your father for what he did, so then he would have you executed too."

Nik tore his eyes away from her desperate look. "I don't know what I would have done," he admitted.

Even now, knowing the horrifying secret, he was conflicted about what to do with it. A demon wearing the king's face had killed his mother. In his heart, he knew that. But Aurialis's words still rang in his head—that his soul was beyond salvation, that death would be a mercy for the fae trapped within the evil grasp.

"I need time. To figure out what to do and come to terms with it. You don't have to explain yourself, Tauria, but I trusted you, and you betrayed that. You watched me agonize over who killed her for decades, and still, you sat silent on the answer to the one question that tore me apart inside." He looked into her sparkling brown eyes again as he finished. "I would never have kept something like from you no matter how hard it would be to tell you. I would have helped you to deal with it instead."

To his surprise, the princess's desolate look steeled. Her posture straightened, and he knew her well enough to know he'd unwittingly struck a chord.

"You can't say that," she said with a hard edge. "You weren't on the run with your life from your home kingdom, hadn't found yourself suddenly in foreign lands where the king who offered you shelter turned out to be a cold-blooded murderer. Your survival didn't depend on the will of that king. Until you know what it's like to be scared, young, and alone—yes, *alone*, Nik, because you weren't yet as dear to me then as you are now—you do not get to tell me what you would or would not have done." Her shoulders fell again, pain returning to her eyes. "Years went by, and I should have told you sooner. It *kills* me that you found out this way instead. But now you know, and I understand your grief. I'll accept it if you need time and space. What I will not accept is the blame for being vulnerable and afraid, the blame for thinking of you, or the blame for wanting to protect your heart."

Nik blinked, taken aback by her passion. With every word she uttered, he found his anger toward her start to dissolve.

Before he could reply, Tauria twisted on her heel and stalked for the door.

He didn't stop her. He didn't know what he wanted to say in response. The call for her to stay, for them to talk it out into the small hours like old times, stuck in his throat as he watched her disappear. The harsh slam of the door was the last echo of her presence.

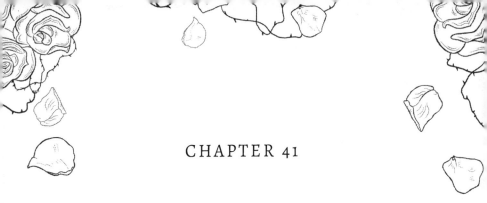

CHAPTER 41

Faythe

FAYTHE WALKED THE halls without conscious direction as her mind reeled over the impossible, the horrifying, and the damned. She couldn't get the thoughts to stop and swayed in rapid, overwhelming panic at everything that seemed so far out of her control.

Eventually, she had to stop walking and pressed her back to one of the walls while she focused on her breathing and wild heart. She tipped her head back and clamped her eyes shut, begging her mind to soothe the storm of emotion that threatened to undo her completely. A tear slid down her cheek, and she clenched her teeth in frustration. Her nails purposefully cut into her palm, hoping the pain would drown the sadness. She was glad for the quiet. No guards loitered in the dark hallway off the main route through the castle.

Just as she was beginning to regain some of her composure, a dark chuckle seeped like poison through the silence. Her eyes snapped open, and her heart leaped at the sight of Captain Varis, alone and creeping toward her with cruel amusement at her obvious distress.

"All become too much for you, has it?" he taunted, coming to a halt in front of her.

Usually, she found the strength to muster her bravado in the face of the monster, but right now, she felt completely at his emotional mercy with the heavy weight of everything else. His presence only added to her rising anxiety, and her chest rose and fell deeply with it.

"This is my favorite version of you, Faythe. The *real* you, beneath all that insufferable arrogance."

Faythe was still backed against the wall, and the captain closed in like a suffocating shadow that filled her lungs with each step.

"Weak, pathetic *human.*" His hand came up, and she lost all her bravery under the flood of fear.

Thinking he was going to strike her while there was no one around to witness the brutality, she closed her eyes and flinched. Varis's hand went to her face, but not with force. His repulsive fingers traced the wet trail of her traitorous escaped tear. She held her breath, trembling now, as she had no fight left in her exhaustion and defeat.

Help. She needed help. And for once, she wasn't afraid to admit it. She prayed for an escape while her veins pulsed and nausea filled her stomach. *Someone, anyone, please.*

"Captain."

At the voice that carried down the hall, Faythe snapped her eyes open, breathing a sigh of immense relief despite the malice that laced the word. When she turned her head toward Reylan, his eyes were livid. He stormed the distance to them, and Varis's eyes also flashed in anger at the interruption. She knew he didn't hold high respects for the general at the best of times, and the feeling was clearly mutual.

"You will distance yourself from her," he warned, low, dark, and calm, stopping deliberately close to Varis.

The challenge for dominance and the fury that rippled from both males trembled every nerve cell in Faythe's body. She shrank farther into the wall as if it could swallow her whole.

"We were only talking—weren't we, Faythe?" the captain said playfully, but he didn't take his eyes off the general.

She said nothing.

Reylan advanced a step, the darkening of his sapphire eyes frightening. Wisely, Varis yielded a step back in response, but rage twitched his expression, and Faythe was surprised he held onto the reins of his violence. Her heart was in her throat at the tension. She almost wanted to put herself between them, knowing how dangerous the captain could be. But Reylan didn't flinch, didn't fear him in the slightest.

"You don't speak her name. You don't cross her path. And if you dare raise a hand to her again, you'll find yourself without it… perhaps without a life, depending on Faythe's mercy."

They stared off for a few long, agonizing seconds. Faythe held her breath in painful anticipation at the way Reylan challenged the captain. She was sure Varis had never been belittled, *threatened,* in such a way before, and she didn't have to try to feel his immense rage piercing her in nauseating waves. The captain's face flexed and creased as he struggled to hold in his hatred. To her great relief and shock, however, his head bowed in a small nod of obedience—something she didn't think she'd ever seen from the wicked demon.

"Remember your station, Captain." Reylan's last words left no room for response.

Varis's jaw flexed, but he turned on his heel, his deadly glare locking onto her for a split second before he was storming away from them both.

As soon as he was out of sight, Faythe released a long breath, finally letting her stiff posture relax now she was in the presence of safety. She turned her gaze to Reylan, finding his deep blue eyes laced with concern but still balanced on the razor's edge of anger.

"Are you all right?" His question was quiet while he diffused his wrath.

She almost came apart, the seams of her grief close to breaking the longer she held everything to herself. The knowledge of the Dresair and everything she knew about her ties to Marvellas's evil. But she couldn't tell him, not without risk to his life, and that thought alone was enough for her to drown out the need to share.

"I'm fine," she answered. Pushing off the wall, she began to walk on weak legs, desperate to make it to her rooms to be alone. Reylan followed, and she added, "Thank you, but you shouldn't have provoked him like that. Varis is… He's dangerous."

"He's nothing but a spineless coward who takes pleasure in dominating those he believes to be inferior." Reylan caught her arm to halt her just before she made it to the door. "But you're not inferior to anyone, Faythe. Your strength is within, and your weapon is internal. It's his biggest mistake to underestimate you."

The backs of her eyes burned because she wanted to believe in his fierce words—but it was as if her mind was blocking any comfort or consolation from being absorbed into confidence. She didn't deserve it.

"You shouldn't underestimate *him*, Reylan. You don't know what he's capable of."

His jaw tensed. "Has he hurt you before?" he asked carefully, his voice as sharp as a blade.

She shook her head. "I've seen inside his mind. It's not hard to guess," she lied, and he seemed to know it.

Reylan always carried himself coolly, collectedly, as if nothing fazed him. Seeing the flash of fury crease his usual stern indifference—it turned him into a whole new force to reckon with, a threat no man or fae would dare to cross or challenge. Despite this, Faythe wasn't afraid. She didn't think she could ever be truly fearful of him.

"It was a long while ago. I took care of it then, and I can handle him now," she said, reading the building temper on his face that made her worry he was fighting against screwing the consequences and confronting the captain with far more than words.

Faythe had to turn away from the turmoil in his expression and kept walking until she got to her long-awaited destination. She wondered why he cared, why he was so affected by the knowledge, figuring it was simply overprotective fae male bullshit. She was about to open the door to her rooms, having every intention of locking herself inside until she came up with a plan to stop the evil at large, when Reylan's voice made her pause with her fingers around the handle.

"You don't have to keep your thoughts to yourself," he said softly.

For once, she wished she could confide in the general to alleviate some of the burdens on her mind. But she couldn't stand to even look at him. She had barely glanced at any of her friends in farewell. She couldn't without thinking it might be any one of them whose days were numbered.

"I want to be alone." Her tone was cold, and it pained her physically that she didn't really mean it.

"If you want to talk about anything—"

She whirled to him, taking all the anger she felt toward the king, the Spirits, and the damned *world* and pouring it into her voice. "We're not friends, General, and we never will be. The sooner you realize that, the better for both of us. Stay away from me."

A flicker of something guarded flashed in his eyes, but it was wiped away quickly as he backed off with a formal nod. Something deep inside Faythe hurt awfully at the look.

Without another thought, she tore her door open and shut it forcefully behind her.

She waited and listened, hearing silence for a long moment. Reylan stood in place, and she could almost feel his desire to defy her wishes and come after her.

Please stay away... she begged internally, fighting against her own want for him to knock and come inside. Then she listened to his few footsteps until his door opened and closed with a faint click.

The moment she heard it…she let herself fall apart completely.

CHAPTER 42

Reylan

REYLAN STARED AT the door he knew Faythe stood behind
after casting him away. His fists clenched as he refrained
from trying to coax her to voice the worries that were clearly
tearing her apart inside.

We're not friends, General.

For some reason, that declaration emitted a small pinch to his
chest. The pain of believing she truly meant it. They had never
said as such, but perhaps foolishly, he had been letting himself
believe she was starting to release those hard barriers around him.
That given a bit more time, she would come to trust him like she so
effortlessly did with her human friends. Even Nik and Tauria.

Then there was the captain.

As Reylan stood silent in the hall, it wasn't only the contemplation of knocking on Faythe's door that froze him still. It took all his
focus and willpower not to damn the consequences and storm back
to find Varis. He feared he'd do something that would cross a
deadly line if he got the captain alone. Faythe's panic around

him…he could feel it from across the castle. And her plea for help, to escape him…

Reylan took a few conscious, calming breaths on the spot. He couldn't allow himself to imagine what Varis had done to instill such terror. He was sure he'd murder the captain without logical thought if given the opportunity.

Cursing under his breath, he turned from the door, making the short stride to his own and hauling it open with more force than intended in his bitter frustration.

He should have detected the presence inside long before he laid eyes on the Prince of High Farrow. He swore again inwardly that he was allowing his guard to slip over foolish concerns for a human who had no interest in even knowing him.

"What are you doing here?" Reylan snapped, in no mood for friendly conversation and angered Nik thought it appropriate to enter his room without invitation.

"Close the door," was all Nik said before strolling out through the balcony doors.

Reylan was too low on energy to object and eager to get the prince to leave as soon as possible so he could have some solitude. He wanted to give in to the torture of silence that fed on his anger and indignation.

It had been far too long since Reylan last allowed himself to be so bothered by someone else. What Faythe did, what she thought, what she felt—he was tormented by it all. He shouldn't concern himself with her beyond his duty to ensure she stayed alive; should instead leave her alone as she wished. Yet he had allowed himself to tangle his long-dormant feelings with her. Feelings of *care*. So slowly, since the day he laid eyes on those golden irises he didn't even know, until it became too late. He couldn't turn his back on her now.

Stepping out against the cool air, he found Nik surveying his city with his back to him.

"Those doors too," he said without turning.

The command flared Reylan's already simmering anger, but he knew better than to voice a disgruntled string of curses to a prince, friend or not. So, he did as he was asked and stood silently waiting for Nik's explanation of the encounter. Though he already had his suspicions.

The prince turned to him, his expression stern and calculating. Reylan braced himself, figuring Nik had worked up a lecture since they left the human town after all the shocking revelations. He had to pity him for finding out how his mother had passed, discovering his father, out of his right mind, was the culprit... Reylan knew the pain of losing parents and more, but he couldn't imagine laying the blame on someone he loved and trusted like Nik did his father.

"Out with it then," Reylan said when Nik continued to silently assess him.

Nik's chest rose deeply before he spoke. "Why did you really come back to High Farrow?"

Reylan blinked. It wasn't the question he expected, as it was one he had already answered, albeit vaguely and withholding some truth. "You know why," he replied, growing irritable at Nik's accusatory look.

"Let's cut the bullshit, Reylan. After all we've been through, at least extend me the courtesy of the truth."

"I'm here to stop a war before your father destroys everything we've built," Reylan snarled.

Nik didn't balk. "I know you well enough. You're a fine war general. Spying in plain sight would be a fool's move with everything you know. Everything you *stole* from Faythe."

There it was. The mention of the human he knew held a place in the prince's heart. He wanted to admire Nik for his protection of her, but he could only see white at the hint that Reylan would ever mean her harm.

"I'll only ask once more," Nik went on, the tone prodding at some primal dominance. Reylan had to focus his breathing. "Why did you come back?"

"I came back for her."

It tumbled out of him so recklessly. Seeing the hard look in Nik's eye, his stance, so ready to protect Faythe...from *him*. Reylan was a fool for exposing himself, but he couldn't stand the thought of being considered a danger to her.

The prince straightened, Reylan's confession having the opposite effect as his whole demeanor changed. His scent shifted, turning threatening. Reylan realized he was in dangerous waters because he couldn't back down, couldn't submit to the challenge. Even against someone above his rank.

He smoothed the edges of his sharp anger, knowing it was he who owed an explanation. "I'm not your enemy," he reiterated.

Nik didn't loosen his posture in the slightest. "What do you want with Faythe?" His voice was dark. A hint of a warning lay in the words, and Reylan's eyes flashed. He clenched his teeth, fighting the damning need to level with it. The tension between them became so thick it was almost palpable.

"I'm certainly not her enemy either," he ground out.

"Are you sure? Faythe doesn't seem to think so."

He knew he should submit to Nik's dominance, not only because he was a prince, but because he had every right to be defensive of his friend. Or perhaps she was still more than a friend to him—it wasn't hard to detect some romantic history between them. The thought riled a different kind of emotion in him that prevented Reylan from seeing sense in the situation.

"You're always around her, always prying into her life when you have no business—"

"And you do?" Reylan flared. He couldn't help it; couldn't stop it. "Do you even know her at all?"

Nik's jaw flexed as he took a step toward him. It was dangerous. Dangerous for the two of them to be alone while they were both high on anger and indignation. He hated the distrust between them, but he knew he could only blame himself for withholding information. Reylan hadn't wanted to confide in Nik before—not because he didn't trust him, but because he didn't want to put him in a position of choice if he knew the truth about the human he so dearly cared for. Faythe's safety came first, by the order of his king. His stomach churned with the seed of guilt that he couldn't be certain Nik would go against his father should the worst of his fears come true.

"You'd be wise to abide by her wishes and stay away," Nik said, authority coating the command.

Reylan huffed an incredulous laugh and shook his head. "Have you ever really *looked* at her, Nik? Have you ever stopped gawking and pining for long enough to *see* her?" It seethed out of him. He couldn't hold it back even though he knew it would erupt into the type of fury that had Nik reaching for his sword.

His hand curled around the hilt, but he made no move to arm himself. Reylan knew it was an instinctive reaction in response to the insult he'd inadvertently thrown.

"You don't have a clue," Reylan went on anyway. "All you see is power to be used and a beauty to admire."

"I have *never* used Faythe. Never."

"No, you sit by and let your father do that."

Nik did draw his sword then and pointed the lethal tip to his chest. Reylan didn't back down but didn't arm himself in response. It would be a grave mistake to physically threaten a prince.

"So, what—you're here because you *care* for her?" Nik mocked.

Yes. No. Yes. Reylan wasn't certain. Not at first. He profusely objected to being sent back north. Yet now, somewhere along the line of duty, he *had* come to care for Faythe. Torturously. He was a fool. Though he would never admit that to Nik—perhaps not to anyone, ever—when it had taken so long for him to realize it within himself.

The prince's face once again turned tight when Reylan didn't answer. "You didn't seem surprised by the fact she's half-fae." The statement held both question and accusation.

"No," he said carefully.

Nik didn't lower his sword. "When Aurialis mentioned Faythe's mother in Rhyenelle, you didn't seem surprised by that either."

Reylan raised his chin in reply, letting Nik put the pieces together in his own mind.

The prince's brow knitted with a hint of disbelief. "You knew her?"

Nik huffed a humorless laugh, finally lowering the threat of his blade as he turned to pace, going over clues internally. Then he whirled back around, face falling in pale dread.

"You weren't…involved with her, were you?"

Reylan's eyes widened a fraction, not believing *that* was the first conclusion he'd drawn. "Gods, no," he responded quickly. "Lilianna and I were somewhat close, but certainly not in the way you're thinking."

Though Nik's expression washed with relief, it was short-lived when his brow furrowed deeply. Reylan instantly knew what had him contemplating.

"You never asked Faythe her mother's name, did you?" Nik locked his gaze, knowing it would strike a chord of familiarity in him.

"Think about it, Nik. Her father is a Nightwalker, a powerful one, just like her mother. But that was never known. A human Nightwalker is not something that should become public knowledge. People fear what they do not know." Reylan could almost see the cogs turning in the prince's mind as he tried to piece together the answer that was right in front of him. "You may not have met her in person as her time at court spanned less than a decade, but her name was common gossip across the kingdoms. Lilianna Aklinsera, the human woman…who stole the heart of a great fae king." Reylan held his breath. Then he saw the exact moment in the prince's emerald eyes that he grasped the truth. The world-shifting truth that fell like a weight on Nik who took a step back as if he'd been dealt a physical blow.

"That can't be true," Nik muttered through a breath, looking away while he mulled it over. "Faythe can't be... *Gods above.*"

Reylan didn't need to insist or even reply. It was clear the prince was fitting everything else together just fine.

With the secret out, Reylan felt the need to explain. "Her eyes...they're just like her mother's. Agalhor's scent is there, but it's faint. I only detected it because I was looking, but the moment I saw those eyes, I knew. Nik—" Reylan dropped his stern posture, feeling his anger fizzle in the presence of a fear so great. "Your father cannot find out."

The prince looked at him, face distraught, and it was the exact reason he initially chose to harbor the secret. It disturbed him to see Nik with a torn heart.

"He would harm her to get to him. To get to Agalhor...he might even kill her." Reylan could barely whisper the last part, feeling the air leave him completely at the thought.

Nik said nothing, his face remaining like stone.

"Please." It slipped from Reylan's mouth, the word he so very rarely had to use.

The prince seemed to snap out of his deep thoughts, locking eyes with the general. His own were hard, and for a split second, Reylan braced for the worst. "Did you really think the worst of me? That I would go running to my father knowing it would put Faythe in danger?" Nik's voice was pained, twisting Reylan's gut out of shame.

"I couldn't take the chance," Reylan said, and he didn't feel guilty for it. Not when it came to Faythe's life.

"Of course I'm not going to tell my father," Nik snapped. He ran a hand through his ink-black hair. "*Shit,*" he swore.

Reylan knew his anger wasn't from the knowledge or even directed at the general for keeping it from him. Nik's disappointment was in himself for somehow not realizing who Faythe was sooner. His gaze targeted him again.

"She's an Ashfyre," he said in no more than a whisper while he

glanced over the stone wall. They were high enough he was confident they were out of hearing range below, and Reylan had already
extended his senses to know there were no lingering bodies on the
other balconies. "You mean to tell me all this time, with everything
we know, we've held an *Ashfyre* in our midst, and you've done nothing!" Nik hissed low.

"Agalhor won't force her to Rhyenelle."

"Then I bloody well will!" Nik seethed, but his voice was torn
with heartbreak.

Reylan found himself in mutual agreement with the prince.
He'd more than once thought to damn Faythe's choice and take
her back to the south with him regardless, back to where she would
be unconditionally protected. He only hoped once she knew everything, she would see sense that it was the safest place for her. In fear
of the opposite, he'd swallowed his confession of the secret he
harbored and hated himself for it. For his cowardice, and for
keeping it from her for so long. More than anything, he feared it
would drive a wedge of deeper mistrust between them when she
found out.

"You haven't told her?"

Reylan recoiled with guilt. "No."

"Well, we have to tell her!" Nik threw an arm out in exasperation.

"I will. I plan to. She just—not yet. Not after everything that
happened in the town and before that. She doesn't need the weight
of anything else right now." Again, his words came out in a
pathetic plea, and he internally cursed at himself for it.

"What do you mean, *'before that'*?"

"She's not been the same since venturing those caves."

Nik's face fell knowingly. "She hasn't spoken to you about that
either?"

Reylan shook his head. Faythe's walls were solid. Her incessant
need to protect those around her kept her worries and burdens on
the side no one could penetrate. The way through was not to take a

hammer to the barrier she'd so expertly crafted, brick by brick, her whole life; it was through patience and persistence without force, to get her to open the door she didn't know she'd attached to it.

"I don't like keeping secrets from her. This…" Nik trailed off, struggling to comprehend the revelation. Reylan sympathized as he'd spent weeks in turmoil after discovering the fact during his first trip to High Farrow. "She deserves to know."

The general nodded. "Agreed." The cowardly part of him was glad not to be the only one who knew. Perhaps when the blow landed, it could be softened by the prince she clearly trusted deeply. Though it pained him to acknowledge it, he knew it would take time to gain the same trust from her after everything he'd done. But all Reylan had was time.

"After Yulemas," he said. "Give her a little more time to sort through her troubles. Perhaps the holiday can bring her some joy. She deserves that at least."

Nik's face softened. "After the holiday," he concluded.

One week.

He only hoped that would be enough time for her to diffuse whatever plagued her troubled mind and find room for another impossible truth—one she silently longed for. To know who her father was.

As for how she would respond… Reylan's emotions were on a knife's edge in anticipation.

CHAPTER 43

Faythe

"**Y**OU ASKED FOR ME?**"

Faythe turned when Caius's voice came through her door after a brief knock. She nodded and welcomed him inside her rooms.

"I'm sorry to ask this of you, but I need to get something to Marlowe. I would go myself, but I can't risk raising the king's suspicions if he happens to have me followed."

The young guard approached, looking ready to accept any task she asked of him. "Of course. Whatever you need."

Faythe didn't know what she'd done to deserve his loyalty, but she was grateful for it. She smiled with suppressed sadness, hating that she had to involve him at all.

She had a plan. Or rather, a death wish.

She'd told no one of it. Faythe had barely left her rooms and refused to see any of her friends over the past week since they spoke to the Spirit of Life.

She had to kill the King of High Farrow. And she had to do it alone.

Her survival didn't play into any of the outcomes she'd drawn over her days of scheming. It seemed sacrificing her life was the only way to stop the fate the Dresair told her would come to pass. If it became a choice between her life and that of those around her, the answer was obvious. It wasn't her way of trying to be the selfless hero. Out of those around her, she determined her life was of the least value. Nik and Tauria had kingdoms to protect, Jakon and Marlowe had a life to grow together. *Gods,* she even took Reylan into account. He was a highly skilled and respected general who would be of far more use in the bigger war to come than she could ever hope to be.

But there were still matters she had to put into place before the main event that would see her commit treason. It was a horrifying, daunting task, and she tried not to dwell on the act out of fear she would succumb to the panic that built inside the hourglass draining faster toward her end.

She would do it during the Yulemas Ball by week's end. A party she wasn't invited to—but now intended to crash. The setting would offer the disguise she needed, the chaos to distract, and the opportunity to get close enough to the king for long enough to strike.

Each passing day added layers to her anxiety, and she'd pushed everyone away for fear they would suspect something was wrong.

Lifting the thickly wrapped package, she held it out to Caius. He took it, wide eyes shooting up to hers as he did.

"Marlowe will know what to do with it, and I'll need it returned at the Yulemas Ball. Can you do that for me?"

He offered a wan smile with his slight nod. "Something big is about to happen, isn't it?"

Faythe reached a hand out to his arm to soothe his wariness as he observed her, perhaps searching for her sanity. "You're on the right side, Caius. Thank you for everything you've done for me and for our friends. You're a picture of the brighter future we all fight for."

Though she didn't mean it as a goodbye, it overwhelmed her all at once that her encounters with him, and with everyone, were short on numbers. She didn't give him a chance to step away when she leaned in to embrace him, grateful and relived when he held her tightly back for a long, bittersweet moment. When Caius released her, his frown was deep with protest and concern.

"Faythe, whatever you're planning—"

"I'll be fine," she cut in, giving her most convincing smile.

Caius looked at her sadly but didn't press further. Instead, he turned and headed for the door. Just before he opened it, however, he twisted his head halfway back. He didn't look her in the eye but stared in thought at the ground instead.

"I'll see you at the ball, and I'll have what you asked for from Marlowe. But Faythe, if we lose you, we lose all hope of that brighter future."

Then he was gone.

The following evening, Faythe felt desperate in her need to release her emotions through the swinging of her blade. She found herself in the training room, an hour into battling it out against a wooden dummy, which she hacked to pieces in her frustration.

Caius's last words did little to motivate her. Having the opposite effect, she hated that she started to feel *guilty* in the sacrifice of her own life. She hated the grief she would cause her friends, which had always been a heavy weight on her decision. Yet Caius instilled a different kind of feeling that made her doubt her choices.

Her life was useless in the grand scheme of everything—against Valgard, against Marvellas. She was of little value in the eyes of battle, though she'd had every intention to fight before she met her new twist of fate. The young guard had succeeded in making her feel guilty for *dying* when she hadn't even told him her intentions.

I have no purpose. She swung her sword, wedging it into the wood. *I am no one.* Bracing a foot against it, she yanked her blade free. *They all deserve to live.* Her teeth ground from the sting in her eyes as Lumarias struck again. *I bring them nothing but danger.* And again. *They're better off without me.* And again, until she finally halted, breathless, and hung her head.

She wished the stationary wooden figure could fight back as she resorted to using her imagination to parry offense attacks. She'd taken several chucks out of the wood, so it was starting to lose its form as she whittled it down. Wood chips carved of self-resentment and sorrow surrounded her. Bracing her hands on her knees, she was about to scream in indignation into the otherwise silent space when a familiar voice cut through her deep breathing instead.

"You know there are servants for that?"

Faythe jolted at the sound of Reylan's words. When she met his deep blue eyes, she struggled to keep her cold façade of hatred, gleaning the concern that lay within them.

Then his words registered, and she frowned wordlessly in question.

He jerked his chin at the battered dummy. "Chopping firewood."

She might have chuckled and even felt the slight tug of her lips, which she forced down. She sheathed her sword instead and couldn't bear to look at his face any longer for fear she would break. Faythe cast her eyes and stepped off the training platform, making to go around him without engaging at all. It was cruel and heartless...but it kept him safe.

His hand caught her elbow as she passed, and she snapped her cold eyes to him. "Tell me what's wrong, Faythe." His voice was achingly tender. She had never heard the pleading tone from the general and wondered why he even cared to try it with her. They weren't friends before, and she'd made it clear she didn't want to be friends now, even though her heart cried the opposite.

"You're wasting your time with me, Reylan. Let me go."

"I can't."

She looked down at his hand still encasing her arm, knowing it wasn't the hold he meant. Losing her fight, she felt the mask of detached loathing dissolve, leaving only desperation—to stop something before it could begin. She couldn't land him on the list of those close to her whose lives now hung in the balance.

"Please," she whispered, begging him to understand and not press the matter further.

She could tell he was conflicted, not knowing whether to accept her wish or stand firm in his assertion that he wasn't abandoning her. Finally, his overprotective fae male bullshit prevailed. He released her arm, but his expression turned accusatory, and he crossed his arms.

"What happened down in those caves?"

Faythe instinctively slipped back into her cold guise at the mention. "Nothing happened. We got what we needed, and that's all that matters."

"You've been pushing everyone away since. You don't have to face everything alone, gods-dammit."

There was only one way she could get him to back down. She felt sick at the formation of her verbal blows, which rose from the dark void of her desperation, leaking like shadows through her chest to encompass her heart. She had to hurt him, or he would never let it go…

"I wouldn't ever confide in you. I don't trust you, and I don't particularly like you. Your place is at the head of an army, and you've only made things worse by being here. There's nothing here for you, General. Go home. Go back to Rhyenelle. You're not *wanted* here."

Her words were cold. So bitterly ice-cold. She felt each sentence chill those shadows, circling, tightening. It would only relent if she stole those words back.

In the flinch of his eye, she knew they'd hit their mark. The flash of hurt was gone in his next blink. On anyone else, it would have seemed negligible. On Reylan, on someone so well-guarded with their emotions, the slither of hurt spoke louder than anything heard by the ear; felt deeper than any cut with a blade.

Reylan was a warrior honed for battle. He'd seen bloodshed and misery, lost family to war, and been on the front lines of devastating tragedies in his four centuries. She didn't think she would be able to invoke pain within him. Yet there it was, clear in the quick pinch of his brow and the flicker of sadness across his sapphire pools.

She didn't mean it—not in the slightest. She'd fought it for so long, holding onto her reserves out of her own fears, but all this time, she *did* trust him. Completely and unexplainably. It crushed her spirit to think she might never get to tell him she was sorry before she met her end.

Without giving herself a chance to beg his forgiveness and give in to her selfishness no matter the risk...she cast her eyes to the exit and marched out of the room.

This time, she didn't feel his need to come after her.

CHAPTER 44

Jakon

J AKON WATCHED MARLOWE wrap her craft delicately, exactly as
Faythe had requested. Then she set it aside, finishing up for
the day.

Exhaustion was clear on the blacksmith's face, and he longed to
take it from her since she'd been working tirelessly for the past few
days. He'd tried to help and hadn't been back to work on the farm
for weeks. He couldn't. A dark cloud had settled over everything,
and he felt himself on the edge, just waiting for the storm to break.
He didn't know why he felt such dread, but he had been unable to
relax ever since they returned from Galmire because he knew
something was coming. Something evil and inescapable.

Marlowe released a long sigh, looking over her work. She wiped
her brow with the inside of her elbow, and then a deep crease of
worry lined her forehead. Jakon moved on instinct and found himself
stepping behind her and pulling her small form into him. She leaned
into his touch with a smile but remained slightly rigid and concerned.
He kissed her temple, then the curve of her ear, then her neck.

"What's wrong?" he mumbled against her smooth skin.

Her arm came around and lazily curled her fingers in the back of his hair. "I'm worried about Faythe," she admitted.

He leaned his head back and twisted her around to face him. "I don't think we'll ever not be worried about that woman," he commented in light humor, though in truth, he'd been a wreck over her since Caius came to them with her request. He dreaded to think what plans she had for such an item, and he was even more riddled with sickening guilt that there was nothing he could do to stop her on whatever reckless course she'd set for herself.

"But how are *you*, Marlowe?" His fingers grazed under her chin, guiding her face back to lock gazes with him. "Since we've been back, how have you been feeling?"

Her brow flinched, giving away her gratitude for his concern. It still pained him deeply, but never again would he allow her to believe her feelings should be suppressed.

"I'm…not sure," she answered vacantly. Where her mind travelled, he went with her. The sense of foreboding danger that couldn't be placed. "I'm concerned for everyone. I don't think any of us are spared from what's to come. And then, should something happen to Faythe before I can talk to her, apologize for how I've been with her and explain—"

Jakon took her face between his palms. "You have nothing to be sorry for. I know Faythe will tell you the same thing. And she *will* tell you, because we will see her again."

It was as much a desperate reassurance to himself as it was intended to soothe Marlowe's worries. A shiver embraced his body as he wondered what pieces of a cracked puzzle the oracle held to inspire such cold trepidation.

Seeing the glittering sadness of uncertainty in her ocean-blue irises, Jakon brought his mouth to hers.

They didn't get the chance to deepen the kiss as a frantic form whipped through the back curtain of the blacksmiths. Jakon tore away from Marlowe, pushing her behind him at the thought of danger from the invading presence.

His alert turned to shadows of dark fear at the sight of Caius, wide-eyed in panic. "You have to leave," he said urgently.

Jakon straightened, his mind reeling over what might cause the guard to be so worried and desperate. "Faythe. Is she—?" He couldn't bring himself to finish the sentence.

"Alive—for now."

Jakon didn't have time to breathe a sigh of relief as Caius went on.

"But they're coming for you—both of you. I think it's to get to Faythe."

He looked to Marlowe in cold horror. "Gather your things, love," he said quickly, trying to keep his calm through the shock.

Marlowe nodded and set to work gathering what she thought was necessary from around the workshop. He didn't know if they had time to make it back to the cottage.

"How?" he asked first, needing to get all the information he could.

Caius's look was grim. "The captain, I think. Nightwalking," he said vaguely.

It shouldn't have come as a surprise. It was always a possibility they could be caught out by such an ability.

"What do they want?"

"All I know is they plan to use you to get to Faythe. She knows something they can't get to without her."

Jakon's mind was a chaos of thoughts. Instinctively, he looked to Marlowe. They shared a moment of dawning before both their eyes locked on the item on the table.

"Faythe once told me if she was ever to be caught, you were to run—and take the ruin with you."

He had to close his eyes for a moment and breathe. Everything in him screamed to go to her. If she was in danger, he couldn't leave her to face it alone.

"Can you get me into the castle?" He met the guard's eye.

Caius shook his head. "I'm sorry, Jakon, but you'll only make it worse for her. She'll give over exactly what they need if they get a hold of you. The only way you can help her is to run far and take what it is they seek with you."

He knew the guard was right, and it infuriated him to no end. He wanted to kill them all, every guard, and even the king who sought to harm Faythe. His friend, his soul mate—he refused to believe there was a chance he may never see her again.

"You can't let them kill her, Caius. Please protect her. Help her to escape, and tell her we'll be heading south," he pleaded like a boy. It was all he had in him as he was painfully desperate.

Faythe *had* to live.

The young guard lifted his chin and gave a fierce nod. "I will," he promised.

CHAPTER 45

Faythe

FAYTHE ADJUSTED THE long dagger strapped around her thigh one last time before letting the cascade of crimson fall over it in disguise. She stood in front of the mirror staring at her gold eyes —soon to be those of a king killer if she succeeded in her plan tonight.

She almost couldn't recognize herself, and it had nothing to do with the elegant new look she donned for the Yulemas Ball. Her dress was a statement in itself. The deep red with gold accents reminded her of fire. *Gave her fire.* Its fierce strength was exactly what she needed. The neckline was scandalously low and almost reached her navel. The transparent mesh of the sleeves and bodice was embellished with weaving lines of crystals, giving the illusion of vines of flame licking up her arms to merge into the blazing inferno that fanned around her. Even her hair was different. Her waves were flattened, and she'd purposefully abandoned the elegant braids that were customary to the ladies of the court. Instead, her hair was held back from her face by one pin above her ear on each side, like two feathered fans of red and gold.

Faythe didn't want to blend in tonight. She wanted for the king to see her and to be heard…one last time.

Nik's gifted necklace lay against her bare chest, and she held it, closing her eyes and imagining him standing next to her with Tauria by his side. Then Jakon and Marlowe. Then Reylan appeared in the scene, and she looked around her friends in her mind.

Out loud, she whispered as if they all could hear her, "I'm sorry."

CHAPTER 46

Reylan

REYLAN WAS NEVER one for grand parties. Back home in
Rhyenelle, it was easy enough to find reason to be busy
when they took place. In his position, there was never a shortage of
problems that needed attention, soldiers who needed training,
patrols that needed organizing. It kept him busy.

Yet he couldn't have avoided the High Farrow Yulemas Ball
even if he wanted to. He knew he had eyes on him, and it would
only rouse Orlon's suspicions if he failed to attend. Still, he didn't
plan to stay long; would only make an appearance to satisfy the
king then retreat back to his rooms where he knew Faythe would be
safe and sound opposite his door.

He hated that even being away from her for this short amount
of time set him irritably on edge. But he had sworn an oath to
protect her. To his king.

When presented with the proposition, he had at first objected to
being sent back to the north. After all, he was Rhyenelle's top war
general, not a babysitter. Yet his king had plead there was no one
else he could trust with the task of watching over the potential heir

to his throne. It seemed impossible to believe, and Reylan found himself often forgetting who she was—who her *father* was—when he was around Faythe.

Reylan had wanted to tell her, but the coward in him didn't want to rain more world-shifting news over the woman who already shouldered so much burden. He wanted to protect her, and it terrified him to admit that as much as he tried to fight it, deny it, through all the horror he'd learned and finding Faythe at the forefront of every danger…he was developing his own deep need to ensure her safety over and above the orders of Agalhor.

The recall of the day he arrived back in Rhyenelle following the kings' meetings made him shudder.

"Orlon's spymaster?"

It was easy to put the pieces together. Lilianna had been gifted as a Nightwalker, which astounded Reylan as she was a human. Coming across Faythe with the immense power she held, he could only assume two Nightwalkers had produced such an anomaly.

Reylan's answer to the king's question was a grave nod.

Agalhor turned away from him, and he saw he was trying to process the life-changing news. Not only for himself, but for the kingdom. He had no other children, and since Lilianna had refused to seek the company of another to marry and produce more, this made Faythe the one true and rightful heir to the throne of Rhyenelle.

There was only one problem: she was human, and no kingdom had been ruled by a human monarch in thousands of years. There was a high chance she would never become queen with her mortality, but whatever children she bore would continue to be the next in line after Agalhor's reign if he didn't produce another heir before then.

"You need to go back to High Farrow," Agalhor said, though he still seemed deep in thought.

Reylan jumped in to protest. "With all due respect, Your Majesty, if Orlon and Varlas are gathering forces against us, I'm better served here." He sounded a little too desperate. He had no interest in going back to the north. He didn't particularly like the lifestyle and arrogance of the kingdom. Their fae were pompous, and they treated their human subjects like outcasts. It was a stark contrast to the freedom and unity of the people of Rhyenelle.

The king met his eye then, and his own were haunted as he said, "If they discover who she is, they will kill her."

Why did that strike a chord in him? He didn't know her, didn't think he held any feeling for her. Yet he dreaded to think of her life ending.

He wouldn't wager on Faythe feeling the same about him.

He'd taken her ability against her will and used it to get the information he needed. It was a desperate act as he could see she wasn't willing to trust him enough to disclose what she saw in the Olmstone king's mind, but he knew she could do it. The king was smart and would have shielded himself against her to keep up his illusion of kindness and friendship. But Faythe was brilliantly intuitive and had caught onto every slight hint he gave her to be wary of the monarchs.

"You want me to bring her to Rhyenelle?" He could do that, as grueling as the round trip would be.

The king shook his head, and Reylan's stomach dropped. "I won't force her here. She has a life in High Farrow. How can I take that from her?" he said sadly.

Reylan knew the king wanted nothing more than to meet Faythe; to look into her gold eyes and make no mistake she was Lilianna's daughter.

Then he asked, "Is she treated well?"

Reylan was conflicted in answer. She was fed and housed, but he doubted her station as the king's spymaster was entirely of her own free will. Faythe was too...*good* for such an invasive position. His fingers subconsciously curled as he imagined what Orlon might hold against her to keep her in his service as a weapon.

"As well as can be expected," he said.

Agalhor's only response was a sad nod before he turned back to the white rosebuds.

"What exactly am I to do in High Farrow?" Reylan dreaded to hear what he already anticipated.

"Protect her. Find out if she is happy, and when the time is right...tell her. Tell her how I loved her mother and would have done everything to keep her safe. Both of them." He looked to him as he finished. "Then let her make her choice."

Reylan blew out a breath at the memory of Agalhor's broken plea.

It was the one thing on his mind that hummed every time she was near. He needed to tell her. She deserved to know who her father was. But he couldn't bring himself to throw the news down upon her. It wasn't a simple piece of knowledge. Far from it. She was the daughter of a great king and could inherit a kingdom if she decided to embrace her heritage. Every day, Reylan saw her more for what she could be—for what she should be: an *heir* to Rhyenelle.

He stood awkwardly by the side of the hall, antsy as he counted down the minutes until it was acceptable for him to leave. Watching the flamboyance and declining several ladies' offers to dance—it was draining. He had to wonder about the talent of High Farrow's suitors to have so many attempting to engage with the most deterring face in the room. He kept hold of a goblet more to occupy his bored hands, giving the wine more attention than he gave a single soul at the hideously over-the-top ball.

Knocking back the last of its contents, he turned and set his goblet down. His hand halted around the jug he intended to refill it with. Slowly, he uncurled his fingers from around the handle, forgetting everything as he felt it.

Felt *her*.

He turned and looked up. His eyes didn't wander, didn't have to search, as they landed exactly on the gold orbs they sought—bright even from atop the grand staircase across the hall.

Yet it was not Faythe's eyes this time that made everything around him distort in a blur of motion, blocking out the loud music.

She met his eyes too, standing proudly above everyone else like a blazing firebird.

Like a Phoenix.

Dear Gods. She had no idea what that symbol alone screamed right in the face of every unwitting and ignorant fae in the hall.

She was fire and ice and all destructive contrasts, much like the storm that stirred inside him at the sight. She was not a human citizen of High Farrow; she was not Orlon's spymaster…

Tonight, she was Rhyenelle's daughter.

And the gut-wrenching irony was that she didn't even realize it.

His feet moved of their own accord as he felt compelled forward. A part of him flared in anger at the thought of anyone else making it over to her before him. He convinced himself it was simply to protect her. On Agalhor's orders.

Yet he knew in his heart he'd developed his own deep need to ensure Faythe's safety, not only as a potential heir to Rhyenelle or as his king's daughter…but as something else. Something *unexplainable*.

He glided through the masses of revelers, and she descended the stairs. Her eyes lit up against the red of her gown like blazing beacons of amber fire. He dared to let himself believe she was the single most magnificent thing he'd ever seen. Strong and beautiful, but she was also *real*. What lay within was always as equally admirable and mesmerizing as exterior beauty.

Reylan didn't care that she might reject him the moment he got close enough. Each step was built on the thrill, the *need* to be near her. As much as Faythe tried to push him away, he just couldn't seem to listen.

CHAPTER 47

Faythe

FAYTHE'S EYES KNEW where to find the general, as if she understood the sight would offer a moment of absolution. He stood idly by the side of the party, and the flamboyance around him became distant, irrelevant, as she took in nothing but the sapphires that beckoned her. Reylan stared at her for a long moment before he started to walk toward her.

She descended the staircase. She looked at no one else, perhaps out of cowardice, but she vaguely noticed the clamor of voices hush slightly with her first steps into the hall.

She'd wanted the attention, and she certainly got it. She didn't have to avert her gaze to know the king was also staring from his position on his great throne in the ballroom, likely blazing at the sight of her disregarding his direct orders.

She kept her chin high in a mask of confidence, and when she got to the bottom, Reylan's deep blue eyes became the calming source to tame her racing heartbeat. His hand was poised for her to take, and she did without hesitation, sliding her trembling fingers into his cool, calloused palm without breaking eye contact.

In that moment, she forgot she was supposed to be keeping her distance from him; was supposed to deny that she had any feelings for him. Allowing herself one night to be selfish, knowing it could be her last, she let Reylan lead her onto the dance floor.

His hand glided across her waist and stopped on the small of her back. The other clasped her own. His skin against hers sent soothing shivers up her arm to embrace her heart, sedating its erratic tempo. Tenderly, the arm that held her pulled her to him so there was no space between the spymaster and the general. She couldn't ignore the warmth in her chest at the movement and relaxed in the invisible shield of safety she always felt when she was close to him.

Faythe didn't know any of the steps, but somehow, she knew Reylan would carry her through it. It was slow, and she found it easy enough to keep up with his guidance. The party faded into background noise, and she forgot the stares, forgot her worries, forgot her fears—all of it became inconsequential while she lost herself in the sea of sapphire and stars.

"I didn't take you for one to participate in such dances," she said quietly, almost breathless. She was spun around with the next movement, her dress fanning around them and encasing his legs in her flames of fabric.

"I'm not," he said, his voice thick, when they came together again.

Her heart skipped a beat at the look in his eye, but she couldn't quite be sure what it was. Not lust or love. Not admiration or appreciation. Something...*more*. And it sparked dying embers inside her.

The heat from his body radiated onto Faythe even through the thickness of his formal jacket. Every time she spun away from him, a new thrill pulsed through her when they joined again and moved together as one.

An ache clenched in her chest like nothing she'd felt before, but she wouldn't get the chance to tell him. Tell him that all this time she'd pushed him away—even before the damning knowledge from the Dresair—she was only doing so to suppress her real fears. She had come to deeply care for Reylan and couldn't stand the thought of exposing him to the danger that followed her every turn if she let him in.

"The color suits you." His voice brought her back to the dance.

A small smile crept onto her lips. "You're duty bound to be biased toward this shade of crimson, *General.*"

He shook his head. "Blue drowns you, but you've never looked more alive in red. You woke every dreary face in this room the moment you stepped out here tonight."

Something in the way he spoke didn't attach the compliment to physical appearance alone. When Reylan looked at her, it was as if he could see right down to the very core of her soul, and he didn't shy from everything she was and all that she wasn't. Feeling so exposed through a mere look should have left her recoiling, but instead, she held onto those sapphires. Held them as if they were her anchor to this world.

She swallowed her building nerves. "It might have had something to do with the human crashing their extravagant fae-only ball."

A smile slowly tugged at the corners of his mouth. "It has nothing to do with the shape of your ears. They see you, Faythe. *I* see you…and I hear you." He didn't just mean the glamor of her gown or the fact of her mortality. This was more than a compliment from Reylan; it was the flare of strength she needed.

He seemed to slow their dance, casting them off from the other pairs. Faythe didn't care as she matched his stare that held something new. Something like *need.* Though it was formed around the small essence of pain that swirled in his irises. Reylan brought their clasped hands to his chest, leaving hers to hover over his heart while his gently poised under her chin. Her breath stilled, skin prickling delightfully at his touch.

Reylan looked over her face slowly, a slight frown of wonder disturbing his brow as though he searched for the answer to his mystifying question. Her quickening pulse as he seemed to inch closer cancelled out all other thoughts. His hand shifted on her back a fraction, enough that his fingertips grazed her bare skin from the low dip of her gown. His touch sent a bolt of warm vibrations up the curve of her spine, causing her body to lean into his tighter. That trail of enchanting desire was felt right to the tip of her spine, in her neck, parting her lips on a shallow inhale and tilting her face to be at the perfect angle for their mouths to meet. His slight crooked smile told her he knew exactly what he was doing.

"We might cause an uproar," he mumbled, but his warm breath across her lips was enough to subside all thoughts of dissuasion.

"I'm already a point of scandal. What's one more act to incite their blatant distaste?"

His wicked grin of agreement made her heart skip a beat. She didn't care for the many eyes of disgust that followed their every movement. All she wanted was to damn everything, knowing she may never get another chance.

The distance closed in slowly. Torturously slow. Each second felt suspended, leaving a chance for either of them to deny; to stop what might become of them should the distance cease to exist. Faythe had no objections. Not now. Not even in the most disagreeable moments did she truly want space from him. With his persistence and protection, Faythe couldn't be sure what it was about the general that sparked her want to *live*. To learn to see whatever it was that caused the flare in his eye when he looked at her. He saw a strength she didn't know she held within. Saw it, and gave unyielding life to it.

His lips came close to grazing hers...

Then the lazy applause of nearby spectators snapped both of them back to their present surroundings.

Faythe's disappointment weighed heavy in her stomach as Reylan pulled his face back, becoming aware of the attention. The dance had ended minutes ago for them, but as the rest of the party caught up, they no longer had the cover of song and bustle.

It was selfish of Faythe to want that kiss, and maybe he would have resented her for it once her life was claimed for the treasonous plan she harbored. Reylan deserved better. He deserved more than she could ever give him. And that fact was enough for her to swallow the hard lump of a lost promise. She looked past Reylan and found Orlon already staring at her, eyes livid. Once, it would have made her shrink in submission. Now, she had a spark of determination to end him, and with it, the hold Marvellas had on her home kingdom.

She cast her attention back to Reylan one last time, needing to tell him, "I'm sorry. For everything. You should know that I do trust you." Her eyes searched his. Savoring them. "I always have." Her hand fell from his firm chest as she stepped away from him, holding her skirts in a short bow to blend in with the other ladies who stemmed off to find new dance partners.

Reylan didn't give her the chance to depart when he swooped in close again, hand going around her waist to lean his mouth against her ear. *"Why do I get the feeling you're about to do something reckless?"* His voice was in her mind, but his breath caressed her ear as he moved his lips to appear as if he were talking out loud. It sent a tremor of desire down Faythe's back, but she breathed deeply to ignore it.

"Goodbye, Reylan."

Those parting words split and cracked something deep within. Faythe was grateful for his internal conversation, not trusting her voice would sound steady otherwise. She didn't give him the chance to stop her, and he wouldn't risk attracting the king's attention by making a scene to keep her close. She slid out of his grasp, feeling cold and vulnerable the second his warmth left her.

The spymaster drifted into the mass of revelers, losing herself and putting distance between her and the general who would surely move to stop her if he caught onto her plan. Faythe paused briefly to scan the crowd, looking for one fae guard in particular who held the key to her plan's success—if he'd succeeded in obtaining it from her brilliant blacksmith friend, of course.

Her eyes found Caius at the edge of the dancers. He was already staring, waiting to catch her eye. The music quietened, and her feet felt unsteady as she beheld the look of panic on his face, followed by a short, subtle shake of his head. Her heart picked up in a wild sprint. She could attempt the assassination without the weapon, but the odds of success were severely diminished.

Every plan she had required quick reconsideration. Faythe turned to glean the King of High Farrow's position, but her view was immediately blocked and her path obstructed by a tall figure. Her eyes trailed up to meet the emerald orbs of the prince.

"Dance with me." He held out his hand, and she would have declined the seemingly innocent offer, but in his look, there was suppressed fear like she had seen in Caius. Faythe filled with heavy dread. This wasn't merely an invitation to take part in the customary dance. The strange reaction made her listen, and she took Nik's hand for him to lead her to the dance floor where they merged with the flow of movement.

"Smile. Engage."

She wisely followed his instruction and forced herself to appear present while the prince sent her a private conversation. Her mind reeled over why he thought it necessary. She looked at him to send something back.

"What's wrong?" she asked in cold anticipation.

"My father knows."

His words echoed, and she swayed with the weight of them. The dance helped to disguise her quickened breathing and uneven footing, but it also added to the beading on her forehead as she became clammy with sweat.

Just like that, the hunter had become the hunted. Perhaps she was a fool to ever think she could get there first. But it was not too late.

Nik's arm tightened around her as if sensing her intentions. *"He planned to bring in Marlowe and Jakon."* Her eyes widened in trepidation, but he quickly added, *"Caius warned them in time. They should be long gone by now."*

She thanked the very bones of the fae guard. She owed him more than he could possibly know as he had responded to their dire need far more times than she cared to admit.

"What does he know?"

"I can't be certain. All I know is that he plans to have you detained and will use your friends to get the information he wants. It's not hard to guess."

She couldn't hear the music from the ringing in her ears and could barely feel the movement as she continued to dance and twirl with the prince. Her eyes knew exactly which direction to turn to meet those of the general who watched her from the side of the hall. She tried to keep her face neutral though it filled her with horrible anxiety to see him there—for him to be in High Farrow at all right now.

"You have to warn Reylan," she said quickly. If there was a chance the king also knew about his involvement, he wouldn't hesitate to have the general killed.

"Caius is taking care of it."

Sure enough, when she looked over again, she spied the young guard approaching Reylan to engage in seemingly boring conversation.

"We need to get you out—tonight."

She tore her eyes from Reylan to meet those of the prince. *"I can't go. Not yet."* Not before she achieved what she set out to do. She wouldn't run—not when she was close to releasing the evil grip on High Farrow.

When she glanced back across the hall, Reylan was gone. She only hoped he had the good sense to flee back to Rhyenelle where he would be safe. He, Jakon, and Marlowe would be far out of the king's reach. It was a huge relief. Now, she only had to pray to the Spirits there were enough fae remaining in the evil grip to spare the lives of the king's son and ward should they be outed for their involvement too.

"It's over, Faythe. You'll only be fighting a lost battle."

With the next turn in the dance, she and the prince switched sides. Her eyes met those of the king then, standing and staring right at her with a wicked smile. Nik was right. With him alert to her intentions, she wouldn't be able to get within five feet before she would be stopped by the guards who stood poised around him. Orlon had her, and he knew it.

Her blood boiled. She almost snapped and forwent the deadly consequences of reaching for her dagger, which had become a dead weight against her thigh, and taking it to the heart of the king against all odds. Feebleness gripped her instead.

"What do I do?"

Every ounce of confidence left Faythe. Strength bowed to panic, and she felt completely and utterly lost and helpless. She had failed.

"You live to fight another day."

When she locked onto Nik's emerald eyes, they were flooded with sadness under the smile he wore for the crowd around them—for the king who stalked their every move.

"Caius has a horse and supplies ready for you to leave immediately."

"Where will I go?" she said desperately. She had nowhere to go, and her friends were already on the run with no indication of where they might be headed.

"Far from here. To where you'll be safe."

The song came to an end, and they stood facing each other as the couples around them bowed down. She forced herself to blend in with the revelers, though all she wanted in that moment was to fall into the arms of Nik. Would they even get a proper goodbye? She couldn't leave him like this—not after everything they'd been through and all that they meant to each other. He smiled sadly as if he could read her thoughts. Then he came close, taking her hand and leaning in as if to thank her for the dance.

"Be happy, Faythe. Take the back exit. Go slow, stop and engage, and don't look back. Tauria is distracting my father as we speak."

Faythe dared one last glance toward the dais. True to Nik's word, the king's attention was now fixed on the ward who kept his back to her.

"Caius will meet you by the stables. Go—now."

Time raced forward, and she begged for it to stop to allow her a few more minutes with the prince. But time was not her luxury tonight, and she met his look with distraught eyes.

"Thank you," she whispered before adding to his thoughts. *"Goodbye, Nik."*

She didn't look at him again as she slipped away, leaving her heart in pieces where she last stood. Her only option was to concede. But the fight was far from over.

She wove in and out of the crowd, being careful not to walk too fast and keeping her face plastered with a smile for those she passed despite their disgruntled reception. Two guards were at the back exit. Her heart was erratic as she approached them, body flushed and turned rigid. To her great relief, they paid her no attention, and she glided through without being stopped. Then she relaxed for all of a few seconds until she quickened her pace down the empty halls. No one usually ventured these passages, and with the Yulemas Ball in full swing, it was even more eerily deserted.

Catching her skirts by the slit, Faythe swept them to the side as her walk verged on a slow jog. She pictured the back exit through the servants' quarters she would take, and in her urgency, the distance seemed so much farther than she remembered. A cruel taunt in her mind that she would never reach it. Every step felt weighted with internal mockery that she was too slow to get there in time. *Just a few hallways more...* She twisted and turned down dark passageways, counting her breaths as a distraction from her fear the king would have noticed her absence and sent his vultures on her tail by now.

She was so close to her destination, seconds from being outside the castle, but her breath of relief choked like ice shards when a voice from behind froze her still.

"Where do you think you're off to, *spymaster?*"

Her spine straightened with a dark coil of dread, fingers curling to tame the trembling as she turned slowly.

Captain Varis's eyes danced with a wicked gleam.

She didn't even try to respond with an excuse as her words were gripped by terror. Two guards flanked him, and she could see in his face that this was not a chance encounter. Footsteps caught up behind her, and she turned her head just enough to see the further four guards approach and block her path to freedom. Too many of them. Her ability was completely useless, and she had no way out as they herded her like cattle.

"How fitting a title. Only, you haven't been entirely loyal in your work to the king now, have you?" he asked in taunting malice.

Knowing what she knew now, Faythe wondered what kind of male the captain would have been before the evil grasped his heart. She struggled to believe such a sadistic, violent personality was completely the result of Dakodas's spell. Heightened, perhaps, but she suspected the captain likely always had some evil in him to call upon.

Faythe lifted her chin, determined to hold onto the dregs of courage she had left. "How fitting that the king should send his prized hound to do his dirty work," she sneered.

The captain chuckled darkly, the sound churning her stomach. "Oh, I volunteered." He stepped closer, and she flinched a step back, her fear overcoming her bravery. "But don't worry, Faythe. The king has many things planned for you." He leaned in so close she had to force back her nausea. Then he pulled away with a wild grin. "Now, are you coming along like a good little girl, or—?" He paused in mock deliberation. "Actually, you don't deserve a choice." His hand lashed out and grabbed her arm, and she couldn't bite back her cry of pain at his excessive pressure and sudden movement.

Another guard stepped forward, adding just as much brutality as he took hold of her other arm. When Faythe snapped her head to him, her fight faltered at the face she saw. She recognized him and racked her brain frantically for why his features struck her with immediate fear.

Then she remembered where she'd seen him before...

In the human boy's memory. The one she was made to kill.

He was one of the guards who had terrorized High Farrow's civilians for information—not about the castle's defenses against Valgard, but to get them to find the Riscillius for King Orlon. Everything started falling into place, and she slowly began to crumble.

All this time, the young boys, Reuben, the guards in the town—they had been purposely made to impersonate the enemy, to make the people believe it was Valgard to fear and not their own king. Then Orlon was killing them when they failed to accomplish what he asked to maintain the guise he was keeping them safe from traitors.

It was heinously, treacherously brilliant.

The captain and the guard dragged her with undue force. She couldn't fight—not physically, and in her spirit...she felt that fight failing too.

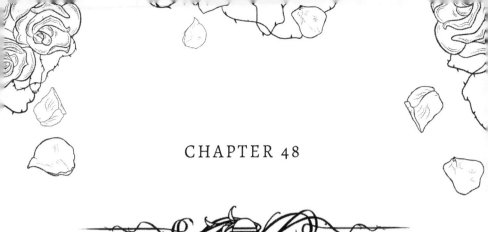

CHAPTER 48

Nikalias

THE YULEMAS BALL came to an end at last. Nik had barely registered any of it. At least, not since he watched Faythe disappear through the exit. His heart broke to think it might be the last time he saw her.

The prince stood from his throne beside his father. He had been quietly desperate to leave for the past hour, wanting to find Caius and make sure Faythe made it out of the city walls.

"Stay, Nikalias," his father drawled with chilling calm.

Nik halted. The command rattled his nerves awfully. He slowly turned back to the demon wearing the king's face who motioned for Nik to take a seat once more. Reluctantly, he did. He was still the king in masterful appearance, and to disobey him would be a grave mistake. Nik didn't know how much of his real father still remained and didn't want to test whether it was enough to spare the life of his son should he step out of line.

He looked to Tauria who sat terrified under her faltering mask of impassiveness, feigning pleasantries as partygoers bid her good night.

As the party ceased and more of the revelers casually left, completely oblivious to the thick, growing tension between the three royals overlooking them all, the hall grew quieter. Nik watched each and every fae leave the hall as if they were the seconds counting down to a deadly confrontation.

Then silence fell.

Nik heard the approach of the guards before he saw them close in, lazily surrounding the dais in the ballroom. He looked over the ensemble—and fell into ice-cold dread at the first thing he saw. Their uniforms were stripped of all hues of High Farrow blue. They stood in all-black instead, robbed of the Griffin crest. To his horror…he recognized none.

The king stood and walked a few paces forward but didn't turn back to them as he spoke. "I'm disappointed," he began, and Nik held his breath in anticipation. "My own son, a traitor." His father twisted his head to him then. Cold, expressionless. Nik didn't yield a reaction either.

"I don't know what—"

"Let's not play games, Nikalias. I raised you better," Orlon cut him off swiftly.

Nik's eyes flashed in rage at being spoken down to. "You didn't raise me," he snapped, rising to his feet. He stared into the black, foreign depths in challenge. "You are not my father—not anymore."

He had all but signed his death sentence anyway.

The king looked bored as he dismissed Nik's anger. "I expected more from you, *Prince*." He switched his gaze to Tauria, and Nik held back the impulse to stand between them. "And you, *Princess*. I give you shelter, and this is how you thank me?" He shook his head with a mocking huff. "Such a waste of talent. Both of you."

Neither of them acknowledged their guilt as the king had yet to outright accuse them of anything. Nik couldn't be sure of exactly what he knew or what he thought their involvement was. He stayed silent.

The king went on. "It's a shame we'll lose an even greater talent thanks to all this treason."

Nik's heart skipped a beat. He couldn't be talking of Faythe. She was faraway by now, safe…

"I rather enjoyed having a *spymaster*."

The room swayed, and Nik struggled to stay on his feet as he felt the ground pull out from under him. His voice dropped into a calm fury. "If you harm her—"

The king waved a lazy hand that flared his temper recklessly. "I'm afraid your plea for the human's life comes a little too late. I'm sure Captain Varis has long since disposed of that problem."

In a flash of reckless emotion, Nik drew his sword, moving fast, and was steps away from bringing it down on his father's neck without pause for thought.

The steel never struck its target. He heard the guards approach seconds before he spun, and his sword connected with another blade. Nik fought against two guards in black who were dangerously quick.

"Nik," Tauria's small voice, along with a quiet whimper, snapped his attention away. He found her within the grasp of another fae, blade poised over her throat.

He instantly stopped fighting, staring wide-eyed in terror. "Let her go," he said, failing to sound stern in his desperation. His worst fear flashed before him—one that had tormented him for decades: seeing Tauria's life hang in the balance…because of *him*. Nik almost fell to his knees as he breathed, "Please."

Nik's sword was taken from him, and the guards closed in to detain him. His father raised a hand, and everyone halted. The king looked to Tauria with bitter distaste.

"You let these females make you weak, son."

There was no way out—not with both their lives. He didn't care about his own, but Tauria…

The king released a long breath. "How disappointing."

He thought he had lost. Nik shifted his position and braced

himself to fight without his blade—whatever it took. Then Orlon turned to address his guards.

"Take them both away. Confine them to their rooms. No one is to enter without my knowledge, and they are not to leave without my word."

The guards nodded and moved around him. Another four circled Tauria, but there was no longer a blade threatening her life. A small relief. Orlon didn't plan to kill them—at least, not yet.

The king cast his black stare back to Nik as he spoke. "We don't want to cause a scene now, do we?"

Nik clenched his fists together in a trembling rage, his breathing hard as he stared off with the King of High Farrow. Then, reluctantly, he was forced to concede and willed his feet to move as he stormed out of the great hall. Six guards flanked him on all sides. To fight would be futile against so many, especially unarmed.

At the corner where he would usually part ways with Tauria to go to their separate living quarters, he stopped. She did too, and their eyes briefly met in a silent promise: She was not going to die. Not while he still breathed.

Nik was pushed forward, and he shot a lethal glare at the guard who dared touch him. When he turned back, Tauria was already walking away, her usual straight and confident poise reduced to a low bow of defeat.

In the confines of his rooms, all comfort was removed as his safe space quickly became his prison, his *cage*. Alone, he was finally left to his own thoughts. And it was perhaps the most dangerous thing the king could have left him with. He'd killed Faythe and threatened Tauria. Now, all Nik had was time.

Time to plan exactly how he would painfully—and slowly—release his retribution on his father.

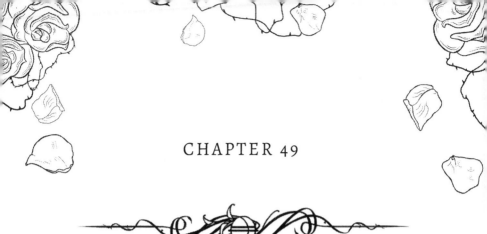

CHAPTER 49

Faythe

FAYTHE HUDDLED IN the corner of her cold, damp cell, grateful for the many layers of her gown as she folded a few up over her arms for warmth. Three days had passed. She knew this from the small box window she spent her days watching from dusk till dawn. She didn't know what the king was waiting for. Perhaps to see if the bitter, frozen nights would claim her life and save him the hassle.

They had her chained to the back wall of the cell, exactly where she had been after her very first day in the castle. It was fitting to think she'd really come full circle.

The only company she had was the guard who brought her a meal and water once a day. It was never a lone guard as two others were always on standby right outside should she try to use her ability. It had taken until now to realize they were drugging her food or water to send her straight into a pit of darkness and prevent her from Nightwalking. She didn't mind, welcoming the numbness it brought through the freezing nights.

She didn't try to use her conscious abilities, but not because she thought it was a wasted effort. In their haste to lock her up, the fae hadn't thought to check her for weapons.

After all, what lady brings a knife to a ball?

She had a chance—one chance—to still carry through on her plan to end the king. She simply needed the opportunity to get close enough.

Faythe heard footsteps before the door to the cellblock groaned open. She didn't bother to move at first. Then she spotted the disheveled, curly brown hair of Caius.

Her chains clanked loudly as she moved, and her bones ached in protest from her stationary days against the hard stone. As usual, two guards were by the main door as Caius came in with a tray of food. She subtly moved forward as far as her chains would allow. The young fae unlocked the door to her cell and stepped inside.

The moment their eyes locked, she heard, *"Can you hear me?"*

She didn't let her face give anything away. *"Yes. Is Reylan—?"*

"He left as soon as I told him of the king's plan. He should be well on his way back to Rhyenelle by now."

A relief. One that stabbed her heart selfishly. But he was safe.

"Nik and Tauria?"

She noticed him place something else next to the tray of bland food. Clothes. Along with a cloak for warmth. Such simple items meant so much to her as she longed to get out of the dirty ruin of her Yulemas Ball gown.

Caius reached forward and unlocked the chains from her wrists for her to change. She almost moaned at the relief of having the harsh metal removed from her raw skin and rubbed her painful wrists as he turned his back to her for privacy while she undressed.

"They're alive. The king has them confined to their own quarters. They're fully guarded at all times."

It terrified her that he knew of their involvement in one way or another. At least he didn't seek to kill them for it…yet.

"Thank you," she said, though it never felt like enough for everything he had done, everything he had risked for her—for *all* of them. Caius deserved far more than the simple words of gratitude.

Her dress fell from her, and she breathed at the weightlessness, quickly stepping into her new garments and tucking her dagger inconspicuously into her boot instead. As much as she was desperate for a full, hot bath, it was a great comfort to be in fresh clothing with a thick cloak to help shield her from the harsh winter nights.

He turned to her when she finished, offering a warm smile. *"I'll visit as much as I can. You're not alone, Faythe."*

Tears pricked the backs of her eyes and started to blur her vision. It was exactly what she needed to hear, and she desperately wanted to embrace him in that moment.

"You're a better friend than I deserve sometimes." She owed him a debt for life for what he was doing for her. For giving her hope and keeping her sane.

Just as another guard hissed at him to hurry up, he gave her one last smile of reassurance. Then he strolled back out, locking the cell once more.

Silence fell around her when everyone took their leave.

She was not alone. Never alone.

Nightfall cloaked her cell in darkness. The only light came from the peaceful full moon that flooded a tranquil glow through the window. It was small, barely bigger than her head, and had a woven metal casing that distorted the view. Not that she could see much anyway as it was too high for her to catch a glimpse of anything except the sky.

The white of the moon brought a different image to mind. She thought of Reylan as she stared at it from her curled-up position on the ground. All she did was think of her friends throughout her restless days. Safe and alive, they would all have a future. The general was smart in choosing to flee. In fact, she was glad it was so easy for him and she didn't have to fight him on the matter. Yet at the same time, a part of her selfishly hurt at the notion.

A small bird landed on the narrow ledge just outside the window. She'd seen it before. White, almost shimmering silver under the moonlight, it came back as if it had no idea of the vast world around it that it was free to take flight to and travel wherever it wanted.

Faythe rose to her feet, wincing as the pain in her bones and abrasions on her wrists got worse by the day. She went over to the window, craning her neck to examine the unlikely friend. Something about the bird brought a small comfort, as if it understood her pain and was waiting for her to join it before it took flight for good.

It was a ridiculous concept, and perhaps she had reached the point of delirium at being left for days without any conversation or human contact. Her madness fully came out when she huffed at the bird that sat still in silence and then started talking out loud to it.

"I was always destined to end up here," she said, voice croaking from her days of silence. "You should go, take in every sight possible, before the war taints the world with black days and red streets." She smiled at the bird sadly, turning away from it to rest her back against the wall. "Do me a favor though, will you? Look out for my friends, Jakon and Marlowe." At the thought of them, her heart cracked, but they weren't the only ones who were fleeing the king's wrath. She found herself adding, "Dammit, Reylan too."

The silence answered back to her. She didn't check to see if the bird was still there. She knew it would be. It hardly left. Perhaps when they took her at last and the cell fell empty once again, in its loneliness, it would fly away and never return.

The groaning of the cellblock door jolted her from her poetic daydream. Her fear rattled in the face of the vicious captain—grinning wickedly as if he got off on her terror before the torture had even begun. She tried to stand tall and keep her mask of confidence, but it faltered more every day in her exhaustion.

"Ready to play?" he taunted maliciously.

Though a cold chill licked up her spine at his tone, she rallied her bravery enough to say, "I once promised to kill you, Varis."

The corners of his smile tugged wider. He enjoyed the fight she had in her, if only so he could relish in the victory of breaking her down to nothing.

"We'll see," he said, darkly seductive. He stepped up close to the bars. "I'm going to have so much fun with you, Faythe." Her name sounded vile in his predator's caress.

Varis jerked his head, and a guard came forward to open her cell. Two stepped inside, and she didn't flinch even when they roughly handled her and she felt her wrists sting in agony as they were let free from their iron grips. She wasn't given the choice to walk with dignity as they took her arms and pulled her from her cell. Her feet fumbled, struggling to step one in front of the other in time with their uneven, wide strides.

She wasn't led to the throne room, and she didn't recognize the east side of the castle where they descended many staircases until she was sure they were underground.

Underground where no one would be able to hear her cries for help.

When they reached the end of the last hallway, she was pulled into a large room that reeked of death. It also resembled the dark force in appearance as the dim torches highlighted every blood splatter around the chamber of pain. Nausea overcame her, and in her panic, she couldn't stop the vomit that rose, doubling over the moment the guards let her go. Her palms slapped painfully to the ground, and she gasped to try to compose herself and calm her raging heartbeat.

The room had one sinister purpose that struck her with cold dread. Torture. The captain chuckled, delighted with her reaction to the location.

Then she spotted the king across the room, so out of place in his finery amid the gruesome setting. He didn't smile, but his eyes held a cruel gleam that told her he was willing to do whatever it took to get the information he thought she had. Without her friends as leverage, pain would be the next best thing.

There was a long, flat bench in the center of the room, and beside it, a far more comfortable chair was positioned in stark contrast.

"Faythe." The king drawled her name. Her blood curdled at his voice. "What a busy woman you've been." Orlon glided toward her like a venomous snake. He paused, looking down on her as if he could crush her like a cockroach with the sole of his boot. "All this time, you held onto exactly what I was searching for."

He gave a nod to the side, and a guard came forward holding an unsheathed sword.

Holding Lumarias.

Faythe's eyes widened in shock, and she fell numb. He took it in his palms, admiring its craftsmanship before settling his attention on the stone set in the pommel.

"The Riscillius," he breathed as if he didn't quite believe it. Then his eyes locked on her again. "Yet you still have one more thing I seek, don't you?" He took a long breath, and Faythe braced herself as he said, "Tell me where you've hidden the temple ruin, *spymaster*."

Faythe tried to keep all expression from her face, hissing through her teeth, "I don't know what you're talking about—"

The back of the king's hand connected with her face. She whimpered at the sharp sting, head twisting so hard it was her own will that kept the blow from snapping her neck.

"Do not lie to me, *girl!*" he spat, his voice laced with venom in his impatience. Then he straightened, composing himself. "I'll admit, I'm impressed. My initial detaining of you had nothing to do with any of this. You can imagine my surprise at discovering what you so cunningly kept to yourself all this time, eluding me and my guard. I have to credit you—it is no easy feat."

Faythe shook violently against the cold ground as the king paced the room.

"I planned to kill you once and for all for your attack on an ally—on a *king!* Your skills aren't as sharp as you believe, it seems, though your manipulation of Varlas's memory did hold out for some time." Orlon stopped his pacing to look down and gauge her reaction to the exposure of her treason. But Faythe couldn't muster a switch of expression while she remained solid, still, frozen in terror. "In his letter, he demanded I hand you over to him, along with the Rhyenelle general. How foolish of him to come back to my kingdom. I do still wonder what influenced his return..." Orlon's eyebrows knitted together in curiosity, but he didn't ponder for long. His black stare fixed on Faythe, rippling with the darkness of death as he stalked over to her.

"You'll be glad to hear I declined his request. Or perhaps you'll beg me to surrender you to Varlas when you sample what I have in store for you instead." He came to a stop in front of her.

Faythe didn't look up, eyes fixed on his polished boots as she forced down the acid rising up her throat once again.

"It made me question what you thought you knew of our plans, and if there was any other time you might have dared to use your ability without my knowledge. I knew I couldn't have a Night-walker enter into your mind—or my son's—undetected. So, I had the memories of my ward searched to see how close you two have become in your time here. Faythe—*spymaster*—it seems you are far more cunning than I took you to be. But I will get the location of the ruin from you one way or another."

The king glanced around the room in lingering threat as he

observed the gore-coated walls. "As much as I would love to see you bleed for your treason and deception, it is not physical pain you should be afraid of. No—I plan to go straight to the source of information. Your mind, Faythe. Your biggest asset becomes your doom." Orlon nodded to the guards behind him and made to walk around her.

Faythe breathed hard in the heat of her frenzied panic. She snapped. Reaching into her boot, she pounced to her feet, dagger gripped in her hand, and whirled to plunge it into the king's back.

A hand curled painfully around her wrist just an inch off her target.

Faythe cried out as Varis's grip turned bone-crushing, and she dropped the blade, her last hope echoing damningly off the stone floor.

Orlon chuckled in mock amusement. "Your fight and dedication is admirable. It will be a shame to see such talent go to waste. You could have been an invaluable ally. You could have helped conquer the world. Yet you fought me at every turn in your own artful way. Your defiance has become your end."

Two guards approached, hauling her away from the king. She thrashed, losing all her strength and dignity as she became completely overwhelmed with fear. They lifted her, feet leaving the ground completely, as she struggled against their brutal handling with everything she had left. It was all wasted energy. In a few quick movements, she was bound by her ankles and wrists, completely vulnerable to the vultures who circled her. Tears burned in her eyes—not from the pain, but at the realization she had absolutely no escape. No one was coming to help her this time.

King Orlon moved to the exit, but before he left, his voice sang chillingly, "I will have what I want, Faythe. By the end of this, you'll beg for your miserable life to end."

Then he was gone, and the demon switched faces as Captain Varis stepped up to her. Faythe shrank inwardly and strained against her bonds, wanting to run far, far away from the monster who grinned with painful promise.

"Let's begin, shall we?" he said with sinister cheer. The captain didn't reach for any tools of torture—didn't even lift a hand to her. Instead, his smile was sadistic and gleeful as he sat in the chair beside Faythe.

He leaned toward her in his seat, and the rope bit her wrists as she instinctively recoiled back. The disgusting heat of his cruel breath caressed her ear as he said, "Now, you'll get to know what it feels like to be powerless in your own mind."

His words struck a new kind of fear in Faythe as she figured out their means of extracting the information. She wished for anything else, even physical pain, in place of having her mind invaded while she was helpless to do anything. Helpless...and aware. In a surge of frantic dread, she pulled wildly against her restraints despite the sharp pain that shot through her weakened muscles and tore her raw skin with every movement. She lost all her dignity and courage, breaking down in a hopeless sob.

Yet she smelled it as someone came up to her other side: a scent that sparked a distant memory; a day so long ago, before she had any idea of her capabilities. When she feared herself, her ability. When Nik stepped in to save her. Back then, that scent offered her salvation. Now, the tonic to stifle her ability would become her worst nightmare...

In a smaller dosage, it can also be used to stifle your ability but still allow another Nightwalker to enter your mind, and you'd be helpless to throw them out. Nik's words from long ago echoed in her ears, and she sobbed in defeat as the smell grew stronger. Closer. She clamped her mouth shut, but a pair of rough hands grabbed her jaw painfully, adding more pressure until she couldn't stand it anymore and cried out. The moment she did, she felt one drop of the foul liquid fall onto her tongue. Then the hands were gone.

Faythe slumped against the hard bench, having lost the energy to fight. It was futile anyway. She was human, weak, *inferior.* She tried to hold onto the shreds of her spirit…but she feared that was soon to be broken beyond salvation too.

"Sleep, Faythe," Varis cooed. "I'll see you inside." His last words echoed with a dark chuckle as she felt her eyelids grow heavy.

She had failed, she had lost, and now her own mind would become a playground for the worst of all creatures.

CHAPTER 50

Nikalias

NIK PACED HIS rooms with simmering rage. He had four guards posted outside his door, and a further six below his balcony. He wasn't foolish enough to try to fight against so many, and he had no doubt there were others who could be quickly alerted if he dared.

No—physically, he was outnumbered. But he wasn't entirely powerless in his confinement. For the past seven nights, he'd entered his full unconscious, building his strength and resting his mind. They could take everything from him except his ability. His Nightwalking. And he planned to use it to bring silent revenge to the King of High Farrow.

He was ready.

That night, he didn't dress for bed. Lying fully clothed, he took a long breath before he closed his eyes and allowed himself to drift off.

Nik stood in the black-and-gray whorls of his subconscious. Before he could head for the king, he had one stop to make. Though he couldn't converse with Tauria in her mind as he'd done with Faythe many times, he could still search through her memories —to ease his worries and be sure she was alive and okay.

Something halted him. At the thought of the human who stole his heart beyond romance...it broke all over again. He'd failed Faythe. It was a guilt and shame he would carry for the rest of his immortal life. He'd lived the past four days in denial, unable to accept that she no longer breathed for fear he would fall apart completely and not be able to exact his revenge.

Then something hideous and hopeful crossed his mind.

Doubt.

It was enough that he wanted to change his destination, desperate to be sure but terrified to meet only empty darkness if he tried. He couldn't stop himself. Despite the pain he would feel to have her death confirmed, Nik found himself picturing Faythe then attempting to channel into her mind.

He met a black wall. It almost buckled him, until...

Something wasn't right. It wasn't an empty void like he was expecting; there was still an essence behind it. Relief crushed him, and he was desperate to get inside. He felt around for any weakness or breaks in the firm barrier. It was a familiar sensation, but he couldn't pinpoint it. Not as if she was in a deep, unconscious sleep. Not as if she was blocking him out. Something else prevented him from gaining entry.

Realization dawned like an ice-cold sheet. He'd felt its likeness before—when another Nightwalker occupied his intended target already. Panic pierced his chest. He didn't have to consider the possibilities, knowing exactly who would be inside—the one called upon for all the king's most heinous tasks.

Captain Varis.

He'd challenged other Nightwalkers before and won, gaining access to get the information first. But it never ended well for the host. He would risk Faythe's life by trying to get inside and cast the captain out without great stealth and even greater power. Even then, he wasn't entirely confident he could succeed without harming Faythe from the inside. Leaving her in the wicked beast's grasp was not an option either, and he knew in his heart that even with the perilous risk, if Faythe had the choice, she would beg him to try.

Nik still hesitated. It was a haunting, gut-wrenching feeling to presume her dead. If he tried and failed, he would all but kill her himself. The thought was shattering, but it was a selfish reason to leave her in the captain's hands. She didn't deserve that fate, and he wouldn't let the captain have what he'd wanted since day one: the chance to end Faythe's life.

He needed more time. While he felt strong enough to break through the defenses of his father's mind, he didn't need to be careful in going there. With Faythe's mind, he had to be able to get in without the captain sensing straight away, and more importantly, without harming Faythe. The task was complex and would require a new test of his ability's strength and precision. He couldn't afford to be even slightly restless or have any loose emotions.

It frustrated and enraged Nik to no end as he knew he had to leave her to the monster's mercy for a while longer. Reluctantly, he forced himself back into his own mind completely. His door to the darkness beckoned him. He would rest and calm and focus until he was confident enough in his strength that he could achieve what he needed to do and keep Faythe alive in the process.

Nik muttered a silent prayer to the Spirits that Faythe would hold on long enough for him to save her.

CHAPTER 51

Faythe

FAYTHE WAS TRAPPED. Paralyzed within her subconscious. Unable to move in her own white-and-gold mist. She could only stare in wide-eyed horror at Captain Varis as he violated her mind. Still, she fought with everything she had to try to conceal certain things from him.

The king couldn't get to the ruin—not only because it would be detrimental to Ungardia if it fell into the hands of Marvellas. It terrified Faythe far more that if he found it...it would mean he'd found Jakon and Marlowe too.

If they did what she asked, they would be far away from Farrowhold with it by now. While finding that out wouldn't give the king their exact location, she knew it was only a matter of time before he would be able to track them down.

Her head pounded with the effort it took to shield the information, and she was close to falling into complete darkness as the captain sifted through her thoughts and memories like a buffet, everything for the taking.

"The Crown Prince of High Farrow," he mused with his back

to her while he went through the motion picture of her past. "I always knew he had a soft spot for you, but this?" He turned to cast her an amused, wicked smirk.

Faythe looked up from her position on her knees and nearly sobbed at the sight. Not from pain or sadness, but because for one moment, she felt comfort to gaze into those emerald eyes. The scene changed, and they were lying on the grass in the Eternal Woods, carefree and laughing. He kissed her. A day that felt within a different timeline. She loved him then, and she still did, only in a different sense now.

Then the vision dissipated into the mist. Not by her will, but the captain's. She hung her head again as he stalked toward her. He kneeled down and reached a hand out to grip her chin. She couldn't resist, couldn't fight, as much as his touch repulsed her. She poured all of her hatred into her eyes instead as she glared back at the demon.

"Now I know *your* deepest fears, Faythe. I guess we're even." His grin turned malevolent. "Unfortunately for you, I don't play fair." Varis's face slowly began to shift, and dread stiffened her spine. His wicked scar smoothed into perfect pale skin. His tied-back hair turned shades darker, shortening, growing sleek, with a few loose tresses over his forehead. Black eyes wove with vines of striking green until they filled completely as sparkling emerald pools. She wanted to find comfort in them as she had so many times before, but all she felt was frozen terror. It was Nik's face, harnessed by a foreign invader. A cruel and merciless monster. Behind him, her white-and-gold mist was snuffed out by a creeping darkness, turning eerily overcast as the scene unfolded into some-thing far more sinister.

She tore her eyes from the distorted familiarity of the prince. They were in the throne room, only the once bright and impec-cable space was now neglected and ominous. Cobwebs clung to the grand chandelier above, distorting its shape and turning it white like a sphere of trapped ghosts—perhaps those of the victims whose blood painted the dais a sickening dark crimson and filled the scars of the cracked stone floor. The room stung her nose with a revolting scent that churned her stomach: death.

Nik stood but didn't take his eyes off her or drop the evil smirk as he walked back toward his father sitting lazily on his throne. Then her eyes fell on Tauria, dressed wholly in royal blue with no hint of her vibrant Fenstead green. She wasn't on her throne next to the king. Instead, she stood by his side, her hand on his shoulder trailing down his arm seductively while she too kept her eyes on Faythe, face plastered with a sly smile of cruel amusement.

Faythe swayed at the sight. Tauria would never show love and affection for the king she saw murder his own mate—Nik's mother. She wanted to scream at both of them to wake them up from whatever trance they were under.

In a flash of confusion, Faythe remembered it was *she* who was under a spell. A trick of her *own* mind. The room tilted, and her vision blurred as her mind fought between reality and imagination. She shook her head. She should be able to wake herself up. She should be in control, and yet…she had lost the fight for dominance over her own thoughts.

"Faythe."

At the familiar broken voice, her head snapped to the side, and she sobbed once at the sight of Jakon, bloodied and ruthlessly battered.

"Faythe, help us."

She whipped her head to her other side, and Marlowe was wraithlike in appearance, her usually bouncing blonde hair dull and snapped, her face drained of color, and barely any bruised flesh on her protruding bones.

Tears streamed down Faythe's face. "It's going to be okay," she choked out, though her weak words were a forced lie. They had been caught and would all die here over the crest of the Griffin, betrayed by their own kingdom at the hands of a demon king. She met the black eyes of the ruler who grinned in delight at her distress.

"You can't help anyone," he taunted from his bloodstained throne.

Footsteps sounded, and she turned again, this time to see the captain. Only, it wasn't his appearance that caught her attention; it was the glint of the large steel blade poised between both hands. Her eyes widened, and she trembled in shock as he lifted the sword above Jakon's head on his approach.

"I should have done this the first time you were on your knees in here," the captain said, and then he brought his hands down.

The waves of her scream thrashed and rose in Faythe's rib cage. It tore through her throat like shards of broken glass and echoed loudly through the room, channeling back to ring painfully in her own ears. She didn't stop screaming as she watched her longest and dearest friend get beheaded in one swift movement. His body fell limp, and his head rolled. Faythe vomited the moment her scream choked into frantic sobs. She retched and spluttered, unable to find breath. The blood pooled around her, soaking under her knees and over her splayed palms against the marble. It fell into the chasms of the broken stone, and she watched it break off into several rivers of Jakon's life.

The captain didn't stop there. He walked right through the thick blood, blade poised once more, stalking for Marlowe. Faythe was screaming again before he reached her friend. Her throat tore in agony as if a frantic beast were clawing its way out. She wanted desperately to clamp her eyes shut to avoid another horrifically gruesome display, but she couldn't. No matter how hard she tried, she couldn't look away.

She couldn't save them, couldn't do anything but watch as they suffered the consequences of her actions. They were here because of her; because of what she was.

The captain's sword fell down over Marlowe's throat... Faythe screamed, she wailed, she sobbed to no end.

Then everything went black.

When Faythe awoke, she wished she hadn't.

Her head throbbed worse than she'd ever felt before, and she found it difficult to adjust to the weak pool of light from the outside moon. She coughed to clear her throat and found it painfully dry and hoarse. She was freezing cold and couldn't feel the weight of the cloak she used as a blanket. Peeling one eye open, she managed to gather that she was still in her cell.

She took a moment against the ground to collect herself, and it all came flooding back to her with bone-trembling clarity. She jolted up despite the shooting pain in her head that blackened her vision. The captain, the mind manipulation, her friends' beheading…

Faythe doubled over on her knees as the vile memories replayed and retched. Nothing came up, but her chest stabbed with excruciating pain, and she trembled against the ice-cold stone. It was all so clear, so *real*, she couldn't tell the difference in her own mind.

She sobbed loudly against the back of her cell, feeling completely lost, vulnerable, and without any hope. She didn't even know how many days had passed since her nightmare ordeal.

A small burst of chirps sounded through her sobs, and Faythe's crying ceased. In her anguish and frustration, she shot to her feet and whirled to face the dammed bird. Ignoring the physical pain and mental insanity, she glared at it while it stared innocently back.

"Go away!" she shouted.

It stayed still, silently watching her.

She stormed the two steps and slammed her palms against the sharp stone, numb to the sting in her frozen state. "You're not in this cage—*I am!* Leave and don't come back!"

When it didn't move or turn away from her in its defiance,

Faythe trembled in another round of cries. She leaned her forehead against the stone and took a few deep, calming breaths.

"I am not alone," she whispered to herself.

The stubborn bird reminded her of that. Though it seemed ludicrous to even think it, she silently thanked the creature.

But when she looked up again…it was gone.

Faythe blinked at the metal shield. Then her stomach dropped, and tears filled her wide eyes as she stared and stared at the empty sky beyond.

It wasn't real.

All this time, being left alone for days—*weeks*—on end in maddening silence…had she conjured the vision of the bird in her desperation to grapple onto her sanity? Her mind's way of not shutting down in its loneliness completely.

Faythe trembled. She sank back to the ground, curling into herself and running her hands through her hair. *Not real.* She gripped tight. The pain in her scalp should have been enough to confirm she was awake, but it wasn't. Her mind spiraled, down and down and down. She fisted her fingers into her hair tighter, not sure what was true and what was a vision anymore, imagining herself still strapped to that metal bench below the castle with the captain pulling the strings of her thoughts. *Not real.* She was losing…she was losing herself.

Before she could fall into a dark hole there would be no escape from, the opening of the cellblock door vibrated over the stone, and she spun around in cold-set fear. She released a shaky breath of relief at the sight of Caius strolling in, a tray of food in hand. The sight of him, and the small comfort he brought…

This is real. This mercy is real. Caius is real.

Faythe breathed deeply to calm her racing heart when he opened the cell door and stepped inside. He gave her a grim look as his eyes trailed over her. She must have looked a ghastly sight.

"I'm sorry for what he's doing to you, Faythe. I want to help—"

"You're doing more for me than I can ever thank you for." She gave a

weak smile, cautious of the two guards still standing by the main door.

He leaned down to place her food but stumbled, sending a few items clattering onto the ground. It was on purpose, to buy them a few more precious minutes as he fumbled to gather them up.

"You should know the King of Olmstone is nearing High Farrow."

Faythe kept her face placid for appearances, but inside, her chest matched the icy chill of the air. Her body shivered in painful vibrations. *Where is my damn cloak?*

As if reading her mind at Faythe's quick glance over the cell, Caius unclipped his own, extending it to her.

"We're not to give the prisoner any items," a guard warned from the cell door.

A flash of rage she'd never seen before flexed in Caius's eyes as he turned to say, "She's to be kept alive, is she not? Varis won't be pleased if she dies of cold before he can get the information he needs." His tone was surprisingly firm and laced with authority, enough that the soldier backed down with a reluctant grumble.

When he turned back to her, his face wrinkled in apology. For the mention of Varis; the reminder that her torture was not over. Faythe offered a small smile to display her gratitude and hide her spike of terror. Gripping the thick cloak, her stiff shoulders fell in relief under its weight and warmth, and she didn't hesitate to sling it over herself. She tried not to pay attention to the color or sigil that felt like a hot brand direct from the merciless High Farrow king.

Faythe asked, *"Are they preparing for war?"* The only reason for Varlas's return would be to set their plans in motion once and for all.

Caius's look said it all, and her heart sank. Had Varis already managed to find out what they needed in her head? It didn't bear thinking about, and she prayed to the *dammed* Spirits Jakon and Marlowe were still safe and out of Orlon's grasp.

"I believe so."

Oh, Gods. It was happening. Everything they wanted so desperately to prevent. The war among allies. There was only one way to stop it: she had to kill the King of High Farrow, and she was running out of time.

Caius finished fixing the items on the tray, and she crouched down to his level. He looked at her then, and she was fierce as she said, *"You have to leave, Caius. It's not going to be safe for those like you— those who want to fight for what is right. There's nothing left for you here."*

The young guard shook his head slightly and gave a warm smile. *"I'm not going anywhere."*

Faythe was about to protest when he stood quickly and strolled out of her cell. As he locked it again, he met her eye once more, and she heard, *"Don't let them break your spirit, Faythe. Don't let them win,"* right before he turned and left her alone in the cellblock once more.

CHAPTER 52

Jakon

"ARE YOU CERTAIN about this?" Jakon's question came out as more of a plea while he struggled with the hard beat of his heart over what they were about to do.

Marlowe's face was desolate, her nod grim. "I don't know how this ends. I can't be certain we will all still hold our lives. But I know we are needed."

Jakon trembled under his cloak, fists clamped tight while they kept hidden in an alley close to the city wall. They intended to flee as soon as they got the news from Caius, and Jakon was fully prepared to leave High Farrow behind if it meant Marlowe's safety. As much as it crushed him completely to imagine leaving Faythe when danger was imminent, Caius was right: he would only be making himself leverage for the king to use against her, and getting the ruin far out of his reach was too important. Or so they all thought.

Marlowe pieced together visions from various dreams, concluding there was only one way to take down the King of High

Farrow. And that was to walk right into his domain and offer up the prize he sought...

He can't stand to lose what he never gained, and what he gains will end his reign.

He didn't think he would ever get used to how Marlowe spoke in riddles and questions that hid answers. He trusted in her and knew she would never give in mindlessly to the guidance of the Spirits without listening to her own gut feelings and rational thoughts.

"It's time," she said, achingly quiet.

Jakon's heart tugged. They had spent nearly a week on the road before turning back, then a further week and a half remaining hidden, making sure what they were about to do wasn't a grave mistake and coming to terms with the fact none of their fates were safe. It pained him to hear the fear in her voice, and he tried desperately to remain strong for her. Taking her face in his hands, he kissed her one last time. When they broke apart, he didn't release her. He stared into the ocean eyes that were his absolution and steadied his breath, finding the serenity to voice what had been weighing him down with nerves, thrill, and fear for some time now. If this turned out to be his last chance...

"Marlowe Connaise,"—his thumb brushed over her cheek—"a simple endeavor to commission a sword brought me to you, and from that first day, you had me. Your infectious wonder, your self-less heart, your incredible mind... I fall for every piece of you harder every day. When we come out of this, I promise to always be yours. And I want everyone to know you will always be mine, as Marlowe Kilnight. There is not a day I want to imagine without you by my side." He watched her face fall a shade paler, eyes widening in surprise. Jakon held his breath. Then the brightest smile lit up Marlowe's entire expression, chasing away the clouded sadness just for a moment.

"Your timing is awful," she breathed in a short, nervous laugh.

"Yes, Jakon, I will take your name. From that first day, you had me too. I am yours, and you are mine. Until the end claims us."

She fell into him, and he gripped her tight, his joy of her acceptance cruelly overshadowed by the grief it could be the last time he held her. He tried not to think so grimly, or he risked never letting her go and fleeing Ungardia with her before they walked through those dreaded city gates.

"Until the end claims us," he all but whispered.

Marlowe held the box he had come to hate the sight of. Together, they stepped out of the shadows, out of hiding, and out of safety.

Hands intertwined, they walked straight into the open arms of the enemy.

CHAPTER 53

Faythe

F AYTHE LOST TRACK of the days. She assumed well over a week
had passed, perhaps over two, since they locked her up in the
cold and dreary cell after the Yulemas Ball.

Varis had dragged her into the torture chamber below the
castle twice more since the first time, and she'd spent a few days
quiet and lonely in between. The captain needed time to rest and
replenish at least sufficient enough strength to riffle through her
mind for the king's answers after each torturous violation. Each
time, Faythe woke up back in her cell with a searing headache from
trying to hide information about her friends. It brought her slight
pleasure to know she'd succeeded thus far in eluding the captain
when he thought he was triumphant in his complete control.

He always played out the same nightmare after reeling through
the memories in her white-and-gold mist. Every time she saw her
friends killed by his hand, it ripped open her heart, and she struggled more and more to bring herself back to reality the following
day.

Faythe stood watching the small white bird. It offered no entertainment and very little movement at all, but she focused on it, afraid to blink in case it disappeared again. But even as her eyes strained and stung, she couldn't be certain it was real. She couldn't be certain what was real anymore.

The cellblock door opened, and she knew it wouldn't be Caius. There had been too many days since her last playdate with the captain, and she stood, anticipating it had come around again. She stopped feeling the initial fear. She stopped feeling anything at all. Faythe didn't turn around as she heard the door to her cell swing open and two guards come up behind her. One roughly unchained her, and she kept her eyes on the bird for as long as she could, holding onto the small, blissful distraction.

Until she was dragged out like routine.

Then she stopped taking in her surroundings and instead focused on her conscious breathing so as not to give in to the panic that rose with each step closer to the room of torture. Still, her trembling was the physical betrayal of her nerves at knowing she was soon to relive the same vivid vision of her friends' brutal deaths. In her mind, it wasn't an illusion. In her mind, every soul-obliterating replay was real.

The captain was sitting in his usual chair when they brought her in and strapped her down. His predatory grin never failed to douse her with a wave of cold terror. Her head was pulled back, and the single drop of ability-stifling serum met her tongue, filling her with the same dread she would never get used to.

Before she could drift off completely, the captain leaned forward in his chair. "We get to forgo the boring run-through of your memories and skip straight to the fun this time."

Faythe dared to turn and meet his eye. He nodded, smile widening, as if he knew the silent question her horror-filled eyes held.

"Yes, Faythe. We have your human friends. I'm sure the king is dealing with them through his own measures as we speak."

She couldn't breathe, couldn't even fight against her restraints as the serum started forcing her into a deep, dark sleep. Varis lay back in his seat with a sinister chuckle, reaching for a different sleep tonic to meet her in the nightmare.

"Tonight is just for fun."

Her lips parted to respond, but the waves of sleep weighed down her words. Then the darkness pulled her under all at once.

Tauria was the first face she met, watching on in amusement as Faythe sobbed on her knees in front of the king she stood next to like a trophy. The wickedness and malice looked so out of place on her delicate features and perfect golden-brown skin. She wondered how she could have been tricked so badly not to see this side of Tauria under the angelic mask. Faythe didn't want to believe the fae she'd grown so close to over the past months was an accomplice to the murderous king standing before her.

Marlowe sobbed at her side, and Faythe looked to her broken friend. "This is all your fault!" the blacksmith cried.

Faythe's heart tore from her chest. "I'm so sorry," she whispered. Her tears blurred her vision and streamed down her face.

They were all about to be executed, and it may as well be Faythe who brought the sword down on their necks.

"Faythe."

She looked up at the voice and found the prince looking down at her from just below the dais. Unlike his father and the ward, he didn't hold the same taunting, cruel expression. He didn't hold any emotion at all as he stood still and straight. Something about him was...odd.

Then she heard the captain's footsteps storming closer, a familiar sound that haunted her waking thoughts. She knew he would be headed with his blade poised to end the lives of her friends. Faythe began to sob in a frantic panic.

"It's not real, Faythe. Look at me."

The prince's voice sounded above everything else in the scene around her, and she realized what was different about it. He wasn't talking out loud—not like Marlowe had. No. His voice was closer. *Too* close considering his position a few meters away.

She tore her eyes from Jakon's executioner and met the emerald orbs once again. Then she felt it—felt *him*. In her mind.

"You have to fight it—the serum. It's just a trick. This is your *mind, Faythe. Take back control."*

She replayed the words over and over in her head.

It's not real. It's not real. It's not real.

Take back control.

Realization dawned, and she became aware of her surroundings, the *illusion* of the captain's making. Yet even as she made the distinction between reality and trickery, she found herself unable to move or change anything about the captain's cruel nightmare.

"You can fight it. You need to. It won't be long until he senses me here."

Faythe found it a miracle he was able to be here at all, never mind remain undetected by the other force in her mind. He could even *talk* to her—and only her—without Varis's knowledge, it seemed, as the captain still approached Jakon and lifted his sword. She knew the prince was powerful in his ability, but this...

It should have been impossible.

A dull headache formed, warning Faythe she wouldn't be able to stand the force of two entities in her mind for long. Especially if the captain became aware of the prince and they fought to be the one who remained.

Varis prepared to drop the weight of his blade down on Jakon's neck, and Faythe knew exactly what came next. She'd never been able to look away, and now she knew why.

She couldn't watch her friend die.

She wouldn't.

Her head pounded harder, but she fought with everything she had to take back control. The sword began to fall, and just before it met Jakon's neck...

Faythe twisted her head.

She didn't hear the thump of Jakon's beheading this time. The captain had paused. Daring a look back around, she found Varis's face was livid. Faythe rivaled him on that emotion as it all came rushing back to her. It was still a struggle as she fought against the serum's hold. But with great resistance, she straightened her back and slowly pulled one leg from beneath her, then the other, before rising to her feet against the weight that wanted to hold her down. She didn't take her deadly glare off the captain once.

"Impossible," he spat, and she felt him attempt to pull himself out of her mind in case she regained full control.

Something else held him there, preventing him from retreating. Not her mind, but Nik's. She felt him draw near, and when she turned, he was within arm's reach, holding a hand out to her.

"Together," he said.

She didn't question it or hesitate to slip her palm into his.

Then she felt it.

His power exploded through her, and she gasped as it merged with hers. No longer was he just another invading force; he was part of her mind, two conscious entities becoming one. The serum didn't hold her back anymore, and she breathed deeply with the wave of release.

"Thank you," she whispered, still not believing he was truly here and helping her.

He smiled back and gave her a small nod. Then they both fixed their attention on the captain who wore his growing rage clear on his face.

"I can still kill you both." He seethed.

His force remained strong and dominant. With her ability still partially stifled by the serum, Faythe only had Nik's borrowed power. It was enough, and it pulsed through her like an electric current. They didn't have long. It would burn Nik out as much as it would kill her if they didn't take down the captain soon.

Varis changed the scene around them. Every other person dissipated into total blackness, dark, angry clouds closed in overhead, and thunder cracked loudly above them. He still had his sword poised in his hand, and she was about to conjure a mirror of Lumarias when Nik stepped past her, carrying his own blade to face off with the captain.

He was stronger than she right now, so she let him go—the darkness facing off with the light in a dance of storms.

Just before Nik moved to attack, she sent one last thought to him through their internal link. *"The killing strike is mine."*

She felt his agreement through that connection. Then steel met steel in the confines of her mind.

Thunder cracked louder, and lightning illuminated the duo with every high-pitched symphony of connecting blades. Clouds weaved angrily around them, and she felt every ounce of hatred and malice from the two of them. Her head pounded sickeningly with the battle that raged on in her head. She held on desperately, trying not to fall into the void of nothingness that threatened to pull her under. She knew if she did, it would not be blissful sleep that greeted her on the other side.

She couldn't stay on her feet any longer and dropped slowly to her knees while keeping her eyes fixed on the pair in front.

Nik was valiant in his efforts. It was impressive to watch him fully engaged in battle as he homed in on the captain and unleashed his full fury. She could *feel* it, mixed in with her own hatred for the monster who tortured her. Nik must have heard her thoughts as he pushed harder against the captain who started to falter against the force of the prince.

Faythe was becoming too dizzy to bear it anymore. She felt heavy...*so* heavy. It was too tempting to give in to the need to completely shut down.

"Hold on, Faythe," Nik said desperately.

She gripped onto his words, his lifeline, held it with her entire being so she wouldn't fall into the dark abyss that clawed at her. It took all her focus, and she couldn't make out the blurred bodies in combat or tell who was winning anymore.

Her palms met the cool ground beneath the mist, her head hanging limp.

Then she felt a sharp sever in her mind, and in panic that it was Nik, she jerked awake, whipping her head up and frantically trying to refocus her vision.

It was not the prince who had lost his control in her head. She breathed in elation to find the captain on his knees in front of Nik who poised his blade over his heart. A weight lifted, and she knew Varis was now completely at her mercy—at *their* mercy, as she still relied on Nik's power to keep control of her own mind.

She raised shakily to her feet again, wobbling on weak knees but feeling a new surge of strength thanks to the prince. She didn't need a phantom sword; Varis's mind was now hers to play with, and she felt its fragile essence. Felt the anger and despair, self-loathing along with hatred for the world. For a moment…she pitied him. He had no love for anything or anyone—perhaps he never did even before his mind was captured and his will twisted by Dakodas and Marvellas.

A life without love was to live in darkness without a glimmer of light. An existence with nothing to lose.

She shuffled over to them, and when she came to stand by Nik, the demon's black eyes snapped to her in a feral rage. Yet he was powerless now, and her fear of him reduced to nothing.

"Get it over with," Varis spat out.

She shook her head, deliberately slow. "You don't deserve a choice."

Faythe reached out her hand, and Nik passed over the sword. Though she could hurt Varis without it, the blade held meaning.

"Just like old times," she said, holding the sharp point to his chest. Her voice dropped, eyes turning hard and cold. "You should never have challenged me in that cave." She applied pressure and felt the tip of the sword pierce through as if it were real. She made it *feel* real—to him, and to herself.

The captain cried out in pain.

"You should never have gone after my friends." Another inch sank into his chest. The feeling was both sickening and liberating as Faythe finally stood to slay the demon that plagued her. "You should never have tortured me." She plunged the blade in farther, and he coughed blood through his choked scream of agony. "And Varis…you should never have underestimated me."

The sword passed clean through his chest and out of his back as she moved forward with the final motion. His blood pooled out over her hand and the hilt, but Faythe didn't take her eyes off his depthless black holes as she took his life. She felt everything and made sure he did too, as if they were both fully conscious and awake, not just inside her mind.

She wanted to remember what it felt like to finally rid herself of the evil that was Captain Varis. She wanted to remember the day she knowingly—deliberately—took another life of her own volition.

With the captain still staring at her, eyes bulging and in immense agony, she wordlessly took the last step to shatter his mind from within her own. When she awoke, he would not.

Faythe felt a new black taint on her soul for killing even someone as evil and malicious as the captain. His body broke off in fragments, floating through the air and turning to dust under her hands as well as the sword that protruded through him.

Then he was gone completely. Turned to nothing.

The black clouds faded, and the brightness welcomed them once again. Her white-and-gold mist returned to chase away the final whorls of darkness.

"He had to be stopped." Nik's voice was behind her.

She knew it was his attempt to console her for the murder she committed. It didn't work, but she appreciated it all the same. Faythe turned to him, and he was close enough that she couldn't stop herself when she fell into his arms. He held her tight, and she sobbed—out of relief, out of sadness, out of fear. It wasn't over. The captain was simply one obstacle less on her way to kill the king.

Nik held her as her body shook with the overwhelming emotions. She ceased her crying slowly before composing herself enough to step back from him. He wiped her wet cheek with a solemn smile, his fingers lingering a little longer.

"I thought you were dead," he said in barely more than a whisper while his eyes darkened at the thought.

Her face paled, and she took the hand still at her face. "You saved me."

He smiled sadly, and then his face turned grim. "We don't have much time. Varlas and his forces will already be here to join with my father. The war is coming."

Faythe took a deep breath, her senses alert to the news, and straightened with a new fierce determination. She had to get to the king before innocent blood was shed for an avoidable cause: a war of revenge and tyranny. She pulled on every last ounce of strength and courage. She was not alone, and Marvellas would not win— not while she still lived to stop her.

She looked into Nik's emerald eyes, just as fierce as hers, as she said, "Let's end this."

Faythe's eyes snapped open. The reek of the room hit her first, like blood and death. Twisting her head, she found the captain slumped in his usual seat beside her. Bile stung in her throat at the sight, at knowing he was no longer simply asleep; he was dead. The other guard in the room would be completely oblivious to that fact.

She turned her head to him then and found the guard leaning lazily against the back wall, looking half-asleep. "Help," she croaked, not expecting him to—but all she needed was for him to be close enough that she could take hold of his mind.

The guard straightened immediately, frowning at her as he made the few steps over. "There is no help for you—"

As soon as he was within reach, she seized his consciousness. He choked when she did, staring wide-eyed in horror. She commanded him to untie her bonds, and then, when her wrists were free, she sighed in relief, the raw, torn flesh no longer stinging against the tight material. She sat up and wasted no time in relieving her ankles while keeping hold of the guard.

Faythe hopped off the bench and turned to meet his eye again. He was just as guilty as the captain and the king in some respects, and she hated that the thought of killing him too crossed her mind. She was not that person. She was not a cold-blooded executioner.

Instead, she willed him into deep unconsciousness with a single thought. Then she hastily made for the door. She swung it open, foolishly not anticipating the guard posted outside. He turned to her, and in the same breath was halfway to drawing his sword, until Faythe instinctively seized his mind, quickly sending him into a deep sleep too.

She swayed on her feet with the mental exertion, catching herself in the doorframe, still recovering from the painful test of endurance with the captain and the prince. She used the wall to lean upright as she tried to regain her physical strength and burn off the remnants of the serum in her system. Faythe forced her feet to move as fast as they could, not knowing how long it would take for the guards to surface again.

As soon as they did…it would be a race to the king.

Faythe breathed slow and steady, finding the strength to stay on her feet finally without aid. She quickened her pace, slowly at first, until the rising panic that she could be too late had her running down the dark passageway and hurtling upstairs. Adrenaline alone dulled the throb of her head and the ache of her bones to keep her moving against physical protest.

She emerged into brighter hallways and recognized the main routes lined with tapestries and ornaments. She knew the way to the prince's rooms from here. Though it didn't matter, as Nik came into view around the next corner, headed toward her. She whimpered in momentary elation at the sight, not slowing her run until they collided. He caught her, and she released a sob at the feel of him. The *real* him. They didn't get a chance to bask in the reunion, however, as his grave look when they parted made her stomach drop.

"It's Jakon and Marlowe."

Their mention brought the world down on her. Along with his words that followed.

"The king has them."

In a gripping flash of desperation, she damned her weak state, screwed the odds, and switched her intended destination. The King of High Farrow would get what he wanted. Along with Faythe's undiluted wrath and fury.

She spun on her heel to head straight for the throne room.

"You're not even armed," Nik said incredulously as he matched her pace.

"You're wrong." Her greatest weapon was within herself.

"You're weakened, Faythe. You can't stand against a hall full of armed fae guards and my father!" he protested, though he made no move to stop her as she stormed the halls.

Guards. It was the first time Faythe realized she had yet to encounter any of them. Not a single one littered the eerily quiet hallways. It should have been a relief, but it made her quicken her pace in a surge of panic over where they might all be gathered.

For the show Orlon planned to make of her friends.

Nik's words made sense, and she should have been rational and listened. But she was unhearing in her need to get to her friends and use every ounce of strength and ability she had left.

Even if it killed her.

Before they reached the end of the next hallway, Nik pulled her to a stop. She was about to bark at his move to delay her until he pushed her against the wall, pressing a finger to his lips in a gesture to be silent. Faythe obeyed, heart racing in anticipation of what the prince's fae senses had picked up on around the bend. Nik strained to listen. He took a deep inhale, and when he released it, his shoulders relaxed. He pushed off the wall just as a familiar brown-skinned beauty came into view.

The ward gasped in startled shock folded with relief that it was friends she'd run into. Nik and Tauria immediately embraced each other tightly, and it pained her to think of what they too had endured these past weeks. Separation with an uncertain fate.

Tauria let out a cry as she hurled herself at Faythe next. "I knew you couldn't be... I just knew it," she mumbled in their embrace.

Faythe only held her tighter in response, overwhelmingly glad for her safety too.

"There weren't any guards at your door either?" Nik questioned after their short moment of joy.

Tauria shook her head, but it wasn't in the naïve hope the king had granted them freedom once more.

Nik's eyes were desperate and pleading when they fell back to Faythe. "You can't go to them. It's a trap."

She would have been flattered that the king had rallied all his forces in anticipation of her arrival, but she wasn't arrogant enough to think it was to protect himself from her ability. Rather, he planned to offer her up as a spectacle. She hated her faltering courage, but she wouldn't leave her friends at the cold mercy of their ruthless king.

"I don't have a choice."

Nik's look softened in understanding, and she knew he wouldn't stop her—nor would he let her go alone. She didn't try to convince him otherwise either. The prince was armed with his sword, and Tauria had the will of the wind around her.

Nik was right: Faythe was exhausted, but she pushed it aside and called upon the remnants of her ability for one final task.

In front of the great doors to the throne room, Faythe paused. She counted her breaths to slow her racing pulse and settled her thoughts to ease her nerves. It was not the first time she had braced herself to face off against the King of High Farrow in this room. But she intended to make it the last.

"Together," Nik said through her worries.

It soothed her to hear the word, and she cast him a grateful smile before looking to Tauria who offered a nod in agreement.

"Together," Faythe echoed.

Nik unsheathed the sword at his hip before taking a step forward to push open the two doors.

Inside, straight ahead, she could already make out the evil smirk and wicked gleam in the king's eye where he sat upon the mighty throne. But it wasn't he who grabbed her focus as she stormed inside. It wasn't that the hall was filled with armed guards down each side either, both blue and purple uniforms alerting her to the fact Olmstone had arrived. And it certainly wasn't King Varlas who rattled her confidence.

It was the sight of her two friends on their knees before them, a sickeningly accurate portrayal of the vision she was made to relive over and over from the captain's influence in her mind.

Her heart raced, body becoming hot and clammy. First, at the thought she could still be strapped to that cold stone in the torture room and this was all a new version of the same horrific nightmare. She consciously breathed with every step toward the dais that flashed between pristine white and the bloodstained version of the nightmare.

She blinked hard.

No—*this* was real.

Second, the notion that perhaps the captain had unwittingly shown her the future threatened her composure completely.

Marlowe and Jakon could still come to meet the brutal beheading he depicted in the illusion, even if not by the captain's hand.

She didn't let it waver her physical façade of bravery. They were still alive, and that was all the hope she needed to make sure they stayed that way.

No one in the room armed themselves, and as she glanced around to take in her surroundings and gauge the many threats, she noted one crucial thing. This wasn't intended to be a fight. It was a gathering for a group execution. And Faythe didn't think the prince and the ward were exempt from it this time.

She stopped before the dais, in between Marlowe and Jakon. She didn't look down at them for risk of losing her nerve. Instead, she glared with powerful hatred and opposition at the king who mocked her with a goading smile from where he sat lazily on his throne.

Orlon straightened and leaned forward to speak the first words in the room. "Now that the main entertainment has arrived, let us begin."

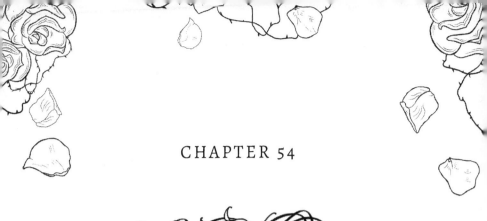

CHAPTER 54

Faythe

T HE HALL WAS still. No one moved, no one spoke, as the spymaster and the king stared off in a deadly battle of defiance.

Faythe made the first move, though not to the knowledge of anyone else in the room as she tested Orlon's mind for entry. His barrier was solid, as she expected. Firm, but not indestructible. The more she became a master of minds, the clearer it was that no one's thoughts were unbreakable. It was simply a matter of being strong enough to shatter the wall or skilled enough to find the faint cracks—neither of which she was confident she was in her current state. Not after weeks of torture by Varis. Maybe never even before that. Nevertheless, she would only get one chance to try, and she had to ensure her friends' safety first.

The king chuckled darkly, feeling the probe on his mind. "Nice try, *spymaster*," he sneered. "I do hope you have something else to offer to those gathered. I promised them a grand spectacle given your reputation."

Faythe didn't take the bait. He wanted to goad her into reck-lessness.

The king stood slowly, assertively, and she tried not to balk at the tall form that cast a sinister shadow from his heightened posi-tion on the dais. His eyes flashed. "My own son stands against me." He shook his head in disappointment, his voice tuning lethal. "And the traitorous Fenstead princess repays the king who saved her with treason."

"Your time of reign is over, Father," Nik said confidently, calmly.

The king shook his head with a wide grin. "And I suppose you think you deserve the crown?" His eyes scanned the onlookers, voice rising in an effort to disparage Nik in front of his guard and allies. "A prince who would stand against his own kind, against his own blood, for a mere human. You do not deserve to succeed me."

Faythe was about to jump to his defense, but she felt Nik brush past her, taking the step up to be level with the King of High Farrow. He faced off with his father with unfaltering confidence.

"It is not I who have failed this kingdom and its subjects. It is you and your will to stop at nothing to gain more power. Even risking the lives of innocents, those you swore to protect. High Farrow soldiers didn't put their heart into training to be led into a battle that will break an alliance built to protect us all against the real enemy. I will not allow them to bleed for tyranny, nor die for greed." Nik's words resonated throughout the great hall, striking the hearts of every fae as he spoke like a leader. Like a king.

Faythe watched the prince before her in awe. The true king the people deserved. It would be impossible for anyone not to see the passion that burned in Prince Nikalias Silvergriff. His love for his kingdom and the heart to do anything it took to keep his people safe.

Yet Orlon still looked at him as if he were less than a servant. She knew it was breaking the prince's heart. This wasn't his father

—not anymore. And she prayed he could see that and not let it shatter his spirit.

"Poetic words, Nikalias," Orlon drawled mockingly. "But it was not words that saw us through the Great Battles. It was not words that kept this kingdom thriving in the face of darkness. You know nothing of what it takes to be king, and you never will."

Anger flared in the prince's eyes, and she saw his hand tighten around the hilt of his sword. Her heart pounded. If Nik struck now...

He didn't get the chance.

Faythe heard the shuffling behind her mere seconds before she caught the glint of the small blade that hurled toward the King of High Farrow. It made its mark. Orlon grunted as the dagger lodged into his side, and he stared down at it in bewildered fury. When his dark eyes snapped up to the culprit, Faythe swore she caught the flicker of shadows swirling over the whites of his eyes. Her mouth dropped in horror as she followed his line of sight. The king's glare, death marked and promised, landed on Jakon, who stood holding a second dagger, positioned to strike again.

The fear that gripped Faythe in that moment was an icy embrace that froze her movement. She could only stare in wide-eyed shock at the reckless, fatal error of her best friend.

Jakon didn't balk. Not even in knowing his first throw had done nothing but attract the strike of the viper far sooner than Faythe anticipated. His face was livid, staring off against the great fae king as though they were equal in combat. His courage was admirable but wholly misplaced, and Faythe could do nothing but give in to the high-pitched ringing in her ears in anticipation of the next move. Marlowe, still on her knees, was pale as bone—Faythe's confirmation she had no foresight into Jakon's act of treason.

Faythe opened her mouth to get him to halt his next attempt with the blade he held, but the words choked in her throat. She was already too late. Jakon clenched his teeth and threw the second blade.

The king caught it effortlessly.

His hand curled around the steel blade that cut open his palm in a terrifying rage, his eyes never leaving Jakon's. Orlon loosened off his fingers as he turned to Faythe's friend fully, his blood and the blade dropping to the floor. She was frantic in her thoughts, but stunned into place. Unarmed, she could do nothing when Orlon advanced a step down from the dais.

On his second step, Faythe snapped back into herself. She moved to stand between them, trembling in the face of the fae king who held a flare of dark emotion that was neither fae nor human.

Black eyes targeted her then, and her spine locked where she stood. Steel sang, and Orlon stopped advancing. His jaw ground as he straightened. Nik stood behind him, the point of his blade to his father's back. But it wasn't the unsheathing of a single blade that blared in a dramatic melody around the room. Faythe spared a quick glance to survey the odds…that didn't exist. Four guards in black equally threatened the prince. A small whimper cast her eyes down to find another poised with a blade over Marlowe's throat. One more held Tauria. Faythe didn't dare look behind to count how many were armed to strike down Jakon.

Her heart pounded at the silence while everyone calculated their opposition. They were damningly outnumbered.

"You dare to harm a king…" Orlon seethed, his voice like ice.

"You are no king," Jakon spat.

Faythe had to blink hard. If she were facing her friend, she might have halted his speech despite the twisted feeling that churned in her stomach at the thought of using her ability on him. While she couldn't fault Jakon for his anger, nor his desire to strike back at the male he despised, his words did nothing but spike Orlon's wrath.

The tension in the room became tangible.

Faythe soothed the edges of her panic to finally speak. "Kill us now, and you'll never get to the temple ruin."

Orlon's eyes flexed—an indication she'd hit her mark.

The king's loathing didn't leave his face, and Faythe's heart beat erratically while he deliberated her words before speaking his next command. With great reluctance, and to Faythe's temporary relief, Orlon yielded. For now. Her rigid posture didn't ease as he slowly turned from them.

"Detain them all. Except Faythe," he ordered.

She flinched, eyes darting wildly between all her friends who were swiftly brought to their knees in front of the dais in the same manner as Marlowe while the king positioned himself before it. She couldn't help the glance she spared behind her. Nik was wild against the three guards who detained him, reduced to nothing in front of his court and neighboring kingdom. He stilled in defeat when a blade rested along the front of his neck, an exact copy of those poised to take all four of her friends' lives in one quick command.

The sight struck her with a terror so deep it strained against the seams of her composure. This was her worst fear made very real. Faythe snapped her head to the scene of onlookers, glancing over them in anger that none would step in and come to their prince's defense. Nik had been more than just their prince; he was a loyal friend. Many of them shifted uncomfortably, looking between each other, at a loss for what to do. Going against their king to stand by their prince would be treason, but Nik was right, and they knew it. Faythe wished she could forgive them for wanting to save themselves, but in her fury, she only saw them as cowards.

She blazed her eyes toward the King of Olmstone who had so far stood in silence like a submissive pet to Orlon. "Rhyenelle is your ally. They helped you when you stood to lose everything in the Great Battles. To turn on them now for personal vengeance is despicable." She seethed.

It should have been her head in an instant to speak to a royal in such a manner. Yet in his eye, for a split second, Faythe swore she saw a hint of regret. Then it was gone, and he flashed livid at her burst of disrespect.

449

"I want her dead."

Faythe didn't flinch at his lethal tone. She turned her attention to the bigger threat in the room who smiled in sly amusement.

"Soon, Varlas. But first…" The King of High Farrow turned expectantly to the side of the hall. A short moment later, a terrified servant woman was escorted through the side entrance. Faythe would have felt sorry for the poor messenger, except what she carried held her full attention as she stared at it in trembling horror. "I'm going to need you to open this for me, Faythe."

The Blood Box that held the temple ruin.

He chuckled in dark amusement at her reaction. "Do you think I'm a fool?" His head tilted with a predatory gleam. "Your companions were so generous to have brought it right to me in a foolish bid to save your pathetic life. Now, I will not only have the power I seek, but I will take great joy in ridding the world of all of you. Consider it a mercy I shall allow you all to die together once this is over."

A black-cloaked guard approached Faythe, and she didn't fight or resist when he took hold of her, extending her arm and poising a dagger over it. She made no sound but flinched at the lick of fire up her forearm where the blade sliced through her shirt. Her blood ran in hot trails down her hand to drip off her fingertips and stain the marble floor. Then another guard brought the box over, placing it on the ground to catch those droplets.

One drop. Two drops. Three.

Everyone waited in silence.

Faythe held the king's stare for those seconds of thickening anticipation. When she couldn't fight it any longer, a dark smile of victory curled her lips.

Orlon's eyes flashed in fury at the mockery. "Who have you used!" he bellowed in outrage. He would have already tested the blood of her friends.

Faythe raised her chin after the guards released her. "You might want to start testing the pigs in the town farm… *Your Majesty.*"

The king roared, the vibration making every hair on her body stand. All tethers to contain his anger shredded at her insolence. Instead of summoning his guards, Orlon went for his own blade. Faythe watched the white Griffin carved into the pommel of the Farrow Sword cry loudly in flight as it was pulled free from its scabbard.

His dark guards grabbed each of her arms and forced her to her knees. Faythe didn't fight it. The king loomed over her like the harbinger of death. He calmed his face once more as he stepped down from the dais and stalked the few paces over to her.

"Here we are, yet again." His eyes flashed to her line of friends behind. "How fitting that you all kneel before me now. I should have ended you so many months ago. Though it has been entertaining to watch you, Faythe, consorting with my son and my ward." He chuckled without humor. "I even commend you for getting the mighty Rhyenelle general under your influence. It is a shame he managed to elude my guard before I could execute him too."

Faythe released a long breath in momentary reprieve. Despite everything, Reylan had remained out of his reach.

"You can die knowing you brought about the death of your friends. Once I torture them for the knowledge of whose blood seals that box." The king raised the Farrow Sword with both palms.

Faythe faintly registered Jakon's struggle, heard Marlowe's cry, and felt the air around her stir from Tauria's influence—and Nik who tried with all his might to break free and save her. None of them could. She raised her chin to lock eyes with her royal executioner, about to throw her whole mental being at the black barrier of his mind—one final attempt to save herself and her friends…

Then the twin doors behind them blast open.

Sharp cries of steel cut through the explosion as every guard in the room became armed ready to fight. Faythe curled into herself to shield against the force of the wind and splinters of wood that flew past. Yet it was not Tauria who caused the commotion as the ward used her ability to deflect the wooden daggers from hitting any of them. Her quick tornado ceased, and Faythe used the distraction to rise to her feet and turn to face the loud intrusion. When she did, she audibly gasped at the sight.

A brilliant white lion. Too large to be of nature, and too perfect in color.

Every guard backed away in terror as the beast growled at them in untamed malice. The vibration of its roar was felt over the stone beneath her feet. Faythe held no fear and did not cower away from it. Her shock turned into relief and joy so overwhelming she let out a short sob as one word, one name, echoed through her to fill her with strength and hope.

Reylan.

His eyes met hers with the thought, and his look softened, curled lips falling back over powerful teeth in his legendary form. Then, after a bright flare of white light, there he was. Shapeshifted back into the intimidating fae male who had every other in the room retreating in fear.

Faythe wanted to go to him but halted her near step as a flood of crimson coats started to file in behind the general. They were all beautifully uniformed and held a lethal focus to protect and defend. It was admirable to see their neat lines and perfect form in the current chaos of the throne room.

Everything was silent. Then the Rhyenelle soldiers cut down the middle, stepping to the side to allow someone to pass.

Not just anyone.

Faythe had never met him, but she had caught a glimpse of the mighty ruler through Varlas's memory. King Agalhor Ashfyre of Rhyenelle.

She didn't have it in her at that moment to question how they gained access into the city, never mind all the way through the *castle*. Their forces were fabled, but still, she was struck by how easy they made it seem. It was no wonder the two kings behind her required something more than an army to conquer their ally kingdom.

The King of Rhyenelle passed the final line of soldiers and came to stand with Reylan halfway across the hall. The general's piercing blue eyes only left her to keep track of the monster behind her, silently calculating every possible way to get between them before the High Farrow king could strike with the blade he still held.

Faythe struggled to believe he was even here at all, too stunned to fear the threat that loomed imminently at her back. She couldn't even turn to gauge Orlon's reaction, though she imagined he was livid at the mockery Rhyenelle made of his defenses.

When Faythe tore her eyes from Reylan, she was instantly met with those of Agalhor. She recoiled a fraction, not expecting the ruler to pay her any attention at all, never mind the lingering look of what she could only decipher as shock.

"This is an act of war!" Orlon thundered.

Agalhor slid his gaze up to the king behind her, not in the least bit fazed by the malice in his tone. "No, Orlon—you took that first step yourself." His voice was deep, calm. He took another step forward, and Reylan drew his sword before following. Agalhor switched his gaze to Varlas. "Though I was greatly disappointed to learn of *your* collusion against me. How many times have we defended your border? Still do, in fact."

Faythe felt awkward at the center of the royal feud. She didn't have to try to feel the waves of anger, distrust, and sadness between the three rulers. She would have stepped out of the way, but it strangely didn't feel appropriate to do so.

Agalhor's gaze traveled to Nik and then over the rest of Faythe's friends who were now standing still under the threat of many swords from the dark guards. "I see not even your own blood agrees with your actions this time, Orlon. If this is how you treat your kin, I feel gravely for the citizens of your kingdom." Then his face fell bored. Despite being a king, she couldn't believe his audacity. "Now, why don't you let these unfortunate humans go so we can discuss serious matters?"

"You arrived just in time, Agalhor," Orlon said in a controlled rage. "The fun is only just beginning. Allow me to demonstrate a just punishment for one who dares to defy. Treason demands death."

Faythe knew he would be bracing to raise his sword to her again, yet the voice of the Rhyenelle king thundered to halt him once more.

"You will not harm her, Orlon!"

Agalhor's tone of voice as he called out to save her was different. Faythe stared at him wide-eyed, shocked by his unexpected intervention, the command that sounded like fear laced with desperation.

It was enough to pause her execution, but she didn't dare turn around.

At the same time, Reylan raised his free arm, and the gesture of his hand immediately disrupted the hall with echoes of shuffling as the front row of Rhyenelle soldiers became equipped as archers in a few impressively fast seconds. Faythe went rigid in fear, ice dousing her, as she looked along the line of lethal arrow tips pointed in her direction. Their aim was on the king behind her, but she couldn't soothe her terror that just one of them might be a fraction off the mark and would hit her instead.

In a delayed counter response, those in the High Farrow and Olmstone ranks who were equipped with a bow drew their arrows and fixed their aim on Agalhor.

Faythe's chest grew heavy with the anxiety that one slipup from the archers on either side could erupt into chaos and tragedy. She found the air too thick to inhale as she waited for the next move. There was no sure outcome in their mutually compromised positions. Every slight flicker of movement made her flinch.

Anger rippled off the king at her back for the threat of the many iron-tipped arrows that now targeted him. Despite this, he chuckled darkly. "I knew you held sympathy for them, Agalhor. You always have been *weak*. But even you are not foolish enough to come to the defense of a nothing *human.*" Orlon spat the word, and she jerked, feeling him closing in behind. Then his voice dropped as he pondered his thoughts out loud. "What is it about you, Faythe?"

She couldn't be sure what he meant by the wandering question and couldn't form a single thought of her own when she felt warm breath brush her ear at his proximity. His hand came up and slid over her shoulder, fingers curling around her throat, but not with tightening force.

Reylan's eyes flashed a dark shade of fury as he jolted a step forward at the contact.

Faythe turned painfully stiff under the king's repulsive touch. His face inched so close to hers she heard his deep inhale, which tremored down her spine and knotted her stomach. She would have doubled over to retch, but she swallowed intermittently to force back her nausea at his dark caress. Her heart pounded faster with every slow, passing second, close to rupturing inside her rib cage. He could crush her neck before she even felt the pain.

Then Orlon retreated from her suddenly and all at once. "Impossible," he muttered slowly, quietly.

The disbelief in his voice had her looking to the general for answers. Both he and the Rhyenelle king stiffened their posture as if bracing to advance, and deep-seated fear filled their eyes at whatever Orlon concluded.

Then his rumbling laughter chilled her to her core, darkly jovial in contrast to the fear and tension that choked the air in the room. "It's almost too perfect to be true. Your compassion for the humans makes clear sense now, as we all look upon the product of your distasteful infatuation."

Faythe kept her eyes on Reylan to try to understand Orlon's words and gauge his movements at her back. She jerked violently when she felt his fingers graze over her shoulder again, tenderly sweeping her hair back to expose her neck.

"What a prize I have held all this time," he said in quiet admiration. Then the Griffin behind locked eyes with the Phoenix in front. "I'm going to take far greater delight in this knowing that with her life, I will break yours, Agalhor."

The world seemed to slow as the eyes of those in front of her went wide with panic. Faythe knew what was coming. The promise of a steel-kissed death loomed behind her. Reylan moved faster than she'd ever seen him react, but even he could not outrun the blade that fell. His face was pale with fear as he raced for her, and she had to look away.

Faythe owed her friends one final farewell and only hoped they could see the apology in her eyes for bringing this mess and danger into their lives. Then she closed her eyes, perhaps in cowardice, as she couldn't stand for any of their distraught faces to be the last thing she saw as she met her end.

With a deep inhale, she braced herself...

The echo of clashing blades pierced a shrill cry through her ears, mere inches above her head. Faythe's eyes snapped open. She turned and was struck by a phantom spear of ice instead of steel.

It was not the crossed swords hovering dangerously close that hitched her breath—but the sight of the young guard who'd saved her life.

Caius! Gods above!

Caius held firm against the strength of Orlon, pushing off his blade. It forced the king back a step. His black eyes blazed in animalistic fury, and he didn't hesitate for a second to advance again toward the guard.

Instead of raising his sword, Caius let his only weapon, his only defense, his only shield...slip right from his grasp.

Faythe's eyes swelled, and her mouth parted, but her scream caught in her throat, gripped by terror at listening to the steel echo off the marble floor. She couldn't move, couldn't hear, couldn't cry out. Caius reached for something else from underneath his cloak, but it did nothing to stop the Farrow Sword that plunged straight through his abdomen.

Time slowed to a crawl and wouldn't reverse. Faythe struggled to accept the fatal maneuver that sealed Caius's fate.

He spluttered, falling to his knees. When he did, she beheld the glittering black cuffs around the king's wrists.

Shackles…crafted of Magestone.

She couldn't believe it. Caius had indicated he'd failed in getting the shackles from Marlowe, who Faythe supplied the material to after a lone trip to the caves below, but all this time, he was saving them for this moment. She didn't know why he chose to keep it from her. Perhaps some foolish notion to try to *protect* her instead. It was a heart-shattering thought that crushed her soul as the price for it would now be his life. His, when it should have been her on the receiving end of the king's sword.

Faythe wasn't capable of feeling an ounce of relief or joy at the sight of Orlon incapacitated. He cried out in anguish as the iridescent stone took effect and his knees gave out to hit the floor.

Nik moved to poise a blade over his father's chest for extra measure.

Caius had saved them all.

Her eyes fixed on him clutching the fatal wound that poured sickening amounts of his blood out across the white marble. Faythe couldn't tear her eyes away from the river of dark crimson. Her heart pounded, and she breathed hard, watching the flow of blood run faster and faster. She heard shuffling around her as the guards in black darted to go to the aid of their fallen master. Her rage was a storm, cancelling out all thoughts of mercy and reasoning. She felt her chaos build and turn all-consuming. She wanted to stop them, to *kill* them, before they could reach Caius. She needed more time with the fae whose breaths were numbered, yet they closed in like merciless wraiths to rob her of the chance.

Faythe tracked the glistening line of red, compelled by it, while ancient words whispered from her mouth of their own accord; a spell so dark and forgotten... The blood met its target, and she watched the item drink its key as she uttered the final verse.

The Blood Box bound by Caius.

She'd asked him to seal it as someone she trusted, someone who had proven their undying loyalty, and someone the king would least suspect. Faythe had taken the task of sealing the box alone so the king could not find out through anyone else's mind who harbored the key.

Faster than she remembered, perhaps even imagined in her desperation, the seal of the box glowed before turning clockwise. A wave of immense power blast from it like a physical blow the moment the closure came loose. Faythe braced her legs and stood firm, recklessly exposing herself to the unearthly magick, allowing it to pierce her being. It ripped through her like a gale in staggering amounts. Straightening, she yielded to that blazing power. It had no beginning and no end—an unparalleled and unforgiving surge of energy not bound for her world. Her veins caught fire, but she fought against letting it consume her. Faythe harnessed that power, adding impossible heights to her ability within. It would kill her. But not before she used it to unleash her rage and retribution.

The guards in black darted toward her, and they were fast. But Faythe's senses were wide and clear, with a reach far surpassing even those of a fae. She could hear the pulse of every mind at once, could see every flicker of motion without looking. Before they could take another step...

Faythe seized control of every mind who dared to move.

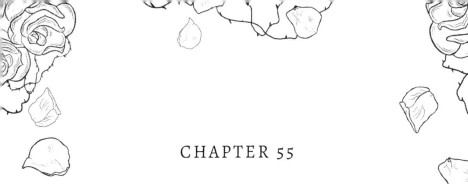

CHAPTER 55

Reylan

R EYLAN HAD NEVER seen anything like it in his four hundred
years.

Faythe glowed under the power of the ruin. He could feel it
coursing through the room as well as his own self, otherworldly
power that didn't belong in their realm, and certainly not within a
human. Within her upturned palms, matching symbols glowed. A
downward pointing triangle within a circle, a single line struck
through its circumference. It rang a faint familiarly, but he couldn't
be sure where he'd seen such an ancient mark before. And couldn't
focus on anything else in that moment except Faythe.

It was a miracle she still stood alive. Reylan thanked the Spirits
for it. Not for long, however, as she would soon be consumed by it
if she kept holding on.

Thirteen fae guards who moved to aid their fallen king were
now paralyzed by Faythe's influence. It shouldn't be possible, yet
there she was, like a storm of light as the air stirred around her and
her veins pulsed bright. The whole hall gawked at her in silence…
then began to retreat with absolute terror on their faces.

Reylan matched them, his own immense fear a kind he'd never felt before, but not for what Faythe could do. He feared for her life, which counted down in precious minutes. While everyone wisely sought distance *from* her, he advanced *toward* her—cautiously, figuring one wrong move could trigger an attack on him too if she mistook him for the enemy.

Her splayed palms and tense arms trembled as if she held an invisible tether to each of the dark guards through every one of her fingertips. She looked deathly pale and slick with sweat. She was faltering and would die if she continued to harness the ruin's power.

The guards choked and spluttered. Then, all in unison, they were brought to their knees, backs arched while their faces contorted in invisible agony. Reylan swallowed hard, throat dry as bone at the horrifying notion she could bend so many wills at once.

Faythe didn't look at him as he edged closer, and mercifully, she didn't turn on him with her deadly power. He sheathed his sword as he approached, taking the final steps until he was standing right in front of her. She didn't pay him any attention, refused to release her hold on the guards who threatened her—or, more importantly, threatened her friends and the young guard as he drew his final breaths. She was protecting them all, even if the cost was her life.

"Faythe," he said quietly, carefully. He got no response, and her trembling turned more violent. Reylan surged with urgency. "Faythe, look at me. You have to let go." His tone turned desperate, but she gave no indication she even heard him. He tried to reach her another way. *"I see you, Faythe. I see you, and I hear you."*

Her gold eyes snapped to his then, blazing so bright they glowed like molten ore. Yet she still did not release the minds she held.

"I'll kill every single fae in this room if they dare to take one step toward you. You need to let go."

"I can't."

Her response was weak, and his eyes widened a fraction in realization. She had lost her control, her own will, to the power of the ruin. And she was fading fast.

In a moment of sheer panic, Reylan reached for her, damning the risks as he wrapped his hands around her forearms. She instantly gripped onto him too, as if desperate for the release she knew he could give her—or, rather, take from her.

The power that raged from her was almost enough to bring him to his knees, but Reylan clenched his teeth and held firm, taking as much of her heightened ability as he could bear in its moment of full, unearthly strength. It pulsed through him— through *them*—like its own physical life source, and he battled to hold it in. Faythe gasped, grappling to stay standing as the darkness threatened to draw her under. He pulled her to him, one arm going around her waist to take her weight.

"*I can't,*" she repeated, head dipping while she fought for consciousness. "*Reylan, I can't hold on.*"

"*Yes, you can, Faythe. Look at me,*" he pleaded.

She did as he commanded, her tired look laced with the pain he wished to take from her.

He raised a hand to her cheek. "*I've got you. I am with you. Always. Don't stop looking at me.*"

Faythe leaned into his palm, her lids fluttering with the claim the darkness tried to stake. Silver lined the fire in her eyes as they strained to hold his. "*Always,*" she echoed in a whisper.

Reylan's heart was hard in his chest, drumming with a fear so great while each second passed with uncertainty. The room around them disappeared, the world around them faded, and there was nothing...*nothing* that mattered but her. The tears in her eyes lapped waves over the sun that was devoured in her irises. She didn't blink; neither did he, afraid it would be enough to make her vanish.

He felt her within, a tether he gripped with everything he had, taking the strain as she faltered. "*I've got you.*" His thumb traced over her cheekbone. "*Stay with me.*"

With his soothing words, he felt her reaching for that tether too, and the tension slackened as she slowly reeled back from the brink of oblivion. Reylan's ability worked with hers. Her power filtered through him, taming the wild storm and returning it back to her in calm, lapping waves.

Slowly, he felt Faythe regain control of herself, and it dropped a ton weight of relief in his stomach. Her breathing was severely labored, but she was no longer rapidly fading as she fought back. Within her own self, she fought to stay alive against the damned odds.

"I see you too, Reylan. I see you, and I hear you."

The words crushed him with elation, and he released a long breath. Both of them focused and reeled back their abilities, slowly letting it dissolve until it was no longer a life-threatening force. He was close to burning out and knew she was several steps closer.

All at once, Faythe let go completely.

The guards around them fell, spluttering for air as the hold on their minds was released. Reylan didn't register any of it, keeping his strength and attention on Faythe as the power within her slowly fizzled out to no longer consume her body. Her golden eyes dulled of their ethereal brightness as she held his stare.

Then she fell limp.

Reylan gripped her tighter, lowering them both to the ground until they were on their knees, forgetting all about the room full of spectators who watched in utter silence. Her forehead rested against his chest as she gasped for breath. Reylan also felt the exertion of the short pulse of all-consuming energy, and he couldn't stand to think what it would have felt like for her. In a *human* body.

"You came back," she said through a short breath.

He broke at the disbelief in her voice, smoothing his palm over the hair at her nape. "I never left."

Faythe peeled her head back to look up at him. Exhaustion trembled her breathing, and sweat gleamed on her too-pale face. Her brow pinched in confusion, but when she opened her mouth to speak, coughing from behind stole her attention and brought them back to the scene of chaos and destruction in the throne room.

With a sharp inhale, Faythe whirled, swaying sideward. Reylan flinched to catch her, but she regained her own balance before shuffling over to the fallen fae guard. He knew Caius vaguely from his time in High Farrow. The guard was always kind to Faythe, but their relationship clearly went deeper at the complete heartbreak on her face. Reylan was torn about leaving her to have her last moment with him. He wanted them to have as much privacy as the situation would allow, but he felt compelled to be at her side. He stood, making the short steps in silence before kneeling down again beside her.

Faythe held Caius's hand. Her soft sobs pulled at something within Reylan, and he wished he could console her. The prince also dropped to one knee to watch in painful silence. Then the Fenstead princess came to stand behind Nik with a hand on his shoulder. Finally, Faythe's human companions came to be at their fallen friend's side, all of them grief-stricken in their own separate ways.

Caius kept his gaze on Faythe. Despite everything, despite the minutes that counted down to his last breath, the young guard smiled at her.

"I can take away your pain," her voice croaked. Reylan had to clench his fists at the noise.

Caius managed a slight shake of the head, knowing if she pushed herself to use her ability now, it would cause her harm. Reylan wanted to thank him even though he hardly knew the fae. His unfaltering courage was rare. He'd saved Faythe—then he'd saved them all.

"Did we win?"

Faythe nodded as a tear rolled from her face and dropped to the floor.

"You saved me."

Caius huffed a weak laugh, wincing in pain as he clutched his abdomen. "I don't know what I was thinking." His head began to drop to the side. Faythe tugged on his arm with a high-pitched whimper, and his tired gaze snapped back to her. Blood still flowed over his blanched skin. He was fading fast.

"Can you promise me something?"

Reylan saw it then. A fear that only crossed the eyes of the dying. A fear he had felt himself before and consoled in so many others who hadn't been so lucky to have been pulled back from death's door. Cruel taunts of an unfulfilled existence, unsated desires, and lost dreams. Reylan saw and felt it as he gazed over Caius's haunted face. His chest pained for the fae while death gripped him with that tragic terror.

Faythe's broken voice sliced right through him. "Anything."

"I don't want to be forgotten."

"Never." Her answer was fierce but tight as if a shard of glass had cut up her throat. "I promise."

"It's okay," Caius whispered slowly, seeing the devastation on her face.

Faythe shook her head. "It should have been me."

Reylan's panic rose at the mere thought.

Caius squeezed her hand weakly. "No, it shouldn't have been. Make this world the one we all dream of. Make it rise." His breath spluttered, and he rasped, "Make it rise from the ashes, Faythe."

"I need you with me to do it, Caius—please," she begged, but her voice broke, casting her eyes skyward with the desperate plea.

"I'm right here." Caius pointed to her chest with the hand she held and tapped weakly over her heart. "I'm always right here." His eyes started to drop and flutter.

Faythe choked a sob and gripped his hand tighter as if it would somehow tether him to their world a little longer. Caius's lids fell over vacant eyes and did not open again. His breath shallowed until it became almost undetectable. Then his body stilled.

Caius was gone.

Faythe buried her face into him. Her cries—*Gods, her cries*—

were the only sound. They echoed heartbreakingly around the hall while everyone stood still in desolate, palpable silence.

Reylan looked up, stunned by what he saw.

It started with the guards in royal blue—Caius's companion soldiers. One by one, they dropped to a knee, heads bowing low in grief for their fallen comrade. But it didn't stop with High Farrow. The kings stayed standing, but behind them, waves of deep purple and crimson joined them to pay tribute. In mutual loss. As allies. The battle between their kings didn't change the righteousness in their hearts.

Faythe's trembling began to ease slowly, and she pulled back to stare at the peaceful fae, still gripping his hand. Reylan didn't disturb her for a long moment, letting her say her final goodbyes. Then, when everyone rose again behind them, he placed a hand on her back without thinking and spoke softly.

"It's time to let go."

He watched her forehead crease with an unfathomable pain as she fought another drowning wave of grief. Faythe closed her eyes, inhaling deeply, before gently placing Caius's hand over his chest. With one last lingering look of despair, she straightened her back.

Along with her posture, the expression on Faythe's tear-stained face turned to steel. Her eyes filled with an ice-cold glaze. She went to rise and didn't protest as he helped her. Then she turned to the hall of onlookers, golden orbs blazing like tangible flame in her sorrow and anger.

"This is senseless," she said, her voice low but compelling, striking everyone to listen.

Reylan should have stopped her before she could continue, knowing she was about to address the kings in a manner that would warrant her execution. Yet she had every right to direct her hostility their way as it had resulted in the death of an innocent. A friend. He knew then he would stand by her side if any of them, including his own king, thought to punish her for it.

"You all hide behind high walls, yet you have already let the enemy inside. The seed of destruction has been planted, and you watered it with your revenge and greed. Without this alliance, the war is already lost. Without the strength of unity, we will all fall."

Reylan watched her in awe. He wasn't alone—all eyes fixed on her. Not with outrage or disgust, but in stunned agreement, floods of crimson, blue, and purple all brought to common ground by a voice of reason. By Faythe. She didn't seek revenge, only unity. To fight a far greater evil that was still to come.

A wicked voice cut through the thick tension. "Who do you think you are to speak out, *girl?*"

Faythe turned to look down on the King of High Farrow, but she didn't get a chance to unleash the wrath that flashed in her eyes at his words when another voice answered for her from across the hall.

"She is her mother's daughter." Agalhor stared wide-eyed at Faythe. The uncanny resemblance was enough to erase any doubt about who she was. It wasn't only her mother she took after in appearance. "*My* daughter," he little more than whispered.

Faythe heard it clear enough, and he saw as much as felt the clash of emotions that lapped over her. The revelation must be sending her already tired-out mind into a wild frenzy.

Reylan knew before she turned her head to catch his gaze that this news would finally call upon the darkness that begged her to rest. Her look was a simple, silent plea for help, and he caught her before she had the chance to fall.

CHAPTER 56

Faythe

FAYTHE SAT BY the warmth of the fire in her rooms. It was the first time she had been able to sit up for long enough to leave the confines of her bed in days. A healer had visited multiple times, and her physical body was near healed from the abrasions of her shackles and aching bones from her nights in the stone cell.

Jakon and Marlowe occupied the rooms beside Faythe's and frequently checked in on her. More than she liked sometimes. It wasn't that she didn't want to see them, but as with Nik and Tauria's visits, Faythe had very little to say. She refused to address the world-shifting revelation that had been thrown down at the worst possible moment. She even refused to see Reylan at all following the events in the throne room.

Since then, she had all but made herself numb to everything. Pain, grief, shock—she was overcome with it all and just one thought away from shattering internally. She couldn't think about the Rhyenelle king's claim—didn't *want* to believe it. So she let heartbreak become the overbearing emotion. Grieved the loss of her friend.

Faythe was doused in guilt. In all her twisted thinking that she should distance herself from her friends and push Reylan away to prevent the Dresair's foretold dire events from coming to pass, she had failed to include the young guard in her worries over who would be taken from her. She could have said more to get him to leave. She could have *tried harder*. Caius was a dear friend and ally, a dreamer of a better world, and his loss was unbearable. Faythe couldn't help but think he deserved to be here far more than she.

The door behind her opened slowly without a knock. She didn't need fae senses to know the pattern of entry was not consistent with any of her friends'. Or perhaps she was gathering a sixth sense for the general. She felt him approach hesitantly, giving her the chance to cast him out as she had done already—three times. But not this time. She knew she would have to face him sooner or later.

Later would be Caius's funeral. She didn't want the weight of anything else bearing heavily down on her for that. So she let Reylan walk all the way up to where she sat, but she didn't turn to look at him. Instead, she chose to watch the dance of the flames in the fire pit. A sight that once comforted her, strengthened her, now filled her with unease at its resemblance to the firebird—to Rhyenelle.

"How are you feeling?" Reylan's voice was soft and concerned.

How she felt... No words existed to convey the depth of her guilt and heartache. She didn't respond.

Reylan wordlessly took up the armchair opposite. Neither of them spoke for a long moment. She was conflicted about what she wanted to say to him.

Eventually, she settled on, "How long have you known?" She looked to him then, needing to see the truth on his face as he answered.

Reylan's brow creased into a frown. Faint dispute filtered into his expression as if the question had him pondering two things at once. He didn't meet her eye, only stared with steely features into the amber sparks. He chose his words carefully.

"Since the day I met you."

Faythe wanted to be angry he kept it from her. She deserved to know. As they came to know each other, started to get close, he still chose to harbor the secret. Yet the emotion failed her when their gazes locked and pain glittered in the night sky of his eyes. She couldn't bring herself to add to it.

"I guess it doesn't matter anyway," she muttered.

"What do you mean?"

"You know what I mean."

"Wouldn't you want to give Rhyenelle a chance—to learn where you came from?"

"I have everything I need here. I don't wish for more than that," she said, but she hated that it felt like a lie, weighing heavier as she voiced it.

"That's bullshit, and you know it."

She flinched a little as he bounded to his feet.

"You can try to fool everyone else, but I see you, Faythe Ashfyre. What are you so afraid of?"

His passion stunned her for a moment. Then his use of the foreign name struck her like an awakening. Her breathing stilled, and she felt a surge of something…something that kindled like a proud flame in her chest. She quickly doused the shallow fire with the waves of her guilt and grief. She didn't deserve to have her ordinary name coupled with that of a mighty house. She wasn't *worthy* of it.

"This isn't a fairy tale, Reylan. A human doesn't just get given a crown and a throne because of some claim to a name she wasn't even raised with."

"You may not have been raised with the Ashfyre name, but you were born with it. By rights, it is yours. And you will rise to it. I've seen it, Faythe. You don't need a crown or a throne or a damn thing to tell you who you are."

469

His words left her conflicted. Humble pride fought with an ugly seed of doubt that grew the longer she pondered the prospect.

"I have no place in a foreign kingdom. No one will accept me there. I don't *belong* there."

"Yes, you do. I think you've known that for some time now. And I think acknowledging that is what scares you the most."

Against the pain that ached in her dormant bones, Faythe rose to her feet. "What scares me the most is that I am *nothing!*" It came out as plea of defeat to get him to understand why she was not worth his determination. "I am nothing but a half-breed nobody with an ability that should never have come to exist. Caius is dead! He died to save my *abominable* existence! I have no claim to anything, no place, and it's better for everyone if I remain here, silent and hidden. *This* is where I belong."

To her surprise, Reylan looked quietly furious at her outburst. "Is that what you really think?"

"It's what everyone will think."

His eyes flashed as he took a step closer. "Let me tell you something, Faythe. This idea you've created that your worth is somehow merited by your blood is wrong." A muscle in his jaw flexed. "Who you are, who you become—that's all on you and what you choose to make of the life you've been given. Don't make yours a waste. Don't throw away your chance to *live* beyond merely existing."

Faythe's argument faltered. Her face wrinkled at hearing the words she so desperately needed to counter the demons inside her mind. "He won't accept me." The fear escaped her lips in a traitorous whisper.

The despairing thought had tormented her for days. A thought so painful it made her shrink back into her confused and vulnerable child-self whose only wish was to know what it was like to have a father. Being confronted with it now, knowing what she was, Nik's words replayed in her head and taunted her mercilessly. *Fae fathers who refuse to tarnish their name with a half-breed...*

"You're wrong." Reylan's hard look softened, and he took

another step until he was close enough to touch. "By announcing who you are in that throne room...he has already accepted you, Faythe." His hand came up to hold her chin, forcing her to stare into his searching blue eyes. "Now, it's your turn."

All she could do was hold his gaze of encouragement, wanting so desperately to surrender; to believe his words and take the leap with him. But all she could see was the burden she would become. To him, to Rhyenelle, and to Agalhor.

"This is my home," she said firmly.

Reylan's expression twitched with the protests he refrained from speaking. His hand dropped, coldness embracing her whole body in its absence.

"When you leave to go back to Rhyenelle, I won't be coming with you."

He shook his head as he paced away from her, and she tried to ignore the twist in her gut at his obvious disappointment. "I can't tell you what to do, but I knew your mother, Lilianna. She was Rhyenelle's queen even without the marriage to Agalhor. Not because of what she was to him, but because of her love and devotion to the kingdom and its people. She knew where she belonged." Reylan burned as bright as the Phoenix of the kingdom he spoke of with such passion. He looked to her with that fierce fire in his eyes, so intense she felt it like heat on her skin, igniting within. "When you figure that out, Faythe Ashfyre, we'll be waiting for you."

Reylan didn't give her time to form a response before he turned to leave. She wasn't even sure she had one as her mouth fell open at his declaration and the mention of her mother. It didn't cross her mind that he would have been alive to know her. He perhaps knew her better than Faythe did after losing her at such a young age. A part of her wanted to go after him. In some ways, being close to him would also bring her closer to her mother. As would the King of Rhyenelle—her father.

She felt dizzy in her thoughts and fell back into her seat, sinking lower at hearing her door click shut behind the general. She wouldn't give in to the temptation. Not when Nik would be crowned king with the exposure of his father's cruel intentions. The guards had obeyed their prince's orders to take Orlon to the castle dungeons where he currently rotted along with his *secret guard*. A new dawn was coming, and High Farrow would thrive once again. It was an age she had only ever dreamed of seeing unfold, and she'd be damned if she left now.

Amber torched the sky as Caius's body was laid to rest upon the tall pyre engulfed in flames. It was nightfall, and the spitting hues of yellow and red were vibrant against the dark sky. Smoke climbed, and she imagined it carrying his spirit high while his ashes fell to feed the soil below.

Faythe stood silent and alone as her friends gave her space to grieve.

She felt...nothing.

Not anymore, as a numbness so detaching had settled for her to be able to leave the confines of her rooms. She'd cried, tormented, for days in solitude, but it would never change the fact Caius was gone. Loss was an eternal shadow. It had clung to her since her moth-er's passing and thickened the moment the light in Caius's eyes went out. It wouldn't diffuse with time; it couldn't be banished with happiness. But it could ease with acceptance, just enough for those still living to bear the passing seasons for however many years they had left in this world. Death was a force that could not be fought, and time was its cunning accomplice. For nothing could prevent death's claim once it sank its claws, and no amount of time could erase the pain it left behind.

Faythe planned to make it count. To honor Caius's life, the life of the human boy whose life she took, and for every other innocent who had been forfeited in a war that was not of their choosing. In aid of a better world like the soul of the dreamer believed in, it was time to fight *back*. In their names, with her last breath, if the end demanded it.

She couldn't deny the inferno before her brought forth the other heavy burden on her mind. Every now and then, she thought she saw the arms of flame cast out like wings and take flight to join the stars before dispersing as falling embers. The cowardly part of her didn't want to face it. She'd made her choice to stay in High Farrow and had no desire to know her father. Even as she thought it, her mind chastised her for the lie. She'd been dealing with the internal tornado of emotions for the past five days.

King Agalhor was set to retreat his forces by morning, and with them, she would likely not see Reylan again either. She refused to acknowledge her sadness over that particular fact. The general had saved her, brought her back when she lost herself to the power of the temple ruin, and risked his own life to do so. It was a debt she didn't think she'd ever be able to repay. She had nothing to offer him, and nothing to offer the Kingdom of the Phoenix.

After a few quiet minutes in front of the pyre, she felt Jakon's presence. She didn't turn to him as he spoke.

"I told him to protect you," he said, achingly quiet. His voice was thick with regret and remorse. When she glanced over at him, Jakon was staring into the flames, face distraught, as if he somehow thought it was his fault.

Faythe slid her hand into his and squeezed. He didn't look at her, but she felt him return the gesture weakly.

"Caius chose to save us all," she said in solace. "It's our job to make sure it wasn't in vain."

Jakon's throat bobbed, holding back the pain he wanted to unleash. Faythe had never seen him cry. Not once in over ten years. Yet now, silver glistened in his eyes, and the stray tear that fell shattered another piece of her fractured heart. He took a long breath to calm himself, quickly swiping the wetness from his cheek.

"It's not over, is it?"

Faythe had no answer to the question that kept them from being able to move on completely. She had to look away. "I think it's barely begun," she answered honestly.

Marlowe came up to her right, and Faythe turned to her. They exchanged a crinkled look filled with heartache, their faces mirroring their unspoken longing, and fell into each other's arms wordlessly.

"I'm sorry," Faythe whispered.

Marlowe's arms clutched her a little tighter. "Me too."

When she pulled back, the blacksmith's eyes sparkled as flames danced through the tears pooling in them.

"You are the strongest of us all, Marlowe. The burdens you carry... I'm sorry I was not there for you when you needed me. I thought you were better off without me, but I was wrong—*so* wrong. I realize now, we're stronger together, and we need each other."

A tear gathered and fell over her glowing porcelain cheek. Faythe's hand lifted to swipe it away with a sad smile. "Can you forgive me?"

Marlowe nodded, her face easing to return to its delicate soft-ness. "Of course. But only if you can forgive me in return. I was hurting and overwhelmed and angry, and I...I took it out on you, *blamed* you, when I knew it wasn't entirely your fault."

Faythe pulled her into another embrace, feeling the darkness lighten enough for her to breathe easy knowing there was no longer a rift between them.

"There is nothing to forgive. You had every right to feel the way you did. It *was* my fault, but I won't ever stop fighting for you. Both of you."

They broke apart, and Faythe turned to Jakon whose expres-sion lifted as he observed them. Faythe's lips upturned contentedly, and she linked arms with him, head tilting to rest on his shoulder while Marlowe folded into her other side.

For one small, suspended moment in time, the three friends

stood in front of the flames listening to the crackle of splitting timber and watching the rain of fire stars. Faythe allowed herself to feel the small essence of joy that weaved through her melancholy chest. She cast her eyes to the sky as she silently, painfully, thanked Caius in one last internal farewell and recalled his final words as a vow she would never forget.

Make it rise from the ashes.

Marlowe's careful voice broke their mournful silence. "Will you go to Rhyenelle?"

Faythe shook her head. "My home is here, with both of you."

Her answering look filled Faythe with dread. She had come to know when Marlowe was speaking to her as more than just a friend. As an oracle.

"You shouldn't give up on the chance to know where you came from. I think there is still so much for you to learn, Faythe. The answers you've silently sought are close."

Faythe felt foolish for wanting to protest to *stay*, as if she needed permission.

"She's right."

Faythe whipped her head to Jakon. His look was pained at the thought of her leaving, but he smiled in understanding. "You deserve a chance to have a relationship with your father. And if you decide the south isn't all it's made out to be, you will always have a home to come back to here in High Farrow."

She held his eyes filled with encouragement, and in his smile of love there was a silent push. He was setting her free. He wouldn't object if she went to Rhyenelle because he would always be here, and nothing, no one, could stop her from seeing him anymore.

"And should you decide to stay in Rhyenelle permanently, damn if you don't think we'll be heading south too," he added, fitting an arm across her shoulders to pull her to him.

Faythe held onto her reservations; she had been separated from them once before. "We only just got each other back."

Marlowe gently squeezed the arm hooked around Faythe's

waist. "Exactly. There is no one keeping us apart anymore, and no one ever will again. But this… This is your destiny, Faythe. Whatever land or sea stretches between us can always be traveled. We will always make our way back to each other."

She cast her eyes back to Jakon. His smile was unburdened and bright as he looked between her and Marlowe.

"What if I don't fit in there?" Faythe asked, admitting the fear that had clouded her mind ever since she saw the path to Rhyenelle as a viable option. She was only human, only *Faythe*, a far cry from any semblance of fae prestige. And to know she would be trading one castle for another… She couldn't ignore where she came from. The sorry, abandoned hut and her careless but impoverished childhood with Jakon. Faythe wouldn't change her past for the world. Not the days they passed on an empty belly in the early years when neither of them were old enough to find proper work. Not the nights that were so bitterly cold they pushed their cots together in the feeble space and stole burlap sacks to use as extra blankets. Not the days she cried endlessly for her mother and wondered what she had done to deserve to be alone in the world.

But Faythe was never alone. Not since the day Jakon entered her life and became her family. For the person she held tightly in her arms in that moment—for him—she would do it all over again. No matter what she learned of her father and why her mother robbed her of the bond they could have had, she would always have him to come home to. Jakon, Marlowe, Nik, and Tauria—her unbreakable found family.

"You weren't born to fit in, Faythe," Jakon answered with a hint of amusement that lifted the somber mood. She smiled, finding comfort in the vibrations against his chest as he spoke. "Not as Faythe Aklin or the Gold-Eyed Shadow, or as an Ashfyre." He took her shoulders, peeling her from his body to look her straight in the eye. "It's time for you to embrace that free spirit of yours. It's time for you to fly."

Her chest opened up with light that chased the shadows of

uncertainty away. Her breathing came easier, clearer, no longer choked by her reserves and protests as she beheld the fierce look in his brown eyes and the warm smile that reassured her nothing could ever sway his opinion of her. No name nor title could waver their bond. And upon turning to Marlowe and seeing the blacksmith's nod of silent agreement, it was all she could do to refrain from pulling her into an embrace of endless gratitude.

Her emotions darted between nerves, excitement and...liberation. This was her choice. She was no longer tethered here by a wicked king or spirit-bound to the Eternal Woods. Her heart beat full and free as she realized her life belonged all to her once again. She would be no one's burden but her own.

The door to Faythe's cage had been opened, and now all she had to do was dare to fly free.

CHAPTER 57

Nikalias

THE PRINCE OF High Farrow wore a brave mask as he entered the castle dungeons. He asked the guards to wait outside while he entered the cellblock, needing to be alone for this harrowing task.

Nik spotted his father immediately, leaning against the back of the dark stone and iron cell. It relieved him that the monster was caged, but equally broke him that it wore his father's face. A once proud and mighty king, used and discarded like an overworked toy. He tried to convince himself there was nothing of his father left, that he died over a hundred years ago when his heart was turned by the Spirit of Death in Rhyenelle. He had to believe there was no saving him as Aurialis claimed. It was the only way he would be able to carry out what needed to be done.

After witnessing the king's madness in the throne room, the guards—the *real* blue-coated High Farrow warriors—obeyed his commands without a thought once it became safe to do so. His fears that they too had turned their backs on him dissolved the moment they seized his father instead of him when Caius rendered him incapacitated with the Magestone shackles.

It was a moment Nik would never forget. He would always remember the young fae for his bravery and sacrifice in saving Faythe's life and ending the reign of terror at the hands of the king. The Magestone was a stroke of brilliance on Faythe's part, and brave Caius carried through on her plan when all hope was almost lost.

His father still wore those bonds that took away his fae strength, chained to the back wall like a dog. Nik pushed his personal feelings aside as he unlocked the iron door and stepped inside. Orlon stared at him through a stranger's black eyes with no regret or remorse for the events he caused.

Despite everything he'd done—killing his mother, conspiring a war, and ruling with merciless malice—Nik's anger and hatred toward his father was overshadowed by another crushing emotion. Guilt. That he had believed all this time it truly was his father who committed such heinous crimes over the past century.

"Ahh, Nikalias, my son..." he drawled mockingly. "And the biggest disappointment of my immortal life." It was his father's voice, but not his words. The male he knew, the one who raised him—he was not the one who looked up at him with cold loathing now. "You're weak, you're spineless, and you let your emotions get in the way of what needs to be done. I saw the future for this kingdom. Power. Strength. I did not spend my life building it all so you could simply let it fall with your soft heart," his father spat.

Nik's jaw tensed, and it was as much emotion as he would show as he raised his chin. "You're right. You led these people. You built this kingdom." He took a step forward. "Then you died at the hands of Dakodas a century ago, and so your reign should have too."

The king's black eyes blazed in fury, and he knew he'd struck the right chord.

"My only regret is that I didn't realize it sooner." He would forever harbor the guilt of failing his father.

Nik looked down at those black eyes, trying to detach his father's face from the evil lurking within as it glared back at him with a powerful malice. He locked away all personal feelings behind a steel guard, going on to address the demon within.

"Did you know of the creature in the caves below the castle?"

Orlon stayed silent, but in the faint flex of his eyes, Nik saw the recognition. He huffed a humorless laugh.

"Of course you did. You were the one ordering for it to be kept fed. But why?"

Nik paced the cell, trying to put the scattered pieces of the puzzle together.

"You will not stand against the might of the dark fae, *prince.*"

Nik halted, eyes snapping back to hold its black depths. It was a snarl meant to scare him, but instead, it gave Nik the confirmation he sought. One that inspired a horrible feeling of foreboding.

The creature in the passage *was* a dark fae.

"Such a savage, unhinged species may be a brutal weapon, but they cannot be tamed and disciplined for battle." Nik chose his words carefully, knowing he wouldn't receive answers by asking the terrifying questions he needed to outright. He wanted to gather what information he could to try to gauge what they were up against.

It seemed to work, as the demon chuckled darkly, each vibration like a cold trail down his spine.

"Those who transitioned too savagely for purpose are but a distraction. They are without any humanity, yes, but they can deliver carnage," he drawled, relishing in the opportunity to strike fear into the prince. "But there are also those who are not so different from you, Nikalias. Perhaps one may have crossed your path, but you would never have known in your ignorance and naïvety."

Nik kept his breathing steady, but his pulse quickened at the haunting possibility they could walk among them without detection. It didn't make any sense.

"Yet they are far stronger. Far more lethal. They are a war you cannot win."

Nik's whole body stiffened painfully to suppress the tremor that swept through him. "Their numbers can't be all that threatening if they have succeeded in remaining hidden. The dark fae are winged," he pointed out cautiously.

A cruel, triumphant grin split the demon's cheeks. "Their numbers span beyond your imagination, *prince*. They are cunning, and there are many with the ability to glamor their dark fae heritage. Without their wings, would you know if one was staring you in the face? The fae are too oblivious to question the shift in scent, too imperious to believe there could exist a species superior to them. Fear the dark fae, Nikalias, for they will make the Netherworld seem like paradise to those who dare defy them."

"You pulled back the forces in Galmire…" The dawning realization that hit him was chilling. "You knew the dark fae were targeting the humans. You—" Nik's breathing hardened in a rage. "You *let* them be targeted." Another puzzle piece shifted into place. "The mountains," he whispered to himself as he fitted it all together. A flash of memory from Jakon's recollection of what he'd gathered in the town: The bodies always turned up near…

"They reside in the Mortus Mountains, don't they?"

The demon flinched as if he knew it was a piece of information he shouldn't give away. His face contorted as if he were fighting within himself to stay silent.

He didn't directly confirm it, but Nik didn't need him to.

"They need humans to feed on, and they need fae bodies for transition."

"Transition?"

The demon nodded. "How do you think they have built their numbers? They have many full-bred dark fae, but to rely on them would take many millennia more to form the army they require after their near annihilation. The Silverbloods are strong, pure, but the Blackbloods—the *transitioned*—add a lethal capacity to their forces. You will not stand against them."

Nik blanched but maintained his outward composure. He stored away the knowledge, unknowing of what he could do with it yet—against an uncharted and absolutely deadly threat, the likes of which no living fae nor human had encountered before. A threat from nightmares and horror stories; a dark fable and historic myth…made *very* real. He swallowed hard to wet his bone-dry throat.

"And Marvellas—does she hear us now?"

"The great Spirit of Souls is everywhere. You cannot hide from her, and you cannot escape her."

"Good."

Nik drew the sword at his hip, and his father flinched back in fear. He blocked out all thoughts of the male he knew, or he wouldn't be able to follow through with his plan. He pointed the blade at Orlon's chest.

"If you're listening, I want you to know…"—the prince's heart hammered, and it took all his strength to keep his hand from wavering and letting his world-shattering pain slip through the length of steel—"we're coming for you, Marvellas." Then he kneeled, thrusting the sword straight through his father's heart in one swift motion.

Orlon spluttered, coughing blood as he looked down to gape at the blade that dealt his killing strike. The king's sword—the Farrow Sword. It would now rightfully belong to Nik.

The prince held firm as he watched in painstaking agony while his father's life faded under his own hands.

Then Orlon's head snapped up to lock his gaze with a sharp gasp that struck him cold.

Regret battered his heart and remorse clouded his mind, at his father's wide-eyed stare and what he saw in it. Through the depthless black voids of his irises, hues of hazel began to lattice. Nik went to retract the blade, horrified he was wrong, that Aurialis had tricked him, but his father's hand curled around his forearm to prevent him from removing the sword in his chest. Nik leaned forward as the familiarity, recognition, and love returned to Orlon's eyes while he stared back.

"Thank you, son," he said in a choked whisper. "I've always... been...proud of you."

"I failed you, Father." Nik's voice was barely a desperate whisper through his tight throat.

Orlon mustered a weak shake of his head. His voice was a slow croak in his agony. "You are smart and wise, my son. You will know how to fight them. You will know how to lead these people." One of his weak, trembling hands raised, a finger pointing to his chest. "You have..." His breathing rasped and spluttered. "You have your mother's heart."

Nik trembled stiffly. He wanted to take it back. *Oh, Gods.* He was wrong. He was foolishly, horribly, wrong...

But over his panic that perhaps his father could have been saved, the pleading look in his brown eyes said it all. This was his wish, and perhaps it had been since the moment he became trapped in his own mind by some dark, evil magick. Nik rested his forehead against his father's, trying desperately to accept what he had done was a kindness, a mercy, better than the alternative of living with a burdened, darkened soul, lost beyond salvation.

"I forgive you," Nik whispered, hoping it would ease his father's guilt as he passed through to the Afterlife. "You're free now."

Nik clenched his eyes together and counted his father's ragged, fading breaths. It was all that filled the grim silence as he shallowed his own to listen. Right until the very last one.

The hand encasing his arm loosened and fell as his body went limp.

His father was dead. And along with Orlon's life, Nik felt a sharp sever from within that pulled him back with a gasp. He knew what it was.

The release of his soul from the Eternal Woods.

Nik hadn't wanted to concern Faythe who had looked quietly horrified at what Aurialis had asked of him to obtain the yucolites and save her life. He didn't think he would ever carry through on his end of the bargain and be free by killing his own father.

Yet in that moment, by his own hand, the prince...became the king.

CHAPTER 58

Tauria

TAURIA BIT HER fingernails nervously as she stood by the fire in her rooms. When her door opened, she immediately spun with pent-up anticipation, shoulders slumping in relief at the sight of Nik. Her heart skipped a beat at his ghostly-pale face. She glanced to his side, finding the scabbard at his hip empty.

He didn't have to speak. She found her feet moving toward him of their own accord. He only stared at her wide-eyed, hands trembling, when she fell into him and his arms instantly gripped her tight, letting her absorb some of his pain through the embrace. He didn't speak, but she didn't need him to.

When she pulled back, Tauria looked up at him. "I'm so sorry."

His hand slowly raised to cup her cheek in silent thanks, and she raised her own hand to encase it. Nik searched her face, but she couldn't be sure of what he was looking for. She stayed silent, hoping that through her eyes he would see there was no judgment for what he had done. For killing his father. She held nothing but love and admiration for the prince before her, and she knew there was nothing in this world that could change that view.

"I don't know if I'm ready," he confessed, his voice so quiet with uncertainty it tore at her heart.

She took both of his hands then and looked at him fiercely. "You are ready, Nik. You have been for some time. And High Farrow is ready for *you* and the new age of freedom and unity you will bring."

Nik smiled as a hint of brightness returned to his eyes. "Spoken like a true leader."

Tauria's chest burst with a warmth of pride. For both of them. "One day, I will take back Fenstead, and we will always be true allies. But right now, it is your time."

Nik nodded in determination. "When the day comes, I will help you take back your kingdom, Tauria. High Farrow will always be your home too."

Her eyes burned with irrevocable love and appreciation for the prince—the *king*—standing before her. She had no doubts about the great ruler he was and would continue to become. Nothing gave her more joy than watching him grow to this point. She embraced him once again, overcome with happiness and relief.

They were safe.

They were free.

He didn't step out of her arms when he pulled back, and her heart fluttered at the familiar gentle look laced with a faint essence of pain. Even after a hundred years together, Nik was a puzzle she could never solve. In the heat of a tender moment, there was always a battle raging within his emerald pools. Since the night they gave themselves completely to each other, a guard had formed around the depths of his desires. He voiced what could not be between them, but those words were often betrayed by his eyes. Perhaps it made her a fool after all this time, but she couldn't give up on him—not while the battle remained that planted the seed of doubt she wasn't alone in her feelings.

Just like every other time, the conflict in his eyes passed, and he stepped away from her. Tauria swallowed her disappointment.

Nik took a long breath. "There's a lot I need to attend to. The lords will demand to know what happened, and I'll have to try my best to convince them not to force my abdication for treason." He huffed a nervous laugh.

Though he looked silently terrified at the possibility, she believed he would convince them otherwise with the help of witnesses. "The joys of the monarchy," Tauria said lightly. "Off you go then, *King* Nikalias Silvergriff." It felt delightfully strange to address him with his new title, but the crown fit.

He rolled his eyes playfully then turned to leave. She watched him right until the door closed behind him and then fell back into her own thoughts.

While she was elated for Nik and High Farrow, Tauria went to the balcony and looked out. Past the glittering city, beyond the horizon. She kept staring as if she could see all the way to the grassy hilltops that flew proud stag banners, knowing one day, she would return to stand on Fenstead soil to make her kingdom rise and the lands thrive once again.

CHAPTER 59

Faythe

AYTHE HAD ONE last endeavor she needed to complete.

She didn't tell anyone when she slipped out of the castle, and now she was a close friend of Nik—the *king*—the guards let her pass without any inquisition. Either that, or they now feared her more than ever before after witnessing the power she harnessed from the temple ruin.

The thing burned a hold in the pocket of her cloak as she headed to return it exactly where it belonged. She wanted nothing to do with it and couldn't wait for it to be out of her possession.

After using the Riscillius to open the temple, she stood in the circle of sun that shot a beam of charged light through the stone in the pommel of her sword. She intended to place the ruin back into its designated spot on the podium behind her and then turn her back on the temple, on the Spirits and their feuds, for good. Something stopped her, however. She knew it was the unspoken words that would always remain unsaid between her and the Spirit of Life if she left now.

And Faythe demanded final answers.

So, she braced herself and poised her sword, guiding the light beam until it struck its stone eye counterpart across the room. Faythe shielded her eyes and adjusted to the harsh brightness for a few seconds. When she lowered them again, Aurialis stood in front of her.

"I am sorry about your friend," were the first words out of the ethereal beauty's mouth.

Faythe's eyes flashed at the mention. "You could have saved him," she ground out.

The Spirit shook her head. "I could not—"

"You're the damned Spirit of *Life!* Where were you when you were needed the most?" she cried. It had been riling her anger for days. How she could demand so much of Faythe and yet not offer her that one mercy in return? "It should have been me." Faythe's voice fell in defeat. "Why didn't you take my life instead?"

In Caius's last moments, she'd put everything she had into trying to plead for his life, and only despairing silence answered.

"I cannot take life. I am not my sister Dakodas. We exist only to keep the balance."

Her teeth ground at the mention of the damned *balance.* "He didn't deserve to die."

"No, he did not."

Faythe and the Spirit exchanged a solemn look—a look of understanding.

"But his sacrifice is not meaningless, Faythe. Nothing is ever without purpose. It triggers so many things in its wake that you cannot begin to fathom. Your role as one of those still living is to ensure the paths opened are taken and carry with you on your ventures the spirit of those who have been loved and lost to carve this world. Every soul stamps the soil you stand on, in life and in death."

Faythe hung her head. A single drop of sorrow fell straight onto the glowing lines of Aurialis's symbol painted beneath her feet. Her mind was racked with conflict. Part of her found solace in the Spirit's words, but a larger part grew with resentment over fate and destiny and everything else that was so damningly out of her control. She hardened her gaze, bringing her eyes up to meet Aurialis again.

"Why didn't you tell me who my father was?"

"It was not for me to tell you."

Faythe's temper flared, but Aurialis continued.

"You must understand there is an order to everything we do. Disrupt it, and the fate of the world can change."

The words sounded so familiar—and they were, as she'd heard them before. Aurialis's words, through Marlowe's voice. Faythe laughed bitterly, despising even more that the Spirit was using her friend too. She had only just regained her life; she wasn't about to bow down to a force Nether-bent on screwing her over.

"I only came to return your ruin. Nik and I owe you nothing anymore." She'd felt the tether to her soul break the moment she stepped into the Eternal Woods that night with the ruin, and she wondered if Nik felt it too.

"You must keep it safe."

Faythe's eyes widened, incredulous. "No way in rutting damn. I don't want anything to do with you or your sister feud. And my friends will not be involved either," she warned.

"You may have freed High Farrow from the reach of Marvellas for now, but the threat is far from over, Faythe. You must keep my ruin safe and seek out the temple of Dakodas before it is too late."

Faythe blanched. "You can find someone else. I want no part in it."

"It can only be you."

"Then the world is bloody well doomed already." She threw her arms out in exasperation.

Aurialis ignored her. "You must go to Rhyenelle. Her temple lies within the caves of the Niltain Isles."

"Orlon was Marvellas's puppet. I won't be yours."

"I seek nothing for myself."

Faythe almost recoiled at the unexpected sharpness in Aurialis's tone.

"Only to protect and save your world before it is too late, as is my sworn duty as a Spirit of your realm. Dakodas and Marvellas lost sight of that, and I'm fighting to keep them from destroying it completely, but I need your *help*, Faythe."

She blinked, a little dumbfounded by the small speech. It no longer felt appropriate to fight against the Spirit of Life—against one on her own side. To hear an all-powerful being almost beg for *her* help... It was more daunting than humbling. While Faythe didn't think she could be of much help and wanted to insist Aurialis find someone else, someone better, if only to give the world a damn fighting chance...she retracted all her counterarguments and listened.

"We are running out of time. Summer solstice will mark the thousand-year anniversary of Marvellas's transition to your world. The day will be one in a millennia when the veil between realms is weak enough for history to repeat itself."

Faythe paled as her mind sprinted to the conclusion before Aurialis had a chance to finish.

"On that day, Dakodas plans to break fundamental laws of our kind, just as Marvellas did, to be bound in a physical form to walk your world. It is why Marvellas influenced the King of High Farrow to locate the Riscillius within his kingdom. The Looking Glass is needed to open the Temple of Darkness for the ritual to take place, and for Dakodas to descend."

Though they had already narrowly escaped it, it seemed death was quite literally close to knocking on their door.

"How do you expect I stop her?" Faythe didn't believe it was entirely in her power to do so. It was a threat bigger than they could have possibly imagined—far bigger than Orlon, and far deadlier than Marvellas alone. It wasn't just her own life at stake if she did nothing. It wasn't even her friends' now either... It was a threat against the whole of Ungardia and possibly even beyond.

"There is only one way. On the solstice, there will be a solar eclipse. As the Goddess of the Moon, it is when Dakodas will be at her strongest. You must reach her temple before this. There, you will have to remove her ruin to prevent her transition into your realm."

It seemed too simple an ask. So easy she questioned why the Spirit seemed so Nether-bent on bestowing the task upon Faythe's shoulders. She was human with a mind ability she doubted would prove useful defense in the face of something as great and powerful as the Spirit of *Death*.

"This thing nearly *killed* me," Faythe said in fear, holding up the arrow-shaped ruin she tried not to think about for too long. It had been silent, emitting only a small hum since she called on its power in the throne room.

"They respond to chaos. Too much of it, and the ruin can consume its bearer," Aurialis explained. "The power you hold within you cannot be glimpsed, and it manifests the more you come to use your ability. But it is not unchallenged. In turn, great power has the aptitude to heighten your negative sentiments. Before you can wield the ruins, you must learn control, discipline, and how to channel your anger. Find the teacher who tames the storm. Only then will you be able to harness them to your own will, not yield all that you are to them."

Faythe shuddered at the thought, refraining from voicing that she was perhaps the least suitable candidate for the role. "Isn't there someone else more…qualified for the quest?"

The Spirit's grim look made Faythe want to groan out loud. "The individual ruins can only enhance what is already there. Without an ability to latch onto, they are powerless."

"I hardly think my particular *talent* is the most suitable against Dakodas or Marvellas. An elemental, perhaps? Someone with a more *physical* ability?" she ranted, trying desperately to pass the baton.

Her hope faded at the Spirit's gaze of sympathy.

"There is a reason you are the only of your kind, Faythe." At her pale look, Aurialis added, "But your triumph against my sisters will also depend on the help and guidance of those around you. Power, strength, wisdom, courage, knowledge, resilience, darkness, and light—you are all soul-bound by the same path of fate."

Triumph. The word awoke something in her, and she wasn't sure if it was deadly fear or fierce determination. Failure wasn't an option. Her friends' lives depended on it—the whole *realm* depended on it. It was a crushing weight that suddenly settled on her shoulders as she knew it was completely possible to fail and for all to be lost to the Spirits that would claim their realm as their own. She dreaded to think what two all-powerful beings could do, never mind one.

They were coming to the end of winter. Summer solstice would follow the spring a little over five months away. It didn't seem like a lot of time to allow her to sample the new kingdom as she'd hoped to do before attempting to seek out the hidden temple on a small island off the coast of Rhyenelle. She wanted to see the kingdom with excitement and adventure. The latter, she would certainly get —only now, it was riddled with terrors and uncertainties. A quest with no definitive outcome.

When Faythe didn't respond, Aurialis said, "Good luck, Faythe. I am always with you. And those you have loved and lost follow in your footsteps no matter where you go."

The Spirit began to fade, and for once, Faythe didn't feel the desperate need to beg for more time. Her path was set, scattered with the answers she sought.

Now, it was on her to find the courage to face them.

CHAPTER 60

Faythe

FAYTHE KNOCKED BRIEFLY but didn't wait long for a response before welcoming herself into the king's chambers. It was highly inappropriate to enter uninvited, but she knew High Farrow's new ruler would not object to her disregard for formality.

She did enter cautiously, however, spotting him outside on the balcony, dressed formally in his royal blue attire. His cloak billowed slightly behind him in the winter wind.

Faythe was also dressed for the outdoors and pulled her cloak tighter as she stepped out to greet him. She walked slowly, taking in the picture of him. Savoring it, as it was likely to be a long while before she saw him again. It pained her to be leaving Nik as much as it tore her heart to leave Jakon and Marlowe.

She had to stop and stare at the image she'd only ever dreamed of seeing.

Nikalias Silvergriff, once a humble prince, now a great *king*. It was dazzling to title him as such, and it brought a smile of pride to her face.

"Are you just going to stand there gawking?" he said, not taking his eyes off the immaculate city below.

Faythe huffed a laugh and joined him at the stone rail. "Would you really object if I did?"

His lips tugged in amusement, casting her a quick sideward glance. Then Faythe followed his longing gaze to look out over the white stone maze of glittering buildings.

"Caius loved this city," Nik reflected quietly, and Faythe's chest tightened. "He loved the town...he loved the people. Human and fae...because he was both. He was a vision of exactly the kind of peace and unity High Farrow needs to be restored to."

"Yes," was all she could whisper through her wave of grief.

"That's why I've made my first decision as king. This"—Nik waved a hand over the beautiful cityscape—"will be renamed. To reflect the dawning of change."

Faythe frowned mildly in question.

Nik's smile widened, and without moving his eyes, he said proudly, "Caius City."

Faythe's eyes pricked. She fought against tears from the burst of emotion that pierced her heart at the declaration. It was perfect. And beautifully fitting to forever commemorate the young fae whose bravery and sacrifice deserved to be honored for generations.

"Thank you," was all she could choke out in her emotional state.

Nik didn't respond. He didn't have to. For a while, they both just stared out at the city that held a whole new meaning now, inaugurated with Caius's memory for the whole world to see. Faythe wanted to remain in the peaceful moment longer than she knew she could. But there were still pressing matters and impending goodbyes to suffer.

It was Nik who broke the silence first. "Varlas and his forces have retreated back to Olmstone. Neither I nor Agalhor forgive him for what he did and planned to do. But you were right. We all have one enemy, and we can't afford to make new enemies out of each other."

Faythe felt her shoulders free of a heavy, looming weight. There would be no internal war. The alliance would remain despite the actions of Olmstone, and she was massively relieved for it. They would need the strength of unity in the face of what was to come.

"I explained what I could to them about my father. They found it hard to believe. I'm sure they still have their doubts that his actions weren't entirely his own." Nik's voice was thick with pain at the mention of his father. When she glanced at his hands, she found them curled into tight fists.

It pained her to ask, but she had to know. "Orlon…is he—?"

"Dead," Nik answered sharply before she had the chance to finish. The muscles in his jaw flexed, and Faythe felt cold with his grief. "It was the only way—you heard Aurialis. So I took the Farrow Sword…and ran it through his chest."

Faythe didn't move or speak to comfort him, perhaps out of shock as she let him continue.

"He was still in there the whole time, and now I see the moments when he fought against the control on his will. He took in Tauria when the demon inside would have killed her too and finished off Fenstead's royal line. All this time, he was still in there." Nik shook his head, the pain on his face cracking deep within Faythe's own heart. She reached out for his hand, and his balled fist uncurled to allow her palm to slide into his. He looked down at their joined hands before his eyes met hers, sparkling with emotion. "Yet when I took his life, he…he thanked me."

Faythe's eyes stung to hear his voice waver. She reached up and pulled him into a tight embrace. She wished she'd been the one to do it, if only to relieve the lifelong burden he would carry as the one who ended his father's life. Even if it was a mercy.

"Then he would have seen the king you were becoming, Nik. He would be so proud of you."

His arms tightened around her, and she desired nothing more

than to take the pain from him through that embrace. She knew it would be his act to shoulder and come to terms with within himself, just as she had learned to deal with the guilt of her mother's passing—her role in it.

When he released her, he looked at her with the same pride she held for him. Then his eyes grazed her from head to toe, a sad but knowing smile spreading across his cheeks.

"You're going to Rhyenelle, aren't you?"

It wasn't really a question, yet Faythe felt compelled to explain. "I will never learn more about myself if I stay," she admitted quietly.

He gave her a small nod in understanding.

"There's one last thing I never explained to you about your Nightwalking. I guess I never thought you would ever have to use it," he said somberly.

Faythe frowned deeply. She didn't think there could be any more layers to the ability.

He huffed a laugh at her look. "Everyone's reach has a limit. Some can walk through the mind only a street away, while others might stretch beyond towns," he said. Then his eyes flashed to her chest before the emeralds pierced through her again. "But with an item gifted by the host, those strong enough can reach between *kingdoms.*"

Realization dawned, and she inhaled, her hand reaching up instinctively to grasp the star pendant under her cloak. "How did you know I would need it?" she breathed in disbelief.

He smiled sadly. "I hoped you wouldn't. But if you were ever lost or faraway, I wanted you to always have a way to visit a familiar face."

Tears filled the corners of her eyes, blurring her vision. Faythe blinked to force them back. "You have no idea how much it means to me, Nik. I owe you everything."

He shook his head. "I only helped you embrace what was

already there, Faythe. Everything you are, everything you're becoming—you always had it in you."

"You saved me more than once."

He huffed a laugh. "You do have a gods-awful habit of attracting danger."

She chuckled sheepishly. "I don't think that's going to change anytime soon." She wanted to tell him what Aurialis told her about what still needed to be done. But she didn't. Not yet. He was about to be crowned king and had his kingdom to think about. She wouldn't get in the way of that.

"At least you'll be in more than capable hands," he said. "I've seen the way Reylan is with you. I know he'll look out for you as fiercely as any of us." He didn't have to add that it wasn't by the command of his king.

No—out of the initial unease, distrust, and denial, she and the general had managed to find something amiable together. Friendship didn't seem like a fitting term to describe what it was. They shared something more…unexplainable, but to be treasured. She also owed a life's debt to him as she trembled to think of the alternative outcome of her harnessing the ruin's power.

"Then there's King Agalhor…" Nik trailed off as if not wanting to use the paternal term in case she wasn't ready for it. She was grateful he didn't. He shook his head in disbelief. "By the Spirits…I never would have thought the strange human I passed that day in the outer town could turn out to have not only an impossible ability, but an inconceivable twist to its origin. The untamed and untrained woman with a golden heart and a will of steel…" Nik looked her over with awe and admiration. She shifted tensely. "I never would have thought that human…would turn out to be Faythe Ashfyre of Rhyenelle."

Her cheeks burned. She was about to protest the new foreign addition to her name, but before she could, Nik went on.

"But it's so clear now. It was always there, yet no one dared to see it until they had no choice. The way you spoke to a room full of fae, of royals…you were the voice of reason in the midst of chaos. It was a moment I don't think any of those there will ever forget." Nik took a small step closer to her. "When you go to Rhyenelle, there will be those who will try to look down on you, Faythe. Always give them no choice but to look up." With those last words, his hand raised to her face, fingers grazing to lift her chin high.

Faythe choked on a hard lump. She had no words in response to Nik's passionate speech that filled her with pride and confidence. "I'm going to miss you so much," she all but whimpered. Then she fell into him, at ease under his warm embrace once more.

"I'll miss you too. We all will. But this is not goodbye. Not even close."

She squeezed her eyes closed and treasured the last moments in his arms. They'd been through so much together, and she struggled to think he wouldn't be a part of her daily life anymore when she'd grown so used to his presence.

"Promise me one thing?" Faythe mumbled against his chest.

"Anything."

"Promise me…no matter how much land is put between us, no matter what conflicts arise, no matter what names or titles might fall upon us…promise me we will always be just Faythe and a fae guard in the woods."

When they parted, Nik's grin was warm and bright. "To Faythe and the fae guard in the woods," he agreed.

Faythe grinned, and they both chuckled, reflecting on their memories in those woods that she would always hold close to her heart. When their laughter ceased, Faythe weighed a final request for the king before she left.

"Before I go…can I suggest something?"

Nik said nothing as he gave a nod of assurance.

"Despite my title as human emissary being a false frontage, it could be exactly what you need to bridge the gap between the humans and fae of High Farrow. Someone who understands the people there. Someone whom they trust enough to speak freely to."

She paused, momentarily weighing up her own thoughts. "There is no one more suited for the role than Jakon."

Nik's expression turned wary. "It's a fine idea, but I worry I would only place him in a position in which he would suffer the same scrutiny and prejudice you did. To an immortal, change does not turn over quickly. There will be many who will rebel, who will disagree, and who will be unaccepting. Do you really want to expose him to that?"

Faythe was conflicted in her answer. She wanted to protect him, but she also knew it wasn't for her to decide.

"I only ask that you extend the offer of the position. I believe he would appreciate the idea, and even if he does not accept, he may want to help in other ways."

Nik's smile lifted her doubt that he might object. It was his choice as king, after all, to grant and remove anyone's station. Faythe looked at him—*really* looked at him—and saw the coat of authority he wore, so proud and humble.

"I will extend the offer. But you have my word that Jakon and Marlowe will receive my protection in High Farrow no matter what they decide."

Faythe gave a nod, overcome with elation at knowing her human friends would be safe and protected in her absence. Though they didn't have to fear a malicious king, it brought her great joy to know her friends would stay united.

The door to Nik's room opened, and Faythe glimpsed the flowing green of Tauria's gown before the Fenstead princess stepped out to join them. Nik and Faythe moved apart, and she exchanged a sad but happy look with Tauria as she strolled over, pulling Faythe into a tight hug.

"I always knew you were destined for more than we could ever comprehend." Tauria released her but took her hands. "This castle is going to be awfully dull again without you." She pouted a little.

Faythe laughed. "You'll have your hands full keeping an eye on

the new king. Someone's got to make sure he's doing his job right."
She cast a teasing look back at Nik who rolled his eyes.

Tauria giggled. "I suppose you're right."

Faythe's grin fell to a bittersweet smile. "You made me feel
welcome in a castle where I wasn't welcomed by many. I can't
thank you enough, Tauria."

The princess squeezed her hands. "No—*thank you*, Faythe. You
helped me more than you'll ever know. You're not just a friend;
you're family."

She gripped Tauria's hands in warm, mutual gratitude.

"Rhyenelle forces left an hour ago. You'd better go now if you
want a chance of catching up," Nik said quietly from behind.

Stepping back from Tauria, she turned to him with a lazy smile.
"Are you kicking me out of your kingdom?"

Nik chuckled softly. "Never, Faythe."

Faythe was jogging down the castle halls when a familiar blonde
and brunette couple come into view around the corner. In her high
of freedom, she didn't slow her pace, colliding with Jakon who
rumbled with laughter as he caught her with a stumble backward.
Faythe held him for as long as she could when they steadied, and
from his equally tight grip, it seemed he was in no rush to part
either. She closed her eyes and breathed his woodsy scent she
would never forget. No amount of time apart could dull any
memory of her dearest friend.

Her feet met the ground again, and the two only separated for
long enough to pull Marlowe into their embrace. The three of
them laughed with no exact cause. Laughed until tears filled their
eyes and their hearts filled with the image they would cherish of the
last moment they had to hold onto until they saw each other next.

Faythe's decision to leave was made all the more bearable
knowing her two human friends could stay in the castle by Nik's

indefinite invitation. Jakon and Marlowe had each other plus the protection and friendship of Nik and Tauria now too. Nothing brought Faythe more joy than to know they would all be safe and together until she returned.

"Don't go wreaking havoc over there," Jakon teased. "I won't be there to bail you out this time."

Faythe wiped her teary eyes, her smile bright. "I can't make any promises."

With a chuckle, Jakon tousled her hair. She batted his arm away playfully, but her chest warmed at the familiar habit she would never admit she loved.

"You're on the right path, Faythe." Marlowe's arm tightened around her waist. "This is only the beginning for you."

Faythe squeezed her back in gratitude, eclipsing her reserves and anxieties. "I'll miss you both. So much."

"We'll see you soon," Jakon said. "You get one letter to us, and we'll be packing to head south—to stay or to rescue, just say the word." While he said it with an edge of humor, he was fierce in his eyes. She didn't know what she ever did right in her life to deserve such devotion, but there was nothing she wouldn't sacrifice or risk for her friends in return.

With a final farewell embrace, Faythe left Jakon and Marlowe where she knew they would be safe and well cared for, within the city. It didn't prevent the twist in her chest to walk away, but she willed her feet to move, knowing it was what she had to do for the chance to discover herself.

She rushed out the side castle door, heading for the stables. She would need to get on the road fast to catch up with Rhyenelle and not risk the long journey alone through unventured territory.

Faythe broke into a jog, and when she rounded the corner to enter the horses' stables, she stumbled to a halt. It wasn't the two dangerously loose horses that skipped a beat of her heart; it was the silver-haired rider who stood lazily by the side of his brilliant raven mare. Faythe was momentarily dumbstruck at the sight of Reylan. Next to him and Kali, another white-and-brown horse was also equipped for riding.

"Took you long enough," Reylan said by way of greeting, a knowing smirk on his lips.

Faythe still gawked. "How did you know I would change my mind?" she asked, stunned he'd stayed behind for her when she had never told him of her plans to go.

Reylan simply turned to the horses, keeping a slight crooked smile. "We'd better get on the road. It's a long journey back," he said, ignoring her dumbfounded look.

Faythe willed her legs to move toward the stallion Reylan stood beside, waiting for her to mount first. She hesitated for a second in her daze and then slid one foot into the stirrup and hoisted herself on top of the large beast with confidence. Something else she had him to thank for despite his taunting teaching methods to get her to overcome her fears.

When she looked down at him, she swore she saw a slight twinkle of pride in his eyes. But it was gone as he turned, mounting his own black beauty in a gracefully swift motion. Faythe's cheeks flamed, and she had to avert her gaze from the thoughts that swirled in her head as she shamelessly observed the movement.

Leaving the castle gates, Faythe didn't turn to look back. She had said her piece to her friends with their blessings to look nowhere but forward.

They trotted slowly through the city, and she tried to ignore the gawking fae and then the humans who stared blatantly in the outer town as they passed. Faythe looked around the dreary brown buildings for a little longer than she did the city. Though it wasn't in sadness. She knew her memories would be forever inlaid in the cracks of the stone streets, and a part of her heart would always belong to High Farrow. This was not goodbye.

When they were past the bustle of humans and fae, slowly walking over the grassy hills, Faythe looked over them as if she could see all the way to the Kingdom of the Phoenix. The sky diffused hues of red and orange, torched and aflame, as if it beckoned her there.

After a long, peaceful silence, she brought up something on her mind that had been left unsaid since their last rocky conversation. "I never thanked you, Reylan." She looked at him through fresh eyes, with a new perspective as it dawned on her. "I might not have survived it without you."

His look softened. "You don't have to thank me. What use is my ability if I can't use it to steal immense power from ruin-wielding humans?" he said in light humor.

She smiled a little, and then it fell in awe as she went on. "I don't just mean for your help in the throne room."

His look was puzzled.

"The white lion was impressive...but I think I preferred the silver bird."

Reylan's eyes flashed in surprise, and he huffed a short laugh. "It wasn't my proudest form. Great perspectives though," he said casually, not knowing just how much it meant to her.

In the darkest moments of her imprisonment, while her mind was toyed with to distort reality, she couldn't be sure the returning stubborn bird wasn't an illusion conjured up in her loneliness. But since the throne room, alongside the horror and heartbreak, three words had chanted quietly on subconscious repeat until she figured it out.

I never left.

Remembering Reylan's transformation from his legendary white lion form slipped the realization into place. Reylan really had never left. Never let her feel abandoned or alone.

"You didn't leave. Why?" He didn't owe her an explanation, yet she needed to ask, to know if he had stayed with her out of friendship or as his sworn oath to his king.

Reylan was quiet, and for a moment, she thought he might refuse to give her the answer. Then his sapphire orbs bore into her, and she almost missed the hint of pain in them when his look hardened.

"Caius warned me of the king's plan to have you detained. I left straight away and had horses ready to leave. For both of us. When it was Caius who showed up at the stables instead of you, and with the look on his face..." His jaw flexed, and his gloved hands tightened on the reins. He looked away from her as he continued. "He told me they took you to the tower instead of the dungeon. The casing on the window didn't even have gaps big enough for the smallest creature to fit through, or I might have shifted into your cell and killed every single guard it took to get you out against the odds." His eyes flinched as he looked over the sun-kissed hills. "I'm sorry I couldn't get to you. And I wish I got the chance to thank Caius for everything he did for you in there—everything he did for all of us."

Faythe's heart cracked at the mention of her lost friend.

"I had to make sure you stayed alive at least long enough for Agalhor and his forces to arrive. I didn't come back to High Farrow alone. Izaiah, a Shapeshifter, remained hidden with orders to send for Agalhor if given the signal. He got word to Rhyenelle immediately, taking the form of an eagle, and I borrowed some of his ability to stay in the only form I could to see you. I've never held onto an ability for so long before and was close to draining myself completely, but you needed something familiar, a regular sight—as obscure as it was—to know you weren't alone. Then the captain..." Reylan trailed off as if unable to finish. A flicker of frightening rage crossed his face. But she didn't fear it. Faythe didn't think she could ever be afraid of what he was capable of.

Reylan was a battle-hardened warrior by glance, cold and fearless, but she wondered how many he let in for long enough to see his armor removed. Above everything else she had to face in Rhyenelle, Faythe was dedicated to him. To discovering everything

Reylan was beneath his fierce exterior, knowing there was nothing that could make her turn her back on him now.

"My only regret is that I didn't get to make Varis suffer for what he did to you. But I found out you took quite good care of that yourself." One corner of his mouth tugged up slightly in bittersweet pride.

Faythe couldn't find it in her to even muster a smile, at a complete loss for words. A lump formed in her throat as she didn't expect the sincerity and loyalty from him. She'd done nothing to deserve it. In fact, she felt overwhelmingly *guilty* for how she treated him before.

"I think a part of me knew it was you all along," she said, reflecting back though it tensed her body and slicked her skin to recall the horrors that haunted her while awake and in sleep. "I'm sorry for shouting at you. You must have thought I was insane." She laughed weakly, admittedly embarrassed by her outbursts.

He shook his head. "I thought you were insanely *brave*. Gods, Faythe, you have far more resilience than even some of the best warriors I know."

Faythe wanted to mention that she might not have made it on her own without his silent presence in the lonely cell. But in his eye, it was as if he already knew.

The evening was peaceful, the still hills serene as each blade of green grass was torched bright amber by the flare of the magnificent descending sun.

"You'll like it in Rhyenelle."

Reylan's thoughtful voice pulled Faythe's gaze from the wavy illusion of fire over the hills.

"How can you be so sure?"

"Because you are your mother's daughter."

Her heart swelled. The comment meant more to her than he could ever know, filling her with new hope and determination.

"It's not every day a *human* queen comes to power," he said, more to himself, with a short breath of disbelief.

She spluttered an incredulous laugh as an anxious defense mechanism. "I won't ever be *that*," she said quickly, unable to even say the title in reference to herself.

He cast her a sideward glance. "It's not impossible."

"It's completely impossible. I'll be long gone with my mortal lifespan before that could ever happen. And just as well too."

"You're half-fae. You could live for two, perhaps even three hundred years."

Faythe paled. She had never even thought having the heritage in her blood could affect her lifespan. The prospect weighed her with dread more than excitement.

She held it together as she said, "And Agalhor could live for another millennia. Besides, I don't want a crown. Of any kind," she added, recoiling at the idea of even being considered a *princess*. It wouldn't be fair to the citizens of Rhyenelle to expect them to call her that. She was but a foreign human in their lands. Though Faythe was committed to doing what it took to prove herself and fit in with the humans and fae there, she didn't expect any different treatment or privileges because of who her bloodline father happened to be. They too were strangers still, and the thought of trying to build a relationship with the powerful fae ruler daunted her more than anything. She'd pushed that to the very back of her mind in fear it would be the one cowardly reason strong enough to stop her from going at all.

Reylan continued. "You have it in you to rule. Don't be so quick to discredit yourself. You have nothing to prove to anyone."

"I have everything to prove."

"Not to me."

Faythe looked into his blue eyes, stunned by the fierce belief in them. She couldn't be sure if it was as her friend or for what she was to his king. Perhaps both. Regardless, she was grateful for it.

"I'm not sure I'm ready for what's to come," she confessed and didn't hide her fear as she made herself vulnerable to him.

He gave her a look of understanding, and his encouraging

smile already began to ease away some of her worries. "Rhyenelle is ready for you. Whatever you face, I'll be right there with you."

Faythe smiled. "I hope you know you have no choice now," she said.

Reylan arched a questioning brow.

"You're stuck with me. Like it or not, General Reylan Arrowood, you've sealed your fate as my friend. This day, until the end of days."

Reylan chuckled—a deep, genuine sound that vibrated delightfully through her. "Spirits help me," he muttered. Then his low laughter ceased, leaving a warm smile that upturned his lips on both sides and created faint dimples in his cheeks. The smile held a rare flicker of contentment that reflected in his eyes and softened the sharp lines of his face. She wondered just how many people had been able to catch a glimpse behind the steel guard he always wore. Faythe treasured the sight.

"I promise to stand by you, Faythe Ashfyre. This day, until the end of days."

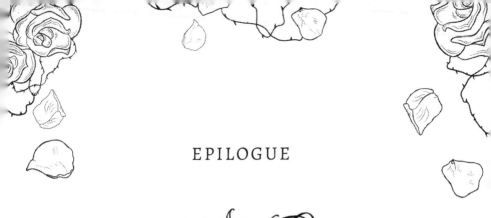

EPILOGUE

Reuben

WEEKS TURNED TO months. Months dragged like years. Time became an imperceptible force, and Reuben bowed to its mercy.

He longed for time to offer him death, for it seemed the only way to find release from the cage of his own mind. There was no door, though it often felt as if he observed the world through a keyhole. He could shout, but no one heard him. He could feel the air, but nowhere was his place to wander freely. Not anymore. Not with the shadow claws that sank into the depths of his mind. It was their domain now, and he was a careless tourist.

Reuben looked straight into the bright gold eyes across from him—eyes that once comforted him. A color that used to bring him joy now filled him with terror every time they met his. What color were his own eyes? He couldn't remember. It didn't matter anymore.

The fae female with hair like a waterfall of flame was devastatingly beautiful and masterfully enchanting. She smiled at him from across the ornate oak dining table where she feasted on a delicious spread of fine meats and cheese. She appeared in every sense of the word a queen. But she bore no rightful crown.

She was brilliant. *Gods,* she was magnificently brilliant. Perhaps even with his free will, he would have fallen to his knees before her, done anything she asked, no matter the risk or cost.

The red-haired beauty popped a grape into her sensuous mouth, chewing slowly, eyes fixed on him. Her sultry smile when she finished caressed his spine with both desire and dread. Then she took a long breath, and he watched the expanse of her marvelous full chest from the low cut of her blood-red gown.

"I'm afraid our time together is coming to an end," she said through the silence they'd sat in for a long while. Hours, perhaps. She stood, floating from her chair like a wave, gliding toward him like a pretty, poisonous snake. How could such beauty be so lethal?

As the enchantress landed at his side, a slender hand came up to his shoulder, trailing over his chest as she stopped behind him. He shouldn't enjoy her touch. But he did. He would bow to that touch.

She leaned in close, her voice an alluring whisper. "Will you miss me, Reu?" she purred in his ear.

No, he wanted to scream.

But his head slowly nodded.

Her fingers gripped his chin, turning his face to stare into those glittering molten eyes. Those of a snake primed to strike. Her rouge-painted lips drew closer, and she kissed him. He didn't feel it —he didn't feel anything. His mouth moved for her, but it wasn't to her approval. She pulled back, eyes flickering with veins of fire while she looked over his face.

"Prove it," she said in that melodic voice, guiding him to stand.

Looking down at her face, he glimpsed something he rarely saw behind her exterior of cold grace. Something that almost made him…pity her. A creature who longed for love but had no idea how to acquire its true essence.

His hand grazed the surface of her chest, over her neck, and held her face as it angled back. Her lips parted in silent invitation for him to close the gap between them.

Another person flashed through his mind while he stared into those gold eyes. With hair darker, browner. With rounded ears, not like the fae. But what was her name?

"I'll tell you what," the seductress drawled playfully, "how about a kiss in return for a memory?"

A memory. Did he want that? Perhaps there was a reason he couldn't remember. A reason he didn't *want* to remember.

Yet he sealed his answer when his lips met hers. Not a small, tender kiss; this female preferred passion. It was in the way she moved. In her poise and her voice: wild and untamed yet perfectly composed. She broke the kiss abruptly, but her smile was feline, not a smudge on her painted lips, not a hair out of place.

Nothing about her was ever shy of perfection.

"That's better," she cooed. "Now, for your gift." Her eyes turned hypnotic.

The longer he held them, the more he saw movement in her irises, as if they'd captured the sun within them. Then he felt the claws in his mind hissing, resisting whatever was trying to pry them free.

No. *No, no, no, no.*

He didn't want them gone. He realized they were his absolution. The barrier that kept him from confronting his past, from seeing what he used to be and all that he betrayed in that life. He enjoyed the numbness those claws brought out; the sedation they filled his senses with. He didn't fear. He didn't think. He didn't feel anything in their embrace.

Reuben screamed when one tore free. But it was not a sound that echoed through the room. The pain, the torture...was within his own self. And somehow, the beauty in front heard it all—*felt* it all—with him. Her hand caressed his cheek, and she whispered things that sounded like soothing notes.

I don't want to know. I don't want to feel. I don't want to see.

None of his wishes were heard. Images slammed into him. Stories played out in his mind with turbulent motions. Reuben went to his knees, screaming. This time, it tore up his throat like shards of glass. He clamped his hands over his ears, begging for it to stop. It didn't. His past slammed into him—memory after memory after memory.

I am Reuben Green.

His throat burned; his cheeks became wet.

I came from High Farrow.

He didn't want to know—not after everything he'd done.

Her name...

Not for what the wicked beauty in front had planned for him.

What was her name...?

Not when he would be used to betray all he held dear.

Faythe.

Reuben gasped when the dark claws stopped resisting. Their grip loosened, but his memories...he remembered them all with bone-trembling clarity. Everything he'd endured these past months. But it was nothing compared to what he was being prepared for now.

It was time.

The dark caress of the female's chuckle rattled every nerve in his body. She crouched too while he trembled on his knees against the stone, the encounter eerily similar to the first time they met. She'd been biding her time with him, had taken everything that made him who he was so she could hone him, craft him, into her own weapon.

Her elegant fingers took his chin. He couldn't fight it—not while his mind remained at her mercy. The dark claws—they were her presence. And she'd relented them enough to make him remember. He didn't want to, knowing what she planned to use him for; why he had to remember her name.

Faythe. Oh, Gods, Faythe.

The female smiled cruelly as if she knew exactly who he thought of. Her next words chilled him right to his core.

"It's time for the fun to begin."

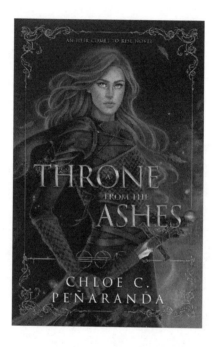

As darkness descends, two destinies will merge. But as embers fly, one may rise from the ashes.

A KINGDOM...

Far from the land she knows, Faythe is beckoned toward the secrets of her heritage. Through trials of her name and a challenge to her claim, does she have what it takes to rule? Faythe bears a future that haunts; Reylan harbors a past that lingers. At his side, what ignited in her heart is kindling, but letting her guard fall could break them...or make them stronger.

A QUEST...

Now faced with a far deadlier evil than the king, a higher calling
seems determined to turn the hourglass on Faythe's quest to save
Ungardia. But she soon learns time isn't the only thing working
against her. Darkness is rising, history is stirring, and the hunters
are about to become the hunted.

A DESTINY...

For fate cannot be outrun. Faythe's powers are manifesting beyond
her control, and if she can't save herself, no one can. Defying
destiny is not without consequence, yet Faythe may be willing to
pay the highest price of all to forge a path to true freedom—for her
kingdom, and for the ones she loves.

PRONUNCIATION GUIDE

NAMES

Faythe: faith
Reylan: ray-lan
Nikalias: nick-a-lie-as
Jakon: jack-on
Marlowe: mar-low
Tauria: tor-ee-a
Caius: kai-us
Orlon: orr-lon
Reuben: ru-ben
Varis: var-iss
Varlas: var-lass
Tarly: tar-lay
Marvellas: mar-vell-as
Aurialis: orr-ee-al-iss
Dakodas: da-code-as
Agalhor: a-ga-lor
Ashfyre: ash-fire

PLACES

Ungardia: un-gar-dee-a
Farrowhold: farrow-hold
Galmire: gal-my-er
High Farrow: high-farrow
Lakelaria: lake-la-ree-a
Rhyenelle: rye-en-elle
Olmstone: olm-stone

Fenstead: fen-stead
Dalrune: dal-rune

OTHER

Riscillius: risk-ill-ee-us
Lumarias: lou-ma-ree-as
Yucolites: you-co-lights
Dresair: dress-air
Niltain: nill-tain

ACKNOWLEDGMENTS

I can't begin to describe the joy I feel to know that you are on this journey, in this world, with me. Yes, you, my dear reader. You choosing to read my books is the reason I get to keep doing what I love. From the bottom of my heart, thank you.

To my mother, Yvonne–number one crazed fan. Seriously, you don't have to keep making accounts for every social platform I join. Despite your near stalker tendencies, I couldn't do this without your constant love and support. Thank you for always being there for me, for cheerleading through the ups and downs. You rock.

To my sister, Eva, things have been hard for you this past year. I wish you nothing but love and happiness. Thank you for supporting for me and this series throughout everything you've faced. You are superwoman.

To the rest of the family unit, I am so very grateful for the unconditional love and support.

To my canine companions: Milo, Bonnie, and Minnie. I never thanked you crazy bunch in the last book because I thought people might find it silly, but in truth, it's not silly to acknowledge you three have seen me through some of my darkest days.

To my absolutely brilliant editor, Bryony Leah. You deserve far more praise than I can fit in this small paragraph. You helped strengthen so many aspects of this book. Thank you for challenging me, teaching me, and being a cheerleader for this series over and above your invaluable edits. I can't wait to do it all again. And again. You're stuck with me indefinitely.

To Alice Maria Power, wow girl, I didn't think you could top the last cover illustration, but you knocked it right out of the park with this one. Your magic never ceases to amaze me. Thank you for coming on this journey with me and perfectly capturing Faythe's growth.

Finally, I've thanked you at the beginning and I'll thank you at the end. To my dear readers, thank you for continuing on this wild ride with me. Your support means the world, and I cannot wait to see you along for the next book. You. Are. Amazing.

ABOUT THE AUTHOR

CHLOE C. PEÑARANDA is the Scottish author of the epic fantasy series, *An Heir Comes to Rise.*

A lifelong avid reader and writer, Chloe discovered her passion for storytelling in her early teens. An Heir Comes to Rise has been built upon from years' worth of building on fictional characters and exploring Tolkien-like quests in made up worlds. During her time at the University of the West of Scotland, Chloe immersed herself in writing for short film, producing animations, and spending class time dreaming of far off lands.

In her spare time from writing in her home in scenic Scotland, Chloe enjoys digital art, graphic design, and down time with her three furry companions. When the real world calls...she rarely listens.

www.ccpenaranda.com

Made in the USA
Columbia, SC
29 June 2023